Single in Buenos Aires

The Polo Diaries

Book 1

Roxana Valea

One thought just entered my mind:
keep calling, 120 dials a day!!! :-)
will never forget that haha

Published in Great Britain by RV Publications.

Cover and interior design by Tabitha Lahr
Front cover images © Shutterstock

First published July 2019.
A CIP catalogue record for this book is available from the British Library.

ISBN: 978-0-9931309-5-3
E-ISBN: 978-0-9931309-6-0

For information, email: roxana@roxanavalea.com

Prologue

I learned three things in Argentina.

The first is *tranqui*. It comes from the word *tranquilo*, which means calm, cool, laid back. They rarely say the whole word, though. That would be too serious. Instead they shorten it to *tranqui*. You get told "*Tranqui*" when you start worrying about something. It's like saying, "Chill out, mate. Everything's going to be OK." *Tranqui* seems to be a magic word. When you hear it, you relax. You stop worrying. You don't think too much about things.

The second thing is *no pasa nada*. That's the next step after *tranqui*. Its literal meaning is "nothing is happening." When you start worrying about something, you first get told "*Tranqui*," and if you don't listen to this advice, then you're told, "*No pasa nada.*" It doesn't matter, so don't worry about it.

This universal form of denial is used for everything. If you did something wrong and you apologise, "*No pasa nada.*" All is forgotten. If you worry about the economy collapsing, which it does regularly in Argentina, you get told, "*No pasa nada.*" If you break a bone and are screaming in pain waiting to see a doctor, you get a comforting "*No pasa nada.*" Whatever it is that's making you unhappy, no worries, it doesn't matter. There is a magic formula that can erase it all. *No pasa nada.*

The third one is *después vemos*. "We'll see about it later." It's used as a general disclaimer for any future plans. Argentines live in the present. Whether this is because of the wild turns and tumbles of their economy or a sense of connection with their vast land is unclear. What is clear is that they have a pretty strong aversion to predicting the future. So they leave it open. We'll see about it later.

Do you want to meet up for dinner tomorrow? "*Después vemos.*" If I feel like it, we'll meet. If I don't feel like it, we won't meet and nobody will feel offended. Not sure how to handle a certain situation? "*Después vemos.*" You'll figure it out later.

These three concepts, when boiled together, form a thick and nourishing soup with a surprisingly sweet but strong taste. It's good for the soul, they say.

I tried it. And I liked it. It was in this soup that my story was born. And it was here that one day it decided to jump out of the pot and start wandering off on a path of its own.

November

SUNDAY 8TH NOVEMBER

I'll do it right this time. I'm determined. I take out my notebook and I start writing. I like writing on flights. It helps me escape the claustrophobic economy-class seats, with the guy snoring on my left and the baby crying two rows in front. If you fly direct from London to Buenos Aires it takes thirteen hours and fifteen minutes. However, I'm not flying direct today, so I have even more time for writing.

My favorite type of writing comes in the form of to-do lists. Trouble starts when these plans don't go the way I imagine. Ideally I should be able to introduce myself as Roxy (short for Roxana), age forty-one, happily in love and married to the man of my dreams. Successful polo player with no injuries. Currently heading to Argentina to enjoy a fantastic polo season.

But something went wrong and my life description now ends in: Single. Currently heading to Argentina to recover from a polo injury .

So I need a new plan to put things straight, and this is it: my to-do list for the three months I'll be spending in Argentina.

1. I will recover my arm—my left one, the one that currently bears an ugly cut on the wrist. I had surgery only a couple of weeks ago. The same doctor who inserted two screws in my bones a year ago had to take them back out because my wrist wasn't moving properly, not even after the tons of physiotherapy I'd had.

I had to have the screws put in because I'd broken my arm really badly. I'd broken my shoulder, too, but at least that didn't need screws. In total, two arms and three bones were broken after one big fall playing polo some fifteen months ago.

Why do I play polo? Well, it's kind of complicated. I'm Romanian and there's no polo in Romania, but I live in London and there's a lot of polo in England. And there's no man in my life, so I figured out I'll find Mr. Perfect on a polo field. I came to this conclusion after I hired a love coach to teach me how to go about this dating business. The trouble is that instead of sorting my love life out, she started asking me lots of questions about my passions. She said I should start loving myself. I had no idea how this self-love would work, but I had a pretty clear idea of what I liked to do as a child: ride horses. So I followed her advice to get in touch with my childhood passions and ended up on a polo field. And it was love at first sight. I couldn't explain why and how it happened, but once I started I could just not stop playing polo—even after breaking both arms and spending three months like a Barbie doll, being dressed, fed, and washed by a nanny. I hired the nanny because I refused to have my mum move in with me. I couldn't face listening to her daily speech about why I should give up playing polo. So I hired the nanny, I recovered the use of my arms, and I went back to playing polo. I played all summer with the two screws still in my left hand. It wasn't too bad and I didn't have another fall—well, I didn't have another fall which resulted in broken bones, I mean.

With the polo season ending in September, I'd scheduled my surgery for October. The screws had to come out, but I wasn't going to have that happen in the middle of my polo season, because I knew how bad it would be afterwards. Just like it is now, in fact—ugly, swollen, and with a big cut. I can't move my hand. Can't hold anything in it. Can't even wash my face with it. But it's OK. It will recover. And with the screws no longer there, I'm determined to make it as good as new.

2. I will play polo. To be fair, this depends on the first point on the list, but I'm confident my arm will recover. I'll make sure it does. I've already done some research and found the address of the Institute for Sports Medicine, Recovery, and Rehabilitation in Buenos Aires. It sounds serious enough for what I need. I'll do physiotherapy, magnets therapy, massage, and whatever else it takes. I will have three therapists working on my wrist if I have to, and it will move again. I have to make sure it does, because I need to play some polo while I'm here.

Argentina is the number-one country in the world for polo. To be honest, it's not like there's a number two and three. It's more like there's a number one, which is Argentina, and then nothing . . . and nothing . . . and nothing again. It's like a big desert, and only after you've travelled some kilometers through it do other countries begin to appear timidly on the horizon—England, the US, Australia, Germany, all clinging together and bitterly competing with each other.

England likes to show off, claiming to be the best in the world—that is, apart from Argentina. This is because it was the English who discovered the game of polo, somewhere in North India in the late nineteenth century, where they adopted the game as a training practice for their cavalry. They then exported the game all over the world, even taking it to Argentina. They wrote the first rules for it, set up an association, and—since the English like to do everything properly—decided it should be played in white trousers. It's still being played in white trousers all over the world. Basically, the English like to think they own polo, even though polo was played in ancient Persia more than two thousand years before they adopted it. An ancient inscription found engraved in stone next to a polo field in northern Kashmir bears witness to its heritage: "Let others play at other things. The King of Games is still the Game of Kings."

However, the English didn't predict what the Argentines would go on to do with the game—which is not surprising, really, since very few can predict what the Argentines will do, not even the Argentines themselves. But they don't really concern themselves with predicting the future, anyway. They like living in the present.

The Argentines took the game and spread it to all their *estancias*—those huge country estates where wealthy landowners with large families and many sons and nothing better to do with their lives rode for pleasure. They took the Criollo horses—bred by the *gauchos* and used for cattle herding—and trained them for polo. In fact the game suited the breed perfectly, since the horses were required to do the same moves they were already trained to do—run, stop, turn and run again.

The Argentines had the time, they had the horses, and they had the landscape for polo—the vast, flat lands outside Buenos Aires—so they became the best in the world. Polo became a national tradition, with the top players in the world passing on their genes and their genius to their sons. A second and third generation of players emerged, and they were even better than their fathers and grandfathers. Polo became a sport of great national pride, coming second only to football. But then nothing comes even close to football in Argentina.

They built a huge polo stadium in the center of the city and called it *La Catedral de Polo*—the cathedral of polo. This is where the biggest competition in the world of polo is played every year: *El Abierto*, the Argentine Open Championship. People travel from all over the world to witness this peak of polo performance, in which the top teams battle it out against each other. Since Argentina is the best in the world, almost all the players who ride their horses into *El Abierto* are Argentine. Which brings me to point three on my list:

3. I will watch *El Abierto*. Every single game, for the entire three weeks of its duration. I'll get myself tickets for all the games and then I'll enjoy the parties afterwards. Many people who go to the polo games do it with their mind on the parties, but that's something else. I'm determined to see the games first, then afterwards I'll enjoy the parties. The parties are actually very relevant for point four on my list:

4. I will fall in love. I'm determined to do so. It's on my list, and I think it will happen at one of the polo parties, because everyone says the Argentines are handsome and they know how to party. And no, it doesn't have to be with a polo player. I kind of gave up on that some time ago. I'm still holding on to many other polo-related illusions, but not that one. In fact it would be better if he weren't a polo player. He must be handsome, which won't be hard, because all Argentines are handsome. He must speak Spanish with an Argentine accent, because I love how they speak. And he must enjoy these fun parties. He will have to belong to this world of polo, just as I do.

Actually point four is a huge one. Perhaps I'd better put it at the top of the list.

For a second or two I contemplate drawing up my list again. But no. I leave it as it is. My hand is more important, and polo . . . well, polo is polo. I can't move polo down the list.

I comfort myself with the thought that I've done enough for number four already. The deal I made in Paris should take care of it. You see, I did something a little bit weird to help with this item on the list—I went to Paris to spend the night. On my own. Not just any night, but the night before my birthday, which was yesterday. Since I was born at 1:30 am, I went to Paris for the actual moment of my birthday. I did this because someone told me about astrolines and I jumped at this new idea. I was feeling desperate enough to try something new that might help me find love. Anything new would do, and since I believe in horoscopes anyway, the astrolines weren't too much of a stretch.

I don't usually think too much about these things, I just put them into practice. The astrolines theory says that if you go somewhere else to spend the few hours around your exact birthday, you can reconfigure your astral chart as if you were born in that particular location. So if love was not well represented on your chart for the place and time you were born, you get a second chance. In fact, you get this second chance once a year, because you can keep on picking better locations to spend your birthday until, as if by magic, your wish is granted.

I had my astrolines done, and it turned out that Venus—she's the one responsible for this love situation—passes through Paris for me. Venus actually helps with a lot of other things, like having a nice comfortable life, creativity, and so on, but I was on a quest for one thing only: love. I have been single for far too long.

Now, I don't really want to tell anyone how long I've been single for. It's kind of embarrassing. And I don't want people to jump to conclusions, like my friend Catherine did when I told her, and she pointed out that this was the exact same length of time I had been playing polo.

"What? You think I'm single because I play polo?" I asked her, irritated.

She said she was only pointing out a fact. We left the conversation there.

One way or another, I was going to solve this love problem. And as I wasn't going to give up polo for it, I had to look for a more creative solution. I found it in the astrolines. If I went to Paris, got a room in a hotel there, and spent the night, I would be sorted. At some time within the new year, I would find my true love.

It actually worked out well. The day before my birthday I got on a Eurostar from London to Paris. Very few people knew about my plan. I couldn't risk explaining to everyone that I was on a mission to make a special deal with the Universe. Or tell them how much I'd paid for it: a return Eurostar ticket, London to Paris, and one very nice room in a very romantic hotel overlooking Notre Dame. Why there? Because it's point zero in Paris, the point all distances are measured from. It's the very center of the city. When you make a deal with the Universe, it pays to take your part seriously. Once I'd done all that, then the Universe would play its part. In other words, it would deliver me one handsome, passionate, Spanish-speaking, preferably Argentine boyfriend, who would love me and make me happy.

My list of requirements for the ideal man was a little longer than this, but I thought I shouldn't overload the Universe. So I left the other points hanging out there on a secondary list. He should like polo, preferably play it as well, should be about my age, or a couple of years older max, as I don't really like older guys. Definitely not younger. I have never dated younger guys. He should have the means to travel and ideally spend half the time in Europe and half the time in Argentina. It would help if we were in similar lines of work. Perhaps he wouldn't need to be a management consultant—an entrepreneur or a manager would do. It would be helpful if he were well-educated. Maybe with a masters degree like me. It would be helpful if he had lots of money too. He can drive a nice car, but not a sports car. I have bad memories of guys driving sports cars and I think they have inflated egos. No, this one will be a real man: strong, reliable, trustworthy, handsome, sporty.

So I went to Paris with my description of the perfect guy in my mind. I visited Notre Dame, went to a concert in an old cathedral, ate a crêpe on my own, and went to sleep in the sexy lingerie I had brought with me. It's good to give the Universe a preview of what you're after. The next morning I woke up and returned to London just in time for my actual birthday party, which doubled up as a leaving do, since the following morning—that is, today—I'd be on my way to Argentina. With a sore head, as I had one too many drinks last night. Which brings me to point five on my list:

5. I will do a Total Body Rehab. I will drink moderately, eat well, take my vitamins, and do a lot of sports. I will use this time off to detox my body and get myself in perfect shape. This will help support point two on the list (play lots of polo), as well as point four on the list—fall in love.

I pause and take a look at my list. I'm pleased with it. Only five points, but the most important things are there—hand, polo, and love. I can be flexible about the rest. And all the best lists have five points, anyway. Not too short, not too long. Just perfect.

The buzzing of the engine fills my ears and my head feels heavy. It's all starting to melt in my mind—the trip to Paris, my birthday dinner last night, the excitement of finally leaving. I'll see what else needs to be on my list when I get there, I tell myself as I slowly drift into sleep. Even the tender left wrist, wrapped in its bandages, stops aching, as if it, too, knows that we are now on our way to Buenos Aires, and we're going to be there for three months, and everything is going to be just fine, because I have a to-do list and I am determined to make it happen.

MONDAY 9TH NOVEMBER

I once worked as part of a consulting project where I was required to travel two to three times a week and stay in a different hotel each time. I used to wake up with this worrying sensation of having no idea where I was, or what I was supposed to be doing there. It usually lasted for a few seconds, and then my memory would slowly return and I would remember that I was there for work and what exactly I had to do there. The hard part was that this sensation also happened on the weekends when I got back home to London. I used to wake up in my own bed, trying hard to remember where I was and what I needed to do.

My first morning in Buenos Aires throws me sharply back to that time in my life.

Awake in the middle of a big double bed, I'm paralysed with anxiety, trying hard to recall where I am. A few seconds of blackout and then it all comes back.

First, the taste of Campari Orange. I remember I had a lot of them last night. Then I see two faces—Rosario and Gabriela, the girls I had the drinks with. Then I remember everything. How I had landed late at night, how I expected to find a taxi driver sent by my friend Gabriela, and how I texted her to say that there was no bloody taxi driver there with my name on a white board as promised. How I got a reply from Gabriela telling me to be patient, to look around, and that's when I saw the two of them, Rosario and Gabriela, and they jumped on me, hugging me and saying, "Roxy! Welcome to Argentina!"

"Where's the taxi driver?" I asked, still not understanding what was going on.

"There is no taxi driver, silly," Gabriela replied. "We wanted to surprise you. We were always going to pick you up from the airport and take you to your flat in Buenos Aires. We'll have a bite and a drink together. That's what friends do here."

I looked dumbly at my watch. It was 11:30 pm. They lived in another city, hours away from Buenos Aires. They'd driven an hour to be here and were going to drive me another hour to get to Buenos Aires. It would be well past midnight before we got a drink and then they would have to drive all the way back home. They'd only get a couple of hours' sleep before they had to get up for work the next morning.

But they are like that, the Argentines. They have big hearts. And they use them well.

With my memory fully returned, I get up and get going. It's day one and I have lots to do—my suitcase to unpack, the language school I have booked myself into, and my first appointment with my hand physiotherapist.

But before any of these things, I need a coffee.

TUESDAY 10TH NOVEMBER

It's not my first time in Buenos Aires. It's my fourth. But it's the first time I'm in the city by myself for a long period, so in a way it counts as a first time. I first came two years ago, for polo, and spent most of my time in the countryside, playing. I'd just taken up the sport and had fallen completely in love with it. Addicted, some people said. I told them they didn't understand. I arrived in December and stayed for six weeks. The great thing about Argentina is that the polo season here starts as soon as it ends in England. I played polo on different *estancias* and even spent a few days in Buenos Aires. I hadn't intended to spend time in the capital, but I was forced to. I'd played so much polo I'd hurt my back, and I had to come to the city for a massage therapist, a chiropractor, and anyone else who could sort it out.

It was then I met Alejandra, the shiatsu specialist. She was recommended by the receptionist at the hotel where I was staying, and she came to my room, carrying her massage bed and dressed in a spotless white therapist's uniform. It took me a long time to open the door when she knocked. I couldn't walk properly. I hadn't broken anything that time, but my back muscles had had enough of riding.

She came in, took a quick look at me, and smiled when I said "Polo," answering the question she hadn't asked.

"I know," she said. "My nephews play. I know all about polo."

I wondered what it was that she knew, and whether she approved of it. But she knew better than to discuss her opinions with a client and she simply asked me to lie down on the floor. No need for the massage table.

I screamed as she used her feet for a few shiatsu moves on my back.

"Why did you do this to your body?" she asked, probably annoyed by my screams.

"*Por amor al polo*," I said. For the love of polo. I thought it was funny.

"*Hay amores que matan*," she answered. There are loves that kill. That was definitely not funny.

Just after she left, Gabriela called. She is the girlfriend of the polo player I'd been training with for the past three days, before I arrived at this non-walking state. I'd stayed with them at their *estancia* as a paying guest. A friend had recommended I go there and I went, just as I went to many other polo places. The difference this time was that this wasn't a commercial enterprise. It was their home. It was a beautiful farm house with seven hundred cows, five dogs, and more than thirty horses. They had a polo field in front of the house. The polo player I trained with—Gabriela's boyfriend—was called Patricio. Their five-year-old son was also called Patricio, as was his seventy-year-old father.

"How long has this been going on for?" I asked.

Gabriela kindly explained that all the first-born males in this family were called Patricio and had been for about two hundred years, ever since they'd come over from Ireland.

The farm was, of course, called San Patricio.

I'd stayed with them for three days and then I'd come to Buenos Aires because I couldn't play polo any longer. I couldn't even walk anymore.

"*Hola*, darling. How are you doing?"

I'd thought it was just a courtesy call. I told her not to worry, that I was doing fine and I had found a great massage therapist.

"Look, tomorrow is Christmas. What are your plans?"

"No plans," I'd said.

"Come back to ours, then. You can't stay there alone in Buenos Aires for Christmas."

I tried to refuse, to say that I was all right, that I didn't want to intrude on their family for Christmas.

"Nonsense," she interrupted. "Either you get in a taxi and come here today, or I'll come there and fetch you. You're simply not staying alone in a hotel for Christmas. It is decided."

And it was done. After only two days in the city I went back to the countryside to spend Christmas with them. I stayed for two weeks. I met the whole extended family, close to a hundred people. I was the only foreigner there. I stayed for New Years, too, and danced in a barn and drank Campari Orange, until the whole world melted away in one big, explosive headache the morning after. And the following year I came back. And then I came back to them again towards the end of that same year for my fortieth birthday, because I had to run away and hide somewhere for this occasion, and an *estancia* in the middle of the pampas, two hours away from Buenos Aires, seemed the perfect place.

That was last year. And now I'm back again, for the fourth time.

And they are here for me again. My big, caring, warm Argentine family watching over me from a distance.

WEDNESDAY 11TH NOVEMBER

I love my flat. I'm renting it through Airbnb. It's quite small, one bedroom only. Actually it has two, but the second is locked up with all the stuff belonging to the owner. She was clearly once a travel enthusiast. The flat is full of memories—little Thai wooden dolls dressed in colourful dresses, a Moroccan wooden windowframe now holding a mirror, old prints with quotes from the Holy Quran on the wall. There is an African cloth painting on the other wall, depicting women walking with big pots on their heads. An Indian goddess—I don't know which one—stands tall in the corner of the living room. She has four arms and looks like she's dancing with all of them. I've only spent a few days in the flat and I feel like I've lived here forever.

"*Hola, cómo estás*?" A neighbor's smiling face pops up beside me as I wait for the lift.

I mumble "Well, thank you." I've never seen this woman before. I've met a few other neighbors who usually talk to me, and I smile back. My Spanish doesn't really support any level of conversation. I can understand the language, thanks to a mixture of my Romanian native tongue, the Latin American soap operas I used to watch as a teenager, and the Italian I learned while living in Milan. I can just about make sense of what I'm being told. Speaking, though, is another thing entirely.

We get into the lift. She carries on talking, not discouraged by my silence. I think she might just be telling me that she likes the color of my t-shirt. I'm not a hundred percent confident, though, so I'm not risking a reply. I just keep on smiling. The small lift carries on moving slowly. I live on the tenth floor. It's a long ride.

The woman carries on talking. By now I'm convinced she must mistake me for someone else. She can't possibly chat this much to a complete stranger. I'm not sure what she's just asked me, so I smile again and try a "*No comprendo.*" I don't understand.

Thankfully the lift reaches the eighth floor, where she gets off. She's in the middle of telling me something else when the doors of the lift start to close. I just catch a glimpse of her waving.

I get to my flat, still not sure if my neighbor has mistaken me for someone else. In my thirteen years of living in London, I have never had such a lengthy interaction with any of my neighbors.

But I'm not in London, I'm in Buenos Aires. And here people talk to each other. Nonstop. More than necessary. Much more than necessary.

Later, I wander down again in search of a bite to eat. Thankfully there are no more talking neighbors in the lift this time.

"*Hola, linda*! *Cómo estás*?" Hello beautiful. How are you? The waiter at the restaurant at the corner of my streets greets me like he's known me all his life.

I tell him I'm all right. I have learned this life-saving phrase in Spanish. I stick my nose in the menu, hoping that was all the conversation necessary. But no, far from it.

"Where are you from?"

Now that's a difficult one. It would take a lot of time and many words which I'm still missing in Spanish to explain that I've come from London, but I'm not from London because I only live there, and I was born in Romania, hence making me Romanian, but I left Romania some fifteen years earlier and have lived most of my adult life abroad, which makes me kind of European. Too complicated.

I decide that London will do for an answer.

"And what brings you here?"

No, he's not going away, and he is not taking my order either, until I tell him my full life story. I attempt a slightly longer answer using a combination of Spanish and Italian words. I just make sure I put an 's' at the end of the Italian words to make them sound more Spanish.

Polo . . . breaking arm . . . accident . . . coming here to recover.

"Ah, so you play polo! How interesting." Where do I play? How long have I been playing for? How come I play? Is there polo for women as well? He thought it was only for men. "Ah, seriously, men and women play together? No, not in Argentina, definitely not in Argentina. Impossible!"

The conversation stretches my language limits, but he doesn't seem to care. He smiles encouragingly as I struggle to explain.

"And are you here by yourself?"

Day three in Argentina and I've already been asked if I'm single. And no, it doesn't feel weird. They have a way of asking this question with a mixture of laid-back curiosity and casualness that makes it actually sound OK. Once his curiosity is satisfied, he finally takes my order for lunch.

Sola. Alone. Or single.

Yes I am *sola* here. I'm here by myself. I have one big caring Argentine adoptive family two hours away, in case I need them. But right now, at this moment of my life, I'm *sola*. As alone as one can be in one big, noisy, busy city, where people simply can't let you enjoy being *sola*, because they want to talk to you. All the time.

SATURDAY 14TH NOVEMBER

I'm quite proud of myself. In one week I've sorted out two big items on my list.

First the physiotherapy. I found the Institute for Sports Medicine, Recovery, and Rehabilitation quite easily. It was on the same street as my language school. I'd known the school was close to it when I booked the course online a couple of weeks before setting off, but I didn't expect them to be only ten minutes apart on the same street.

My first appointment at the Institute was with Sabrina. I told her my life story in the few words I could manage in Spanish and filled in the gaps with Italian. I thought she got the picture, but just to make sure I showed her the x-rays before the screws, after the screws, and with no screws at all. My screwed-up wrist, which even after two operations and lots of physio still refused to move properly.

"*Tranqui*," she said. "We'll sort it out." And then she decided to talk to me non-stop to divert my attention from the pain as she pulled and twisted my hand.

It had to be done this way, she said.

At the end of the session I booked a further one-hour appointment for every day of the week, Monday to Friday. Sabrina worked there only three days a week. The other two days my appointment was with a colleague of hers who only talked about half as much as she did. During the rare moments when they were quiet I could hear the radio in the background, always on and always tuned in to a chat show. These people do like to talk a lot.

Next, I sorted out the language school—my intensive Spanish course which I'd pre-booked from London. I needed to be able to communicate with these people and my half-Spanish, half-Italian words wouldn't get me very far. So I decided to do it properly—two hours of Spanish classes every day. And because I'm not a beginner, but I'm not an intermediary student either, I got put alone in a class. Just me and a teacher who patiently started hammering every single Italian word out of my vocabulary.

I don't mind. If the price to be paid is to lose my Italian, so be it. I'll learn this language and I'll speak it like them, with sweet, rolling 'j's that make it sound more Portuguese than Spanish. I'll speak it with the funny second-tense verbs which aren't to be found anywhere else in the Spanish-speaking world. I'll call them *vos*, not the boring Spanish *tu* that actually sounds Romanian. I'll speak it fast, just like they do, and eat an 's' every now and then, just as they seem to like it. I'll speak it as sexily as my teacher does.

For a moment, I contemplate adding "Learn Spanish" to my list as number six, but in the end I decide not to. The best lists only have five points. No more, no less. I will stick to five. I always stick to five points. Learning Spanish will just be a bonus.

But Spanish is not just Spanish. It comes bundled with the sexiest guy I have met in a while—my teacher. By the end of my first week of classes I'm already fantasising about this friendly, well-built man with thick, dark, curly hair who happens to be my teacher. He's got the moves of a salsa dancer and the looks of a Greek god, and whenever he sees me a big smile breaks out on his face. I think he likes me, too.

Our conversation classes revolve around him asking many questions and me trying to answer them to the best of my ability. In Spanish.

Am I single?

"Si, sola." My *sola* sounds much more encouraging than the *sola* I had thrown at the waiter the other day.

Am I looking for a boyfriend?

"I prefer to let the next boyfriend look for me," I answer, feeling very proud of my increased proficiency.

Why am I single?

Ah. Now this is too difficult. I don't know enough words in Spanish.

And for how long have I been single?

Ah no, wrong question again. That's actually a secret, and—

Having come to the end of the list of questions that can possibly revolve around the single status, he then enquires further into my romantic history.

Have I been married?

"Yes, I have."

He looks shocked. He clearly didn't expect this.

"A long time ago," I hurry to add. "It only lasted six months."

I stop, unsure whether this makes it sound more reassuring. I wish he hadn't asked.

He abruptly changes the topic and starts asking questions about London. Maybe he doesn't like me anymore. Maybe he's not interested in divorced girls.

Actually, a divorced woman. One forty-one-year-old woman, divorced after a six-month marriage more than seven years ago. Currently with only one functional wrist, due to being slightly addicted to playing polo. A woman who speaks a mixture of Spanish and Italian, and who has a to-do list that features looking for love as the fourth point. Who thinks maybe this guy asking all these questions could be the answer to this fourth point, if he happens to fancy her. But at the present moment not quite sure whether the guy actually does fancy her any longer.

The rest of the lesson continues in a neutral tone. The flirting is over. Oh well, I think, there will be others.

And yet on Friday, just before the end of the class, he tells me about the *Feria de Mataderos*, a Sunday fair where a lot of artisans come to sell their goods. And he tells me he will be there, dancing salsa. He says it casually, as if he's not aware that his sexiness has suddenly increased, just because he has mentioned he is dancing salsa. I have no idea how to dance salsa, so anyone who does seems to have supernatural abilities in my eyes.

And then he writes down the address of the place for me, just in case I want to come. It's on the other side of the town, some forty minutes away by taxi. But I instantly nod. Of course I'll come.

And then he gives me his phone number. So that I can call him if I get lost. My heart fills with hope again.

SUNDAY 15TH NOVEMBER

The same hope is still there as I look for a taxi on Sunday to go to the Feria de Mataderos to meet my curly-haired teacher.

"*Hola. Cómo estás?*"

The taxi driver sounds like he's known me for a lifetime already.

"*Bien, gracias.*"

I tell him I'm going to the Feria de Mataderos. It only takes this sentence for him to figure out I'm not an Argentine.

"And where are you from?"

Again London, Romania, Europe. I give him a quick explanation.

He knows all about Romania, he tells me. Nadia Comaneci, the Romanian gymnast who broke all Olympic records in 1976. Nicolae Ceaușescu, the communist dictator who was overthrown twenty-six years ago. He talks to me about the history of my country with such ease, I start to suspect he is a history teacher with an occasional part-time job as a taxi driver.

"And are you here by yourself?"

"*Sola*. Yes."

"How come?"

No, it doesn't matter that he is just a taxi driver, supposed to take me from A to B. He is incidentally also an Argentine man, and as such, when presented with an opportunity to chat with a lady, he just can't resist asking the question, "Do you have a boyfriend?" which is politely rephrased as, "Are you here by yourself?" And then the inevitable follow-up question, "How come?"

How come I don't have a boyfriend? Well, I don't know. I don't think about the question like this. Should I absolutely have a boyfriend?

"*Por supuesto*," he says. Of course. "Because you are beautiful."

I start to feel uncomfortable. I'm not really sure I want compliments from my taxi driver, but he continues unperturbed.

"It is not normal for a beautiful girl like you to be alone."

OK, I get it. *Sola* equals *no good.* We are in agreement, mate, I want to tell him. But I don't, because I haven't got the words.

So I just listen. He tells me I've come to the right place, to this country, to this city, because it is absolutely impossible for a *linda* (that means beautiful woman) like me to stay here *sola* (that means alone) for too long.

"Impossible," he repeats. "Not while Argentine men still have eyes."

This is my hope as well, but I don't tell him. I get out of the taxi and start looking for one specific Argentine man with curly hair. Hopefully with good eyes too.

It turns out he's not there. Or maybe he is, but I just can't find him. Too many people, tourists, locals, all mingled together in a never-ending crowd, moving like a huge human snake through the hundreds of stalls. Everything is for sale here—leather belts, shoes, clothes, prune marmalade, huge round lumps of home-cooked bread, hard yellow cheese, and kids' toys, probably Made in China.

Smoke from the *parrillas*, the famous Argentine meat grills, rises from the stalls and dances above the crowd.

On a stage in the middle, a man dressed like a *gaucho* in a white shirt, loose beige trousers, thick leather belt, and riding boots shouts something into a microphone. It sounds like he is reciting a poem. My Spanish isn't good enough to get the whole thing, but I manage to catch a *patria* (fatherland), *amor* (love), and *gauchos* (local cowboys). The words are repeated a lot and it sounds like the whole poem is about these three things.

As I stretch the limits of my Spanish comprehension and decide it's really not good enough, he finishes the poem, and a group of kids dressed in traditional folk costumes takes the stage for some local dances. The girls wear long bright dresses, the boys the same *gaucho* outfits as the guy with the microphone. Everyone holds out what appears to be a very long handkerchief, and the whole dance seems to revolve round it. At least I can follow this much better than the poetry.

Then, in front of the stage, a few locals start dancing too, and these aren't dressed in any specific costume. They're just ordinary people who've been browsing the stalls.

I watch, fascinated, as whole families dance casually in the middle of the street in front of the stage. After a dance or two, they carry on with their walking, shopping, talking routine, but then others start. For a moment I panic, thinking someone will drag me into this dance, and I have no idea what it is and how it's supposed to work. But no, no one bothers with me. I'm just another tourist planted by a food stall, watching them dance with the joy of life glowing on their faces.

The dances start to get repetitive, and I decide I've had enough. It's time to look for the next attraction. I carry on through the many rows of stalls, looking for *gauchos* and horsemanship shows. I doubt there can be any horses in this huge crowd of people, and sure enough, I find none. Maybe it's too early, maybe it's too late, or maybe today is not the day.

Forget about horses, let's look for this guy, I tell myself, remembering my priority of the day. But it's impossible to actually find anything or anyone in this crowd. I take another look around, get pushed by the crowd towards the other side of the fair, and find myself face to face with a *mate*-cup seller. Now this is an interesting sight. Maybe I should get one, I think. Just to complete my full immersion into the Argentine culture. The cups are made of metal but are covered in brown or black leather and look rather cute. And drinking *mate* is as close to becoming Argentine as one can possibly get.

Made with the leaves of a bush called *yerba mate*, this tea tastes more bitter than anything I have ever tried before. It's usually served in a metal cup and drunk through a silver straw, called a *bombilla*. The cup is filled with the leaves and boiling water is poured over them. The *mate* is then offered around, each person taking turns to drink from the same long straw until it's finished. Then the leaves are replaced and more boiling water is added and the cup offered around again. It's a big insult, apparently, to refuse *mate* or to just take a sip and give it back to the person offering. Being offered *mate* is a big thing here. Like being offered friendship. The trouble starts when you know how horribly bitter it tastes, and you also know you have no way out but to politely accept and take a few sips, without making it too obvious how you really feel about it.

Argentines are addicted to *mate*, and it is widely drunk in Uruguay, Paraguay, and parts of Brazil as well. Once you start drinking it and have got over the initial bitterness, you are likely to carry on. I remember a drive I had with my friends Gabriela and Rosario, where Rosario required *mate* every ten minutes while driving, and Gabriela and I, two strangers to the *mate* culture, spilled boiling hot water from a thermos all over the car in a desperate attempt to keep the *mate* supply going.

But maybe I don't need another addiction. Polo is enough. I decide against buying my *mate* set and carry on looking for love at the Feria de Mataderos—although the name has very little to do with love, *matadero* meaning slaughterhouse. This was the place where the cattle would be brought in and killed, and their meat sold to the city-dwellers. This is no longer done these days, thank God, but meat is still everywhere, at every food stall. Argentine cuisine is heavy on meat, which is a problem, since I've been a vegetarian for nearly thirty years. I look around the huge food stalls, trying to find a more suitable option. I ignore the *choripan* (grilled sausages) and the *panchos* (hot dogs) and make sure I keep well away from the *parrillas*. And then I find my thing—an *empanada* stall.

An *empanada* is a traditional pastry filled with either mince-meat, cheese, corn, onions, vegetables, or whatever else they can get their hands on. I buy a cheese version and then examine the contents of a huge bowl displaying *locro*, or corn stew. I'm not quite sure it's meat-free, though, so I decide against it.

I'm quite happy with my first week here, I decide, as I sit down on a plastic chair in front of the food stall and eat my *empanada*.

I've settled into my flat.

I've started Spanish classes.

I've started physio.

I got asked about twenty times if I'm here alone. Yes, *sola*.

I flirted with my Spanish teacher.

I ate an *empanada* and decided I like it.

Not bad for just one week.

I take another stroll through the stalls, just in case the Universe has decided to deliver Curly Hair in the meantime, but no, it's a missing delivery. He is definitely not here. I have his number, though. For a moment, I contemplate calling him.

"Hi, I'm here. I'm lost . . ."

Ridiculous. I would sound like a desperate tourist. Maybe I am a desperate tourist. No, I'm not, I decide. I'm not a desperate tourist. I'm almost a resident, eating *empanadas*, and I can even understand about half of what people are telling me. And I'm on my way to becoming a full resident and speaking fluently. And I really am not desperate. Not at all. I have outsourced my desperation to the Universe in Paris, and all I need to do now is wait for the delivery. So, no calls. Plus, if he was interested he would have been here. I look around one more time and take a deep breath. There will be others.

On the way home I decide to take the bus. It's the first time I've taken a bus in Argentina. I have no ticket. Can I buy a ticket inside? No, you cannot. Where can I get a ticket? You have to have one before you get on the bus. I switch back to being a desperate tourist in the blink of an eye. I look around waiting for a miracle to happen as the driver patiently waits for me to get off the bus. And then the miracle does happen. The woman behind me tells the driver she's got my ticket and produces one from her bag.

I say, "*Gracias.*"

She smiles. I ask how much I owe her.

"*No nada.*"

"Thank you."

"*No pasa nada.*"

She waves off any further attempts to express my gratitude. It's what people do here, her smile seems to tell me. Look after one another.

Maybe the Universe sent her instead of Curly Hair. Maybe there was a delivery mix-up somewhere up there at the Universe fulfillment center. But hey, if this is the case, I'll take her for now. I have sore feet, a belly full of *empanadas*, and I have no idea where to buy a bus ticket. And she has miraculously solved all these problems in one move. So I'm positive she must be a delivery from the Universe.

TUESDAY 17TH NOVEMBER

It's during week two that it fully hits me—what am I doing here?

I try to tell the question that I've got a to-do list and I know exactly what I'm doing here. I've got five points on that list. But the question ignores my reply, clings to me, and won't go away, however hard I try to push it. It comes back again and again, pulls up a chair next to me, sits down and tries to strike a conversation. And it really isn't a conversation I'm looking forward to, because it threatens to evolve into a much bigger one, along the lines of what I'm doing with my life. And I really don't want to think about this just now.

But the question is always there, walking with me, sitting with me, eating with me, sleeping with me. It's there and there's no way I can pretend it isn't.

"I'm going to recover my arm," I tell the question. "Don't you understand? I need to do physio every day to recover the use of my arm. Is this not enough for you?"

Apparently not. The question remains where it is, unimpressed by this first answer.

"And I'm going to learn Spanish, you'll see. I'll speak it really fluently in three months. And it's going to benefit me in my consulting work. At least I'm doing something with my time off."

My time off from work is dangerous territory. It's best not to go there, but now it's too late. I'm starting to feel like I'm talking to my parents, rather than trying to answer my own question. To my parents, my working life as a freelance consultant is a source of constant wonder, impossible to understand. I work on projects for about half the year, then the other half of the year I spend looking for more projects, or else doing other things when I want to avoid work. Other things, like playing polo, breaking my arms, recovering my arms, going to Argentina to recover my arms, and to play polo again. Basically I earn money, then I spend it, then when I feel I really need to be earning again I look for another project and I earn some more money. It's not a regular job, it's not 9 to 5, and it doesn't come with twenty-one days of holiday per year. But I make more money than if I were employed, and I have about six months off every year. It works for me and I've been doing this for the past ten years. I still haven't managed to convince my parents, though. And now the question seems like it's siding with them. I detect a hidden "You should be back home working on a project right now" behind the innocent "What are you doing here?"

No, I shouldn't be back home. It's winter in England and freezing cold over there, and it's nice and hot here and I want to be here.

I really want to be here and play some polo and fix my wrist and learn some Spanish and . . .

I leave "looking for love" out of the picture for now. When the question comes by, I've learned that it helps to keep things businesslike. The question tends to react badly to stuff like the "I came here to look for love" type of answer. It labels it "blahblahblah" and starts a full-frontal attack, and the last thing I need right now is a full-frontal attack from my question.

So I keep it businesslike. I tell it that learning Spanish will make me more desirable in the consulting marketplace and will help me get a new project. When I'm ready for it. Just not now.

It's a good try, but not good enough. The question refuses to give in. I decide to ignore it and carry on with my week. I go to my language classes. I go to physiotherapy. I eat a lot of *empanadas*. I call Gabriela and Rosario. They are far away in Lobos, so I don't see them. Gabriela tells me to go out and meet some guys. I tell her I will, I'm just settling into my new life.

More language school. More physiotherapy. More *empanadas*.

What am I doing here?

Desperate to silence the question, I hide in my flat and watch the last season of *Downton Abbey*. This is exactly what I would do if I were back in London on a rainy November evening, with too little energy to leave the house. Maybe this will put the question to sleep for a while.

THURSDAY 19TH NOVEMBER

Not only does the question continue to bother me, but to make matters worse Curly Hair has abandoned me. His replacement is called Santi, short for Santiago. Argentines love short forms. He is twenty-something, still a student, and incredibly tall. He seems nice. He doesn't flirt, though. This isn't good. I need a man to flirt with me, if only to make me feel I'm making progress on my to-do list.

Curly Hair is still around in the school and I meet him in the corridors. He doesn't talk much. I feel sad about having a different teacher and I contemplate going to the director of the school and asking to get Curly Hair back. But this would not be fair on Santi, who is actually doing a pretty good job. And since my mind is not set on flirting with Santi, I'm actually making better progress with my Spanish words.

I'm also making progress with my recovery. After a week of physio, my wrist has started to move much better. I'm so distracted by the continuous chatter of my physiotherapists that I forget to scream, and I let them pull and twist and push and force my wrist into submission. It works.

My daily routine is now firmly established:

1. Breakfast at the café on the corner of my street, where chatty waiter brings my coffee.

2. Walk to school, which takes five minutes.

3. Talk to Santi for two hours and diligently let go of all Italian words.

4. Ten-minute walk to physio, grabbing an *empanada* for lunch on the way.

5. Physio session for about two hours. This includes waiting, chatting, saying "Hi" (which takes a long time, since lots of people are involved), saying "Bye" (ditto), the actual one-hour physio session, and then some magnet therapy. Magnet therapy is the best part. It's a kind of *siesta* in which I have a rest while my arm is inside a machine that's supposed to create magnetic fields around

it. I'm not sure what the magnetic field is actually doing to my bones, but I enjoy the *siesta*.

6. Optional extras in the afternoon.

I'm very proud of my optional extras. Two days a week I go to the gym, one day a week I have a massage, and another day I go to a lady who gives private Pilates sessions. This should take care of point five on my list, get back in shape, and support point two, play polo. My program during the day is as packed as that of a pre-teen with pushy parents. I feel good, though. This program achieves two main things—it keeps the irritating question at bay and ensures a smooth progress with my to-do list.

In the evenings I go home and watch another episode of *Downton Abbey*.

But the question I struggle so hard to keep in check is still there with me throughout the day, walking with me from the café at the corner of my street to the language school, and then on to the *empanada* place and then on again to the physio center. It sits with me in the waiting room, lies on the physio bed with me, then walks with me upstairs to the gym, where it sits down again and watches me lifting weights. It's always there, patiently waiting for me to come up with a better answer.

What am I doing here?

FRIDAY 20TH NOVEMBER

After too many evenings watching *Downton Abbey* at home, I decide I'm going to go out.

Gabriela will be pleased. She keeps sending me pushy text messages. She's actually in Switzerland at the moment. She had to leave a few days ago because her mother was ill and about to undergo surgery. But distance doesn't stop her from looking after my social well-being.

Go out, woman! What are you doing hiding in the house???

Up until now I haven't felt like going out. I've been too busy wrestling with my question. I'm still not really sure why I am here. But I can't tell her that; I can't admit to her or to anyone else how little confidence I have in my own to-do list.

But tonight is different. Tonight I will go out, because Curly Hair has invited me.

Actually he's not just invited me, he's organised drinks with all the students in the school, but it's still good. I'll go and we'll have a drink and maybe a chat. He saw me in school today and asked for my phone number.

"To send you the address of the place," he said.

Wow, that's progress!

I continue my Spanish lesson with Santi with a big smile on my face. I will go out tonight! My thoughts dance around my head. Finally I will go out. But Santi doesn't seem to share my dreamy mood, and he points out that I seem to have my mind in the clouds and I'm not focusing on the Spanish words. Then he puts on a tape with a song I'm supposed to translate.

"Listening and comprehension exercise," he says.

Sola en Baires . . . the singer's voice fills the room. *Sola en Baires . . .*

Sola I know very well. But Baires?

"The short form for Buenos Aires," says Santi.

Ah, yes. I remember now. They love short forms of everything.

And I won't be *sola* for long, I want to tell the woman screaming from the small tape recorder on the table. But she doesn't seem to care and the song goes on and on and on.

Sola en Baires . . .

LATER THAT EVENING

I do go out. After a week of diligently carrying on with my classes, physio, and gym routine and hiding in my flat every single evening to watch *Downton Abbey*, I finally manage to go out.

I text Gabriela. *I'm going out tonight!*

I get back lots of red hearts.

So I go out with high hopes that I'll meet lots of red hearts, even if it's only a language school get-together with fellow students, most of whom are German or Swiss guys in their early twenties, and a far cry from my ideal partner.

Curly Hair is there too, but unfortunately he comes accompanied by three beautiful girls, all of them staying at his place. Couch-surfing, apparently.

"I like to share my house and make new friends," he says.

I wonder what else he's sharing, and whether it's with all three of them.

It soon becomes apparent that the girls seem more concerned with their phones, texting the whole evening rather than flirting with him, but I'm disappointed nevertheless. A professional flirt, that's what my Curly Hair is. Ah well, there will be others, I tell myself again, and decide to take a good look around.

Looking around in a bar full of Argentines is not a hard job. They all look around, too. All the time. I remember a friend telling me a story back in London when I told him I was thinking of spending three months in Argentina.

"Take care with the guys there," he said. "Don't believe them. They will say anything. Anything. Really. You have no idea."

He'd been living in Buenos Aires for a few months, he told me, and once went out with an Argentine friend to a local bar.

As soon as they got there, his friend looked around, picked a girl, went straight to her and said:

"Your eyes are the most beautiful eyes I have ever seen."

The girl didn't even bother to answer.

Unfazed, the friend looked around again, picked another one, went to her directly and said:

"Your eyes are the most beautiful eyes I have ever seen."

Another rejection. He then carried on. My friend watched him target half a dozen girls, delivering the same message about the supposed beauty of their eyes. In the end the guy was unsuccessful, but he swore his method would eventually deliver results.

"So," my friend concluded, "take care. Don't believe everything they tell you. Don't believe the guys."

Argentine girls know this, which is why they are hard to get. Or play hard to get, as Gabriela says. She complains a lot about the Argentines. She's not one of them, not by birth at least, but she's an adopted Argentine, as I point out to her all the time. She tells me I don't understand.

Half-Mexican and half-Swiss, Gabriela came here more than ten years ago and decided she liked the way they spoke Spanish, so she would stay. She bought a flat, refurbished it, then when it was all done she bought the one next door and tore everything she'd done to pieces again to make one bigger flat. Gabriela is like that—she likes things to be perfect. Then she fell in love with a polo player and moved to his *estancia* with him. She still has the flat in Buenos Aires and uses it once in a while to get away from the farm and live like a carefree city girl for a few days. She says it gives her breathing space.

Gabriela had also warned me not to take Argentine guys seriously, but tonight she needn't have worried. Although I sense a lot of keen looks around, no one actually initiates any conversations. I'm a bit puzzled. How come nobody approaches me to talk in here and yet everybody wanted to talk to me elsewhere? All the taxi drivers, waiters, shop assistants, language teachers, and physio trainers I interact with—they are all very talkative and they all ask me if I'm *sola*. Maybe it's just their way of being polite.

I decide to go home early. Curly Hair is busy with his harem and the guys from the language school are speaking English to each other, and this means I can't even practice my Spanish. No one comes to tell me my eyes are the most beautiful eyes they'd ever seen. I drink my beer and leave. I comfort myself with the thought that at least I made an effort to go out.

And I will persist. I have to. For the sake of point four on my list, which says, "fall in love." I'm not going to fall in love if I'm hiding in my flat watching *Downton Abbey*. Gabriela is right. I have to go out again.

SATURDAY 21ST NOVEMBER

Buenos Aires has a surprisingly well-ordered traffic system. Although the way they drive is wild—with sharp turns, sudden braking, near misses while overtaking and a tendency to cut up those unfortunate pedestrians who are just about to cross the street—there is a basic sense of order and predictability in the way their streets are designed. You have the *avenidas*—the big streets. Then you have the *calles*—the smaller streets. On the *avenidas* the traffic flows in both directions; the *calles* are one-way. In between them, they form a grid of rectangles with buildings nicely aligned. At every junction there is a traffic light. It's pretty easy to navigate.

Recoleta, with its beautiful French architecture from the beginning of the twentieth century and its luxury-goods shops and elegant people, is considered to be the city's best district. It's also the most expensive neighborhood. Palermo comes second to Recoleta and is considered the trendy neighbourhood. People here are younger than in the aging Recoleta, more international and easy-going. It's a very traveler-friendly area. And right in the middle of Palermo, the Argentines have built the only polo stadium in the world to be found in the middle of a city.

Palermo has it all. It's safe, and it's got the polo stadium and all the entertainment you need on your doorstep. Plus in my case it has another great advantage—the physio center.

Some travelers prefer Puerto Madero, which has a similar atmosphere to London Docklands, where I lived for a few years—old warehouses converted into luxury lofts, lots of fancy hotels, and wide-open spaces, but lots of concrete and iron, and seagulls flying over the sea. Well, not really the sea, only the Plata River, but it's so big it could be the sea. Puerto Madero is far from everything else, and in the same way London Docklands is not really London, this area is not really Buenos Aires. And because in London I now live in Notting Hill, I decide to make Palermo, the equivalent neighborhood in Buenos Aires, my base.

Palermo is divided into several sub-neighborhoods, with names such as Palermo Soho, Palermo Hollywood, and Palermo Chico. The atmosphere varies greatly as you move around these sub-neighborhoods, passing from squares filled with bars and restaurants to quiet, tree-lined residential streets. Palermo Alto, which is where my flat is located, is a middle-class area with tall blocks of flats, convenience shops, a big shopping center called Alto Palermo, and a busy road passing straight through the middle of it all—Avenida Santa Fe.

I'm walking around my neighborhood today because it's Saturday and I have no school, no physio, and no gym, and I'm not quite sure what to do with myself. *Sola en Baires.*

I'm walking down Avenida Coronel Diaz, which is at the junction of my street. This is handy, since most taxi drivers take instructions in terms of a junction. To them the name of my street, Charcas, and a number doesn't mean anything. Charcas and Coronel Diaz, well, that's another story. I learned that on day two and it has ensured my safe return home in a taxi ever since.

I'm not really sure what to do in the absence of a program, so I decide to do chores. It's a safe choice, and it stops the old question from coming back. First I need a to find a shop to have my favorite earrings repaired. Hopefully I can muster the words to explain what I need.

"Hi, do you repair earrings here?" I try my luck in the first jewelry shop I come across.

"Hola." She smiles. *"Cómo estás?"*

How am I? Why does she care how I am? I'm not here for me, I'm here for the earrings.

I show her the problem. She says they can repair them and that I should come back in a few hours.

My next stop is the launderette. My flat doesn't have a washing machine. Very few flats in Buenos Aires actually have one, and dishwashers are even rarer. But here, there are launderettes at every corner and they cost next to nothing. Sixty pesos for a full load works out to about £5. I've discovered that £5 in Argentina buys you pretty much anything—a blow dry, a manicure, one lunch with drinks, or half an hour of physio.

"*Hola. Cómo estás*?" I ask the old man behind the counter at the first launderette I spot. I'm freshly trained by the jewelry shop to take things slowly.

He smiles and tells me he's doing great, and how am I?

"Good, thank you." I point to the bag of clothes, thinking we're done with the niceties and can now get straight down to business. But no, it's not so easy. He wants to know my name. Roxana, I say, and then I give him my short form: Roxy. They all like short forms here. But he sticks to the full length of it and pronounces it the way most Argentines do: Rosanna.

"And where do you come from, Rosanna?"

"Ah, from a long way away. From Romania."

"How interesting. How is Romania these days?"

Well, I don't know how Romania is, because I live in London and have been living there for the past thirteen years. I struggle to explain, wondering for the hundredth time why I don't make up an easier story about where I come from.

"Ah, even more interesting. And what brings you here?"

"I need to strengthen my wrist. I broke it badly last year and had surgery just before coming here."

By now I'm impressed I can say all this in Spanish. Two weeks of language school have done miracles. Or maybe the second week did it all, since I spent my time actually studying with Santi instead of flirting with Curly Hair.

"No! Really? And what happened? How did you break your wrist?"

"I had a fall in a tournament. I play polo."

"Seriously? I thought only men played polo."

"No, ladies too. We play mixed in England."

"Do women play polo here as well?"

"Yes, they do, but not mixed. Guys with guys. Girls with girls."

He smiles. This makes sense to an Argentine psyche. Men and woman flirt with one another here; they don't play rough games together.

"And how long are you going to be here?"

"A few months, perhaps. I'm not sure." I glance back nervously at the two women who are also waiting with bags full of washing. They don't seem to mind that it's taking a long time to get through this customer-interrogation phase before we can arrive at my laundry bag.

"And where do you live?"

I tell him I live around the corner.

"And are you *sola* here?"

Ah yes, back to the *sola* question again.

Yes. *Sola*.

"How come?"

He is now leaning over the counter watching me attentively, as if he's watching an interesting TV reality show, and I'm the star. The women behind me are clearly listening to the conversation and they, too, are interested to hear what I'm going to say next.

"Well, I'm alone. No boyfriend."

"How about in London? Have you got a boyfriend waiting for you?"

"No, I don't."

"*Pero cómo*?" the old man exclaims. "*Están ciegos en Londres*?" Are they blind in London? He points at me and carries on in the same stunned voice. "A beautiful girl like you alone? *Sola*? Alone in London as well? They must be blind. Men in London must be blind."

The women behind nod approvingly. One smiles at me. "*No te preocupes*." Don't worry. Here, a girl like you won't be *sola* for long!

I nod, smiling to hide my embarrassment. It's not like I'm a top model in the prime of her youth. I've just turned forty-one, for God's sake. I may look a lot younger—I've been told so many times—but the reality of the situation is that I'm divorced, I'm over forty, I have a wrist that doesn't move, and I have been single for longer than I'm prepared to admit to anyone.

I talk to the guy for about twenty minutes before I finally give him my bag of dirty laundry and agree to pick it up the next morning.

Just before I go, the old man adds, "And don't worry. If no one asks you out in a week from now, I'll do it."

I glance at him. In the back, I can see an old woman, his wife probably, ironing shirts. She doesn't look like she would mind. I don't mind either. I smile.

"*Dale*," I tell him. "We have a deal."

At least I have a fallback option.

SUNDAY 22ND NOVEMBER

I'm going out again today., I've been invited to an *asado*—that is, a barbecue. An *asado* is not just a barbecue, but a full Argentine tradition. Too bad I'm a vegetarian, but I'm sure there will be something for me there. The *asado* is being given by some friends of my friends in London. They don't really know me, but here people are very welcoming and don't mind inviting you for an *asado* just because a friend has put you in touch.

I buy a bottle of wine and head over to pick up my earrings.

They have been repaired. Beautiful work. I ask how much it costs.

"No-o-o. *Nada.*"

"What do you mean, *nada*? You just repaired my earrings."

"It's nothing." She waves her hand. "Really nothing. *Tranqui.* Lovely earrings, by the way. Enjoy wearing them."

I stand there with my purse in my hand, still not believing she doesn't want me to pay for the repair. Maybe she'll try to sell me something else instead? But no, she doesn't. She just reaches out, takes a small jewelry bag from under the counter, and puts the earrings inside.

"They'll keep better in a bag."

"*Gracias.*"

She smiles and nods. Thanks received. There's nothing else to add. I go without paying. I still don't understand how this works.

LATER THAT DAY

The friends of my friends own a beautiful penthouse apartment in a normal block of flats which they have converted into a guesthouse. From the outside, there's no sign that this is now a luxury guesthouse. No name on the door, no sign on the building. But once you step inside, a lavish staircase greets you, and a lovely, cozy lobby that would rival that of any boutique hotel in Europe. At the back, a large terrace and a professionally refurbished kitchen complete the picture. They have six rooms available for guests and are permanently booked up.

It's a secret place, but Argentines love secret places. It's part of the *puerta cerrada* culture, which literally means "closed door." The *puerta cerrada* restaurants, for instance, are a well-established presence on the Buenos Aires culinary scene. It works like this: you find a place to have dinner, usually advertised online as a seat at someone's dinner table in a normal house. You book weeks in advance and then you turn up at someone's living room, where you meet up with six to eight other guests while the host cooks a feast for you. It's not a cheap experience, but not crazy either, and you get to enjoy fine dining and meet other people at the same time. Lots of the diners are locals, so the added bonus is that you can get to practice your Spanish.

The *puerta cerrada* dining experience was definitely something I wanted to try, and my *asado* at my new friends' came close to this. Someone's living room—actually a terrace in this case—people I didn't know, great food, lovely conversation. In no time at all I feel I've known them for a lifetime. This is what tends to happen in Argentina.

I enjoy the *asado* with them and their guests. We are about twenty people around a long table on the terrace. A couple of the hotel guests mingle with their Argentine friends. The conversation is mostly in English, at times reverting to Spanish when the Argentines become animated while talking about politics. It's election day today. On a grill nearby, tons of meat is being cooked. I look around trying to spot something else, something I can actually eat. I can't see anything.

The Argentine *asado* consists of meat, meat, and then some more meat. Because the friend of my friend is English, I'm lucky to get a potato salad on the side. This is unusual for an Argentine *asado*. Normally there's only tomatoes and lettuce. But the meat is grilled in copious quantities and is cooked throughout the day.

Strongly rooted in the *gaucho* culture, cattle raising, and the vast farmlands, the *asado* is intertwined with the Argentine soul. It's not just the Spanish word for grilled meat, it's a social event consisting of slow food, where a typical meal lasts for five to seven hours. It's the backbone of the Argentine social life and provides endless opportunities for socializing. The *asador*, the person actually grilling the meat, is always a man and usually gets a round of applause as he delivers the last plate of grilled meat to the table. The fire needs to be a wood fire, and any serious Argentine would despise propane gas or even charcoal.

Women have little to do at an *asado*. They prepare the salads and the sweets, and then gather in groups to chat while different cuts of meat are added to the grill.

I had come to understand the extent of the *asado* culture at my Argentine polo club in London, where the grooms would wake up at 5:00 am on a Sunday to make a huge fire that would die down while they were getting the horses ready. Then they would stick a couple of whole lambs on two huge forks right on the edge of the fire and leave them there to cook for hours as we played the games. Afterwards, everyone would gather around to eat the meat—everyone but the vegetarians like me, who were forced to turn to the potato salad.

Here there are no whole lambs, but the quantity of meat added to the grill is much bigger. People eat, chat, drink Malbec, and eat again. I get to know them all—their stories, why they're here, what they are doing. About half are tourists, the other half locals. There's a fat Canadian lady in her mid-forties who decided to take six weeks off from her post as a university professor and tour South America, but now that she's in Buenos Aires she can't bring herself to leave. She loves the cultural scene and every single evening she finds another theater, dance, or music show to go to.

Then there's a tango enthusiast—an American guy in his fifties who has come here to practice tango and go to the best tango clubs. Known as *milongas*, Buenos Aires has quite a few of them. There are also a couple of Brits on their honeymoon, too absorbed in each other to notice anything around them. They make me wonder why people would want to go traveling on honeymoon. There's a guy from Australia who is packing in as many South American countries as possible in a ten-day trip. There are also two Argentine couples in their mid-thirties, but I have no idea what they are doing with their lives since the fat Canadian lady has planted herself next to me and talks non-stop. In English. Not good for my Spanish practice, I think.

Everyone talks about the elections. The Argentine political scene is always a drama, but feelings are running particularly high today. It's a big day. After eight years of leftist Peronist rule, today the Argentines are voting for a new president. The choice is between Scioli, a left-wing candidate who will continue the populist mandate of the current president, Cristina Fernanadez de Kirchener, or Macri, a right-wing candidate who wants to turn Argentina towards the outside world and promises an ambitious list of political and fiscal reforms.

People who are poor vote for Scioli, I'm told. They rely on the subsidies the Peronist government pledges to hand out. People who have businesses vote for Macri. This is because he promises to reduce the red tape, bringing the official exchange rate in line with the more realistic black-market one and thus boosting the economy. I don't understand much about their politics, but everyone around the table supports Macri, so I decide I'll support him too. Not that I have a say anyway.

But they don't expect Macri to win. It would be too good to be true, they say. I have learned that Argentines have a tendency to be fatalists.

By 6:00 pm, yet more quantitates of meat have been added to the grill. I can't imagine how people can possibly still eat. But they can. They talk, they drink, and they eat slowly. The lunch started at 1:30, and we've been going on for more than five hours now. I munch on a piece of bread and some potato salad. Occasionally I add some tomatoes.

At 7 pm they bring out the dessert. Two types of cake—one a tiramisu and the other a round fruit tart. I dive into them both and serve myself twice from each cake. It feels like I'm finally eating.

At 8 pm, after more than six and a half hours sitting around a table, the lunch slowly starts to come to an end. People begin to leave—Argentines to their homes, tourists to their rooms. I remember I'm supposed to meet my friend Marco tonight, and I say farewell to my hospitable hosts.

I rush home to change my clothes and find five annoyed messages from Marco on the English phone which I had left at home.

Where are you? Just landed. Am I having dinner by myself?

Now, I can't possibly let Marco have dinner by himself. He's one of my closest friends. I have known him for more than fifteen years, ever since we met on the corridors of the Bocconi School of Management in Milan as students for a Master in Business Administration. Marco is my old classmate, and much more than that—my soul brother, business adviser and, even more importantly, psychotherapist. Every time I've been though a messy breakup (and there have been quite a few in the last fifteen years), I've ended up calling Marco. Extensively. After one particular messy breakup, I called him every day for about three months. He listened. He picked up the phone on his way back from work and talked to me as he got home, as he got changed, as he started cooking his dinner. Marco loves to cook. His secret dream is to own his own restaurant one day. Too bad he's too busy with his life as a business consultant.

But back to this particularly messy breakup. Marco saved me. He talked to me as he sat on the toilet and as he washed the dishes.

He talked even when he had his mouth full of his evening meal and he couldn't talk any longer.

"But I can listen. You talk now," he would say.

And then I would talk. I would pour all of my broken heart into that phone and tell him over and over again the same old story.

"Aha," he would say. And then he would carry on listening. After about two hours on the phone, he would say he needed to watch some TV dramas to escape my real dramas and that I could call him the next day if I needed to chat. Which I did. I always did.

All this was about twelve years and three breakups ago. With time I became less obsessive in my post-breakup need for therapy, but he was still there for me. Every time I needed him. It didn't matter that we lived in different countries and only saw each other in person once every couple of years. It didn't matter that over the years we both got engaged, married, and divorced (to different people, obviously). Marco was always there for me when I needed him. Full stop. And his extremely cynical view of the world was there, too. It came bundled together as an all-inclusive package.

"So tell me, have you screwed up your business career completely this time?" he asks casually as he cuts a big slice of pizza.

Marco is Italian. Like every Italian, he is obsessed with how exquisitely food is cooked in Italy and how terribly it is done everywhere else. But tonight he told me he would take me to one of the few places in Buenos Aires which actually knows how to make a pizza.

"No, I'm not going to screw up my business career. I just took a break. It's not a big deal. I need to recover my arm."

"How long since you worked?" he carries on, unimpressed.

As usual, Marco displays a very precise ability to hit the nail on the head and smash my own head in the process. All in one go. I dread this question. The only other question that's worse is how long have I been single. And Marco is one of the very few people in the world who knows the answer to this one.

"I haven't worked since July, actually. I wanted to play some polo. And then I needed to have my surgery. And now I'm here, to recover."

"We're in November." He points out the obvious. "So there will be at least eight months' break before you get back to work. And you tell me this doesn't matter for your career?"

Before Marco became a management consultant, he was an accountant. I hate the ease with which he deals with figures, especially when they don't work in my favor.

"Look, you don't understand. I'm a freelance consultant. I've done this job for a while. A long while—almost ten years, to be exact. It's OK. I'll get back to London and I'll get another project and I will—I will—"

"What are you living off now? I hope you haven't re-mortgaged your flat in London to come here."

He carries on savoring his pizza while he continues the questioning. Now he sounds like my parents. But he is still Marco, which means I can't get angry with him, like I would do with my parents if they were to ask the same question. I'm just a little bit annoyed. I tell him I haven't remortgaged my flat and that I'm all right.

"You hear me? I'm all right. Absolutely all right. Enough with lecturing me."

He nods and moves on to the next subject. "How long since you last had sex?"

He can ask this because he is Marco. He knows all about me. He knows it's been a long time. He does not know about this, though . . .

I tell him about the handsome guy I met while on holiday in Barbados and about the hot night we spent together before I left, and in justification I tell him I had to do it, otherwise I would have forgotten how sex is done.

Marco stops chewing his pizza, takes a long, pitiful stare at me, and concludes, "Roxy, you need a proper boyfriend."

"Yes, I do. That's why I'm here. I'm going to find him here. It's point four on my list."

But Marco isn't impressed with my list. There are too many extracurricular activities on it, he says. Regarding point four, he tells me to take care.

"Don't believe the Argentines," he warns me. "They seem very friendly, but in the end they are very superficial. They will tell you everything you want to hear to get you into their bed, and then they will break your heart." He pauses, giving me a hard stare. "And I don't . . . you hear me? Don't want to deal with that again, because I know what happens. You will call me. You always call me. Oh God." He rolls his eyes at the thought. "You'll start calling me again. Soon. Roxy, please take care this time."

"I will." I smile. "And if I call, you'll be there to pick up that phone. Like you've always been. And it won't be that bad this time, I promise."

Somewhere in the corner of the pizzeria, the TV is tuned to the election channel. They're counting the votes. The whole country is in turmoil. At 12:30, just as we finish our meal, it turns out that Mauricio Macri has won the election. Against all odds.

MONDAY 23RD NOVEMBER

After just one evening talking with Marco in Italian, my Spanish has gone into hiding. The next day Santi is incredibly frustrated with the return of the Italian words.

"No more Marco. No more. I just got rid of all those Italian words from your vocabulary and now they're all back."

"Yes, I know, but you see, Marco is Marco. I have to speak Italian to him. We could speak English or Spanish, but it won't be the same. And I only see him so rarely and he's now gone. He was here on a quick business trip."

"OK, but keep away from the Italians. We are going to turn you into a Spanish speaker. A proper Spanish speaker."

He means an Argentine Spanish speaker. At least here we are in agreement. I nod, diligently repeat my verb tenses, do my homework, and overall try to be a very obedient schoolgirl.

This week I have a new goal. I really need to sort out this going-out thing. Gabriela is losing patience with me. Her text messages are getting more direct.

Have you met anyone?

Hmm. Curly Hair sent me a flirty text message yesterday. Well, at least I assume it's flirty, because it said: *How's the most beautiful student of the language school doing today?* I told him I was busy with an *asado* and dinner with a friend. It didn't sound very encouraging in case he wanted to ask me out. I got ready to let him know that I wasn't always that busy in case he sent me another message. But a second message never came. Then today in school he acted as if he didn't see me. Maybe he felt rejected? I have no idea, but I decide this puzzling behavior doesn't count as meeting anyone.

No, but I will, I reply.

Go out, woman, she texts back. This is followed by lots of bottles of Champagne. Gabriela loves her emojis.

I will go out, I have a plan. Someone at the *asado* told me about Spanglish. It's a great concept. People meet in a bar to practice languages—in this case English and Spanish. It works like a sort of speed dating, except there's no dating involved. Or so I understand. You sit at a table and get paired with a stranger. It can be a man or a woman, young or old, it doesn't matter. It will be someone who also wants to practice their language. You start speaking one language for five minutes. Then the organizer says "stop," and everyone changes language. You then speak the other language for five minutes. Then the organiser says "stop" again and you rotate the table, find yourself in front of another stranger, and the process gets repeated. And then again. All for about two hours, then everyone has a drink, and if you want to hang out, you all go out dancing afterwards.

It sounds perfect. I have researched it, and I know where it is. It happens almost every night of the week. I decide to go. Some day.

FRIDAY 27TH NOVEMBER

Ping. Message.

Have you gone out?

Gabriela is relentless.

I think hard. What can I possibly find that would fit her definition of going out?

No, I decide is the truthful answer.

Why not??? What the fuck is wrong with you??

Gabriela swears a lot. I've learned not to take it personally. She actually claims she has Tourette's, that condition that makes people say a lot of bad words.

I don't know what's wrong with me. I really tried to get myself to go out. I've even finished the whole *Downton Abbey* series, so I have no more excuses not to go out. Even if it's scary to be alone in this big city. And I don't even know what I'm scared of. Not the city and not the people here, definitely not. It's the most friendly city I ever lived in. Maybe I'm just scared that my search for love will leave me disappointed once again. Or maybe I'm just tired to start again from the beginning: new city, new life, new friends, and hopefully a new love. And yet . . . he may be out there. The man of my dreams might be out there just waiting for me to finally get out of the house. I have to make an effort. Gabriela is right.

I look at her question again and I tell her I've been to the *asado* with some friends and to a dinner with Marco.

Doesn't count, she texts back. *Go somewhere you can meet new people! How about that Spanglish?*

I wanted to go, I tell her. But on Wednesday I didn't feel like it. Thursday I didn't feel like it, either.

You have to go tonight!!!

OK, I will, but tonight I have agreed to meet the friends who own a guesthouse and some of their clients . . .

Fuck them. Go out. Now. No emojis this time.

It turns out that it's possible to do both. "Go out," which for Gabriela means go out alone to meet new people, and "go out" with my new friends and their guests at the same time. Well, not exactly at the same time, but in the same evening. The guests are English. This means they want to meet up for drinks around 7 pm. No sane Argentine would go out at 7 pm for drinks. They are all at home taking a nap.

Siesta is a powerful word in Argentina. In the countryside it's done properly, after lunch. They eat around 1:30 and then they all disappear to their rooms for a couple of hours' sleep. That is, when they have a normal lunch that only lasts for about an hour—not an *asado* that goes on for the whole afternoon and replaces the *siesta*. If you don't feel like sleeping, that's your problem, because everyone else does, so all you can do is retire to your room and pretend to sleep.

Last year I spent two weeks with Rosario, who is the cousin of Patricio (the polo player and Gabriela's boyfriend). I met Rosario at the Christmas gathering the first time I was in Argentina. Rosario is two years older than me, an artist at heart and an art teacher in one of the schools in Lobos in her everyday life. She also speaks impeccable English after spending more than ten years in the US. She eventually came back to Argentina to give her son a better chance of growing up in a supportive environment. Rosario is the single mother of a teenage rebel son with whom she spends many days and nights arguing about studying, passing exams, cleaning his room, and not staying out late when he goes out. Typical teenager stuff.

Rosario is also a passionate admirer of Frida Kahlo. Soon after I met her, I developed a strong suspicion she was the reincarnated version of Frida Kahlo herself, because of the numerous portraits of the painter scattered all over her house, and the huge green parrot she kept in a cage. Just like Frida's.

Rosario and I became instantly close. Like twin sisters, despite the fact that we're not that similar physically. I have blonde highlights and Rosario's hair is dark brown; my boobs are too small and she thinks hers are too big. I wish I had boobs like hers. But women are like that, never happy with the size of their boobs. Physically we didn't look alike, but we felt like soul sisters inside from the moment we met at the Christmas Eve family gathering. Two days afterwards, the three of us (it turned out that Gabriela liked Rosario a lot, too) decided to go on a girls' road trip to the sea. Four days, 300 kilometers, and many bottles of wine later, we came back, and it was as though we had known each other for a lifetime.

The three of us have remained close ever since, and later that year, when I turned forty and panicked, not quite knowing what to do on my birthday, Gabriela came up with a brilliant idea.

"Why don't you come to the farm? And don't worry, we'll help you turn forty, darling, and you'll be all right."

So I did. I told my boss at work I absolutely had to take a long weekend off to go away for my birthday and I told him he didn't want to put up with me on my fortieth birthday, anyway. The best solution for everyone concerned would be for me to be too far away to cause damage. My boss agreed. He was a wise man, my boss. I got myself on a flight and went to Argentina for five days. Gabriela picked me up from the airport in a 4x4 pickup truck, a bottle of beer in one hand. We celebrated my birthday at the farm, eating a chocolate cake with a horse's head on it (chocolate, of course), and I got as a present a basket with forty polo balls. Patricio told me I had to score a goal with every single one of them. I said I would, eventually, but I had to leave them at the farm for now, as they were too heavy to carry back to Europe. I took only one back with me—one small, white polo ball on which they all wrote their happy birthday wishes.

The day after my birthday I went to Buenos Aires with the girls for another dinner. They helped me survive that scary fortieth birthday just as they'd promised, and it was not as bad as I'd feared. And then I flew back to London after only five days, and life started smiling at me again.

But back to the *siesta* concept. In the two weeks I spent with her, Rosario taught me everything there is to know about *siesta*. After we had lunch, I used to ask her, what do we do now?

Now? *No pasa nada*. It's *siesta* time.

So we would sleep after lunch. Every single day, for two weeks. By the end of it I really got the concept.

City-dwellers with 9-to-5 jobs don't have this luxury. They can't sleep after lunch, because businesses don't close for *siesta*. But they can sleep as soon as they get home from work, which they do without fail. They get home by 6 pm, take a nap till 9 pm, wake up fresh, do their things, have a bite to eat by midnight, and maybe go out later. They come back home to sleep around 2 am and still manage to clock around eight hours' sleep. It's just that it's made up of two parts.

As a result, nobody in Argentina would go out at 7 pm. For them, going out starts at 10:30 and can go on until about 12:30-ish, if not later. This, on a weekday. On a weekend, it's a different story. Going out on a weekend involves drinks from 11 pm , dinner around midnight, drinks again after dinner around 2 am, and going to a disco from 3 am onwards. It doesn't make sense to go to a disco before this, because discos are usually empty until about two or three in the morning. People are busy eating. At six or even seven in the morning, discos close and people go home with the sunrise.

This pattern meant I could actually go out twice in an evening. Meet the English at 7 pm for drinks, have dinner with them at 8 pm, hang out for a couple of hours, and by the time they were ready to go home to sleep, I could carry on and meet the Argentines for a new set of drinks.

So I go to a small and noisy jazz bar where I meet the English group and spend a few hours listening to a local band trying hard to damage the hearing of the twenty or so people crammed around the few tables inside. The music is loud and not really to my taste. I've never been a jazz fan anyway. The bar serves food as well and we manage to eat and even talk a little when the band takes a break. I wish they would take breaks more often.

After a couple of hours, I finally excuse myself and go in search for the other bar where the Spanglish event takes place. It's easy to find it, since all the trendy bars are usually lined up in the center of Palermo.

This place is bigger and, thank God, does not have loud music. Just some wooden tables that wait half-empty for the crowd to gather. It's 10:30 already, but Argentines are not really punctual. I'm told to take a seat at one of the vacant tables and wait for a while. More people are due to come.

I try to accustom my eyes to the very dark room that is lit only by the candles placed in colorful terracotta jars on the wooden tables. The place looks trendy, although a bit empty. A few other people are seated at the tables around and seem to be waiting for something to happen. I'm starting to feel uneasy.

But just before I decide to forget about Spanglish and call it a night, the organizer comes around to announce we're finally starting.

A woman in her early thirties comes by and sits at my table. She wears a black top and a short skirt. She seems dressed for a disco, I think. She also seems very friendly, says hi and asks me if

I've been here before. I say I haven't. She tells me I'm going to love it, it's just a friendly chat with some people and then everyone goes out dancing. Ah, that explains the short skirt and the black top.

She tells me she's an English teacher who teaches in a number of schools simultaneously, using video conferencing. I'm impressed. She says there aren't enough teachers, so the government uses distance teaching for English. Fascinated, I ask for more details. We change language and now she explains to me in fluent English how this distance-teaching business works. I want to speak to her for ages, but the organizer comes around and asks us to switch tables.

My second speaking partner is an older guy. He's deeply into politics. He tells me about the pain of setting up a business in Argentina. His small company imports sports equipment and distributes it to shops. They have no access to foreign currency, which they need to buy the goods. They have to apply for lengthy permits and sometimes they get them, other times they don't. He tells me his main job as the managing director of the business is queuing at the Ministry of Industry, hoping he will get authorization to buy foreign currency. Once, he only went in to have a rest from the heat outside, since he knew the waiting room so well, and a employee came out and asked him what he was waiting for, and he wasn't really waiting for anything, but actually the employee said he could help him . . . and . . .

The organizer comes round again to tell us the ten minutes are up and we need to exchange tables once again.

"Hang on, I want to know—I want to know what happened!"

But we have to move. The businessman stands up and goes to the other table while still carrying on talking to me. I'm not sure I get the full story, but I think he tells me he got the authorization to buy foreign currency just on that one day, when he didn't expect it, when he had gone in there by chance.

I sit down at the next table in front of my third speaking

partner, and my mind is still with the old man from the previous conversation. I hope the results of this election are going to make life easier for him.

My new speaking partner doesn't talk much. He asks about me.

I'm here to recover my arm.

What happened to your arm?

Polo, bones, screws. The same old story. By now I can say it pretty fluently.

"Wow, how interesting. Tell me more."

I tell him more. Polo. Horses. Excitement.

"Why do you play?"

Joy. Feels like flying. The wind on your face. Friendship. Doing something out of the ordinary . . .

"Tell me more."

I speak and words flow out of me. All of a sudden I'm back on a polo field talking about the sport I love so much. I fill the full ten minutes with talking about it. I can't believe I have enough Spanish words to fill all this time.

The organizer comes round and asks us to change once again.

I stop, suddenly realising I haven't asked the guy in front of me one single question. But it's too late. I need to go.

"Would you mind if we speak again?" he asks, just as I stand up to change tables. "I mean, if we meet up to practice our languages again?"

"Uh, yes. Sure. Why not?"

"Can I have your phone number?"

I look at him. The light that comes from the candle on the table is so dim that I can barely see his face. He seems polite, well-mannered, and calm. He also seems very interested in everything that interests me.

Yes, why not?

I give him my number and we switch tables again.

In a corner I see the old man from before, talking animatedly to another guy. Probably telling the same story of trying to buy foreign currency unsuccessfully and getting the permit just that one day when he didn't try.

I start talking to my fourth speaking partner. He is a computer programmer who wants to go to Europe and find a job.

This is quite fun. I decide I like Spanglish.

SATURDAY 28TH NOVEMBER

I didn't stay long last night. I didn't go out dancing afterwards, didn't even linger for a drink at Spanglish once the ten-minute talking rounds were over.

I went home and triumphantly texted Gabriela.

I have been out!!

And?

Nothing. Nothing had happened, but I had been out, and that was the main thing.

Today I'm going out again, this time to see Rosario. I'm going to travel two hours to Lobos by bus to spend the weekend with her. Gabriela isn't with us. She's still in Switzerland, hopefully due to come back next week.

I get on the bus happy, anticipating being in the *campo* again. I love the Argentine *campo.* When I first got to San Patricio, the *estancia* where Gabriela and Patricio live, I thought I'd arrived in heaven. I kept on marveling at every tree, every leaf, and every animal, as if I was a person who had never seen nature in all her life.

Gabriela had tried to be polite, but eventually her down-to-earth nature overcame her patient smiles.

"What the fuck, girl, have you never seen a tree before?"

"Yes, I have. But do you know how it feels like to be on a 7 am commute on the underground in London? Every single day?"

No, she doesn't. She doesn't commute to work. She lives on a farm, designs handbags in her spare time and sells them at the polo events where her boyfriend plays. No, she doesn't know how it feels to commute on the London underground in the morning, and she has no idea how many people in thick winter coats can be crammed into one square foot. No conception of the metallic sound of the carriages, while a continuous stream of grey passes in front of your half-closed eyes—grey corridors, grey stations, grey coats worn by grey-skinned people, all going to their grey workplaces on the same cold, grey early morning in London.

So I told her that once she knew that, she would understand why I kept marveling at every tree and every dog I meet.

But that first visit was two years ago. I'm slightly more normal now.

And yet, going to see Rosario and spending two days in the *campo* still fills me with joy.

Ping. Message.

Hola. Cómo estás?

I look at the number. I don't recognise it.

Soy Rodrigo de anoche.

Ah, the guy I spoke to last night. What did we speak about? Can't remember . . . Ah, yes, polo. I can't remember his face well, though. It was too dark.

The next message is in English.

Was nice meeting you. Maybe we can meet again and speak some more.

I text back. *Yes. OK. Nice meeting you too.*

Ping. Another one. This one is from Curly Hair.

Hola beautiful! How is the most beautiful student in the language school doing this morning?

That's his standard phrase. I smile. He's probably just a player and I'm sure he sends this message to everyone. But still, no harm done for answering a flirty message. If nothing comes out of it, at least it counts as training.

LATER THAT DAY

Rosario isn't as cynical as Gabriela, but she too laughs at my attempts to find love in Buenos Aires. She tells me to have fun but to keep my eyes wide open, my heart firmly closed, and above all not to take things seriously. Or, God forbid, fall in love.

"Why? What's wrong with falling in love?"

"Not here," she says, and then she gives me a long list of why not here.

Argentine men don't fall in love. They play. They want sex. They give sex. For this, count on them. They will give you the time of your life. They will call you *linda*, they will make you feel wonderful. They will boost your self-esteem. They will take you to heaven. For one night only. Or a few more. That's it. Then they will move on and do the same with another girl.

"Come on, they can't all be that bad."

"Yes, they are. Trust me. I know what I'm talking about. I'm Argentine."

She's also a single mother. Maybe she knows what she's talking about.

"Roxy, listen, *amiga*. Have all the fun in the world. But please don't get hurt. Remember they're not serious, OK?"

I tell her about Curly Hair and his text messages. She looks at me with that "here we go again" expression in her eyes.

"Did he invite you for dinner?"

"No."

"Did he invite you for a drink?"

"No."

"Did he actually invite you anywhere, suggest anything?"

"No."

"Forget about him. He's a player."

"What do you mean?"

"A player, flirty, nothing serious, *nada*. It doesn't mean anything."

"But the messages . . ."

She takes a look at the long list of them but doesn't bother reading the details. Just a quick scan is enough. She dismisses him with a shake of her head.

"Forget about him. He's a player. I know what they're like. Don't waste your time. And don't get hurt, Roxy. Remember this. You can have all the fun you want with the Argentines, but it's rare they're ever looking for something serious. Got it?"

"Yes. Yes. Got it," I say, but I still think she must be exaggerating. There are also Argentines who settle down and have a family—otherwise this country would disappear!

We go for a walk. Rosario's little house in the middle of the *campo* is an oasis of tranquillity. She lives surrounded by her family, as they all do in Argentina. Her two brothers live down the road, her sister a little bit further on. Her mother lives in town, some ten minutes' drive away, and her father in the big country house next to hers. Her son is growing up surrounded by his cousins and countless aunts and uncles. Patricio's farm is a little bit further away, around twenty minutes' drive. They have many more relatives scattered all around the town. They are a clan, and it was for the support of this clan that she gave up looking for a life outside Argentina. After ten years in the US, she gave it all up—her life there, her green card, the money she could make. She came back to this small town, got her son into a local school, and woke up every morning to the sound of birds singing in the trees. No regrets.

I breathe in deeply that fresh air of the countryside. I love it here. And I love her, too. My Argentine sister with a very big heart, who cares.

SUNDAY 29TH NOVEMBER

Patricio comes to pick me up from Rosario's home and drives me to Buenos Aires. He's going there anyway, to watch the first polo game of the Abierto. This works out perfectly, since I'm going to watch the same game. He comes with Lisa, a German client who has been training for polo with him at the farm. Gabriela is still in Europe for another week or so.

On the way to the capital, I mentally revise my list. The most troubleful point is still number four—"fall in love." Maybe Rosario is right and I need to change that to "have some fun." At least temporarily.

The other points on the list, however, are getting ticked off nicely. I'm quite pleased with my progress over the past three weeks. My wrist is moving much better. Three weeks of daily physio every day is more physio than I had in London in six months. I can see it's working. My hand bends, twists, and only hurts a bit when I get to the end of my range of motion and I press on a little harder. There's still work to do—it's got to be perfect. It's got to move just like the other wrist. This is my goal, and I'll make sure it happens. And until it does, I'll keep on going to physio once a day, every day.

Next in line is point two on my list—play polo. I glance at the front seats where Patricio is talking to Lisa. I will need to find a moment to talk to him today. It's time I start playing again, and what better place to do so than at their farm? There's just one slight difficulty: I need to make Patricio accept payment for it. Ever since that Christmas with them two years ago, he and Gabriela have refused to accept payment for polo. Patricio doesn't want to hear about it. Not when I came to train at his farm, and not when I met him and Gabriela in Spain last spring, where Patricio was contracted to play a tournament. At that time, I hadn't played polo for ten months following my polo accident, and I was rather apprehensive about starting again. They told me to come and see them and spend a few days with them. I came and booked myself a room at the same hotel where they were staying. He got me on one of his horses—the horses that he keeps in Europe, where he plays polo professionally all summer—and we went on the field for a training session. It went well. I had no fear. Then I played a *chukka*, which is one period of a polo game lasting seven-and-a-half minutes. I left after three days, ready for the season that was about to start in England.

Patricio didn't want to hear anything about payment.

"Come on," I told him. "This is your work. You are a professional polo player. You make money playing polo, training people to play polo, and renting out your horses so that people can play polo on them. We can't go on like this forever!"

He just shrugged his shoulders. *"Después vemos,"* he said.

It's an Argentine thing. You become friends, and then they don't want to charge you. It's pretty bad business for them, because they become friends very easily here. As a result, I feel awkward playing polo with him again, but since he's my friend and the main pillar of my Argentine family, I really want to play polo with him again. So I really need to sort this out.

I once tried to sort it out by pulling Gabriela aside and asking her about it, but she cut me short immediately.

"Talk to him. I don't deal with his polo stuff. I don't want to get involved. For me you are a friend. You come to our place whenever you want. The horses, he deals with them."

So I'll have to talk to him today. At the Abierto. Which brings me to point three on my list. I'm seeing the Abierto. Finally.

The Argentine Open Polo Championship, or simply "the Open," or el Abierto, has been going since 1893. History has been made on this polo field in the middle of Buenos Aires. The fathers and grandfathers of today's best players in the world have fought hard for the titles here. The level of horsemanship and game skills one can witness here is unparalleled. There's only one Abierto, and everyone who flies to Argentina to watch these games knows they are in for a treat.

I've bought tickets for every single game, next to Patricio and Gabriela's seats . We'll watch the games together. This is going to be very exciting. I can already feel my mouth dry and a knot in my stomach only when I think about it. These games are the best in the world. I'm also feeling something else in my stomach—more like butterflies this time—when I think about the parties I'm going to go to afterwards, the polo parties. The best in the world as well, they say.

As to point number four—well, I'll sort that one out. I definitely will. In its new form of "have some fun," it shouldn't be that difficult. I take a deep breath in and finally decide it's far better than "fall in love." Yes, definitely better. Rosario might be too harsh in her judgement of Argenine men, but since I haven't made any progress with the original version, maybe I can try this new version for a while. I need to see progress here.

Maybe Marco is right, too. I can still see his face as he concentrated on cutting the perfect slice of pizza, casually asking me how long since I last had sex. And for that, there are plenty of options around. Almost every man I meet here gives out the vibe, "I'm interested and available." The waiter at the corner of my street who still chats me up every morning when I have my coffee, the taxi drivers, the guy at the grocery shop whose face lights up every time he sees me . . .

But I'm getting carried away. I won't just have sex with any random waiter, taxi driver, or shop assistant simply because I've decided to give up on finding love. No, it needs to be a bit more classy than that. What about Curly Hair? Even if Rosario has dismissed him as a player, he's still an option for "having fun only." His messages are definitely getting more daring. The last one from yesterday stated he was very good at giving massages if I was interested.

No, it won't be Curly Hair, I decide. Rosario called him a cheap bastard because he hasn't invited me anywhere. She also told me that in this country men invite women on a date and pay for the food and drink. They also expect sex on the first date too, but at least they pay for the meal. If they don't invite you anywhere, it's a really bad sign. Plus he's still ignoring me at school, which is even worse than not inviting me anywhere. Maybe he's not that interested after all.

So if Curly Hair doesn't invite me anywhere, he'll never know I've seriously considered him as a "have fun" candidate. But then, there will be others. Maybe I'll meet someone at the games today. Or maybe tomorrow. At some point, sooner or later, I will meet someone.

My thoughts are brought to a sudden halt. We've arrived at *La Catedral de Polo*. The Polo Cathedral. The huge polo stadium in the center of Palermo, the neighborhood I'm currently living in. People come from all over the world to watch the best players compete here for the most valuable trophy in polo.

I take a deep breath in as I make my way through the huge crowd gathered at the entrance gates. I manage to produce my ticket and keep close to Patricio and Lisa, careful not to lose them in the crowd. Everyone is dressed casual, shirts and jeans or chinos for men and long summer dresses for women. Polo in Argentina is a much more casual affair than in England. Here, it does not have that ring of exclusivity to it. Everyone plays polo here, and everyone comes to see a polo game, like they would go to see a football game.

The sun is out and it's blazing hot. We head straight for the ice-cream stand, ignoring the many bars that line the way to the tribunes. There's no point trying to buy anything there—the queues are too long.

We finally take our seats and I take a good look at the huge expanse of lush green field that stretches empty in front of us. It's about the size of nine American football fields. At first sight it seems too big for two teams of four players each. But I know that once they get their horses into a gallop they will cover the whole ground in less than a minute.

I ask Patricio why there's no goal awarded on handicap difference at the start of the game, as I would expect. In polo, all players are rated according to their skill level on a handicap grid that starts at minus two and goes up to ten.

In the low-level version of the game that I play, which is also called "low goal," the handicaps of the players are added together and a complex formula is then applied to translate the handicap difference into goals awarded to the lower handicap team at the start of the game. This is to balance out the game and make it a fairer encounter.

He takes a long look at me. I can tell he's amused.

"Of course there are no goals awarded based on handicap difference. It's Open, this championship. Open. *Abierto.* Do you have any idea what that means?"

Aha, I get it. No handicap difference. Should I have known this? I wonder.

"You're the one writing about polo, maybe you should know this." Patricio reads my thoughts. He means my polo blog. It's called "Seven and a Half Minutes," which is the duration of a period of play in polo. I'd been writing and posting polo stories during the time I couldn't play because of my broken wrist.

I may write a blog about polo, but I still don't know a lot of things. I ask Patricio why the names of some players on the board have an "H" in brackets.

"*Hijo.* Son. They have the same name as their fathers, so they are given an H to differentiate."

Ah, I'd forgotten about this, just like his son has the same name as him. Patricio. This is a very Argentine thing.

Then I can't ask anything any longer because there's a sudden gasp from the crowd. It must have been a foul, I deduct, because the umpire has blown the whistle and the game stops. I have no idea what happened—the game is too fast to follow.

Patricio patiently explains that the one of the riders has taken the right of way of another one. This is a big thing. It's like a car suddenly changing lanes on a highway, cutting in front of another one. Players and horses can get seriously injured as a result.

I decide to shut up and not to ask any more questions while the other team executes a sixty-yard penalty. It's an impossible one, but they score.

In polo we have several type of penalties. First there's the thirty-yard penalty, undefended. This is usually an easy goal—well, at least to players better than me. Then we have a forty-yard, defended. This is a particularly nasty one when you are playing on the side trying to defend the penalty. That's because you have to line up with your fellow players in the goal post, trying to stop a hard plastic ball coming at you at speed with nothing but a mallet. It scares me deeply. Every time.

Then there's the sixty-yard penalty, which is a far dream for me. My teammates would not even let me try to take it. I'd have no chance. But here at the Abierto, a sixty-yard penalty is easily converted into a goal.

In the break I get a moment with Patricio alone while the German client goes for a wander. I tell him I want to play again.

"Sure, come over. Whenever you want. I'll let you know if the fields are good."

He means if they're dry. Polo can't be played on fields that are too wet, even though it can be played while it's actually raining. It's complicated, and it has to do with how much water has been retained in the fields, because this can lead to horses sliding and falling. Last week it rained a lot, so the fields are still too wet to play.

I tell Patricio if I come to play polo, I want to make a deal about how much money I pay him. He waves me away.

"Don't worry. We'll talk about it afterwards."

"Afterwards, when? You always say this."

"*Después vemos.*"

"No, no more *después vemos*. I know what you're like. If we don't discuss payment, I'm not coming. I'm serious."

He smiles. "Shall we watch this game now?"

The next chukka is about to start.

"Yes, but—"

"*Después vemos*. Relax."

The game has started again and there is nothing more to say.

The thundering sound of hooves hitting the ground rises up to the stands and everyone watches, in silence, the impossible dance of eight players fighting for a small plastic ball.

For a second I close my eyes and I remember how it feels to be on a horse in full gallop trying to score a goal while someone rides you off. The surreal speed of the game, the fear in my guts as I feel how fragile my balance is in the saddle. The unexpected movements of the horse, bringing up the panic in me. No, not another fall, I don't want to fall. And then the pain in my ribs as another player crashes into me at full speed.

But these players seem to feel none of these things. They dance with grace in their saddles, their sticks nearly always finding the perfect shot. They ride each other powerfully, the sound of man crashing against man mixing with the short shouts they throw at each other. Words of encouragement, like "*Buena-a-a*," indications for a teammate as to where to send the ball (like "Tail" or "Open"), and at times a scream of frustration. Never swearing, though. Polo is a gentleman's sport, and swearing on the field could result in a penalty against your team.

I feel their strain as I watch the game. I feel their rising tiredness as chukkas go by, I live their hopes and their disappointments. All of a sudden I am no longer watching from a distance. I am them.

I feel their breath and I smell their horses. I hit their shots. I love their victories and I cry for their defeats. I am all of them.

The game ends and I need a few minutes to extract myself from feeling one with the players and come back to myself. I slowly let the game go and come down from the stands, heading towards the bar areas. After the games, everyone mingles here. There are several smaller bars and one big one, the Chandon bar, which is where they'll turn up the music full blast later on. It's where the biggest parties happen.

People stroll around, stop to talk, have a drink, then mix and mingle some more. It's a small world, the polo world. Everyone knows everyone. Patricio starts talking to some friends. I don't want to seem clingy, so I leave him and his German client and start wandering around.

My mind is still replaying the shots of the game as I walk around absent-mindedly and bump into a group of players from my former polo club in England—the one where I broke both arms falling off a horse. We kiss the Argentine way, with a quick peck on the right cheek. We wouldn't kiss in England normally, but here we're in Argentina, and here everyone kisses everyone.

I had trouble with this kissing business in the beginning. My first visit here two years ago felt like a cold shower. I realized pretty quickly you're supposed to kiss your friends, but when the massage therapist gave me a kiss I started to doubt her manners, and then when I went to see a chiropractor and his secretary gave me a kiss, I was even more shocked. Then the chiropractor came out of his office to greet me for the first time and he gave me a kiss too. Then I went to the family Christmas gathering with Gabriela and Patricio, and I was told I had to kiss everyone when I got there and before I left again. So it was there I finally got used to it. I must have kissed around a hundred people, including old people who couldn't move from their chairs and toddlers in the arms of their mothers. And it was there that I got it. In Argentina everyone kisses everyone.

"Do I have to kiss taxi drivers as well?" I asked Gabriela. Just to be sure.

"No, you can draw the line at taxi drivers. Also, you don't need to kiss a receptionist at the hotel or the waiter who brings you coffee. Or a shop assistant when you buy bananas. But apart from this, just kiss everyone else. You can't go wrong."

So I did. I went to school and gave Santi, my Spanish teacher, a kiss on the cheek every single day. I gave a kiss to all the other teachers as well, and I kissed the receptionist too. I gave a kiss to Curly Hair who hurried to give me a kiss back, although the rest of the time he pretended I wasn't there. He was only daring in his text messages. It was actually great that Santi remained my teacher. I couldn't have focused on studying Spanish with Curly Hair, not after his very suggestive messages.

I kissed the physiotherapists, I kissed my trainer at the gym, and just stopped short of kissing the receptionist, but only because I didn't interact with her a lot. I kissed my cleaner as she came to the apartment to clean, and I kissed my landlady as I paid her the rent. I did my best to fully integrate into the Argentine society and went about kissing everyone, just as Gabriela had told me I should.

So now I kissed my English acquaintances, and I kissed the friends they introduced me to. Other people came to talk to us and I kissed them, too. I drank my Campari Orange, kissed some more people, spotted Patricio in the distance busy kissing other people in another group, and decided to stay where I was and chat with the people I had already kissed, just to escape further kissing.

This is when I met Andrea. She lives in London, just like me. She plays polo, just like me. She also loves polo, just like me. But unlike me, she hasn't broken any bones. Yet.

But then the list of similarities continues. She's in Buenos

Aires for three months, just like me. She's studying Spanish, just like me. She's going to watch every single game of the Abierto, and she's here *sola*—just like me.

Great, just what I need. A new friend to help me navigate this confusing world of Spanish phrases, kissing on the cheek, glam parties, and handsome Argentine guys. I instantly decide I like her. A lot. And that I'm going to hang on with her.

I watch her as she chats casually with the people in the group. She is very, very beautiful. She looks like a princess in her long, pale pink silk dress, with a chic Cartier bag hanging on a golden chain from her shoulder. She wears very high heels, smokes a lot, and drinks Champagne.

I am fascinated by her and I'm not yet sure why. I have this feeling that we might have met before, and yet I have no memory of it. But polo is one big family; maybe we did meet somewhere on some polo field in England.

She seems to like me too, and after some small talk she asks me if I want to have a walk around with her. She heads straight for the VIP tent.

"Hang on, I haven't got tickets for that," I say as I figure out where she's going.

"Neither do I." She smiles. "But don't worry, they'll let us in."

I doubt they will, but I still follow her. And then she shows me how it's done. She walks straight to the bodyguards with such poise that they lower the chain immediately without asking us to show any tickets. Andrea just smiles at them as she floats by. I follow her closely. I want to ask how she did it but there's no time because a guy is just approaching us.

"*Hola*, how are you?"

"*Hola*. Good, thank you."

"Wasn't that a lovely game?"

"Amazing."

Would she like anything to drink?

Yes, of course she would. Champagne, please. And for my friend as well, please.

I drink Champagne with her, and before I know it some friends of the guy who brought us the drinks are coming to greet us and now we're in the middle of a circle.

How does she do it? The thought does not leave my mind.

I watch her chat, a glass of Champagne in her hand, a pleasant smile on her face.

My mental note book is wide open, and I am taking some serious notes.

It's clear she dresses like a princess and she walks like a princess, and therefore she is treated like one. I must learn how to do this.

She'll be a perfect teacher, I decide. And once I learn all this from her, maybe I can make some progress with the troublesome point four.

More Champagne comes our way. We are still inside the VIP area and in the distance I can see Patricio watching me with a wide smile. It's not hard to understand why. I have about five guys around me and my new friend, all trying to talk to us. Actually they are trying to talk to her, but that's good enough for me; I don't mind being treated as the second choice. I decide to enjoy my shadow place, sip my Champagne, and just feel good about life.

The music grows louder. I'm on my third glass of Champagne. This is as good as I thought it would be. Andrea gracefully disentangles herself from the conversations with all the guys who have bought us Champagne and heads out of the VIP area.

"Let's go for a walk," she says. "See who else we may meet."

I nod and follow her. I doubt I'll get offered Champagne if I'm on my own.

And then we meet him. He's out there walking alone and stops when he sees us, as if dazzled. We don't know him, but it doesn't matter. Not to an Argentine, anyway. He starts talking to us immediately. Friendly, polite, easy going. Casual conversation. Did we like the game? Do we like polo?

Yes, we play polo.

Wow, beautiful ladies playing polo. How extraordinary. Would we like a drink?

Yes, thank you. Champagne, please.

He goes to the bar and asks us to wait for him.

"How do you do this?" I ask Andrea in total disbelief. "You need to teach me. How do you do it?"

She laughs. She tells me she's not doing anything special, and that all Argentine men are like this. They will just come over to talk to you.

"Yes, I know that, but no one has offered to buy me Champagne before."

"Well, have you gone out a lot?" she asks.

I count in my head. One dinner with Marco, one day with Rosario. One Spanglish session, one bar encounter with people from the Spanish school, the *asado* at the guesthouse . . .

"No, actually, I haven't been out a lot," I admit.

She shoots me a reassuring smile. "Don't worry, we have all the time in the world to go out."

Mr. Perfect is back with the drinks. I have no idea what his real name is and have decided to call him Mr. Perfect in my mind. He must have told me his name at the moment of the initial kiss on the cheek, but I was too overwhelmed to register it. He is the sexiest guy I have seen in a while. Even sexier than Curly Hair, with his air of smart street boy who can dance *salsa*. Definitely no street boy look for Mr. Perfect. He's got class. His pale blue shirt, open a few buttons at the neck, is of the finest quality and smartly tucked into dark blue chinos. Elegant brown belt and brown leather shoes. He smells of perfume. Not too much, just enough to be sensed at the moment of that kiss of introduction. His handsome and perfectly shaved face is relaxed, and his smile is easy-going and confident.

The only slight disadvantage is that he isn't very tall. He's shorter than me with my heels on. Argentines are not very tall. The average Argentine man is my height. If I wear heels, I will inevitably be taller. Andrea is not as tall as me. She would be a better fit for him, I think, with a stab of envy.

Unlike the guys we've met before, who seemed so spellbound by Andrea that they mostly ignored me, Mr. Perfect talks to both of us equally. His body positioning is carefully neutral, in between us both. He looks to each of us in turn, taking care to not linger on one more than the other. I study him as we talk. I like his haircut—brown wavy locks, rather long, some of them touching his shoulder. It gives him a creative air. Maybe he's a creative guy? Age-wise he seems in his mid-to-late-thirties, I would say. Maybe a bit too young for me? Andrea is in her early thirties, maybe more suitable for her.

I'm tired of my own thoughts. I like this one, I decide. I really like this guy and I'm going to make a move to show him that I like him. Just as I make this decision, a guy throws his arm around my neck.

The owner of the arm then leans his head casually on my shoulder and smiles.

"Hey Roxy, here you are. I've been looking all over for you. I had no idea where you'd disappeared to."

Patricio's arm is still around my neck. I freeze.

"Come on," he carries on, blissfully unaware he's ruining my chances with Mr. Perfect. "We need to go. It'll take more than two hours to get home with this traffic. Sorry to interrupt, but we need to go."

We don't need to go. He and Lisa, the German client, need to go. I look around, desperately trying to locate her to save me from the misunderstanding which by now has surely started to form in the mind of my Mr. Perfect. But Lisa isn't there. There is no other woman around. Patricio leans on me as if he's known me all my life. He has known me for a lifetime—just not in that way!

I'm wracking my brain for something to say to save the situation, but I've got nothing, except to introduce Patricio as a friend—stressing "*friend*" to make sure Mr. Perfect understands. They all exchange kisses. In Argentina, two guys will kiss to say hello when they're friends. Sometimes in informal settings, when they are introduced as friends of friends, they kiss too. When he emerges from the kissing procedure, Mr. Perfect's body language is irremediably changed. He is now completely turned towards Andrea.

"I've left a bag in my *friend*'s car. Sorry." I'm still struggling to explain. "I need to pick it up before he leaves for Lobos."

But it's no use. Mr. Perfect is now lost in conversation with Andrea. We all kiss again, a goodbye kiss this time, and I go.

"What the hell were you thinking?" I burst out as soon as I find myself alone with Patricio.

He looks at me with puzzled eyes.

"You came up to me and gave me a big hug in front of that guy! He was trying to chat me up. He was really hot. Now you've blown it. He will think you are my boyfriend!"

He starts laughing. "Come on Roxy. *Tranqui*. Friends hug here in Argentina, you know."

"Yes, I know, but he doesn't know you're only a friend. He stopped talking to me as soon as you came."

"Well, it looked to me like he was talking to both of you when I got there. I wouldn't have interrupted otherwise."

"He was," I admit. "I think he was trying to decide which one of us to chat up. At least until you came. Afterwards, it was pretty clear which one he chose."

Patricio is still laughing, but I'm really upset. That was it, my absolutely magnificent chance to meet Mr. Perfect at a polo game, just as I had always imagined I would, and Patricio has blown it.

"Well, if he couldn't decide, maybe I did you a favor by scaring him away. You deserve a man who clearly wants you. You want to be more than just a 'maybe.' Don't worry, you haven't lost anything." And then, with a guilty edge to his voice, "What was his name again? If I meet him again I'll talk to him and let him know you're single and interested. How about that?" He winks reassuringly.

No, I'm still not feeling better. We walk in silence to his car. His German client, now entertained by my little drama, asks more questions. I don't feel like answering. I pick up the bag I had left in his car and get ready to head back home, feeling like the world has just ended.

"See you for polo this week, OK?" Patricio says just before leaving. "I'll text you tomorrow to let you know if the field is dry enough to come and play. Otherwise, see you later in the week. And don't worry," he adds. "There will be plenty more guys to talk to."

Ah, yes, the same old phrase. There will be others. I know this phrase. I use it a lot. Still, it doesn't give me comfort.

A brief Argentine kiss on the cheek and he's gone. In my heart, I still haven't forgiven him for blowing my chances with the handsomest guy I've met in a long while.

MONDAY 30TH NOVEMBER

The next day Patricio texts me to say the field is still too wet for polo. We need to wait until later in the week.

I give up my hopes of playing and content myself with another week of routine—language school, physio, gym. Maybe I'll go out. Maybe I'll go to Spanglish again.

Andrea has left town. She's only here at the weekends to see the games. During the week she plays polo in one of the *estancias* outside the city. She'll be back next weekend. I ask her what happened between her and the cute guy after I left. Nothing, she texts back. They just chatted.

Curly Hair has gone back to texting me. I didn't hear from him over the weekend. Maybe he was busy charming other girls. He asks me if I'm going to play polo this week.

No, can't. La cancha está mojada . . . I'm in the middle of writing back. The field is wet. I almost press send, then I take another look at the text and freeze. My iPhone's automatic spelling has changed *cancha* for *concha*. *Concha* in Spanish means shell. In Argentine slang it also refers to a woman's genitals. I'm horrified at what I have just written. My pussy is wet. Literally.

I very carefully change the "o" back to an "a," which makes the sentence innocent again, and I think that maybe Marco was right.

Too long without having sex.

December

TUESDAY 1ST DECEMBER

I'm back at the launderette. My friend, the old man, is still there and greets me like I'm his best friend.

"*Hola, lind-a-a-a*. How are you?"

"Good. I'm good. I'm really good."

"So tell me," he says, ignoring the bag of dirty clothes I put on the counter. "Tell me how it's going. Have you found love?"

How does he know love is point four on my list? Although, actually, it isn't any more. It's been replaced with "have some fun." I'm not making much progress with this revised version, either.

"No, I haven't found love, but hey, my wrist is moving much better and my Spanish is improving, and I have met nice people, and I have been to the *campo* to see my *amiga* who I met two years ago, and—"

"*Bueno, bueno*," he interrupts. Not interesting enough, I guess. "How about guys? Anyone out there?"

I think of Curly Hair and decide that he doesn't qualify as "someone" yet.

"No one."

"What do you mean no one?" He opens his eyes wide. "No one has asked for your phone number yet?"

"Yes, actually one guy has. A guy I met in a bar."

"And?"

"Nothing. He says it would be nice to meet sometime to practice speaking English."

"And?"

"He didn't say when, and I'm not going to ask him."

"Do you like him?"

"Not sure. I can't remember his face. The bar was too dark. Now can I please leave the laundry bag? I'm late for school."

WEDNESDAY 2ND DECEMBER

Polo is the best substitute for sex I have ever known. In fact, I've only managed to remain single for so long because I've been playing polo. And when I haven't been playing, I've been recovering from broken bones, and one doesn't feel very sexy recovering from broken bones.

Polo causes a mixture of adrenaline rush and physical exhaustion which completely replaces the need for sex. After a game of polo, I feel I don't need anything else from life. Content with eating, sleeping, and caring for my aching body, sex became a distant thought, a disposable extra. And I disposed of it. If it doesn't happen, no harm done, I thought. At least I have polo.

But after two full months away from the game, the calming effect it had on my body has completely worn off.

Two months is long enough, I think, as I board the minibus for Lobos. It's time to play again.

San Patricio is just as I remember it. Wide green spaces, a sense of calm radiating from the tall trees in front of the house, grooms getting the horses ready at the pony lines beside the huge polo field stretching away in front of the farm. Lisa, the German client, is still there. Gabriela is still in Europe and is due to come back next week.

Patricio gets me on a horse the moment I arrive, and he mounts another. He's got his serious face on, the same expression he always wears on a polo field. Off the polo field he may joke a lot, but for him polo is serious business.

"Roxy, listen, take it easy, OK? See how you feel. You haven't been riding for two months now. See how your wrist feels. *Tranqui*," he tells me, as we walk towards the field.

I get it. I get *tranqui*, I think, checking my position in the saddle. I hope the horse gets it too. He must, he's Argentine. My knees automatically grip at the first movement of the horse, and then I feel the familiar rocking of the canter and I take a deep breath. I'm back.

The stick in my right hand feels familiar, too. My left hand, with the injured wrist, is safely protected by a wristband and is holding the four reins in a fist. There are always four reins in polo, not just two, as in ordinary horse-riding. There's always a lot more tack in polo. They say it's for the safety of the rider. Thankfully I didn't break the right wrist, the one that's holding the mallet. That would have been a nightmare, since in polo all the moves of the mallet come either from the shoulder or from the wrist. The left hand doesn't have a big part to play. All it needs to do is hold the reins and pull to stop the horse. And since Patricio gave me a really easy horse, I don't even have to pull a lot.

We start to stick-and-ball. This is what training is called in polo. Basically it involves a lone rider on a polo field cantering around and hitting the ball on her own. Or in my case today, with Patricio by my side, just making sure I'm all right.

And I am all right. I'm back on a horse. My heart dances happily. My body remembers all the moves, and the swing comes back naturally as if my arm has only been asleep for the past two months. My wrist doesn't hurt. Patricio says I'm hitting much better than when he last saw me. I laugh and tell him that's because I played all summer in England. Of course I hit better.

I return to Buenos Aires that evening still buzzing. I'm planning to come again to stick-and-ball a few times, and then I will be ready to play a game.

THURSDAY 3RD DECEMBER

I wake up with the familiar sensation that I can't walk. Polo tends to do this to people. I thought I was over that phase, that my body was by now accustomed to doing what it takes to stay on a horse in full gallop and hit a small ball at speed. But no, it looks like I was mistaken. My body is in pain. Only a two-month break, and my body has reverted back to an ordinary, non-polo body. Coming back is painful.

I drag myself to school, then to physio, then to the gym. One needs to carry on with the program, no matter what.

"Listen, we need to do something about this," I tell Fede. I point at my legs.

"This is ridiculous. One hour on a horse and I'm like this? Even though I've done three weeks intensive training in this gym?"

Fede is my personal trainer. He comes with the gym, actually, and the gym comes with the physio. I love this deal. I get one hour of physio per day and access to the gym any time I want. And whenever I want there's Fede, a personal trainer who will design a program just for me, specifically for polo players, and who will keep in mind my wrist recovery as well. These people take sports seriously. No wonder they are the best in the world at polo. And at football . . . and at hockey . . . and at basketball . . . Well, if you believe the Argentines, they will say they are the best in the world at absolutely everything.

Including the best lovers.

Well, I will have to see about that. This is my fourth week in this city and I'm still single. *Sola. Sola en Baires* as the song goes. Bloody Santi! How did he know to put that song on?

I bring my thoughts back to the task at hand. I need to get my body moving again. Fede smiles mischievously. I bet he has a plan. He always has a plan. I tell him it's serious. I need to be in a condition to play a full game in two weeks' time. I will train again a few more times with Patricio, just to make sure I can ride and hit the ball as I used to do, but then I will play.

Back to polo. My heart is singing. That's point two on my list almost ticked off.

SATURDAY 5TH DECEMBER

It it wasn't for the troubleful point four, my list would look pretty good, I think, as I get ready for another day at the Abierto.

Sort out wrist. Done. Well, almost, but I can consider that a tick.

Play polo. Done. Just a stick-and-ball session, but hey, I did it. It counts as done.

Fall in love replaced with "have some fun." Pending. Today at the Abierto, maybe I'll get another chance.

Get into shape. Done. Almost. Fede is trying hard and I crawl diligently on the floor of that gym and do everything he asks me to do.

And the later addition, learn Spanish, is a half-tick. I can speak it. Really. The Italian words left on the same flight as Marco some two weeks ago. I can communicate. I can express myself. I can even write flirty texts.

Ping. Message.

Hola. Cómo estás?

They always start with *"Cómo estás?"* here, as if you could reply anything other than, "Great, thanks."

Great, thanks.

It doesn't matter who's asking. It's always "Great, thanks."

I was wondering if you'd like to meet up for lunch. So we can practice languages again. How about Tuesday? It's a public holiday here.

It's Rodrigo, the guy from Spanglish. I haven't heard from him in ten days. I thought he would never text back. I try hard to remember his face, but it really was too dark in the bar.

Would be nice to meet. Not sure about Tuesday though. I might be off to Lobos to play polo. Can I let you know later?

It's too complicated to explain that if it rains we can't play, and if it rains the day before and the field is too wet, we can't play, either. And only if neither of these things happen will I be free to have lunch with him. Otherwise, I would rather play polo.

Dale. Let me know.

Hmm. Abrupt message. Is he disappointed? Never mind. Polo has priority. And he wrote *Dale* which means OK here. So it should be OK.

I forget about him and I get myself back to El Abierto. Women in elegant dresses hang on the arms of men in linen shirts. The smell of horses is everywhere and the excitement is in the air, carried away in the wind like the buzz of animated conversations. The huge expanse of lush green grass is shining right in the heart of the city, surrounded by white skyscrapers. La Catedral del Polo, the place where people come to worship the gods of this sport.

I make my way through the crowd, looking around, trying to spot people I know. Easy enough, I think, as I see Patricio in the distance. There's someone with him, but it's not the German client this time. Gabriela is back!

I jump up to give her a hug.

"*Hola*, darling! How the fuck have you been?"

Gabriela is loud, fun, and swears like a cowboy. I've missed her.

"Patricio tells me you're back on a horse. That's great. And your wrist? Let me see. And how is your Spanish?"

I don't want to speak Spanish with Gabriela. She speaks Mexican Spanish and I like to speak Argentine. Plus, I can't tell her all the stories I need to tell her in Spanish. One day I'll be fluent enough, but not today.

We catch up over a Campari Orange. Patricio asks me if I've seen Mr. Perfect again, the guy he scared off last time. He's still feeling guilty, I assume. I inform him that no, I have not seen Mr. Perfect again, and likely never will. And if he can be more careful next time when he interrupts a guy trying to chat me up, that would be much appreciated.

The sun is shining, and a huge Argentine flag is waving in a corner of the field. I watch the blue and white stripes and I remember my polo helmet has the same colors. And my car, the little Mini I bought three years ago in London, has a white roof on a bright blue body. In a weird kind of way I feel I at home here. Plus, I'm sipping Campari Orange with my friends and life seems just perfect. With or without Mr. Perfect.

After the game I meet Andrea again. I know where to find her. I just walk by the VIP area and sure enough she's there, drinking Champagne and chatting to guys.

"Roxy! Come on in." She points to one of the guys. "Can you please make sure they let my friend pass?"

Of course they do. Andrea always gets everything she wants. Just like that, with no effort. I must learn how to do this.

I kiss Gabriela and Patricio goodbye. They're heading back to Lobos. I, on the other hand, am heading inside the VIP tent.

Before they go, Patricio tells me to come over to play on Tuesday. I nod. *Dale*. But I can't think of polo right now. All I can think of is how Andrea manages to gather that impressive number of handsome guys around her.

But the best thing about Andrea is that she is great at sharing. She shares her Champagne, she shares the guys around her, and she has more than she needs of both. And she shares a lot of gossip too, and gosh, how good it is to gossip with a girlfriend, sipping Champagne while watching the most handsome men in the world gather around us. I'm in heaven.

"*Hola*, girls! Here you are again."

I almost drop my Champagne glass in shock. Mr. Perfect is back and he's wearing another of his sexy linen shirts, a few buttons open at the collar. He pushes a hand through his wavy hair and I notice drops of perspiration on his forehead. It's hot outside, or maybe it's just the excitement of the game.

Andrea smiles. I detect a small smile, though. It's the type of smile she keeps for guys she's not really interested in. Oh, good. I feel the tension in my shoulders easing. If she was interested, I'd have no chance. But now it looks like I do.

I turn around and chat to Mr. Perfect, trying to imitate the ease and poise of my girlfriend. Pale comparison, I think, but hey, I'm trying.

It seems to work. He asks what I would like to drink. I say, Champagne. This is what Andrea always says, so I do too. The magic happens. He goes to the bar and comes back with two glasses of champagne. One for me and one for her. Wow. It's the first time a guy has ever bought me Champagne, just like that. I'm thrilled.

Andrea smiles encouragingly. She approves of my learning.

"Ah, these Argentines. They're so insistent," she says. "Don't you find them a bit too insistent? A bit annoying? You can't get rid of them sometimes."

"No, I don't." I really don't want to get rid of Mr. Perfect.

She sips her Champagne while scrolling down a list of WhatsApp contacts.

"Look at this," she says. "After watching just four games here in Palermo, I don't even know who's who. They all want my phone number and they all text me. It's too much, don't you think?"

To be honest, I don't think so. I've only had one assado invitation in four weeks in Buenos Aires, and a date invitation that will only happen if the weather is bad and I can't play polo. And I can't even remember his face.

I must really learn what Andrea does and how she does it.

"It's easy, darling." She laughs when I ask her. "There's nothing you need to do. Just be."

And I watch in awe as she does it again. Just as her glass becomes empty, a guy magically appears, says *hola* and asks her what she'd like to drink.

"Champagne, please," she says, then points at me. "And one for my friend."

He brings us the drinks, we say "*gracias*," and talk for five minutes before moving on. As we finish our glasses, other full glasses appear. All the guys ask for her number. No one asks for mine, but I don't mind. I'm too busy watching her, trying to understand how this flirting business works.

Mr. Perfect went for a walk round after bringing us the Champagne, but now he's back. He fills our glasses once again. I almost drop mine as I hear his question.

"Can I have your phone number?"

He is asking for my phone number. Obviously, since he already has Andrea's. Still, I can't believe this is happening.

"Yes, sure," I mumble. I give him my phone number and I watch in disbelief as he sends me a text.

"So you have mine, too." He smiles. I'm afraid to breathe. The miracle has happened. Just by keeping close to my new friend I'm getting some of the mysterious quality that makes men want to have her phone number.

The night has fallen, but the discreet lights of the bars create an intimate ambiance. The music is loud—only the latest international hits here, no Latino tunes like you find in the discos. Drinks are flowing and people start dancing. I'm feeling a bit dizzy. I've had too many glasses of Champagne. I haven't eaten anything since lunch and it's now close to midnight. Alcohol on an empty stomach is not a good idea.

"Girls, would you like to go for dinner?"

Someone has just read my mind. Mr. Perfect is back from another wander and this time he's brought a friend with him. Of course he has. Argentines are very skilled at these things. A guy can buy drinks for two girls but will invite them to dinner only if he has a friend nearby, so it looks like it's a chill friends' gathering.

"I know a great pizza place just around the back of the polo field," he continues.

Las Cañitas is a well-known area filled with cozy bars and restaurants that start just where the polo stadium ends. It's where people who have come to enjoy a polo game and have had one too many drinks go for a bite to eat afterwards.

We walk out of the stadium and onto the small streets packed with terraces, where people sit outside in big groups to sip drinks and share food. The neighborhood feels like one huge restaurant with tables everywhere. Music spills into the streets from the bars. There are so many people eating. Girls in summer dresses lean in together chatting happily, while guys strike up separate conversations, laughing loudly. In this country, men and women tend to cling to different ends of the tables when in a big group. The smell of all the different grilled meats mingles in the air. Thankfully we're heading to a pizzeria, so I'll be able to eat something.

I feel I'm living in a dream. Point four on my list—and he will be handsome and I will meet him at the Abierto and he will ask for my number. And maybe "have some fun" can be converted back to the original "fall in love."

The best night in a long while, I think, as I sit down at the table smiling at Mr. Perfect. The pizza is great. The conversation is great. I'm enjoying every minute of it. I'm half-drunk so I'm careful not to speak too much. Andrea is half-drunk too, but she isn't worried about not talking too much. All goes well. Mr. Perfect sits in front of me, his friend in front of Andrea. This is a good sign.

And then he turns pale. All of a sudden.

"I don't feel well," he says.

He looks like he's about to throw up. If he does it will be straight on me, because I'm sitting in front of him. We try to give him some water. Something. Anything. But nothing seems to help. He excuses himself and says he needs to go home right now. He had one drink too many.

I look at him, desperately hoping a miraculous solution will fall from the sky and save this evening. But nothing falls from the sky. Instead he looks like he is the one about to fall off his feet. Maybe it's better he goes home.

He instructs his friend to look after us, apologizes once more and disappears.

His friend tries to talk him out of driving his own car home but no, no chance of that. An Argentine will drive his car back home, no matter what.

As Mr. Perfect vanishes through the door of the busy pizzeria, so do my hopes for the night. The rest of the evening goes by in a blur. His friend talks to us, pays for the dinner, and drives us both home. A perfect gentleman. Just not the one I was interested in.

MONDAY 7TH DECEMBER

I can't believe I've done this. I've texted Patricio and told him I can't come to play polo.

Why? he texts back. *The field is perfect. No rain.*

Can't. I have a date.

What????

I'm not sure if the question marks refer to his surprise that I finally have a date, or his irritation that I'm cancelling polo for a date.

Yes, sorry. I have decided to go to lunch with this guy.

Why?

What can I tell him? That in four weeks it's the only guy who has asked me out properly? That Mr. Perfect vanished Sunday night in such a state that it's clear I'll never see him again, that Curly Hair keeps on sending me sexy messages and offering to show me his massage skills but never invites me anywhere, not even for a Coca Cola?

I let the question hang.

I'll come on Wednesday instead, I text back.

I can't believe you're giving up polo to have lunch with a guy, he answers.

Well, I can't believe it either. I've never done it before.

TUESDAY 8TH DECEMBER

Instead of rushing to catch a minibus for Lobos to play polo, I'm getting ready for my date, still uncertain it's the right decision.

It's not really a proper date, I tell myself to calm my nerves. I remember the guy said, "Let's just meet and have a language exchange." There was no suggestion of an actual date. We'd met in a pretty neutral setting at the Spanglish language exchange. He didn't invite me to dinner or for a drink. He just suggested lunch. Lunch can be a friendly affair. Right?

I contemplate what to wear. Definitely not too sexy, just in case this is only a friendly thing. Not too elegant either. It's only lunch. And no, not a polo shirt. Definitely not a sporty look—I just gave up polo for this bloody lunch!

In the end I give up waiting for inspiration. I get dressed in a pair of jeans and a plain green t-shirt. I bought it at Victoria's Secret, where I buy my sexy underwear, but I have a slight suspicion it was from the pyjama section. Never mind. I've done enough for this date by cancelling polo. I don't need to put any more effort into it.

I meet him just at the corner of my street.

"Hola, cómo estás?"

Brief kiss on the cheek, the Argentine way.

I look at him, wondering if he can tell how nervous I am. It almost feels as though I'm on a blind date. I can't remember much about this guy. All I know is his name: Rodrigo.

He has big brown eyes with a kind and somewhat serious expression. Black hair, rather short, not wavy like that of Mr. Perfect. Strong jaw, full lips, and a big crease in between his eyebrows, suggesting he frowns a lot. He's wearing blue jeans and a black t-shirt, showing off strong, tanned arms. Not very tall. About the same size as me without heels. A typical Argentine guy.

And just like a typical Argentine guy he looks relaxed and in charge. He suggests we drive to a place close to Plaza Serrano for lunch. This calms me down a little. At least he knows where he's going.

I know nothing about this guy, I think, as I get into his car. I remember our previous conversation was all about me and polo, so I try to make up for it by asking him questions. He works in a cable factory. No, he's not a manager, he's just a worker. An employee in the maintenance department. More exactly, he repairs big machines that produce cables. He has always wanted to learn English, but never had the opportunity to study it. He learned it by himself, he says. He tells me all this in English, switching effortlessly from his initial words in Spanish.

"Wow, really?" I'm impressed. He speaks English pretty well. Better than I speak Spanish, despite all those classes.

He says he would like to travel. He's only been outside his country once, to Brazil, last year. He's never been to Europe. He's got a cousin living in Germany whom he'd like to visit one day. He's also teaching himself German, in addition to English. I tell him he must be crazy. No one teaches themselves German.

By the time we reach the little café he has in mind for lunch, I feel I've accumulated a decent amount of information about him. And all of that in English.

"Shall we change language now?" I say, smiling. "After all, we're supposed to practice both languages."

He compliments me on my Spanish. He says my accent is perfect. I'm starting to feel more relaxed. The conversation about languages gives us both a perfectly acceptable reason for this encounter. It's just two people practicing languages. Definitely not a date.

I order a Campari Orange. He orders the same.

"It's my favourite drink," I say.

"Mine too."

I suspect he's probably making that up, just because it sounds like a nice thing to say.

We carry on chatting and the Campari relaxes me even more. He's smiling a lot and the words flow easily. We're back to speaking Spanish. He talks all the time, and this puts me at ease. By the end of my drink I've learned about all the factories he has worked in—a chocolate factory, a dairy, and plastic materials. And then the steel cables. All the time in the maintenance department.

"I'm good at repairing things. I've always done it, ever since I was a kid." He laughs. "I used to tear apart all my toys, just to see how they were built."

He's got big strong hands, with very short nails. Clearly a guy who works with his hands. I like guys with strong hands. And muscular arms, well, that's a bonus.

"And when you can't repair something?"

"There's always a way. Sometimes it takes longer, but I sit there with the machine until it comes to me. If I'm patient enough, the answer always comes."

It sounds almost like meditation to me. I have no other source of reference to better understand what he does. At least he sounds like a patient guy.

"And you? What do you do for work? That is, when you don't play polo."

Ah, work. Yes. I'm not sure how I can explain to him what I do for work.

"I'm a management consultant," I say, hoping he won't ask more.

"So what does a management consultant actually do?" He does ask more.

This is a hard question. A lot of people would say we don't really do much. What can I tell him? That I go to factories just like his and talk to the boss of the boss of his boss about how to restructure the factory, which often involves laying off people who work in the maintenance department, just like him?

"We just talk a lot and write reports," I say instead. "My Spanish isn't good enough to explain more." I'm relieved I've got this excuse.

The pasta arrives and I switch the discussion back to him.

"Tell me about your family."

"There's not much to say. I've got a mother and two sisters. They live far away in the south. I'm on my own in Buenos Aires."

"And your father?"

"I have no idea. I haven't been in touch with him for a long time."

"How long?"

"Over ten years," he says.

"Why?"

"It doesn't matter."

Clearly he doesn't want to talk about it. Maybe it's too much information for a first date. He goes back to the list of factories. I feel there's something he's not telling me about his life. There must be more to it than working in different factories and teaching himself English in his spare time.

Despite these thoughts running through my mind, my body feels relaxed. There's warmth coming from him and a sense of calm confidence, of ease and strength. My body registers the close proximity of his body, and I feel warm. There's definitely chemistry flowing between us.

When we finish eating the pasta he reaches out over the table and puts his palm on top of my hand. Just like that, casually. He looks straight into my eyes as he does it. I know if I withdraw my hand he'll get the message and he won't try again. We'll just have a friendly lunch and nothing more.

I'm not sure what I want but I don't withdraw my hand.

He smiles. A big, relaxed, open smile that lights his eyes. And lights my eyes too.

"*Linda*," he says. It means beautiful.

I've been called *linda* here before by a lot of taxi drivers, shop assistants, and waiters. But when he says it, it sounds different. It's like this is the first time I really register someone calling me *linda*.

I'm not sure why, but as soon as I hear that word my body relaxes even more, and I smile back as if I've known him for ages. I like him.

After lunch he suggests we take a walk. He wants to show me the neighborhood. He takes my hand casually as we leave the restaurant and I don't withdraw it. I like the touch of his hand. Solid, warm, relaxed.

And I like the touch of his lips, too, when he kisses me some twenty steps later.

Hand in hand we walk through Palermo in silence after the kiss, as if both he and I are not quite sure what just happened. I can't stop smiling, though. There's something about this guy that just makes me smile.

He asks me more questions. I tell him I've been here before, to play polo with the friends I met here who have become my adoptive Argentine family. I tell him I spent my birthday here last year.

"How old were you?"

This is a straightforward question. I look at him. He must be younger then me. Late thirties, I guess. Definitely under forty. He may be shocked to find out I'm over forty, so I decide not to answer. Better to ask him some more questions. I still have the feeling he's not telling me the whole truth about himself. When he talks about his life, it feels as though there are some years missing. Maybe he's married? Maybe he's hiding family? Kids? Or maybe he's been to prison? The years just don't add up.

He answers all my questions, but I don't find out a lot more than what he's already told me. We get back in the car and he offers to drop me home. And then he kisses me again, passionately this time. I'm surprised at the intensity of his kiss, and I'm surprised at my own reaction, answering his kiss with the same hunger. My heart is beating fast and it tells me I like him.

"Tell me something," he says after a while. "Why did you not want to tell me how old you are?"

It's impossible to avoid his gaze. "Well . . ."

"Are you worried you might be older than me?"

So he feels this is the case, too. I thought I looked younger, but my hesitation in talking about my age might have betrayed me.

"Yes. Maybe."

"*Tranquila*. It's OK," he says. "You can tell me how old you are." And then he smiles. "*Linda*."

I can't resist when he says this word. My body relaxes instantly.

"OK, but you first," I say. "Tell me how old you are."

"Sure. Twenty-seven."

"*What*?"

"Twenty-seven. Why?"

I can't say a word.

"Are you older?" he asks.

I watch him in disbelief, and I feel the earth is opening up under my feet and I am free-falling into an abyss with no end. "You are twenty-seven years old," I finally manage to say.

"Yes."

"You can't be."

"Why not?"

"You look older."

"So I've been told." He smiles. "It's not a big deal. Your turn now. How old are you?"

I can't possibly tell him how old I am. All I can think about is how to escape from this car before I die of embarrassment.

But he kisses me again and I melt into his soft lips.

"*Tranquila*. It's OK if you're older. I don't mind."

I still can't say a word.

"Over thirty?"

"Yes," I whisper.

"I wouldn't have thought so, but well, I told you I don't mind. How much over thirty?"

"A lot."

"What do you mean, a lot? Like thirty-three?"

There's surprise in his voice.

I shake my head. I can't tell him. I also can't not tell him.

"No. More."

"More than thirty-three? Can't be! You can't be older than that. Thirty-five?"

"More."

"More than thirty-five? Impossible! What, thirty-seven?"

His voice has gone up in alarm.

"More. Much more." I've stopped breathing.

His eyes are now wide open. I am closing mine.

"There is no possible way you can be forty!"

"Forty-one," I whisper. "Since last month."

He's speechless. When I open my eyes to look at him, I find he's looking back at me in total disbelief. I wish the earth had really parted and swallowed me up, after all.

"I don't care," he says when he regains his voice.

"Yes, you do," I reply. "Are you crazy? There are fourteen years between us."

"We can pretend we are both thirty-four, then, so we can meet in the middle."

He's good with numbers. He actually does look thirty-four, and so do I, I'm told. But this isn't enough. Nothing we can possibly say or do right now can sort this out.

"Why don't you drive me home," I say.

He drives in silence. I'm convinced this is the first and last time I'm ever going to see him again. I feel utterly and totally embarrassed by the situation, and the only thing I can think about is getting out of his car and locking myself in my flat for the rest of the day.

We arrive. I'm not looking at him, but I feel his hand on my shoulder. I wonder if I should give him a brief Argentine goodbye kiss on the cheek, or whether I should just get out of the car without a word.

"*Linda*," he says.

That makes me look at him.

We kiss again, passionately. He bites my lips and I bite his with a bitter realisation—that this is the last time we will ever meet. The first and the last time. We kiss and hug desperately, with the intensity of two teenagers told they will never see each other again. We kiss until I lose myself in a kiss that wipes out everything else that happens around us—the street with the busy traffic, my racing heart, and the question about my age that should have never been asked. We kiss until I feel I can't hold my tears any more, and then I pull myself away and open the door to get out of the car.

"I want to see you again," he says, just before I step out.

I don't answer. In my mouth, a faint taste of blood. Mine or his, I don't know.

I have never been kissed like this before.

WEDNESDAY 9TH DECEMBER

I'm on a bus heading to Lobos. I'm going to play polo at last. I should have bloody gone on Tuesday instead of staying in Buenos Aires to kiss a teenager in a car, I tell myself.

There have been no messages from Rodrigo since that lunch and mad kiss we had in the car. Of course there haven't. What is he going to say to a woman fourteen years older than him?

Patricio comes to pick me up from the bus station.

"Well?" I can detect the rest of the unspoken question in the air.

"Well what?"

"The date. How was it? Worth giving up polo for?"

That just rubs it in. No, it wasn't worth it. I sigh. "Yeah, nice guy. But *nada*."

"Why *nada*?"

"Because it's impossible. The guy is twenty-seven. What can I do with a twenty-seven-year-old guy?"

He keeps a straight face as he answers. "*Todo lo que quieras*." Everything you want.

"What?"

"Everything you've ever wanted to do, you can do with a twenty-seven-year-old guy. I can tell you for sure. He wouldn't mind."

"Patricio!" I look at him, scandalized. On the back seat, his seven-year-old son is playing with an iPhone. Not the right environment to carry on discussing my secret fantasies involving one particular twenty-seven-year-old man.

"Anyway, he hasn't called back, so *nada*." I don't say any more than this, but my mind is racing. I don't think he wants to see me again. And it's better that way. What are we going to do if he does? It's impossible.

Patricio drives in silence for a while and then comes up with the solution. "I've invited my cousins to play some chukkas this afternoon. I have one in mind for you."

Now, Patricio and his cousins are a long story. It started two years ago when I spent Christmas and New Year's with them. Having decided that I was *buena onda*, which is a very Argentine expression for cool, literally translated as "a good wave," Gabriela and Patricio started thinking of available bachelors to pair me up with. Preferably from their own family. Preferably from around Lobos, so I can be forever happily married and settled next to them.

They are like this, the Argentines. They like match-making and they put a lot of effort into it.

As a result I found myself surrounded by nice-looking guys at the New Year's party. They kept coming up to talk to me and offering me a drink. It would go like this:

"Hi, I'm Patricio's cousin. He told me you like Campari Orange. Here's a drink."

I would talk to one for a while and then another would show up with another glass of Campari Orange.

"Hi, I'm Patricio's cousin. He told me you like Campari Orange."

"How many cousins have you got?" I asked Patricio when I finally got hold of him later that evening.

"As many as it takes." He smiled back.

But then I was leaving for London the next morning, and the whole cousin story was put to rest. Until now, that is. I wonder whether Gabriela has something to do with the cousins' polo gathering this afternoon. She must have given up on me finding love by myself in Buenos Aires.

Sola in Baires. The song comes back to my mind.

Not for long. Screw that song.

LATER AT THE FARM

I'm back on a horse and that's enough to make me forget about it all—the kiss, the lunch, the unsuitable Argentine date, Mr. Perfect nearly vomiting on me half-way through eating a pizza, and that song with the depressing lyrics about being alone in Baires. I even forget about the cousins I'm playing with, because I'm back on a horse, holding a polo mallet in one hand, the reins in the other, and that's all that matters. And not even the kisses of that twenty-seven-year-old guy can match the adrenaline rush through my body as Patricio hits the ball into the field and shouts "Pla-a-a-ay" to mark the start of the game.

And we play. Gabriela on her horse, wearing her beautiful cowboy boots. She's a trendy girl. Normal polo boots would be too ordinary for her. Patricio on his stallion—the crazy black one I'm too scared to get close to. Two of the grooms on other horses. And three guys I've never seen before. They must be the new cousins.

We play, and the joy of playing takes over and I fly again. My heart sings. There might be no man in my life right now but there is polo, and that's more than enough.

The game is fast. Faster than I can remember, and faster than I'm comfortable with. I try to take the ball and fail. I almost lose my balance in the saddle and I stop the horse in one sudden movement, not caring that I am now lagging way behind the other players.

Then I try to reach them again and I suddenly find myself in the possession of the ball. That's because Patricio has sent it my way. I panic trying to hit it as I see the players from the other team coming towards me at speed and I expect them to ride me off. They don't. For a reason I don't yet understand, they just stop and watch me hit it and then they proceed to take the ball as I miss my hit and my horse gallops past it.

Then I try to remember which way we are going and I get confused for a few moments. That's because in polo we change the sides of the field every time a goal is scored. So if you're not careful to remember which way you're supposed to go, you may end up scoring a goal against your own team. But Patricio shouts at me from far away and I get my bearings right again. He passes the ball to me once more and I lose it the very next second.

But I ride on, content with the feeling of once again being part of a polo team. I ride on with the smell of the freshly cut grass in my nostrils and joy in my heart, the joy of seeing the ball expertly hit by one of my teammates. I ride on and I don't really care that I am the worst player on the field today. I'm quite used to this position. And like my trainer back in England used to say, it's the best position really. It means I've got an opportunity to learn.

"Why did no one touch me in the game?" I ask Patricio, struggling to get my breath back after the chukkas. "You guys all play so well. So much better than me. And yet no one came to ride me off."

"Of course they didn't." He laughs. "I had a word with them beforehand. Are you crazy? No one is going to be rough with you here. You're only just recovering. It's your first game in two months, right? Plus you're a girl. Of course they won't come to ride you off."

They are like this, the Argentines. They don't usually play tough sports against women, and when they do, they do it softly.

"Well played," he added. "Come back to train. We'll make a polo player out of you."

THURSDAY 10TH DECEMBER

Mauricio Macri, the new president-elect of Argentina who managed to surprise everyone by winning the elections last month, assumes office today.

I am in a café having lunch after my language course when it happens. The TV is tuned to Macri swearing on a Bible. I can't fully understand what he says. Something along the lines of country, love, duty, and honor.

Every single customer in the restaurant applauds at the end of it. I turn and look around. All the waiters and the kitchen staff are gathered to watch, and they applaud, too. There's a huge hope that the new president will turn the failing economy around and bring financial stability to the country.

The politics in Argentina resemble a soap opera. Last night I heard helicopters all over Buenos Aires as thousands of supporters of the outgoing president, Cristina Fernandez de Kirchener, gathered outside the presidential palace—or Casa Rosada, as it is known here—to hear her last speech. She told them she loved them. She said she would give her life for them and for Argentina. She cried. She complained about the new president, who requested a federal court to rule that her presidency end at midnight rather than the following day at noon, when Macri would be sworn president. As a result, Argentina found itself without a president in office for twelve hours, because Cristina and Mauricio could not agree on how the ceremony of handover was to be conducted. He wanted it at the presidential palace. She wanted it at the Congress. If she were still the president, she would have had it her way. So Macri made sure she wasn't the president any longer.

As a result, Cristina decided not to attend the ceremony the following day. She vanished in a helicopter at midnight straight from Casa Rosada just as her term ended, and she did so in front of the tens of thousands of her fans assembled outside.

"I am going to turn into a pumpkin at midnight," she'd declared earlier that day.

And late at night she said a tearful "I love you all" before boarding her helicopter. She cried. People in the street cried.

Macri won it all. He won the election battle and he also had the ceremony the way he wanted it. The only problem was that he found himself without a key player at his inauguration ceremony, since the custom is for the outgoing president to hand over the presidential sash and scepter. But Cristina had decided that since she'd been kicked out early, she would go. Early. He could take the scepter himself if he wanted to—she wouldn't be there to hand it over. She boarded her flight and vanished from sight, going to her home province of Santa Cruz, where incidentally her sister was sworn governor the following morning. Presidential ambitions run high in the family. She also left her son Maximo behind as a congressman.

Meanwhile in Buenos Aires, the leader of the Senate assumed interim presidency of the nation and was there to hand over the scepter and the sash to Macri. I bet Macri would have loved to have Cristina do it, but she managed to give him one last blow before she vanished.

Macri now has a hard job ahead of him. The country is divided. Nearly half the people voted against him. Argentina's economy is struggling, and the dual exchange rate of the peso with the dollar—the official one and the unofficial one, which everyone (including me) uses—is just one of the signs that there's a lot of work to do.

The applause in the small café dies down, Macri assumes office, and the presidential soap opera comes to an end. This episode, at least. There will be others. The beauty of soap operas is that they never end. And in Argentina, there's one for every occasion.

FRIDAY 11TH DECEMBER

I'm not going to contact him. Whatever happens. I'd rather die than send him a message.

And yet . . . his kisses.

Screw his kisses.

I go back to the launderette. I need therapy.

"*Hola. Linda-a-a-a.*" The old man is still there. His *linda* sounds encouraging but not as sexy as Rodrigo's. No *linda* can ever be as sexy as Rodrigo's.

Stop it!

"*Hola.*"

"*Entonces*? How is it going?"

I sigh.

"News? Anyone taking you out for a meal?"

"Well, yes . . ."

"Finally," he exclaims. "Excellent news. I was actually getting ready to invite you myself. How did it go?"

"Nice."

"Did you like him?"

"I did, but—"

"Perfect. When are you seeing him again?"

"Well, this is the problem. He hasn't called back."

"He hasn't called back? When was it?"

"Tuesday."

"Three days ago. And he hasn't called back? Hmm."

I can see his enthusiasm dwindling. I don't need him to tell me this isn't good news. I also don't need him to tell me why Rodrigo hasn't called back. I know exactly why.

"Hmm," he repeats. "Don't worry, there will be others."

Just like this, Rodrigo is dismissed.

"You mean if he doesn't call, I shouldn't call him?"

"Estás loca? Are you crazy? Calling a man? A man who invited you out? Absolutely not. You must be out of your mind to even think about it."

"So, never?"

"Never." His eyes are serious. "The man calls. Is he Argentine?"

"Yes."

"Then he'll know what he has to do. If he doesn't, don't worry, *linda*, there will be others."

I nod. I put my laundry bag on the counter and leave before he can see the tears welling up in my eyes.

Back to my usual status. *Sola en Baires.*

LATER THAT EVENING

By 6 pm I have officially given up waiting for a message. I'm going to get myself into my sexiest short black dress and go out. This city is full of men, many of them as sexy and handsome as Rodrigo. Or even more sexy and handsome. And I'm going to find out if they kiss better, too. I am determined.

After four weeks of my once-a-day physio treatment, I've been invited to the Christmas party of the Institute for Sports Medicine, Recovery, and Rehabilitation. It's normally a party for the staff, but because they are Argentines, and the Argentines always like to invite more people to a party, they've put an announcement next to the reception saying clients are welcome.

So I signed up to go. I already know a few of the physiotherapists who have treated my wrist, and they know all my polo stories. We talk nonstop for an hour every day while they pull and twist my wrist. Plus there's my gym instructor, and he knows my polo stories, too. There are also a number of girls I've met who all give me a friendly kiss on the cheek and chat, so I feel I know enough people to have a decent night out.

Except for the Abierto parties, where I hung out with Andrea and drank Champagne, I haven't been out as much as I'd planned. I've been to Spanglish twice, had a couple of student evenings organised by Curly Hair, and a few meals with my friends who run the guesthouse. It isn't much.

But tonight it's going to be a good night, I decide, as I put on my sexy little back dress and head over to the party venue.

In Argentina, parties start late. Even though I know this I'm still surprised to find that at 11:30 there's still not much happening. The women are chatting in one corner, the men in another. I move between the groups awkwardly, speaking to people I don't really know.

But then they put on some music and the distance disappears, and the awkwardness vanishes, too, in the rhythm of reggaeton. Or maybe it's *cumbia*. I've never managed to tell the difference. There is no Campari Orange, but there's beer and I have a lot of it. I start to relax.

By midnight I'm being taught how to dance *cumbia*. I'm not sure who the guy is.

By 12:30 I'm on my third beer and chatting to another guy in a dark corner. He wants my phone number. He makes sure he mentions he is single.

By 1 am I'm agreeing to carry on to a disco. I get in a car with one other girl and two guys. I don't know them. I've seen the girl before, but I don't know the guys. She knows one of the guys though, and she says they are OK. "*Buena onda*," she calls them.

By 1:30 am we are driving across Buenos Aires, drinking vodka mixed with the remains of a carton of orange juice. The girl and I try to mix the two liquids and end up spilling half of it on the back seats. It's not our fault. The driver is pressing down hard on the accelerator. We must be well over the legal speed limit.

Half an hour later we are still driving. We are going to La Boca, I'm told. I've never been out of Palermo, the neighborhood where I live. La Boca is on the other side of town.

"What are we doing in La Boca?" I want to know, in between sips of vodka and orange juice.

"We're having a drink with some friends before we go to the disco."

Ah, I'd forgotten people don't go to clubs before 3 am here. We have time.

More vodka and orange juice. I'm starting to feel like I'm floating. But I'm happy. For the first time today I'm not thinking about a text message that's definitely not coming.

The others are happy, too. We all drink vodka orange, including the driver as he stops the car at a traffic light, right next to a police car.

"There's a police car," I shout from the back seat. "What if they see you drinking?"

"*No pasa nada*. The police here, they are *buena onda*."

Buena onda seems to be the explanation for a lot of things here.

From the radio of the car, Enrique Iglesias is crying about the love that he lost.

That's his problem, if he's desperately looking for his lost love on the streets. I am not. I'm drinking vodka orange and having a really good time driving at lightning speed through Buenos Aires. Tonight, it's going to be a good night. In fact, it already is a good night.

We arrive in La Boca. We park outside a lonely block of flats and head up to the second floor.

"What are we doing here?" I ask again.

"Having a drink with some friends," comes the same answer.

In the flat about ten guys are drinking around a table. The room is big but empty, except for a large table in the middle, covered with plastic bottles and cups. No food. The only light comes from one bulb suspended from the ceiling. There's an old battered sofa in the corner. We are the only two girls. The music comes from a small stereo and it's loud. *Cumbia*. Or maybe regaetton. One of those Latino tunes everyone dances so well here.

Brief kiss on the cheek with all of them. Of course. And then we get asked what we would like to drink.

"Do you know anyone here?" I ask the girl in a whisper, although they can't hear us anyway, because of the loud music.

"No, not really. But it's ok. They are *buena onda*."

My heart is still dancing to the rhythm of Enrique Iglesias, but I'm starting to feel a chill down my spine as I slowly take in the situation around me. Two girls and ten guys in an apartment in the middle of nowhere. At 2 am. Alcohol flowing. Music on loud. The average age of the guys must be under twenty-five. They might be *buena onda*, but I still have enough reason left in me to tell me I need to get out of here right now.

I stand up in panic.

"What's the problem?" asks one of the guys who brought us here.

"You said we were going to a disco. Let's go!"

"*Tranqui*. We're having a drink here, then we'll go."

"No, let's go now."

"It's too early for the disco."

"It doesn't matter. I want to go now."

No one has said or done anything wrong. They poured us a drink and resumed the conversation around the table. Nothing was happening to feed my paranoia. But my survival instinct takes over and decides this is a setting that can lead to trouble.

I grab the other girl by the hand.

"Listen, we need to go. This doesn't feel right."

She looks at me in disbelief. No one can make sense of my sudden paranoia.

"OK, OK. *Tranqui*. We go." The guy who drove us here looks puzzled. "We'll go now. As you wish."

"*Chicos*, we're going to the club," he announces to the group.

"It's too early. Sit down. Have a drink, *boludo*."

There doesn't appear to be much enthusiasm about moving.

Boludo means crazy and is a common way of addressing friends here. But this particular *boludo* is on a mission to make my wishes come true.

"No, we have to go now. The girls want to go to the disco, so we're going."

They don't argue any more. All ten guys stand up and we go. Just because I said so.

"See? *No pasa nada*," the girl whispers as we come down the stairs. "They are *buena onda*. I told you so."

We're back in the car and it appears now we're going to San Telmo. This is a different neighborhood, the other side of town again. We drink some more vodka with orange juice, since all the drinks have been loaded in the car along with us. The rest of the guys are crammed in two other cars behind us. The drivers appear to be enjoying a race through the big boulevards. I suspect we are well over the speed limit again.

At 2:30 am we get to San Telmo. They park the cars and then the boys gather to pee in the street around a lamp post. The girl and I keep a safe distance.

"Sorry, we had to," one of them says afterwards. "We had too much to drink in the car."

Yes, definitely too much. My head is spinning. But we're entering the disco and the sound of cumbia makes my head spin even more. Maybe it's reggaeton after all. I must remember to ask them.

The guys buy the tickets. They pay for us girls. I offer to pay, but there's no way.

"*Tranqui*. You're in Argentina. We pay for girls' entry to discos here."

More drinks. They pay for the drinks too.

"Listen, is this OK?" I ask the girl. "Do these guys imagine we're going home with them afterwards? Why do they pay for everything?"

"*Tranqui. No pasa nada.*" She smiles. "No one imagines anything. We're just here to dance."

And we dance. By 4 am my cumbia moves are solidifying. By 4:30 I'm a born natural and I even don't care if it's cumbia or reggaeton any longer. By 5 am I'm deciding that one of the boys in the group is the best dancer in the world.

By 5:30 I'm kissing him. Or maybe he's kissing me. I'm not really sure who started it. And this one is definitely under thirty. No doubt about it. He tells me he's a professional football player. He tells me where he plays. I'm really not into football, so I have no idea if this is a big team or not. He tells me he loves kissing me and that he wants to do it all night long.

Perfect. Just what I need to hear. We do some more kissing.

Then I have to go to the toilet and on the way there I dance with three other guys. They simply don't let a woman walk on her own in a disco. They come to you, look you straight in the eyes, smile, and start dancing with you. If you respond, fine. If you don't, they smile anyway. It's OK. Everyone is out to have some fun.

"*Linda.*"

For a second my heart stops beating. I turn round, expecting to see a pair of deep brown eyes looking straight into mine.

But no, it's not him, my twenty-seven-year-old date of four days ago. It's not him, because I will simply never see him again. A new face looks at me, smiling, hand outstretched, inviting me to dance.

Well, at least they all call me *linda*, I think, as I dance with the newcomer.

By 6:00 I finally make it back from the loo. It's taken me thirty minutes to get there and come back, on account of all the different guys I've danced with on the way.

My cute football player is now kissing someone else on the dance floor.

Shit.

Oh well, it doesn't matter, I guess. There will be others. There are others, in fact. The disco is full of them. Just as I decide to retreat to another corner of the disco, the football player turns around and sees me. Very swiftly he lets go of his newfound love and smiles at me. The music is so loud I can't hear what he says. I grab the arm he stretches out and we dance again.

Out of the corner of my eye I see the girl he's just dumped casually dancing with someone else in a corner.

This is madness, I think, as my body rotates to the moves of cumbia, guided by the expert hand of my football player. Kissing here doesn't seem to mean anything. Everyone is here to have a great night out and they make sure they do. They dance, they kiss, then they dance with someone else and they kiss with someone else. About half the people around me have a wedding ring on their finger. And still it doesn't seem to matter at all.

For a second I hear Rosario's voice. "*Roxy, don't fall for the Argentines. They are players . . .*"

But then she's gone from my mind, to be replaced by the pounding sound of the Latino music, and the sensation of the lips of my football player hungrily looking for mine. We lock again in the sensual dance, our bodies drenched with sweat, our minds filled with lust.

The night becomes morning as Enrique Iglesias's voice continues to pound from the speakers, tearfully declaring his love.

By 7 am, as the disco finally closes, I'm floating above the earth. My body has no adrenaline left. My lips are swollen from too much kissing. My feet ache from too much dancing.

"Shall we go to your place now?" The cute football player is still with me.

I smile. This feels good for my ego boost.

"Well, do you remember my name?"

Let's just test the strength of this relationship.

"Aurora? Luisa?"

He gives up after a while and admits being confused.

"Roxana."

"Ah, Roxana, of course Roxana. The most beautiful name there is. Shall we go to your place?"

"How about we see if you remember my name after you wake up later today?"

"Of course I'll remember. Are you joking?" He looks offended.

"OK then, give me a call then and we'll see what happens."

"So we don't go to your place now?" his voice drops in disappointment.

"No, I don't think so."

He sighs, accepting defeat graciously. "OK. I'll call you when I wake up."

If you can remember my name, I think as I grab the hand of the girl I came here with and we both get into a taxi in the light of the morning sun.

I go to sleep with a mask on my face and the music still pounding in my ears.

See, it's not that bad, I tell myself. They all kiss well here.

But somewhere in the back of my mind Enrique Iglesias is still singing about roaming the streets all drenched in alcohol, looking for his lost love.

SATURDAY 12TH DECEMBER

I wake up to the sound of my mobile ringing. I have no idea how long I've been asleep.

"Yes."

"*Hola*."

"Yes, *hola*. Who's this?"

My memory comes back slowly. It must be the football player. He promised he would call.

"Rodrigo."

I almost drop the phone. "Who?"

"Rodrigo. Don't you remember me? We met on Tuesday."

By now I'm wide awake. I'm also very conscious my voice is hoarse. Too much drinking. And singing. And kissing. Oh my God, the football player . . .

"Ah, yes . . . of course I remember. Yes. How are you?" I try to control my voice.

"I was waiting for you to call me," he says.

"What?" I almost drop the phone again. "Me to call you? Why were you waiting for me to call you?"

"I thought you didn't want to see me any longer so I waited to see if maybe you did."

Silence. This guy needs to talk to my launderette mentor. He needs a quick refresher course on basic Argentine man behavior.

"Well, I was waiting for you to call me," I say finally. "I thought in this country men do the calling."

"They do. But . . . never mind. I want to see you."

I swallow. Silence. My mind is a void. My body, alive. I can't think. Don't think.

"I want to see you too."

"Today?"

"No, I can't today." My lips are swollen. I can't tell him this. But today is also the last day of the Abierto. I will meet Andrea and then we will go out again. The best polo party is always on the day of the finals.

"Not today. I'm going to see a polo game. Tomorrow?"

"OK, tomorrow. I'll pick you up for lunch."

I put my head back on the pillow after I hang up, and the mask back on my eyes. But I can't sleep any longer. All I can think of is that sometimes the Universe gives you a second chance. Or a second lunch.

LATER THAT DAY

By 4 pm I'm a decent version of myself again. I've had a few hours' sleep, refreshed my eyes with an eye mask, used generous amounts of cream on my swollen lips and applied my makeup. Next up is an appointment with Sol.

Sol is my hairdresser. She owns the salon at the corner of my street. She's got three kids—two boys under seven and a girl who's just two. She also has an ex-husband who mistreated her and the kids, to the point where the police got involved. She took the kids and left. She looks after all three of them, gets no support from the ex-husband, and runs the salon as well. She is twenty-seven and has given up any hope of decent treatment from men.

I tell her it's too early to give up on love at twenty-seven. There will be someone else.

"No, not for me," she sighs. "I've got three kids. Three devils to raise. Who will want me, since I come as a package with them?"

Sol is very pretty. Long blond hair, round plump face, full lips, green eyes with lots of makeup. She is a professional makeup artist too. Short skirt, nice legs. Everyone wears incredibly short skirts here. I'm contemplating how I can best pass the message that she still has a lot to offer a potential suitor, but I have no opportunity to dive into this.

"No! Stop it!" She shouts. "Stop it now!" She puts the hair drier down and launches at her son, who is busy banging the telephone against the hard floor.

More shouting follows. I don't understand anything. It must be slang. I must tell Santi to teach me some slang. Here people don't talk like they do in his textbooks.

"Sorry darling," she says, picking up the hair dryer again. "These kids are like devils. I don't know what I'm going to do with them. You know how kids are . . ."

Two more clients are patiently waiting their turn and they nod their heads knowingly. Only I don't know. I have no kids. I don't know how kids are. Listening to her, I'm not even sure I ever want to find out.

Sol usually complains either about kids or about men as she does my hair. She tells me not to trust them. Men, she means. Especially not if they are Argentines. Fun yes, love no. Don't get your heart broken, she says. I feel like I'm listening to my friend Rosario. But today there are not that many complaints on the list. She wants to know how my evening went.

I tell her about the Latino dances, the kisses, the football player, mixing vodka and orange in a car . . .

She smiles. "Yes, we know how to have a good night out here."

I tell her I've never had a night out like that before. Not as a teenager, not as a student, not as a traveler, not as a single girl. Ever. I ask her if they all kiss like that.

"Yes, they do. Argentine men are good at one thing only. Don't fall in love, though," she warns me again.

The two clients waiting their turn nod again. All seem to be in agreement on this. One of the clients is a very fat woman in her fifties. The other one is a teenage girl. They nod at the same time, with the same level of female solidarity. Yes, men are like that, they seem to say.

Who's talking about love, anyway? I think.

"Did he call you back, then? The guy you kissed in the disco?"

"No. He's probably still asleep. Either that or he doesn't remember my name."

"Oh, don't worry, there will be others." She gives a wave of her hand. I have seen this gesture enough times to know its meaning. *Dismissed.*

But one man did call me back. My heart is dancing. I'm going to see him again tomorrow. But I don't tell her anything about this one. Let it be my little secret.

Sol is interrupted again when her toddler shits in her nappy. She changes her right there on the chair beside me, under the bright fluorescent light that fills the small salon. It doesn't smell too bad, and I don't mind. The other clients don't seem to mind, either. Sol is a single mother and somehow she needs to do it all. Run the shop, straighten my hair, look after her kids, and give me dating advice as well. She blends her work with her life, and somehow miraculously makes space for both. And she does it all with a big smile.

Because they are like this, the Argentines. They don't let work take over their lives.

THE EVENING

It's the last evening of the Abierto and emotions are running high. The top two teams in the world are facing each other. It's impossible to see this level of polo anywhere else but here. Everyone on the field is a handicap-ten player. The handicap grade starts at minus two. I'm a minus two. It took me two years and three broken bones to become a minus two. It also took me countless sessions with my chiropractor and acupuncturist in London, a couple of weeks of not being able to walk in Argentina, and more than one crying fit in the tack room as I wondered what was stopping me hitting the ball properly.

It also took a lot of shouting on the polo field from my trainer in England, the Old Man. Lots of cigarettes as he smoked patiently, watching my failed attempts to score a thirty-yard penalty. Countless encouraging comments from fellow players along the lines of, "You'll make it, don't you worry," and countless worries on my side that I would never make it.

So as a minus two–handicap player I can perfectly recognize the abyss that separates me from a handicap-ten player. They and I are not from the same world. They are gods on horses. I'm a poor mortal. I can hardly breathe as I watch a game in which eight players, all handicap ten, line up to play the final of the Abierto. The only non-Argentine player on the field is from Uruguay, a neighboring country. And to the Argentines, Uruguay is like a province of Argentina, anyway.

Adolfo Cambiaso, the legend of polo and the best player in the world, is captain of one of the teams. I have long ago given up trying to understand how this man does what he does on a horse. But Cambiaso is going to have a hard ride today, because the captain of the other team is Facundo Pieres, my idol. Officially Pieres is number two in the world, right after Cambiaso. To me and many others, he is better than the current number one. He is the young wolf challenging the established alpha male. It's going to be a fascinating game.

I met Facundo Pieres in London after a charity game he'd played at another club—a club where a friend of mine also played. My friend is the only other Romanian polo player I know, and we spent many hours brainstorming how we might find two more of us, so we could put together the first-ever Romanian polo team. That's becase polo does not exist as a sport in Romania and we both started playing while living in London. So we figured out we must try to find other players who play outside our country. And if we did, we would maybe get sponsored by the embassy of Romania, and we could play a charity match. On my friend's side there was an extra ambition—inviting Facundo to play with us.

For me this was pure fantasy, but my friend actually did invite him. He walked up to Facundo at the end of the game, just as the well-known player was chatting with people who had come to ask for autographs. My friend walked up to him, dragging me along, and proceeded to introduce me as "the only Romanian female polo player in the world."

While this description is technically correct, since this sport is non-existent in my country and I don't know of any other Romanian women who play polo, I was mortified by the introduction. I shook hands with Facundo, and just as I was trying to extricate myself from the scene, my friend went one step further. He actually asked Facundo if he would mind playing a charity game with us. Next year. It would be our first-ever game as a Romanian team.

"You know, you could really help us out," he added, looking straight at Facundo as if this were the most natural request in the world.

I wanted to die on the spot. Facundo took it lightly. I could tell he was amused. This guy is being paid millions per season and plays with the top players in the world. He had a good sense of humor, though, and genuinely laughed as if he had heard a good joke, and then fortunately he was called away for a press photo and I was released from the most embarrassing moment of my polo life.

Now, as I watch Facundo ride his horse out onto the field, I hope I'll never again meet him face to face. Just in case he remembers our previous encounter.

Patricio shows up with his good friend Bernie, and they take the seats next to mine. He's a nice guy, Bernie. Handsome, like all Argentines. I suspect the only reason why Patricio hasn't tried any match-making is that Bernie is not only married, but recently had a baby as well. Even for Argentines, this is no-go territory.

I get compliments from both of them. In my short summer dress and high heels I look pretty, they say. I'm still in my blue phase, and the electric blue bag I carry matches my nails. Gabriela would disapprove, but then again she disapproves of pretty much everything I wear. We have different tastes in fashion, that's clear.

The bright shade of my bag makes me think of the light in the disco last night. And the kisses of the football player. Just as I'm starting to daydream, I get another confirmation that Argentines can read minds.

"So how's it going with the *chicos*. The guys. Anyone new?" Patricio asks.

"Yes, a probably underage football player in a disco last night."

"*And*?"

"*Nada*. Just kissing."

They both look disappointed. I'm sorry my news isn't more thrilling.

"Are you going to see him again?"

"I suspect he doesn't remember my name. So probably not. I'm seeing the other guy, though."

"Which one? The one you said I scared off?" Patricio hasn't forgotten my obsession with Mr. Perfect.

"No, not that one. We had dinner with that one and he looked like he was going to vomit on the table in front of me. I haven't heard from him since. I'm meeting another one. The twenty-seven-year-old guy I went to have lunch with. I'm seeing him tomorrow."

Our conversation ends abruptly as one of the players suddenly flies off his horse in a violent ride off. I wouldn't have survived either the ride off or the fall. I broke both arms in something a lot milder. But he gets up and gets back on his horse as if nothing has happened. A sort of *no pasa nada*. This strengthens my suspicion that these polo players are really not human.

I watch Facundo score an impossible goal out of a spot penalty awarded somewhere in the middle of the field and all of a sudden all the guys in my mind dissolve. There is no other guy in the whole world who can stand next to Facundo scoring a goal.

By the third chukka it starts to rain. On the field the game carries on, regardless. The rain is the last thing on their minds, and in any case, polo can be played in the rain until the field is soaked and it becomes dangerous for the horses.

Unlike in England, there is no commentary on the game. It goes on in silence, and all you can hear are the hooves of the horses hitting the grass, the brief shouts the players throw to each other, and the click of the mallets hitting the ball.

Also, unlike in England, people don't need any commentary to follow the game. They all understand what is going on, and a collective "ahhh" from the stands accompanies each spectacular shot. Impossible shot, rather. I'm convinced that even if I reincarnate ten times as a polo player, I won't even get close to those shots.

The three of us huddle under the only umbrella we have. Patricio tries to get more info about the guy I'm meeting tomorrow. He's unsuccessful, because for me, right now, there is one guy and one guy only, and his name is Facundo.

In the end my idol loses. The old wolf Cambiaso takes the title again. It's his third consecutive title. I'm getting tired of Cambiaso. I bet Facundo is getting tired of him, too.

After the game I let Patricio and Bernie go their own way while I go and search for Andrea. I need to maximize my chances to talk to nice, available guys. After all, it's the last night of the Abierto and I need to make the most of it. The man of my life might be just here, waiting to meet me tonight. My chances of meeting him while I'm squeezed under an umbrella in between Patricio and Bernie are slim. But finding Andrea, and spending some time with her sipping Champagne, will instantly increase the probability. Or so I hope.

Andrea is, of course, in the Chandon bar. Not yet in the VIP area, which is good for me because I can approach her without an effort.

She is, of course, talking to two guys. She waves to me as soon as she spots me approaching. We all exchange kisses, and a guy immediately asks what I would like to drink. Champagne for both of us please, she answers. And so, in a fraction of a second, I'm back to where I belong—learning from Andrea how to be a lady.

My disappointment for Facundo's loss dissolves in the first glass of Champagne, and many more glasses follow. I meet more people. I meet people I've been playing polo with in Argentina or in London, people who play at the club where I used to play, people who play at the club where I play now, people who know people

I played with. People I trained with. People I had met before but didn't remember meeting. Polo is one small family scattered around the globe. If you're a player then you're automatically part of this family and it welcomes you wherever you go. Or, as Winston Churchill put it, a polo handicap is a passport to the world.

The music in the Chandon bar gets turned up. It's party time. And no, it's not Enrique Iglesias this time. They tell me cumbia is for the masses. We're with the élite here and they only play international hits. I drink Champagne and then Campari Orange and then some more Champagne, and I'm even persuaded to try out their national cocktail, Fernet and cola. Everyone is in the mood to party, even if only to forget that this is the last night, the last game. The final. From next week onwards there will be no more Abierto, no more games, no more Chandon bar with music, no more sipping Champagne with Andrea and talking to all the guys who cluster around us. It's over until next year, and the problem is, I still haven't met my dream man.

Andrea is alarmed when I tell her about my adventures with a close-to-underage football player in the Latino disco last night.

"You're crazy. Forget about that stuff. We need to find you a proper boyfriend. Here, let's see. Do you like any of these?" She scrolls down her WhatsApp chat list. It's a long list. I don't think I've had so many guys ask for my phone number in all my life. And I've lived longer than she has.

She tries to bring up their profile pictures, but the internet connection is bad and it takes ages.

"Forget it. Let's just look around. We'll find you someone."

She looks around and they come. Dark hair, handsome faces with that wild, unshaved Argentine look. I love the Argentine wild, unshaved look. Most of them are tall. Taller than the average Argentine. Maybe polo attracts taller guys. They all wear white or blue shirts, a few buttons open and not tucked into their jeans. They all smile. They all seem relaxed. They all say *hola* and ask if we would like to have a drink.

Given my disco experience, I'm now a little bit more confident. But Andrea is still by far more advanced. Her shining self-confidence attracts them. They come straight to her. I'm just part of the package.

We drink Champagne. We stroll around. We chat with the guys who buy us drinks. Then we move around and others come. It only takes Andrea a quick glance, followed by an enigmatic smile, for two new guys to instantly appear in front of us. Argentines tend to hang out in pairs.

"*Hola*, ladies, *como están?*"

Before she answers, Andrea takes a good look to work out whether it's worth the effort. The guys seem young, possibly about the same age as my football player last night. She smiles without answering. The guy carries on talking. He doesn't realise he's being dismissed. He carries on innocently, but he stands no chance. I recognize that look on Andrea's face. She has decided. It's not worth talking to this one. Her eyes start flashing warning signals. The guy still speaks and he does so in Spanish. This is a big mistake. He should have figured out we are foreigners and should have switched to English by now. Andrea's look tells me she's starting to get annoyed.

"What have I done?" The guy finally seems to realize something isn't quite right. He turns to his mate. "Do you think I said something wrong?"

Nothing wrong, but you have no chance, my friend. You're not going to last another five seconds.

Andrea has spotted someone she's met before and she smiles graciously at him. The guy registers this and approaches. The others leave immediately. They've lasted about three seconds since the death sentence issued by Andrea's annoyed smile. I guess Argentine men also have a code to understand when they have lost in front of a rival.

"*Hola*!"

We're now with the newcomer. Andrea introduces him to me and he goes to the bar to get us two glasses of Champagne.

"Polo player," she whispers to me, watching him walk away. "Really handsome. Nice horses too. I think you will like him."

Maybe this is my last chance. I cast a glance at the guy, who is now back with our drinks. Broad shoulders, black hair, full face, sensual lips. Feels familiar. Have I met him before? But no, I haven't met him before. He just happens to look like Rodrigo.

Stop it, silly, I tell myself and I sip the drink he has brought me. This might be my true chance at happiness. I tell him I'm in love with this country and with everything Argentine.

"Really? I'm not," he says. "I left this country ten years ago and I live in Spain now. I left precisely because I can't stand anything Argentine."

After this revelation, the conversation dies pretty quickly. Cultural incompatibility, I would call it. He leaves, we move on. New guys come to talk to us. Andrea laughs and whispers something in my ear, but the music is too loud and I don't catch it. I nod, I smile, I drink, I talk. But deep down I'm still thinking of Rodrigo.

Some hours later I go home drunk, happy, and alone.

I have to talk to Santi, I think, as my head hits the pillow. I need another song. It's all the fault of that bloody song.

Sola en Baires . . .

SUNDAY 13TH DECEMBER

I wake up with another hangover. I'm not used to drinking this much, and definitely not two nights in a row.

But it was the final of the Abierto. Now I'll go back to a healthy routine. Back to the gym. I will play polo. I will eat well and sleep enough. I will refrain from kissing nearly underage football players in discos. Enough with all this nonsense.

Still, I'm sad it's all over. Andrea is leaving Buenos Aires to go traveling in southern Argentina with a couple of friends. Maybe I should join her. But I can't. I have a to-do list to complete. I'm still doing physio for my arm, and I think I'll carry on until the end of December. My wrist has improved a lot. It doesn't bend like the other one, though, and I'm determined to get there. Both my wrists need to bend in the same way. And I'm still going to language school, and Santi's efforts are starting to bear fruit. I can now have a fluent conversation in Spanish. I remember yesterday speaking fluently with Patricio and Bernie under the umbrella. Definitely big progress. And I will play some polo. I agreed with Patricio to come back on Tuesday for another training session. And this time there will be nothing preventing me. Not even a date.

Which brings me to point four on my list, and the thing I need to do now—get out of bed, get into the shower, and try to compose myself for the lunch date about to start in two hours.

And yet . . . what am I doing with this guy? To be honest, it would have been better if he hadn't called. It would have been the perfect clean break. We accidentally got talking to each other, we accidentally kissed like two love-struck teenagers in a car, and when we found out there were fourteen years separating us, we should have agreed like two grown-ups never to speak to each other again. Yes, that would have been the decent thing to do.

And now? I contemplate my options as I lie wide awake.

Option 1: text him to cancel lunch. Say I have a headache. Which is true, by the way. Definitely the most sensible option. He'll get the message. He'll never call again.

Option 2: meet him for lunch. Only for lunch and nothing else. Discuss the situation. Tell him it's impossible. Agree to part friends. Then, never see him again.

Option 3: go for lunch and possibly kiss him again. No, hang on. I don't want to think about kissing him again. If I really want to think of kissing someone, I should think of the football player from Friday night. Who has never actually called back. Probably because he doesn't remember my name.

I try to keep my thoughts in check and get back to my list.

Option 3: go to lunch and kiss him once more. Just once more and just to see if his kisses really are better than those of the football player.

I know they are. I don't need to try again.

Stop it. You are playing with fire!

And what happens if I kiss him again? Just like that, for fun?

I'm now annoyed at my own sensible self.

"Ha? What happens? It's not going to be the end of the world. When was the last time you felt like this? Can you remember?"

No, she can't. She—the sensible part of me—tries to convince me that last night in the disco she felt like this. No, you didn't, liar! You were kissing the football player, imagining you were kissing Rodrigo. Come on, be honest!

My sensible self doesn't want to be honest. She only wants to be sensible, and nothing else. She reminds me that the guy is twenty-seven years old.

"Yes, but the football player is close to being underage!" I point out. "What's the problem?"

"You will never see the football player again," she replies. "But you will see this one in exactly one hour and twenty-seven minutes from now, unless you cancel."

"It's just a lunch."

"No, it's not."

"Yes, it will be. Lunch and a kiss."

"Why do you need another kiss?"

"Because I do. I don't know why. Because no one has ever kissed me like that before."

"It's just an Argentine kiss. They all kiss well here."

"Says who?"

"Rosario. And Sol. Gabriela too."

"They also say you should be careful not to get hurt," my sensible self says.

"I'm not getting hurt, you stupid, I'm just having some fun."

"Really?" My sensible self is far from convinced.

"Yes."

"Really?"

"Screw you. Yes. Only fun. No love. Look, I have erased love from my list. Replaced it with fun. Happy?"

No, she is not happy.

"You will fall for him," she says.

"No I won't. I can't. He is twenty-seven and I'm forty-one."

"Precisely. I'm glad you acknowledge that."

I've had enough of talking to this irritating voice. I just can't get my point across. So I get out of bed, have a shower, and then head straight downstairs to the café for some light-hearted flirtation with my waiter. I need urgent male attention, and I'm in the perfect country to get it. I don't need to do anything. Just enter the coffee shop, sit down, and ask for a coffee. It comes with flirting on the side.

But neither the waiter nor the football player can save me from this situation. At 1:30 I get a text message from Rodrigo telling me he's here. His car is parked downstairs and he's waiting to drive to a restaurant he has chosen for lunch. I'm wearing a skirt this time. No more jeans. I'm also wearing a big fake smile to cover that silly voice hidden inside which is still asking what exactly I think I'm doing.

I get in the car quickly so Sol can't see me from the window of her hair salon. At least I won't have to explain this.

And then I see him and all of a sudden I feel I really don't need to explain anything to anyone. A quick kiss and he drives on. He doesn't ask me anything. I'm so tense I think I'll burst into tears. I'm not sure where we are going, but as I get into the car I'm sure of one thing. I missed him.

Rodrigo drives on through the crowded streets of Palermo. Silently he takes his hand from the gearstick and finds mine. *Tranqui*, he seems to say. *No pasa nada. Después vemos.* And my heartbeat gradually goes back to normal.

We finally arrive at a restaurant, one of the many small cafés in Palermo open for lunch, and we each order a Campari Orange. I casually mention how I've been out dancing. I stay away from any reference to football players, close encounters while dancing cumbia or maybe reggaeton on the way to the ladies' room, or the vodka and orange juice shared with four others as we raced well over the legal speed limit through the streets of Buenos Aires by night.

Rodrigo tells me he also went out last night and only had three hours' sleep. It takes him an hour to drive to his suburb. He tells me the name of the town where he lives. I forget it as soon as he says it.

I stare into his deep brown eyes as I sip my Campari Orange, and then he calls me *linda* again. Like that, out of the blue. I feel I'm melting like a naive teenager. It's definitely been too long since someone called me *linda*.

We kiss right there at the table, on the terrace of that restaurant, beneath the tall tree that shades us from the strong afternoon sun. We kiss as the waitress patiently waits to leave the bill on the table. We kiss, oblivious to everyone and everything around us, and this time there's no blood in my mouth as we stop to take a breath, just a deep longing for more.

With the meal finished, the bill paid, and the heat of noon upon us, there are not many options left.

"What are we doing now?"

He stares at me, one long stare and then says, "Look, don't take this the wrong way but I have a one-hour drive now to get back home, and I didn't sleep much last night. I could do with a *siesta*."

He wants to have a *siesta*. With me. He wants to go home with me, lie down in my bed, and have a *siesta*. And he makes this proposal in such a straightforward, friendly tone, as if indeed all he wants to do is have a *siesta*.

I don't buy the *siesta* story. But my mouth holds the memory of his kisses and my eyes are lost in his. And even the silly me inside seems to have stopped talking. Maybe she, too, has remembered that point four on my list now says have some fun.

Let's have a *siesta* then.

The drive home passes in a second. Rodrigo continues to hold my hand in his, occasionally changing gears before returning to hold my hand each time. My body relaxes instantly at his touch, and even my mind, with its constant internal chatter, is forced to take a break. When he holds my hand, time stands still.

Time stands still later too, in the cool shelter of my apartment, far from the maddening heat, as I melt under his kisses. No more desperation this time. Just the strength of his arms around me and the fullness of his lips, and my body inexplicably but deeply knowing his, my mind completely and firmly shut.

"What are you doing?" He stops kissing me and I note the look of surprise on his face.

I'm taking off his t-shirt.

"Are you sure?" he asks.

Well, yes, I'm about to say. We've been kissing for thirty minutes and it didn't look like you were making any move to take my clothes off, so I thought I'd better start with yours.

But no explanations are needed. The shocked look on his face makes me think for the first time that maybe he hadn't anticipated taking his clothes off when he came up with the *siesta* idea.

"Why, do you mind?" I ask.

"No, not at all, but—are you sure?"

For a split second Patricio's voice rings in my ears, telling me I can do everything I possibly want to do with a twenty-seven-year-old guy, and he won't mind.

"Yes, I'm sure," I whisper and carry on with my task.

A little bit later, I ask him, "Have you got a condom?"

"No."

"What do you mean, no?" I look at him in disbelief. A guy who wants to have a *siesta* after lunch should have a condom with him, surely.

"I haven't got one. Have you?"

"No." I'm about to add that my dating life isn't so active I need to keep a supply of condoms in my house, but then I decide some things are better left unsaid.

"Why have you not got a condom?" I ask him instead.

"I didn't think I would need one. I don't expect sex on the first date."

"Most Argentines do."

"Says who?"

"My Argentine girlfriends."

"Well, I'm not like most Argentines, then."

Back to the condom problem.

"So what are we going to do now?"

We could technically just get dressed again and carry on with the original plan of taking a *siesta* which involves no kissing, no touching, and no taking our clothes off. But this would be a very difficult thing to achieve, given the state of extreme arousal we are both in.

"I suppose we could go and buy one. That is, if you think we need one. If not, we can just have a *siesta*."

He laughs. "There is no way I'm only having a *siesta* right now. All your fault."

"OK. Can you go buy one?"

"I don't know the neighborhood. Are there any small shops here?"

I don't want to think about waiting for him in bed as he gets lost in my neighborhood trying to buy a condom.

"I'll come with you."

"No, you can't."

"Why not?"

"What? You think I'll buy a condom in a shop with you standing next to me? Can't you see what everyone will imagine?"

"So?"

"I can't do it! It's embarrassing. It's like making love in front of them."

"Fine, I'll show you where the shop is and I'll wait outside."

We get dressed. This is not how this whole "having fun" business was supposed to work. I'm getting slightly irritated.

But then he kisses me just as we are about to leave the flat and my body relaxes again.

"*Tranquila. No pasa nada.*"

Why can he not say "*tranqui*," like all other Argentines?

We're back on the street, in the scorching heat of the afternoon sun. I locate the shop. It's two streets away.

"There." I point it out to him.

"OK, wait for me here."

I wait in the middle of the street as he goes inside to buy a condom. I hope he buys more than one.

"So?" I ask as he comes out.

"They don't take cards. I'm out of cash. We need to find an ATM."

A surge of frustration washes over me. "Here, take my wallet. I've got cash."

I wait again in the middle of the street as he goes in with my wallet to buy a condom. Not exactly how I imagined the start of a romance.

He comes out again.

"Well?"

"Done." He hands me over the wallet. "I left the receipt inside."

What for? I wonder. It's not like we're likely to return it.

We go back to the flat and awkwardness sets in. We're both fully dressed now and the whole shopping trip has broken the spell.

"I suppose we can still have a *siesta*, right?" I say tentatively. We don't need to do anything else, I think.

But then he kisses me again. "*Linda*," he whispers.

And then there's no more need for words because the whole world has melted into nothingness.

TUESDAY 15TH DECEMBER

I'm going to play polo today. I board the minibus to Lobos in the morning and my heart dances. There's no particular reason. It's just been doing this for the last two days and I can't seem to return it to its senses, no matter how much I try.

I've also developed a worrying habit of smiling non-stop. I smile at my waiter in the coffee shop and this encourages him a lot. I smile and let him talk to me and I just smile back. I smile at the jacaranda trees in full purple bloom and marvel at their beauty. They deserve a smile simply because I've never seen a more beautiful blossom and they are all over Buenos Aires and they've become the most iconic spring image of this city.

I'm starting to worry about the state of my mental health. Staring for twenty minutes at a tree in bloom and smiling all the time is not something I would normally do.

I smile at Santi, my language teacher. I smile as I stumble over the irregular verbs and I smile at my own mistakes—the same ones I used to get so annoyed with. I smile when Santi asks me to read a Jorge Luis Borges novella as extra homework to compensate for the fact I'll be missing school on Tuesday in order to go to San Patricio to play polo. I smile and he smiles at my constant smiles, not really understanding what's going on with me.

I don't blame him. I can't understand it either. I'm under a spell and I can't break it. I just keep on smiling at the world like a total and utter imbecile, and I don't really know why.

Nothing has changed in my life. We made love that afternoon. I told myself it was just sex. But then why has it left me smiling like this two days in a row?

Because you haven't had sex for a very long time. I can imagine just what Marco would say. *Don't take things out of context. It was just sex. Just what he wanted. What else could he want from a woman who's fourteen years older than him? And it was just what you needed. And just what you planned, remember?*

Yes, I planned it. As soon as Rodrigo called to propose another lunch, I thought about it. I thought that since the age difference effectively ruled out any further development between us, at least I could have some fun. Tick off point four on my list. Get it out of my system and get myself free to concentrate on point two again. Play polo. Preferably in Mar de Plata, with the Old Man, just as I promised him. And he won't let me off the hook, not this time.

The Old Man is my trainer from England. He's Argentine and he owns the polo club where I play back in England. I call him the Old Man, even though he's not actually that old, because the grooms all call him "*el Viejo*," and in Argentina this is a common way to refer to someone of a different generation. So I decided to call him the Old Man as well.

Would a fourteen-year age difference qualify as a different

generation? The question catches me off guard. Surely not. Borderline maybe. Stop it! It doesn't matter. I'm going to see Rodrigo again once, maybe twice. If he calls back. I rather think he will, this time. And then I'll go to Mar de Plata. A perfect exit plan. No harm done. Just fun. See? It's possible, I tell my sensible self. She keeps quiet today. She's not in the mood to argue any longer.

Back to the Old Man. He put me back on the horse after I broke both arms playing polo. Actually, I broke my arms playing at another club, not at his, and he got very angry when he heard about it.

"Why do you play at other clubs?" he asked. "Come play here. Nothing bad happens to you when you play at my club."

This was true. Up until then I'd had the odd fall or two at his club, but had never had an injury. Maybe because the Old Man is Argentine and governed by the *no pasa nada* law. Or maybe because he has better horses. Or maybe because he shouts at me so much while I'm on the field that I actually ride better. Or maybe it's pure luck.

He had promised me then, after my fall, that I would ride again. That I would play polo again, as well. And that he would see to both. I told him it was a long road to recovery. I had to have surgery on my left wrist and then tons of physio, and the right shoulder blade would need more than six weeks to get back to one piece.

"*No pasa nada*," he had said then. "I will put you back on a horse. I promise."

He did. As soon as I got out of the cast I got a phone call from him.

"Are you coming down to the club or am I coming to fetch you from London?"

I told him I was barely out of my cast and my arms weren't moving properly yet. And that the polo season had already ended. It was October already.

"You need to get back on a horse," he said. "Not to play. Just ride. Just to be back on the horse. It's important. For your mind. Trust me, I know what I'm talking about."

He did know. He was missing half a finger and had broken a number of bones, all from polo. He'd recovered each time, though, and he always played again.

I trusted him and I went to see him at his farm one sunny October morning. He put me on one horse while he got up on another and then he walked with me on the polo field for about one hour. He didn't let me trot or, God forbid, gallop.

"No running," he said. "It's too early. This is all you need to do. Walk. Be back on the horse. Remember how it is. This is what your mind needs."

I inhaled deeply and the familiar smell of freshly cut grass hit me with a power that surprised me. I felt the wind on my face and I looked beyond the ears of the horse at the immense, empty polo field stretching all around me. My body fell back into the rhythm of the mare's hooves. She walked slowly. I went with her. I remembered. I relaxed. I let the fall go.

Still, I will never forget the accident. It will be with me forever, deeply imprinted in the cells of my soul—that fraction of a second when everything went dark, the unexpected fall, the horse landing on his shoulder. The short flight in the air as I left the saddle and went flying up above his neck. The sharp landing on my right shoulder. The clear sound of a crack from under my ribs, which I heard inside my skull. It's impossible ever to forget the sound of bones breaking somewhere inside your body. My left hand came forward, still carrying the whip, trying to stop the fall. And then another crack. A smaller one this time. Two bones in my left wrist were broken, too. The sound of the ambulance that had been waiting patiently on the side of a polo field. Now I know why they are always there. The whistle of the umpire. My friend shouting behind me, "Roxyyyy!" as she jumped off her horse and came running towards me. And the huge shot of pain that blinded me momentarily and which I turned inwards. I hadn't cried out. But the shout I didn't dare to free turned inside and broke something else in the depths of my soul. It broke my courage.

Somehow, without any words or explanations, the Old Man understood this. He must have read it in my eyes. The deep hidden fear, the panic that woke me at night, making me relive the moment again and again and again. The shout I didn't let out as I lay broken on that polo field came back afterwards to haunt my nights.

The Old Man must have sensed it, or maybe he even knew all about it himself. Maybe it was the same for him when he broke his bones. Maybe his falls had broken his courage, too, and maybe it also took a long time for him to recover, because it's one thing to recover from a broken bone and quite another to recover from the memory of it. And maybe it took time for him to become whole again. But one way or another, he knew exactly what I needed—a gentle walk with a horse on a polo field on a sunny morning after the polo season had ended and there was no one else around. Just me and him. Me silent, him talking casually, about falls, about bones, about polo, about passion, about not giving up. About recovery.

"You'll be fine, you'll see. Now you've been back on a horse, you'll be fine. Go recover, go do your physio and the gym, do whatever you need to do. And when the spring comes you'll be ready to play again. I'll make sure you do. And I'll make a polo player out of you, of this you can be certain."

It took me all winter to recover. That was last year. I came back to Argentina for just five days on my birthday and went to San Patricio, but I didn't touch a horse. I took time off, just as the Old Man instructed me, and I knew I would be fine. Because that walk on the polo field in October last year had done its part.

And then Patricio did the second part. He told me he would be in Spain playing polo in April, just before the start of the polo season in England, and that I should come too, spend a few days with Gabriela and him, and he would help me get back on a horse. I went and I met them. I cantered again. I hit the ball. I tried to jump from one horse to another just as he does between chukkas. I failed and found myself lying across the saddle like a bag of potatoes. Gabriela took pictures. We laughed. I healed.

When I returned to the club, the Old Man was there waiting for me. He did make me into a polo player that season, just as he had promised. I played fifteen tournaments and won two of them. He screamed a lot. He shouted at me a lot. He pushed me a lot, far beyond my comfort zone.

There were days I had to explain him why I didn't want to hit it—"it" being the ball, which lay peacefully on the ground, mocking my failed attempts to touch it while in full gallop. I had to endure his jokes about my confusion between a horse and a motorcycle while turning. I had to put up with the embarrassment of him shouting at me in the middle of a game.

"Come on, come and take the ball from me—if you can!"

I couldn't, but I tried hard. I tried really hard the whole season, and at the end of it, when he told me my handicap wouldn't be increased as I had hoped, I found myself crying in the tack room.

"Believe me, I'm doing you a favor," he told me. "You're not ready to be a minus one yet. You are a strong minus two handicap. And you'll stay so until you're genuinely better. And I'll see to it that you do. Come and train with me in Argentina," he added, and then left me to my misery.

I hated him for it. I thought he was unfair. He had promoted other players to minus one, and I was playing just as well as them. Other players told me I should look on it as a gift not to have my handicap increased, but my ego wanted it badly.

I wanted it especially since I knew exactly why I hadn't got it. For some weird reason, although my hits had improved a lot, I still wasn't able to score a goal. I hadn't scored a single goal in all the tournaments I'd played. I assisted others. I did my part. I marked well, I passed the ball. I hit well. But I didn't score. Whenever I got close to that damn goal, something happened to me and I missed it. Every single time. I missed again and again, until one day the Old Man asked, "Want my glasses? So you can see the goal post better? Maybe there's something wrong with your eyesight."

I kept on failing to score a goal and I had no idea why. But he knew.

"You need to train some more," he said. "Come to Mar de Plata in Argentina." That was his hometown. "I'll be there in December. I'll make you score. And when the season starts again in England you'll be a different player."

Maybe the last part of my broken soul needed to be mended before I could score a goal in a tournament. Or maybe it was just pure skill and I simply had to work at it. Whatever it was, I was determined to have it fixed. I would score.

Soon I'll train with him, I think, as I board the minibus for Lobos. I'll go on one more date with Rodrigo, next weekend. And then I'll go to Mar de Plata and train with the Old Man. Maybe I'll stay there for the rest of my time in Argentina.

LATER, ON THE POLO FIELD

"Let's see what moves this guy's taught you," Patricio shouts across the field. The grooms are within earshot and I find myself hoping they don't understand much English.

"Give me a break," I shout back.

He grins. "There's only one thing that helps with polo riding, you know. And that's what you have been up to last weekend."

Oh God, why did I tell him? Why could I not keep quiet? But the smile all over my face was there when he came to pick me up from the bus station. And Gabriela was there, too, and asked me what I'd been up to. I told them both that, yes, I had a big tick on my point number four, the former "fall in love," now replaced with "have some fun." And that his name is Rodrigo.

"Rodrigo what?" Patricio asks.

"Ah. Not sure. I can't remember."

"You don't know his surname?" I detect suppressed laughter in his voice.

"I haven't actually asked."

"Where does he live?"

"Somewhere outside Buenos Aires. Maybe an hour away."

"What's the name of the town?"

"I can't remember."

"What does he do for a living?"

"He works in the maintenance department of a factory. Something to do with cables, I think."

"What's the name of this factory?"

"Can't remember."

"Do you remember anything about this guy?"

"She remembers a lot, I'm sure." Gabriela jumps in to help me out. "It must have been great if she's smiling like this."

The interrogation lasts until we reach the polo field. Then polo does its trick again and manages to clear my mind. Once on a horse, everything that isn't polo simply vanishes from my mind.

There's a saying in polo, "What happens on the field, stays on the field." Well, it's more like whatever happens off the field doesn't exist when you're on the field, I would say.

We play. There are no cousins this time. Just Gabriela in her sexy cowboy boots, Patricio, their grooms, and Lisa, the same German client who had been at the Abierto on the day Patricio blew my chances with Mr. Perfect. She plays well—much better than me. She's faster and a much better rider, and she rarely misses a ball. That's why she's a minus one handicap and I'm not.

After the game we have a drink. I'm out of breath, sore, and happy. Polo happy this time. Even sex happy is not as happy as polo happy. Nothing can come close to polo happy.

"Listen, you should play a tournament with us," Patricio says.

A tournament? I think, excited. Really?

"Do you really think I'm good enough?" This is the main question. In polo and everything else.

Tournaments are tough, because unlike practice games, where no scores are kept, in tournaments people play to win. It wouldn't be like the practice chukkas where his cousins received clear instructions not to touch me. In a tournament, they would touch me. Except they wouldn't, would they? Because they are Argentine and play tournaments against other men. But many of the clubs are filled with foreigners who come to play, and they play mixed. They also play a much quieter level of the game than Patricio's cousins. I should be fine, I tell myself. There's nothing to worry about.

"You'll be good," he echoes my thoughts. "It won't be difficult. We're playing at Estancia Don Manuel. It's a mixed tournament. You'll play with us." He indicates Gabriela and Lisa. "We need a fourth. You'll be perfect."

I nod. This is exciting. I've never played a tournament in Argentina before. I've never played one with Patricio and Gabriela, either. Just the chukkas on their field with the many cousins, the grooms, or his other clients. And that was fun. A tournament would be super fun!

We agree on a plan. I'll head back to Buenos Aires and return at the end of the week for the two-day tournament on Thursday and Friday. The rest of the plan takes shape in the privacy of my mind. On Saturday, I'll go on my date and after that, I'll travel to Mar de Plata to play with the Old Man. It'll all work out perfectly.

WEDNESDAY 16TH DECEMBER

There was another reason why I absolutely needed to go back to Buenos Aires. I had booked a tango lesson.

They say tango is as close to the Argentine psyche as football and polo. I don't know much about football, so I can't comment, and I know too much about polo, so I can't judge impartially. But tango was love at first sight, ever since I first saw it at a tango show during my first trip to Argentina.

Developed in the late nineteenth century in the working-class neighborhoods of Buenos Aires, tango was born out of the national dances and the music European immigrants brought over to the new world. It had a bit of polka, of waltz, of flamenco, and anything else these young, poor people—people who'd arrived here from all over Europe in search of a better life—wanted to throw into it. It used to be the raw dance of courtship of the lower classes and was often danced in brothels. It then made its way up in society, and by the 1940s the Golden Age of tango had spread to Europe and North America. In Argentina it became a national institution.

I was keen to try out tango because I thought it would be a good counterbalance for a woman playing polo, which is as masculine a sport as it gets. A highly competitive sport with fast speed, rough ride offs, dangerous plays, accidents—polo is hard work. The adrenaline makes up for the hardship and is responsible for getting us players addicted to the game. But the beauty of this sport is surreal, and the sense of connection you feel to the horses and the people you play with or against is beyond anything I've ever experienced. However, it's not really something that makes me feel very feminine.

Maybe this was why I had been single for so long, I thought, when I first contemplated trying out tango. Since polo was taking me towards the masculine, I needed something to make me feel like a woman again.

I wait for my tango instructor impatiently as I try out my new tango shoes. They are gold leather, open toe with standard four-inch heels. I can barely walk in them. But a polo player can't be a proper player without the boots. This must apply to tango as well, I thought, as I bought my first pair of tango shoes just before my first lesson.

Halfway though the lesson I think I'm in love with my tango teacher. He's a handsome guy with dark hair and the standard Argentine unshaved look. Most of the men in Argentina look like this. In addition, he's well built with a broad chest, and he smells of tabacco and a hint of spicy perfume. I can smell him pretty well, since I spend all the time with my nose tucked in his neck. Surely this isn't enough for me to feel I'm falling in love with this guy. It's ridiculous, but it's beyond my control. There is nothing I can do about it. He touches me and I shiver. The current of energy moving between us is palpable. If the energy doesn't flow, he doesn't move. He made that clear from the very beginning.

"Tango is all about connection. No connection, no movement."

So when I try not to feel anything, he simply stops. And in tango, when the man stops, the woman can't do anything. The woman doesn't move on her own. She moves exactly as much and as fast as the man wants her to move. No initiative. None of that "I know better" attitude. No independence. A complete lesson in utter submission.

"Why did you move? Did I ask you to?"

"No."

"Then don't."

We stay there, embracing. A tango embrace. Uncomfortably close. My breasts pressed to his chest, my face almost touching his. Cheek to cheek, but at least he doesn't breathe in my face, because his head is slightly turned, watching the dance floor behind me. We stay there until I let myself feel the tension—the sexual tension that builds up when a man and a woman embrace. And he is a very attractive man. For a second I wonder if he's going to have an erection. If he does, I'm definitely going to feel it with my body pressed to his like this. But it turns out my tango instructor is very professional. No erection, nothing out of place. This is only about tango and nothing else.

But the energy is there and it runs through me. The blood pulses hot in my veins. My temperature rises and I wonder if my face is turning red. Along my spine a weird sensation of electricity is running up and down. There's no way to check, but I bet my nipples are erect under my padded bra. Thank God for padded bras.

"*Bueno.*" He smiles approvingly. "This is it. Now we move." He obviously felt the energy too.

He tells me I don't need to know the steps. I don't need to know where I'm going. He is the man and he will lead. All I need to do is keep the connection to him and follow him.

"It comes from the heart," he says. And then, resting his hand on my back, "Where are you? Where have you gone? I can't feel you."

I was in my head, thinking about it. But he waits there with the music playing in the background, waits until I come back into my body and feel the tension once again. And only as I do that does he finally move.

"Close your eyes," he says. "It'll be easier to let yourself follow. And don't worry. I know what I'm doing. I'm the man. I'm in charge. In tango, the man is always in charge."

In tango and everywhere else the man is always in charge, he means to tell me.

I thought I would feel offended. I thought I would tell him I play polo and I know how to be in charge, too. That I can ride off men and win the ball from them. I expected to fight with him over control. The old me—the me that stepped into that tango room some thirty minutes ago—would probably have said all these things. But something has happened. He waited until I let myself feel. And once

I feel the delicious tension building up inside me, I can't do anything but let myself follow wherever it leads me.

With my eyes closed and all my attention focused on my heart, I dance.

For a second I imagine Rodrigo's lips on mine, the smell of his skin in my nostrils and the strength of his arms around me, and my heart tells me I'm safe to let myself melt away. Then I bring myself out of this daydream and back to my tango instructor and our little tango taster session. Then I close my eyes again and I'm back to daydreaming and I discover that this actually helps me dance better.

"You see, it's not that difficult," he says. "The hour is finished. You can book another one at reception if you like. We'll make a tango dancer out of you."

For a second I remember the Old Man promising me he'll make a polo player out of me. How can these two extremely different personas coexist in the same body? A polo player. A tango dancer. Who's the real me?

And yet. There is only one flow. One energy. In polo as in tango. And when the flow comes to you, your body knows what to do with it, even before you have taken the time to think about it. It knows it and it dances with it.

I walk home happy. And it's not about Rodrigo. It's not about the tango, either. It's not even about polo. It's all of it. It's about being here in this city, where for some inexplicable reason I feel so much at home. It's about wearing the new Argentine clothes I've bought here and feeling my hair, all silky after a treatment Sol recommended. It's about feeling I can speak Spanish for the first time in my life—really speak Spanish fluently, although I'm not sure when exactly that happened. It's about being alive. And sex, polo, and tango all in one week is an explosive cocktail of aliveness.

THURSDAY 17TH DECEMBER

I'm back on the minibus headed for Lobos. I'm going to be late, I realize as I contemplate the utter mess of traffic ahead. It's chaos. Cars are at a standstill and people are swearing out of their windows.

I text Patricio. *On my way. Might be a bit late.*

No answer. I hope he's not annoyed. Actually, I've never seen Patricio annoyed. When he is, he hides it well. He is usually serious, very polite, and very busy. At least that's when it's about polo. Off the field he relaxes a bit, and that's when he makes comments about the guys I'm dating and the guys I should be dating.

Gabriela, on the other hand, is explosive. If she's angry, I'll know it. Everyone will know it. The frequency of the "fucks" in her speech increases dramatically. The trouble is that the frequency of "fucks" in her speech also increases when she's happy, or surprised, or excited about something. So at times when a lot of "fucks" pour out her, it's actually a hard job trying to pinpoint the exact emotion that's provoked them.

She'll be annoyed I'm late, for sure. The German client, too. They will all have to wait for me and the other team will have to wait as well. You can't start a tournament game if one player isn't there. Well, you can. A really tough umpire will start the game with three players against four, but it's a really nasty thing to do since the three-player team will stand no chance. Or they could find a substitute, but this takes time, plus . . . I'm not really going to be that late. And we are in Argentina. Everyone is always late here.

I'm feeling somewhat apprehensive about the tournament. And no, it's not the wrist. The wrist is fine. Sabrina, my main physio at the recovery center, was a little annoyed when I told her I was going to play a tournament, and she asked me when exactly I had heard her telling me I was ready to play? I wasn't aware I was supposed to ask permission to play polo again, but they take things seriously at the Institute for Sports Medicine, Recovery, and Rehabilitation. But the thing is that I don't usually ask for permission. I tend to do things when I feel they come to me. And this tournament came to me. I didn't look for it, it simply came. And I said, "Yes."

Sabrina, being Argentine and therefore pretty laid back, even in her position as a physiotherapist, took a deep breath and let it all go. "Well, I guess you can play. Your wrist is fine. Just don't force it, OK?"

I won't force it. Patricio knows about my wrist and he'll give me easy horses. I'll need at least two horses for this game, but he likes to take care of his horses so I bet he has three or four lined up for me. I also bet they will be easy ones—the type that stop immediately when you pull the reins—so I won't need to dislocate my wrist in the process. I'll be fine. Just fine. Don't worry, I tell myself.

It's not my wrist that's playing on my mind, however. It's my old problem of scoring goals. I wonder if I'll score this time. I have to score this time. I remember all my tournaments in England and all the times I haven't scored. I did score a few goals in tournaments towards the beginning of the season. But then something happened—I'm not sure what. Something happened in the middle of the season and I didn't score a goal again.

I really need to get over this problem, I tell myself. And it would be great if I could get over it here, before I go to play with the Old Man and have him give me a hard time for it. I have to score. I will score today. I have to.

I arrive on the field determined to score but also very late. Patricio greets me politely and doesn't mention anything about my being late. Gabriela does, however.

"Where the fuck have you been? We've been waiting half an hour to start this game. Get a fucking taxi next time!"

The German client says nothing but is clearly pissed off.

Still, the owner of the club where we play greets me with a big smile. I know Emi. I stayed here, at his club, the first time I came to

Argentina, before I got to know Gabriela and Patricio. He's dressed in a white shirt with black vertical stripes, polo boots, and helmet, and he looks ready to get on a horse. It's clear he'll be the umpire of the game. It's also clear to me that he, like everyone else, has been waiting for me to arrive.

"*Hola*, Rosanna." Most people call me Rosanna in Argentina. It must be because of the strong Italian influence present in this country.

"*Hola*, Emi! I'm so sorry I'm late. The minibus—"

"*No pasa nada*, Rosanna! *Tranqui. No pasa nada.*"

I instantly relax. I locate Patricio's car and start changing into my polo gear behind it. We always change behind a car by the polo field. I get into my white jeans, then into the boots, the knee pads, the elbow protectors, the team shirt. I'm playing as number one, the position reserved for the worst player in the team. I have no problem with that. The great thing in polo is that you always know where you stand. The order of the pack is pretty clear to everyone. I'm at the bottom of it. I pick up the number one t-shirt without even questioning it. Everyone on this polo field today is going to be better than me. But I'm not here to compete with them. I can't. All I can do is hope to make a decent play. And I'm here to compete with myself. I will score.

But it turns out I don't. I miss a couple of balls, and then I'm too afraid I'll miss again, and I don't go for the shots. I don't ask for the ball. I let Gabriela and Lisa go for them. Sometimes they miss too, but other times they score. They both score. I don't. Patricio doesn't score either, but that's because he makes sure he doesn't. It's not his job to score. He is the professional player on the team, handicap four. He's a million miles away from where the rest of us are. He and his equivalent professional player on the other team have a gentleman's agreement not to score goals. It would be too easy for them. They simply pass the ball to the rest of us, get the game moving, defend. They play *tranqui*, as they say. They don't play at their full force. A minus two player like me would stand no chance on a field against a handicap four player. I know this well, and they know this, too. They stick to marking one another and steer away from the weaker players.

We win the game and the memory of my late arrival on the field is drenched in the victory drinks. The girls are happy. We won and they scored all the goals. Patricio is happy, everyone had a great time and his horses are all right. Emi is happy, too. There were no particular incidents in the game, and it was easy to umpire. The other team is less happy, but polo is like that. One day you win, one day you lose. There is no win-win in polo. Not on the field, anyway.

I'm half-happy. The happy half is because I've played a tournament again, and this marks the full completion of point one on my list (recover my wrist), and also point two—play polo. I have two big ticks. The unhappy half is because I didn't score. I didn't even trust myself enough to try to go for shots at goal.

As usual Patricio reads my thoughts. He teases me a little for my unspoken worries.

"Roxy, next time you see one of the girls trying a difficult shot, talk to them. Shout, 'Leave it.' They'll leave the ball to you if you come from behind them and have a better angle shot. You could have done it a few times today."

He's right. Playing at number three, the strongest position in the field, he can see how the game unfolds in front of him. I know he's right. I haven't told him about my quarrel with scoring goals. It's enough that the Old Man knows about it and uses it to constantly make fun of me. I don't want to put more pressure on myself. Don't want to talk about it. Don't want to think about it. I dread thinking about it.

"I'll do it tomorrow," I tell him.

We have another game tomorrow. The second game of the tournament. There are always at least two games in a tournament.

Emi invites us for dinner and we stay on and drink and eat with the other polo players around a big table. My muscles are sore, the t-shirt still wet from the sweat slowly drying and my white jeans are dirty again, brown with the dye of the saddle and the sweat of the horse. I wonder again, as I have done many times in the past, who decided polo should be played in white jeans, and whether we can eventually do something about it. I also wonder if the launderette has any Vanish, since I know how many packs of Vanish it takes to get the stains out of white polo jeans.

We talk about the game as we eat and I'm back to where I belong—part of one big international polo family. And then I'm reminded that I'm also part of one particular Argentine family, as Gabriela and Patricio get ready to drive home, dismissing my kind request to be driven to the bus station.

"Are you crazy? You're coming home with us. Why do you want to go back to the city? It's already late. And you need to be back here tomorrow anyway."

"But will you have room for me to sleep at your farm?"

I know Patricio's sister and her family are there as well, which makes five adults and four kids staying in the house.

"We'll find space for you, darling. Don't you worry. You're one of us."

"Plus if we let you go to the city, we'll have to wait for you again, because you'll be late tomorrow. Fuck the minibus. You're coming with us," Gabriela declares.

They are like this, the Argentines. They like to welcome you into their homes and into their hearts. And that even applies when they are half-Swiss and half-Mexican, with no actual Argentine blood running through their veins.

FRIDAY 18TH DECEMBER

I wake up in San Patricio in the bedroom of Patricio's sister. Not the sister who lives there, but another one. Patricio has three sisters. One lives at the farm with her husband and three kids. The second lives about 1,500 kilometers away in Bariloche—too far to come over for a day at the farm. The third lives twenty minutes away in town and has a bedroom at the farm for when she comes to stay.

"She won't come," they tell me as they point me to her room. "You can sleep here. The bed is changed."

"But what if she comes?"

"*No pasa nada.*" Patricio is convinced.

"You're becoming like the English, darling," Gabriela continues. "Stop worrying so much and just make yourself at home. If she comes, we'll deal with it."

So I make myself at home and go to sleep in his sister's bedroom and get woken up in the middle of the night when she actually does come home. I freeze, half-awake in the bed, as she opens the door.

She turns on the light, letting out a muted sound.

"Oh, sorry!"

I jump out of bed. "I'm so sorry! Oh my God, so very sorry. We didn't think you were coming. They—Patricio and Gabriela—they said I could sleep here."

"*Tranqi, no pasa nada.* Go back to sleep. I'll find somewhere else."

She leaves before I can add anything else.

I look for her at breakfast to apologize again for taking her room. She smiles.

"*No pasa nada.* Really. We are happy to have you here."

"Where did you sleep?" I knew there was no other bedroom available.

"In the kids' room. There's an extra bed there."

"Ah. So sorry."

"Darling, stop apologizing like the English do." Gabriela has joined us at the table. She opens up a jar of her exquisite marmalade. "Remember this one? I made it when you were here last year."

I remember. Gabriela cooking marmalade in the kitchen and me sitting on a chair and watching her. I couldn't move, since I had hurt my back. Playing polo, obviously.

The marmalade is delicious. Gabriela is an amazing cook. I love the tarts she makes for lunch. One day I'll ask her to teach me how to make them, I think, helping myself to half the jar of marmalade. Not that I've ever been good at cooking, but maybe it's not too late to start.

Breakfast at San Patricio is a lavish affair generally, but today we have a game to play and one German client to collect from a hotel nearby, so we get going.

I will score today, I think, as I get into a fresh pair of white jeans. I will score. I am determined.

And I do score. Just not how I imagined I would.

The game starts well. But then in the second chukka one of the guys from the other team takes a nasty fall. No one touched him, no one rode him off. It's not clear why he fell, but such things happen in polo.

A sharp cry of pain and I hear the whistle of the umpire. The game stops. The game always stops when there's a fall. I remember that well.

I also remember that when someone falls in polo, the other people shouldn't dismount their horses. The friend who jumped off her horse and ran to me when I fell a year ago clearly ignored this rule. You're supposed to stop and wait on your horse. Help usually comes from the sidelines. If everyone were to dismount, you would have nine horses running wild on a polo field, and you really wouldn't want to have that sort of madness around a player who is lying on the grass, likely with something broken.

So you stand still and control your horse. It's the best you can do to help. Also, when someone falls, he or she must be left there where they have fallen, until the ambulance comes. The player is not to be moved. This is because there could be other, more serious injuries. A fall from a horse running at full speed is no joke to the body. People die falling from horses in polo. And it doesn't only happen to beginners. Very experienced players have died on the polo field.

We gather around the fallen player on our horses, while the people on the sidelines run on to the field and try to keep him still. He knows there's not much they can do for him. He needs to remain where he is and wait for the ambulance. And they will be there talking to him, keeping him company, until it comes.

I sit still on my horse, my mallet down, my helmet securely fitted under my chin, wearing my protective Oakley glasses with their dark lenses. I just sit there in all my gear—the one I put on ready to go to war and which is no longer needed. I will not cry, I tell myself, I will not cry. And if I do, thank God I have the glasses on so that nobody sees. I hear the screams of the injured guy as if they were in the pit of my stomach, and I know that what I'm really hearing is my own scream, the one I didn't dare to let out on the polo field some fifteen months before, when I fell, just like he has now. When I broke both arms—unlike this guy today, I really hope.

We take the horses to the pony lines. The game has stopped and it will be stopped for a while. The ambulance will come and then we need to find a substitute. We will have at least a couple of hours' break.

I feel dizzy and suddenly very weak, although the guy on the field is not screaming any longer. Someone comes to tell us that it appears he has nothing broken. They keep him on the field waiting for the ambulance, just in case.

The good news doesn't ease my nausea. I need to eat something. Urgently, otherwise I will throw up. I notice I'm shaking as well. This is ridiculous, I tell myself. Nothing really happened. It was just a fall. People take a fall every now and then in polo. The guy is fine. And my own fall was more than fifteen months ago. And I have played many tournaments since. Enough! Enough with all this nonsense.

"Yes, but you haven't heard this cry before," my mind reminds me.

I go to Emi and ask him for something to eat. He takes me inside the kitchen and points to the fridge.

"Help yourself to whatever you want," he says.

Typical Argentine—he likes sharing his food, his drink and his home. Likes sharing life.

Just as I would do in my own home, I open the fridge, take out some cheese and butter and make myself a sandwich. I need to eat, otherwise I will faint. In my mind I can still hear the screams of the guy on the field.

Time moves slowly as I sit in one of the large armchairs on the veranda of Emi's place and I eat my sandwich. I love Emi's place. It's one of the most beautiful farm houses I've seen in Argentina. It was a family home and Emi has converted it into a polo guesthouse. It has six or seven bedrooms arranged around a huge living room full of his polo trophies. Emi has played a lot of polo in his life, and judging by the trophies he has won a lot of tournaments, too. A large veranda with confortable seats surrounds the house. There is a well looked after park with nicely trimmed grass, and a swimming pool some twenty meters away. At the back of the house, a quick walk takes you to the stables. In front, after the trees and bushes, the polo field stretches to the horizon. The same polo field where right now a guy with potentially broken bones awaits an ambulance.

It's close to two hours before the ambulance eventually arrives. They lift him carefully. They say he looks all right, but they'll take him to the hospital anyway. Everyone takes polo falls seriously here. They've seen far too many.

Patricio comes to find me on the veranda. "Come on, we need to get ready. We've found a substitute player and we can start again."

I'm feeling better. The sandwich has done the trick. Plus, the guy isn't there any longer. He's safely on his way to hospital. I can forget about him and his screams.

I get back into my boots, elbow pads, knee pads. Oakley glasses. Helmet. Gloves. Mallet. Whip. Ready. The groom is holding the horse for me.

We don't talk as we ride back onto the polo field. There is nothing to say. Someone fell, the game was stopped. Now we start again. Polo is like this.

And then I score. It happens in the first two minutes of the second chukka in my second tournament game in Argentina. I finally score.

I follow my teammate close behind, but not too close. I follow her by the book, just as they say you should, leaving enough space between us so I can do a full swing on any ball she might miss, but not too big a gap to allow a rider from the other team to get between us. My teammate tries to score, but she misses and rides on in full gallop, past the ball that is now waiting for me. It's my turn. I tighten my grip on the the mallet. Steady gallop. I swing and hit. A nice clean swing, and a good hit. The ball takes off towards the goal and it looks like it's going to go in. But no, it hits the post instead and bounces back, coming to a standstill in the grass some three meters away from the goal.

Bloody ball. I'll teach you a lesson. This time I will score. Whatever it takes.

I carry on in full gallop. My second swing won't be as clean as the first one. This one is a difficult shot. The ball is now at a very sharp angle to the goal post. I need to do an "under the neck" shot to get it in. This means I need to rise out, far out of the saddle, then hit the ball and bring the mallet under the neck of the horse. All that without hitting any part of the horse's body and while still staying mounted, although half my body is hanging outside the horse.

I will do it, I tell myself as I approach the ball. I have to score this goal. I will do it. I hit and watch it go towards the goal. It's almost there.

But I can't see if it goes in. I lift my head for a second and see the two-meter-high goal post just in front of me. I'd been concentrating so hard on the ball, I'd forgotten I was going at a full speed towards the goal post.

A thought flashes through my mind in a speed that matches that of my horse—the goal post will fall. Goal posts are designed to fall on impact. It won't hurt me as I hit it. Because there is no doubt I'm going to hit it, the very next second.

But it's too late to do anything with this thought. My body is half out of the saddle and the horse is running wild, straight for the goal post. It just misses it and the pole comes in between me and the horse and I fall. I let myself fall over the side of the horse running in full gallop, with both hands stretched out instinctively so as to protect my face from the impact with the ground. Arms will always stretch out instinctively to protect the head.

As I fall I hear it again. In my head I hear the clear crack of a broken bone.

And the cry I've kept inside for the whole fifteen months since my last fall finally finds its way out of my lungs and takes off towards the sky, carrying with it the pain that explodes inside my body.

I have broken another bone. From the abyss of pain, this thought appears calmly and clearly in my mind.

I'm not sure how long I lie there, but I'm sure I've never cried like this before.

My initial scream is so loud it dissolves the world around me. My eyes are squeezed shut and my whole world is full of the pain in my right arm, the one still holding the mallet, and the deafening scream that has broken free from the depth of my lungs.

Someone's hand touches my shoulder and suddenly my chin strap is loosened and my helmet pulled off. A voice speaks in alarm, and as my scream dies down I realise it's Patricio.

"Roxy, Roxy! It's OK. We're here."

I feel him push the helmet under my head as if it were a pillow, and for a second I marvel at how I can register all these things with the explosive pain coming from my right arm.

I have no more air left. The scream has taken it all. I inhale sharply.

"I've broken it," I scream on the exhale. "Again! I heard it. I heard the cracking sound. Again. I can't believe I've broken it again!"

I take another deep breath, but I don't scream this time. Instead I start sobbing so hard, my whole body shakes.

Patricio's hands are on my shoulders. He tries to keep me still. Thank God he's there, pushing my shoulders firmly into the ground, otherwise I would just disintegrate into nothingness, all eaten away by the pain.

"I have broken it," I scream again as I get a fresh breath in between the sobs.

For a second I dream I hear the words, "No, you haven't. It's OK, silly. It's just a fall."

But nothing like that comes. Lost in the darkness of my firmly closed eyes I hear his voice again. This time he sounds calm.

"It's true. It's broken. I can see it. Don't look at it. It's gonna be OK. We are here and we are going to take care of you. It's gonna be OK."

He's still trying to keep my shoulders from shaking.

The enormity of his words reach me in the middle of sobbing, and for a second I stop. Then I take in some more air and let out another scream.

This one comes from my mind.

"I can't believe it!"

My mind starts replaying in fast motion the full movie. The hospital, the surgery, waking up after the anaesthetic, the screws in, the screws out, the many other hospital appointments that follow. Not being able to move, stuck in bed for six weeks, not being able to dress, not being able to eat. Not being able to play polo.

Not being able to play polo.

Again.

"Roxy, we are here. You are not alone. We are here. We'll look after you. You're going to be OK. You're not alone." Patricio continues in the same calm, soothing tone.

Alone. *Sola*. My mind clings to his last word as if there's something in there, there's something I should think about, but can't. *Sola in Baires*. But I wasn't alone any more. No more *sola* . . .

Rodrigo!

Another inhale and another scream. This one is for him. I was supposed to see him tomorrow. For lunch. And maybe a *siesta*. Not any more. I will never see him again.

I shake with another series of uncontrolled sobs and this time it's because I so wish he were here holding me in his strong arms as I cry.

Rodrigo isn't here, but Patricio is and he's doing a good job. And his arms are strong, too, and this makes me feel I can let myself cry without the fear I will disintegrate, becase a woman always needs a man to hold her when she cries.

After about ten minutes of uncontrolled screaming, there is nothing else to come out. I'm slowly calming down. The pain is gone, drenched in the sea of adrenaline the body produces in these events. I remember well how it is. It has only been fifteen months since the last fall. I didn't cry like this then. There was no one to hold me still.

I finally dare to open my eyes slowly and take in the sight around me.

I'm lying on the polo field just as I expected. The same place where I fell. They won't move me until the ambulance comes. I hope they've called it already. It's going to be a long wait under the midday heat. We were not supposed to play in this heat but our game was delayed by the first fall.

My head is resting on my own helmet. Patricio sits on one side of me with both hands still on my shoulders. Now, as my sobs are slowing down, he releases the pressure a little. No worries, I think. I'm not running anywhere. I must have cried like a mad woman. How embarrassing. But I'm too exhausted to care.

Then I see Gabriela. She's pacing up and down. She sits, she stands. She can't sit still. I can see the shock on her face, the utter shock. I expect a lot of "fucks" but none come out.

"Oh darling, I'm sorry, I'm so, so sorry, I'm so terribly sorry. I'm so sorry darling."

"Gabriela, stop talking like a reincarnated Englishwoman," I manage to get out, in between deep breaths. "What the hell are you sorry about? It's not your fault."

A smile starts to take shape on her face. At least she can see I've returned. I think my screams must have shocked her more than the actual fall.

I really need to let them know I'm back to my senses.

To my right Emi touches my shoulder. "Rosanna. You will be OK. Really."

How does he know? I wonder.

"I know." He answers my unspoken question. Just like Patricio, Emi is also equipped with a special detector to read my thoughts. An Argentine thing, I imagine. "I know you'll be OK, because I've broken a lot of things too. Look, I broke my elbow and my collar-bone and my leg, and I tore muscles too, and muscles are worse than bones, believe me. I'm all broken and I'm all right again. Polo is like this, Rosanna, polo is like this. You break, you recover, then you break again."

This is not encouraging. This is not what I want to hear as I lie on that field with a broken arm. At least one broken arm, if not more.

"*No pasa nada*," Emi continues encouragingly.

"*Cómo que no pasa nada*? I broke my arm. Again! Just as I recovered the other one."

"Yes, I know. *No pasa nada*," he repeats. "You will recover this one as well. Just like you did with the other. But then—" He smiles. "What a goal. What a goal you scored."

"Did I score?" The blood rises to my cheeks. "Did I really score?"

"You did," he says firmly. "And what a goal it was. Amazing. Under the neck of the horse and straight in."

He must know. He was the umpire of the game.

"Once upon a time I would also go for shots like that. The risky ones," Emi continues. "But not any more. I've learned now to let these shots go. It's not worth it. Really not worth the risk."

I'm not sure this is approving of my beautiful goal. But Emi doesn't understand. Of course he doesn't. How can he? He doesn't know about my private quarrel with the goal.

Noting that I'm actually talking coherently, Patricio lets go of my shoulders. He takes his own helmet off and keeps it above my head to shade me from the sun, which is getting hotter and hotter.

"We've called the ambulance. They're on their way."

Earlier this morning it took them close to two hours to arrive. I wonder how long it will be this time.

"It took some persuasion," Gabriela adds. "They thought we were calling about the same accident from this morning and they said they'd already picked up an injured person from this address. It took some time for them to understand there was a second injured person."

The ridiculousness of the situation finally hits me. It's very rare in polo that two players get injured one after the other.

There's nothing to do but wait. Gabriela takes my boots off without moving me from the position where I fell. Patricio continues to keep his helmet above my head.

"You don't need to do that for the next two hours, you know," I tell him.

He takes his helmet away for a second and the sun blinds me.

"See?" He smiles. "I do."

The helmet comes back to shade my face.

Emi lies on his back next to me on the grass of the polo field. His head is touching my head. He is carrying on with his *no pasa nada* encouragement.

"You'll recover. You can take some time off from polo, go to the seaside, to the beach."

"What do you mean, go to the beach? I'll be in a cast. What can I do on a beach with my arm in a cast?"

"You can still have fun. So what if you are in a cast? You can sunbathe. You can get in the water. OK, maybe just a little bit. You can go out, you can have a drink. Guys will come to talk to you."

"With my arm in a cast? Are you crazy? Nobody will come to talk to me."

"Ah, they will all come to talk to you, you will see. They will ask you what happened. It's a great conversation starter. And you will be the heroine of the day."

I doubt it.

"*No pasa nada,*" he repeats. "Come to Mar de Plata. We have a summer house there. Come stay with us. We'll look after you."

I don't really know Emi. I only met him briefly last year when I came over to spend two days at his *estancia*. And today we have interacted for a total of ten minutes, most of which involved me finding my way around his kitchen to produce myself a big cheese sandwich. I'm a little surprised to be invited to his summer house just like that, just because I happen to have broken a bone on his polo field.

But they are like this, the Argentines. It doesn't matter how long they know you, it only matters how deeply they know you. And one polo player with a history of broken bones lying on the grass next to another polo player with a freshly broken one feels like a deep enough connection.

Mar de Plata. Another thought shoots through my mind. Shit! The Old Man. I was supposed to call him today to tell him when I could come next week. We had agreed to set a date and I missed three calls from him yesterday. In the excitement of the game I forgot to return his calls.

Oh, no! He will not like this. He will really not like this.

I'm not quite sure how much time goes by. I'm suspended in a place where there is no time. My arm is completely frozen, packed with adrenaline and thankfully not hurting any longer. One of the other players eventually brings out a parasol so Patricio can finally put down the helmet he's been holding above my face. Emi lies there with me for a while, then goes to look after his guests. It's lunch time, after all. Gabriela goes back to her usual quota of "fucks" per sentence, and this is a powerful sign that things are slowly sliding back to normal. Patricio tells me he needs to check on the horses. I think he must have spent more than an hour holding that helmet above my face.

The guys go and I'm left with Gabriela. With her I feel I can relax into crying again. But she won't let me.

"Don't you start crying again, now. Didn't you hear we're going to look after you?"

"Yes, but—"

"No but. No more crying. It's just a broken bone. It will recover."

"Yes, but—"

"No but. We're going to the hospital now. We'll see what that fucking hospital can do for you. If they can't do much, we'll take you to the best hospital in Buenos Aires."

"Yes, but—"

"No but. You'll get the best doctors, is that clear?"

"Yes, but—"

"No but. Then you're coming with us to the farm and you're staying there. Fuck your apartment in Buenos Aires, you're staying with us. Until you recover."

"Yes, but—"

"No but."

"I can't."

"Why?"

"I have a life."

"No, darling, you don't. Not any more. Not until you recover."

Silence. She's right. There's no reason why I should be in Buenos Aires. No reason whatsoever. With an arm in a cast there is no language school, no physio, no tango. No Rodrigo. Specifically no Rodrigo.

I don't argue any longer. No more "buts." I'm just grateful to have her there with me. I'm grateful to have them all.

"And how the fuck did you manage to break it again?"

"It's the other one."

"I know it's the fucking other one. How did you do it?"

"I don't know. I must have put my arm down. Instinctively."

"Stop putting your fucking arms down when you fall. You need to learn how to fall properly. You can't break something every time you fall."

I know she's right. But I just can't begin to think about another fall right now.

The ambulance eventually arrives. It has taken less time to come than this morning.

"Here's the *empanada* delivery van," Gabriela announces cheerfully.

I take a look. It's not a proper ambulance. They must only have one at the hospital, and that was used for the first guy that fell. What I have now is the spare car, which really does look like an *empanada* delivery van.

And with her sense of humor retuning, I finally get it—it's not that bad. I will live through this, just as I lived through the fall before, and I will recover, and maybe Emi is right, and at some point in time I will be able to look at what's happened and tell myself, "*no pasa nada*."

I'm just not there yet.

LATER THAT DAY

I get taken to the hospital in Cañuelas. This is the nearest town to Emi's place, about halfway between Lobos and Buenos Aires. Incidentally, Adolfo Cambiaso, the top polo player in the world, has an *estancia* on the outskirts of the same town. And it's the same hospital where his injuries are treated, and he must have broken quite a few bones during his polo career.

Knowing this doesn't make me feel any better. I get taken straight to the x-ray chamber. The pain comes back, explosive. It's inevitable, as they are trying to manipulate a broken hand on an x-ray table. I scream. Outside I can see Gabriela's face. She's pale.

Then they take me into another room and two nurses come over to me, talking in Spanish. I'm not sure what they are saying. Either my Spanish has just vanished, or it's the strong painkiller they injected into my bum just before the ambulance took me from the field.

"*Mamita . . . gordita . . .*" The nurses talk to me as they undress me.

My hazy mind tries to make sense of reality, but fails. Two unanswered questions persist.

> 1. Why are they undressing me? I hope they don't touch the polo glove which is still on my right hand. It will hurt like hell if they do.
>
> 2. Why are they calling me fat? *Gordita.* And Mammy? *Mamita.* Why the fuck do they think I'm their mother?

I'm starting to speak like Gabriela. I gradually let go of my thoughts. The drug is slowing my mind and I feel heavy. And fine. I feel just fine. Great stuff, these painkillers.

Next I'm on a moving bed being taken around the hospital corridors. I'm not sure I'm wearing anything any longer, but I'm covered in a white sheet. The polo glove is still on my right hand. Thank God they haven't touched it.

Then bright light. I'm in another room. Cold. I'm cold. I don't like being cold. I remember how cold the surgery room was when they put the screws in my wrist. I don't want screws again. Please. Anything but screws.

"Have you got any allergies?" he asks.

Why is he dressed like that? I wonder. Full medical gear. Blue. A mask on his face. A cap over his hair. Why is he dressed like that?

And why is he looking for my veins?

Then I stop thinking. The needle is in my vein, and the anaesthetic flowing through it brings with it that familiar sensation of falling into a dark abyss.

I know this feeling, I know it well.

Surgery.

Again.

~

I don't know how long I'm out, but I wake up with my mind a void. Just as I remembered waking up from the other two operations the previous year. Screws in, then screws out. I wonder how many screws they've put in this time.

"No screws, darling." Gabriela is next to my bed, holding my other hand. The unbroken one. That is, my non–recently broken one.

"They have no screws in this fucking hospital. So they had to reset your bone. Put it back in place without screws. They say it's better like that."

She seems well informed. I ask her how long I was unconscious for.

"Pretty long. Long enough for us to have a bite to eat."

Patricio had taken the German client to the airport to catch her flight back and then returned to the hospital. They had a chat with the doctor, saw the before and after x-rays and received reassurances I was going to be OK. And they were now waiting for me to wake up so that we could go home. To their home obviously. To San Patricio.

I look around slowly. I'm still naked under the white sheet. Well, almost. I'm in a hospital surgery gown. My right arm is covered in a cast past my elbow. I can't feel anything.

"Of course you can't, darling," Gabriela says reassuringly. "They have given you enough painkillers to put an elephant to sleep."

I don't find this so reassuring.

The nurses come back, the same ones who undressed me. They are here to dress me again, back in my dirty polo jeans.

"Gabriela, these women . . . Why do they call me fat? They said *gordita*."

"Don't be silly." She smiles. "It's a way to show they care. It means fat, but not really. They don't actually mean you are fat. It's more like *sweetie*."

"Sweetie? Why do they use the word for fat for sweetie?" I ask in disbelief.

"Because the Argentines are fucking crazy. They can't help it."

She should know. She is de facto married to one of them, even with no papers. That makes her an Argentine too.

"Gabriela, will you do me a favor?"

"Yes, darling. Of course I'll fucking do you a favor."

"Get my phone. There's a number for the tango school. Please call them and cancel the lesson I booked for tomorrow. And . . ." I hesitate. But it needs to be done. "And please send a message to Rodrigo. You'll find him on my WhatsApp chats. Tell him I won't be able to see him tomorrow as planned."

She nods, takes my phone and goes out of the room, leaving me with the two nurses who gently start dressing me again. I watch carefully as they manage to get my polo t-shirt back on top of the huge cast. I need to learn how to do this, I think. It will come in handy.

LATER THAT EVENING

I fall asleep in the car on the way back to the farm. Patricio is driving slowly, careful to avoid any bumps in the road that would make my arm move. They're both joking with me, trying to make me feel better. Gabriela says something along the lines of "learn to fucking ride better, so you can stay on the horses rather than keep falling off," and Patricio reminds me about the goal I scored. I fall asleep knowing they're there for me and they're taking me home. And that I don't need to worry about anything.

At home I'm put back immediately into the sister's bedroom.

"And she ? Where will she sleep?" I ask.

"*No pasa nada*. We will manage. There's enough space."

I contemplate the bed. Now what? Sleep, eat, and sit. For the next six weeks, probably.

"Gabriela, did you call the tango place?"

"Yes, all cancelled, darling. Don't think about it. Not the right time for it now."

"And . . . Rodrigo?"

"Him, too. Nice guy."

"How do you know?"

"We spoke, he called back."

"He what?"

"As soon as he got the message. He called back. He wanted to know how you are. He wanted to come to the hospital, or at least speak to you."

"And?"

"I told him not to come. We were going to leave. And you were half-asleep. I told him we were going to the farm. And that you were all right now and would go to sleep."

He called back!

"Don't worry about him, either. Not the right time for it."

He called back! My heart is singing.

"He said he'll call again to speak with you."

That would be more difficult. There was no phone reception at the farm, and the internet signal was forever coming and going. How was I going to be able to speak with him?

"Who's this guy?" Patricio asks. He has just come in and overheard the last exchange with Gabriela.

"Rodrigo. The guy I dated in Buenos Aires. My date from last weekend."

"And? He disappeared?"

"No, he called back. He wanted to come to the hospital."

"Really?" I detect a note of surprise in his voice. "Have you got a picture of this guy?"

No, I haven't got a picture. But I have his Whatsapp and he has a profile picture on there.

I grab my phone to show it to Patricio, but then I stop. No need. Even if Rodrigo did call back, it doesn't mean anything. Of course it doesn't. He's just being polite. He can't disappear straightaway. But now he will probably not call again. And since I'm at the farm, with no signal, I won't even know if he tried to call or not. It's pointless. Stop thinking about him. Just stop.

"So?" Patricio is still waiting. "Are you going to show me his picture?"

I open the chat but he's no longer there. Our messages are there, but his face—the smiley picture he had as a profile—is gone, replaced by another image. The new picture is of graffiti on a wall. It says, "Everything will be all right in the end. And if it's not all right, it's not yet the end."

I freeze, not understanding why I'm staring at this image, what it means, or where his face has gone.

"So?" Patricio is losing patience. "Are you going to show me his picture or not?"

I hand over the phone to him without a word.

"What the hell is this? Roxy, this is a wall, this is not a picture of a man. Is this guy real?"

This, I'm not sure of any longer.

SUNDAY 20TH DECEMBER

But it turns out he is real. It took a bit of struggle, with the internet connection coming and going, but Rodrigo did text me and I texted back. He wanted to come and see me at the farm, but I told him to wait. I was going to return to my flat in Buenos Aires.

"You must be mad," Gabriela says. "Why do you need to go back home?"

Because I haven't got a thing here. Nothing with me—no clothes, nothing to change into. Just one dirty pair of polo jeans which Gabriela threw in the washing machine while I was asleep. Plus I've got two more days of class at the language school which I need to finish. And I need to go to the physio and tell them what happened. I need to pack a few things from the flat. Then I'll come back.

"You'd better be back. It's Christmas in three days."

Once again I was going back to Buenos Aires broken after a game of polo. Just before Christmas. Alone. And once again Gabriela was insisting I should come back to the farm to spend Christmas with them. Time was going backwards.

With a feeling of *déjà vu*, I promise her I will be back for Christmas.

Gabriela arranges for a driver to take me home. She's concerned I won't be able to survive with only one arm, but I tell her not to worry, because I've had lots of practice. My Barbie Doll episode is still fresh in my mind, and compared to having both arms broken, having only one unusable arm feels like a much better deal.

I have to go. Rodrigo told me he would come to see me on Sunday night if I was at home. And I really want to see him. I told myself it would be a friendly and respectful goodbye chat. Nothing major. After all, we had only known each other for a couple of weeks. It would only be a friendly chat. No kissing, absolutely no kissing. Well I don't need to worry about that, I told myself. With one arm in a cast, looking like a broken doll, there would naturally be no kissing. He probably wants to come by just because he's a nice guy. He'll ask me if there's anything he can do, I'll tell him there's nothing he can do, and then he'll leave.

And I'll never see him again.

LATER THAT EVENING

Rodrigo doesn't come in the end. I arrive home to find Buenos Aires in the middle of a power cut. These power cuts are frequent during the summer months when everyone turns on the aircon units. The old electricity network can't sustain all the demand and it fails. When this happens, it normally lasts for a while. Lifts don't work in apartment blocks, there's no light, and, what is worse, there's no power in the sockets.

The driver comes up with me, carries my small bag, and helps me get into the flat.

"Are you going to be OK?" he asks.

"I will," I whisper. I'm out of breath. I have just climbed all the ten floors to my flat carrying the heavy cast with me.

There's no way of charging my phone. The battery was already dead when I left the farm, and until the power in the flat returns there's nothing I can do about it. No way of talking to Rodrigo. Nothing to do. I drag myself into the bed before the sun sets and the apartment is left in darkness.

Tomorrow will be a better day, I tell myself, as the tears start rolling down my cheek one by one. But today is just a miserable one. I'm back to being *sola in Baires.* With a broken arm this time.

MONDAY 21ST DECEMBER

The power is back. My battery has charged and five messages all from Rodrigo appear on my phone at once.

Are you back?

Yes I'm back. No electricity, my phone was dead but I'm back.

I'll come tonight, he writes back.

He comes and I go down to open the door for him. They don't have electric buzzers here. Thankfully the power cut is over and the lift works again.

Rodrigo gives me a long, measuring look, taking it all in. My face, my dress, my arm in a cast all the way up to my shoulder, my sadness, my pain.

"I can't believe it," he says finally.

He holds my other hand, my healthy one. We can't even embrace. It's too awkward, the cast is in the way.

We go inside and sit down on the sofa. I want to tell him how it happened, but all of a sudden it doesn't matter any longer. I feel my eyes heavy with tears.

"*Linda*," he whispers.

And then I cry. "Hardly beautiful," I say. "More like Frankenstein."

"Don't be silly. You are always *linda*."

"Even like this?"

"Even like this." He smiles.

And then we kiss again. For a brief moment, and the first time in three days, I forget I have a broken arm.

He tells me he wants to be here with me. He wants to spend Christmas with me. Maybe even New Year's Eve. Perhaps we can go somewhere on the beach for New Year's Eve.

"Are you crazy?" I point at the arm. "I can't go anywhere like this. As for Christmas, well, Gabriela and Patricio have invited me to the farm for Christmas. I promised them I'll go."

"Stay with me. Please. At least Christmas Eve, if not Christmas Day. Let's spend Christmas Eve together. It's in three days, in any case. I'll cook for you."

"What? You don't want to spend Christmas Eve with your family?"

"No," he says. "I want to spend Christmas with you."

"But you barely know me."

"*No pasa nada*."

I'm happy. I know I shouldn't be. It doesn't make sense. But I am.

TUESDAY 22ND DECEMBER

I have to go to the physio. Not that I can do anything there, but I have to let them know. There are three physiotherapists and two personal trainers who have been looking after me. I want to wish them a Merry Christmas.

I know they'll understand. They've seen a lot of people injured. This is what they do for a living at the Institute for Sports Medicine, Recovery, and Rehabilitation.

But still, I feel apprehensive as I make my way inside. I'm such a joke, I think. Argentines have a slang word for joke—*joda*. It means a joke but it's used for many other things—to have fun, to be kidding, to have a good time out. For me right now it means to be a loser. *La joda del Universo.* The joke of the Universe.

I meet all of them. I parade my broken right arm covered in the enormous cast all over the place, downstairs to the physiotherapists and upstairs to the personal trainers. I can read the pity in their eyes. Some amusement too, as if this is somehow funny. I can relate to that. It is somehow funny that I came to this place every single day for a month and a half to recover my left wrist so that I can play polo again, only to fall during my second game and break my right arm. I am a joke.

After I'm done telling the story for about the tenth time to all the physios and personal trainers, I continue to my next stop—the language school. They give me a couple of pillows to rest my cast on as I continue my lessons with Santi. I can't write with my right hand covered by the cast, but Santi can, and he patiently writes in my notebook the new verbs.

"No excuse for not studying them," he says. You don't need your arm to speak Spanish. And then he gives me tons of homework for my two-week Christmas break.

Everyone tries to encourage me. It will pass, they say. I feel like a clumsy dinosaur as I make my way around the school, listening to everyone's words of encouragement. Curly Hair is there as well, politely commenting on my news. I suspect this will put an end to his sexy messages.

I walk back home. I'm pretty much self-sufficient, even though my right arm is in a cast. I can take a shower all by myself, using a plastic shopping bag to protect the plaster. I can dress and undress. I can eat. I can't cook anything, but even with two healthy arms I wasn't much of a cook. I can still study Spanish, even if I can't write. I can send text messages.

Gabriela wants to know when I'm coming back.

I can't come to the farm for Christmas Eve. I'll come on Christmas day, I text her.

Why not? What the fuck will you do there by yourself?

I won't be by myself. Rodrigo is coming to cook for me.

What???

He says he wants to spend Christmas Eve with me.

What??

No big deal.

Are you crazy? Why does he want to do this? Doesn't he have a family to spend Christmas Eve with? Argentines spend Christmas with their families.

I don't know.

What exactly do you know about this guy?

I don't answer. Not a lot, I think, but enough to know I want to spend Christmas Eve with him.

THURSDAY 24TH DECEMBER

By the time Christmas Eve arrives I've almost changed my mind. Not content with texting, Gabriela gives me a call and the concern in her voice makes me rethink the situation.

"Do you mean he'll come to your place and cook and then what? Spend the night there?"

"I guess so."

"What are you going to do with a guy in your bed and one arm in a cast?"

"Sleep, I guess. I don't think we can do much more."

"And do you think he wants to come there to sleep?"

"Look, I don't know. He was nice. He was sweet. He was supportive. He said he wants to cook for me on Christmas Eve and I said yes. What's the big deal?"

"I spoke to Patricio. We are both concerned. You don't know this guy. Maybe he is a serial killer."

"Well, no harm done so far."

"But you have a fucking arm in a cast now." Gabriela has lost her patience. "What the fuck were you thinking? Who the fuck is this guy and why the fuck does he want to spend the night with a disabled woman? We are concerned!"

I get that she's concerned. It's not that difficult to tell, judging by the increase in the number of fucks in one phrase.

"Listen, we need to know more about him. Last name. Address. Where he works."

"Do you want a copy of his ID as well?" I laugh.

"That would be the minimum you could do to put us at ease."

I tell Gabriela that I won't be able to give her all the details she wants, but at least I can find Rodrigo's last name.

Then I go to have my hair done at Sol's. There are limits to my self-sufficiency with one arm in a cast. There is no way I can wash my hair, for instance. I think I'll just have to go to Sol's every other day and enjoy having the hair of a princess for all of my disabled weeks.

I ask her if she does makeup, too.

"Yes I can do, why?"

"I need some makeup done today."

"Why?"

"I have a date tonight."

"You what?" She looks at me and then at my arm in the cast.

I tell her about Rodrigo and the cooking date tonight.

"You are kidding me. Who is this guy? Why does he not want to spend Christmas with his family? Maybe he is a maniac. Have you thought about that? A serial killer?" She points at my huge cast, without mincing her words. "What normal guy would want to spend Christmas Eve with a disabled woman he barely knows?"

Not only that, I think. A woman fourteen years older than he is. But Sol doesn't need to know that just yet.

By the time we're done with the hair and makeup, I'm seriously convinced I'm going to get chopped into pieces tonight and stored in the freezer.

Gabriela calls again. "Roxy, listen. I want frequent updates. I want text messages to tell me you are OK all through the night. You get it?"

I promise frequent updates.

Then Patricio picks up the phone. "Roxy, we are concerned."

"OK, I got that."

"If something happens and you are not confortable with the guy just call or text. We will drive straight there, OK? Have you got the surname of this guy?"

By now I know Rodrigo's surname. I asked him via a text message. Feeling smug, I give Patricio the name.

"Address?"

"No, that's too much. I haven't got his address yet."

"Call if you need anything, OK? Promise?"

"For God's sake, it's just a date."

By the time the date actually rings the bell, I'm wearing a short black dress, flat shoes—since I can't be sure I can keep my balance on high heels—and professional makeup which makes my eyelashes look huge and fake. My arm is in a sling and my spirits are rock bottom.

I'm actually shaking as he gives me a long warm kiss.

"*Tranquila*," he says. "Everything is going to be OK."

This is one thing about Rodrigo that is not Argentine. He doesn't say *tranqui* like everyone else. He says the whole word. Maybe he only does it with me because I need the extra length of the word to actually relax. It works.

He comes in carrying a number of bags. The meat he's going to cook for him, a big frying pan just in case I had none, the pasta for me, and drinks—one bottle of Fernet and some Coca Cola to mix the classic Argentine cocktail, some beer, and a bottle of red wine.

Then he says he needs to fetch some more things he left in the car. I can't possibly imagine what else he can bring. It's just a meal.

He comes in with no more bags this time, just a big smile. He grabs my healthy arm and leads me to the bathroom mirror.

"Merry Christmas, *linda*," he says, putting a pretty silver necklace around my neck. "I wanted to give it to you at midnight but I can't wait. I hope you like it."

I touch the necklace and feel so absurdly happy just because he has brought me a Christmas gift and because he couldn't wait for midnight to give it to me.

"I love it," I say.

I wasn't sure we were going to do gifts, so I had hidden the t-shirt I bought for him in the wardrobe. I wasn't going to give it to him if he had no gift for me. But now it's my turn to take him by the hand and lead him to the bedroom.

"Merry Christmas to you, too."

"I can't believe you have a present for me," he exclaims, his eyes wide open with surprise. "I really didn't expect this."

Just like I did not. Maybe we are very much alike, despite our differences.

It's just a black t-shirt with a picture of a crossroad and an inscription about the future being hard to predict. I thought it was funny. He tries it on and it fits perfectly.

"I love it," he says.

And then he kisses me again. We are still in the bedroom. I'm not sure it's such a good idea to start our evening by kissing in the bedroom, given the current state of my arm. I'm still tense. There's a knot in my stomach and I just can't seem to relax.

"*Tranquila,*" he says again, reading my feelings. "*No pasa nada.* Everything is going to be all right." He takes me towards the bed.

There's only one thing that can relax me right now and help me get over my anxiety attack, and despite our very short acquaintance Rodrigo knows exactly what that is. And he is determined not to let an arm in a cast stand in the way.

Later as we lie down in bed, I start laughing.

"*Mi amor. Estás bien*? Are you OK?"

It's the first time he has called me "*mi amor.*" My love. Given that we've just made love, it doesn't feel out of place. Given that I've only known him for two weeks it does.

I'm laughing at my own fears. I'm naked, in bed with a guy fourteen years younger then me, and I have a bulky cast on my right arm which is now comfortably sitting on two pillows. And I feel really good.

Ping. Message. Gabriela. *Are you OK*?

Yes. All good.

Then I turn over to my date and say, "How about that cooking?"

With sex out of the way now, the awkwardness is gone. We get dressed again, he in the black t-shirt I gave him as a present and the dark jeans he came in, me in my elegant black dress which seems a bit out of place compared to his casual look. He cooks pasta for me and *asado* for him. Of course it's *asado* for him. No decent Argentine would cook anything else for dinner on Christmas Eve.

Ping. Message. Gabriela.

Are you still OK?

Yes I am. All good.

"*Mi amor.* Why don't you eat meat?" he asks casually, as he struggles with the pack of pasta. He didn't seem to have any difficulty with the *asado*.

I tell him it's a long story and it's been like this for many years. I'm not going to change now.

"Too bad," he sighs. "I'll never be able to cook an *asado* for you. You have no idea what you're missing."

"So are you a great *asador*?" In Argentina, *asados* are cooked by men.

He shrugs. "They say so. My friends. I'm always the one cooking the *asado* when we get together."

"Are you as good an *asador* as you are a lover?" I ask flirtatiously.

"This is for you to judge, *mi amor.* But you will never know how good an *asador* I am, since you will never taste the meat I cook, so I guess you'll never know the answer." He's now concentrated on the meat. And then after he's put the lid back on the pan, he asks, "Am I?"

"What?"

"A good lover. Do you think I am a good lover?"

I laugh. "Yes, *mi amor.* You are."

"Oh, good." He seems relieved. "I want to make you happy."

Does he mean happy in bed or happy in general? I wonder. Definitely no complaints about the first part.

I notice the pasta looks overcooked already. One cannot have everything. And if I have to choose I would go for good in bed rather than good in the kitchen, anytime.

I change the subject. "Doesn't your family mind you spending Christmas Eve with me instead of being with them?"

"They're not here," he answers casually. "My mother is on the other side of the country. My father, no idea. One of my sisters, with her boyfriend. The other one, no idea."

"Have you spoken to them tonight?"

"Yes."

It's a short answer and he gives no more details. I get the message. He doesn't want to talk about his family.

Ping. Message. Patricio. *Are you OK?*

Yes. Just texted Gabriela, all fine.

After dinner Rodrigo starts kissing me again.

"*Linda*," he says, in that soothing, sweet voice.

"How can you still call me *linda* with my arm like this?"

"Because you are always beautiful. The arm doesn't matter. It will recover."

"Yes, I know it will, but right now it looks horrible. And it really doesn't make me feel sexy."

No answer. Just another kiss. So intense, it convinces me he really does still find me beautiful.

Ping. Message. I decide not to answer. I'm busy finding a comfortable place for my arm while Rodrigo and I are kissing on the sofa.

"Just rest your arm on my chest," he says after a while.

"It's heavy."

"*No pasa nada*."

"The cast will scratch your skin."

Rodrigo's shirt is off by now. "*Tranquila*."

He lifts my cast and places it on his chest. I can now comfortably lie on his shoulder.

"See? It's better like this." He smiles and embraces me, cast and all. "I like to feel you close to me."

Ping. Ping. Two messages at once. I bet one from Gabriela, one from Patricio. Are these people not talking to each other? I can picture them at that huge family table in the living room at the farm, each reaching out for their phone to send me a text message.

I'm fine!! I answer. Not answering is not a solution. It makes them send more messages.

"You seem to be getting lots of messages tonight," Rodrigo says tentatively. Maybe he imagines I have another suitor.

"Yes. They're from my friends in Lobos. They're worried."

"Why?"

"Because I told them I was spending Christmas Eve with you."

"And what's the problem?"

"They don't know you. They are kind of protective, so they're checking up on me. To make sure I'm OK."

He laughs. "They should relax. You've known me for two weeks now and nothing bad has ever happened to you while you were with me. I should be the one who worries. You spend two days with them and come back with an arm in a cast."

I leave that out of the text message I send back to my friends.

"Talking of which, how could you do that to yourself?" His dark brown eyes are serious now. I wonder how he does it. He can look sweet one moment, teasing the next, and then change to being serious in a second. His face is an open book, betraying his emotions at every moment.

"Do what?"

"That." He points at the cast. "It's crazy. When I met you at Spanglish you talked about your broken arm. I can't believe you've now broken the other one."

"Well, it's like that. Polo is like that."

"Why?"

"Why what? Why do we break bones? Because we fall at great speed. It's a rough game."

"No, why do you do it?"

"You mean why do I play polo?"

He doesn't answer. Clearly he doesn't get it.

"Look, I don't understand. For me, if something hurts me I don't do it. If something breaks a bone in my body, I don't do it any more. But you—you keep on doing it and then you break another bone. Why?"

"It's not that easy to explain." I'm defensive now.

"No, it's not. I really don't get it."

Ping. Another message. This time I'm relieved. It gives me an excuse to leave the conversation there.

We go back to the bedroom to sleep and end up making love again. He makes love to me with a tenderness and with an intensity that takes me by surprise. He does it looking straight into my eyes and calling me *linda* so many times that after a while I really start to believe I can be sexy and beautiful, even though I'm much older than he is and have an arm in a cast. We make love in the dark and the whole world around us disappears, until nothing else is left but two embracing bodies falling asleep exhausted, protectively cradling one big cast in the middle.

"Rodrigo."

"*Si, mi amor.*"

"You're snoring."

"Sorry, *mi amor.*"

He turns around. I fiddle with the pillows to find a comfortable position for my cast. We fall asleep again. Not for long.

"Rodrigo."

"*Si, mi amor.*"

"You are snoring again."

He gives me a kiss and turns around.

Ping. My phone, left somewhere in the living room, continues to receive messages. I can't get up to answer right now. I hope they don't take this as a sign that they need to start driving at once to come rescue me.

FRIDAY 25TH DECEMBER

A combination of making love through the night and Rodrigo's snoring meant that when morning arrives I haven't slept very much. Which makes me rather grumpy.

He's grumpy too, and this is a new experience for me. I've never seen him grumpy before. But then again, I've only seen him a total of three times before.

"What's wrong?"

"No, *nada*."

He doesn't call me "*mi amor*" any longer. And there's been no "*linda*" since he opened his eyes. And no kissing either. Something is definitely wrong. Maybe he's coming to his senses and has realized he's been making love all night to an invalid. Not to mention the age thing.

"Yes, there's something. Tell me."

"Well, it's that—" And then he explodes. "You can't do this to a man."

"Do what?"

"You can't wake a man up like that."

"Like what? You mean throughout the night? You were snoring!"

"Yes, but still. I think you woke me up fifteen times."

I hadn't counted, but he's probably right. I had woken him up many times.

"So? You were snoring. I couldn't sleep. I had to wake you up."

"But don't you know you can't do that to a man?" He is genuinely puzzled. "You can't wake up a man just because he's snoring."

And then I remember how the "Sorry, *mi amor*" had stopped pretty quickly. The kisses, too. A sense of irritation had descended upon us as neither could sleep—me because of his snoring, and him because I kept on waking him up.

It must be an Argentine thing, I think. Some kind of forbidden territory of waking up a man because he's snoring. Or maybe it's a sign we shouldn't sleep together.

LATER THAT DAY

I'm in the minibus again, headed for Lobos. Rodrigo didn't stay long this morning. We had a quick kiss before he went, a far cry from the passionate kisses we had shared through the night. He didn't offer to wash the dishes piled up in the kitchen sink. He didn't offer to drive me to the minibus station. He didn't say when we were supposed to meet again. He didn't mention anything about New Year's Eve.

I tried to look nonchalant as I casually mentioned that I might stay with friends until after New Year's. Our next meeting was left in the air.

"*Después vemos,*" he said before he left.

At least he gave me a Christmas present. I touch the silver necklace that's still around my neck. It makes me feel warm inside. He must care about me if he brought me a Christmas present.

And yet something inside me is telling me I'm never going to see him again. Maybe all there was from him was pity for the situation I had got myself into. Maybe he had only come because he didn't want to hurt me by disappearing straight after I had broken my arm. Maybe that was it. I still thought it was nice of him to show up and spend Christmas Eve with me. But now that it was done, it was also easy for him to disappear. I couldn't even hold a grudge against him if he did. For a casual love affair, he had done more than enough.

A casual love affair. Nothing more. I have to remember that. I decide to take the necklace off, just in case it reminds me too much of him.

MONDAY 28TH DECEMBER

San Patricio welcomes me back with the same timeless calm and joy as always.

The large living room, with its table long enough for fourteen people to dine comfortably, is decorated for Christmas. There is no tree, but the huge fireplace, surrounded by three big sofas, is filled with pine tree branches. And something else. I'm not sure I identify the smell correctly, but then Gabriela confirms it's Eucalyptus leaves and branches from one of the many tall trees surrounding the farm. The kitchen, too, is decorated with Christmas-tree lights above the big oven, and there's a bunch of freshly cut flowers on the round kitchen table. I have had many breakfasts here with various members of the family joining in as they wake up, the kids still in pyjamas.

The whole family is there. Patricio, Gabriela, and their son, little Patricio. Patricio's father, the owner of the farm, his two daughters, one of them with her husband and three kids—two boys and a girl. At six and nine, the boys have started playing polo already. The girl is twelve and she rides but doesn't play. In Argentina, polo tends to be a masculine affair. Gabriela plays, though. Gabriela is non-conformist enough to break every possible Argentine custom.

We have breakfasts in the kitchen, lunches at the table outside on the veranda, with two wooden benches facing each other, and dinners at the long table in the living room, set with beautiful china. There are always many people around for the meals—the family, friends, neighbors, or relatives who just stop by, whether previously arranged or not. One morning I witnessed Gabriela receiving a phone call to announce the imminent arrival of six people for lunch. Not a problem, she said. They'll just put more meat on the barbecue.

They cook *asados* on the huge circular grill outside the house—a grill big enough to accommodate a whole cow. The meat is well-done for the Argentines. Only Gabriela prefers hers half-raw. There's no meat for me, but usually pasta or one of the many exquisite tarts that Gabriela bakes herself, nudging the maid aside in the kitchen.

The afternoons are lazy. Lunches usually last a long time, and once the last glass of wine has been emptied and the guests eventually leave, people retire to their rooms one by one for an afternoon *siesta*. Everyone has an afternoon *siesta* in Argentina.

There is no polo at Christmas, as the grooms have taken a few days off and the horses have been set free in the fields. We watch them running in herds, far in the distance. If you walk to them they will come to say hello. The cows are further away and we can't see them from the house. They are meat cows and there are many of them, around seven hundred, according to Patricio. They live wild in the fields and they mate in the wild. They give birth to their calves alone in the fields. And every year a portion of the cows are selected and sent to the slaughterhouses. The rest are kept for breeding in the fields and the same cycle continues uninterrupted, as it has for many hundreds of years. Untouched by modern farming, antibiotics, or crowded stable conditions, these cows roam around as cows are supposed to do. The intervention of man in this landscape is almost non-existent.

Patricio tells me they have only one employee at the farm for all the cows. His only task is to go out in the field every day to check they are OK. And also to check that the windmills work, so that the pumps have power to get water out from the ground. As long as the cows have water, they will be fine.

Funnily enough, with all these cows the family still buys milk from the supermarket. It's because the cows are bred for meat, not milk. Milking cows is a messy business, Pati tells me. It's not worth the effort.

"Better to go to the supermarket and spend a few pesos on a liter of milk," he says.

They have sheep as well, all huddled in a stable close to the horses' yards. They are released into the field every day and only brought in at night, so that the little lambs can be protected from the foxes roaming the pampas. And there are five dogs, the proud guardians of the house, except they're so friendly with everyone who comes by I actually doubt they are any good as guard dogs.

We spend many early evenings with a glass of wine before dinner, watching the night fall and talking about everything. Argentines usually eat late, and the time just before dinner—when all the chores are done and everyone has taken a shower and dressed in clean clothes—is a special one at the farm.

There's silence at this time. The birds that are so loud in the morning usually calm down at nightfall. Sometimes, if it has rained, you can hear the frogs all around the fields, and they are loud. Other times, it's just the silence, the stars shining incredibly brightly above our heads, and little fireflies shining like tiny nuggets of gold in the night. The dogs usually come to sit with us on the veranda. Occasionally a frog will jump around, attracted by the lights of the house.

My friends ask about Rodrigo. This time I have a picture to show them. I still don't have his home address, though. They ask about Christmas Eve. I tell them it was nice, but that I had no hopes it would go anywhere. They don't ask any more questions, probably sensing the sadness behind my words, and I try hard not to think of Rodrigo for the reminder of my time at the farm.

We talk about the accident, too. A few times, in fact, as if I had to get it out of my system and they had to get it out of theirs, as well.

Patricio still can't believe I've broken my arm on one of his horses.

"It wasn't the horse," I tell him for the hundredth time. "There's nothing wrong with the horse. It was the goal post. I hit the goal post."

"Yes, but what I don't understand is why you threw yourself out of the saddle when you hit it? You know the goal post isn't solidly anchored into the ground. It's loose, so that it can fall. It's designed to come down in cases like that. It would have fallen on impact."

Once again, he's right. Patricio sees everything in a game. It's his job as a professional player to see everything, and he does it well. He must have seen the fall, every single detail of it, and he saw me hitting the goal post, and he probably even caught the moment when I decided to fall.

"Why did you let yourself fall? If you had clung onto the saddle, the goal post would have fallen and you would be just fine now."

I can't tell him why. I close my eyes and I relive that second. I can see the huge goal post coming at me at full speed. I can feel the jerk of the horse under me as he avoids a last-minute collision. The horse doesn't know that the goal post is not stuck deeply into the ground. So the horse acts out of fear and avoids the hit. I know the goal post will fall before it does too much damage, but even though I know it, I feel the same terror as the horse feels. Enough terror to make me want to fall rather then hit the post.

I keep quiet. I don't tell him that it was fear that made me fall.

TUESDAY 29TH DECEMBER

"Gabriela! Where are you! Gabriela!" I scream as I race through the house in search of her. I find her in the bathroom.

"What?" she screams back.

"Your son! He's riding a horse in full gallop. Across the polo field. With no saddle!"

Gabriela's head pops around the bathroom door. "Oh woman, you scared me. Why the fuck did you scream like that?"

"Your son!"

"It's OK. I know. He does it all the time."

"How about if he falls?"

"He falls all the time. *No pasa nada*."

I wish this was true for my falls as well.

"Now can you calm down? You're in Argentina."

In Argentina, kids as young as seven gallop across fields on polo ponies. With no saddle. With no helmets, either. To be honest, the whole concept of riding helmets is not quite understood in Argentina.

Helmets are obligatory by law when playing polo. So everyone wears them. Only that in Argenina there are a few exceptions. Like when they hear the national anthem at the start of a game and then they take them off. Or when they take them off to salute the crowds in full gallop at the end of a game.

But apart from playing a polo game, there's little use for helmets in this country. Argentines stick and ball without helmets. Sometimes they wear *gaucho* berets when training, sometimes a simple golf cap. Neither of these would do anything to protect their heads. And nobody puts a helmet on just to ride across a field.

I remember the first time I showed up at San Patricio fresh from England. After the first training session with Patricio, he told me he wasn't impressed with my balance on the horse. He asked me to get up early the following morning to go for a ride in the fields. At 7 am the next day I found him and Gabriela patiently waiting for me. I was ready—polo t-shirt (Ralph Lauren, since they have nice colors), white jeans (we only wear white in England even when we train), and my polo helmet, which is so much cuter than a normal riding helmet. Plus gloves, whip, boots of course, and Oakley glasses. I love my Oakley sunglasses, which double up as protective glasses.

They looked at me as I emerged from the house in all my gear. It was a long, quiet stare that told me there was something not quite right.

But I didn't know them well enough then, and even Gabriela kept her "fuck" in check. She just pointed at my helmet, saying, "What are you doing with this? We're not playing."

"We're riding, aren't we?"

We went riding. The two of them in blue jeans and cowboy boots, and hair flowing freely in the wind. Me in full polo gear, starting to feel a little bit out of place.

They didn't say anything else, but I got the message. The second time I came to Argentina I made sure I had some normal blue jeans with me and left the helmet off when I was only riding.

THURSDAY 31ST DECEMBER

Tonight is New Year's Eve. Rodrigo hasn't messaged me. There hasn't been any suggestion to go to the seaside. No "I miss you." No "*linda*," no "*mi amor*." Nothing.

I hide my tears in a glass of wine, with Rosario and Gabriela by my side.

"Roxy. This guy is not for you." Rosario is Argentine and therefore she can read minds.

"But it was nice. He was nice."

"Of course he was nice. He's Argentine." I can detect a hint of national pride in her voice . "Men treat women nicely here. They make them feel like princesses."

"Like calling them *linda* all the time?"

"Of course. They all do this. It's nothing new."

"I've never had someone call me beautiful so many times."

"You've never dated an Argentine, that's why. But listen, *amiga*. Listen to me. It doesn't mean anything."

"What do you mean, it doesn't mean anything?"

"Like I said. It's nothing. It's just being nice. It's not serious. They don't mean it. I mean they do mean it, of course." She must have seen the sudden abyss in my eyes. "But not like you imagine. Of course you are beautiful, and of course he will see this. And of course he will tell you that you are beautiful. But that's it. It doesn't mean anything else."

"But he called me *mi amor*," I say stubbornly.

"Everyone will call you *mi amor* here. Even the taxi drivers."

I must admit she's right there. A number of taxi drivers have called me *mi amor* and I doubt they were in love with me.

"So this doesn't mean he loves me?"

"Roxy, what the fuck is wrong with you?" Gabriela joins the conversation. "Are you forty-one or eighteen? Of course the guy doesn't love you. You only met three weeks ago, for God's sake. And had sex twice."

"Three times. And we made love, not sex."

"Ah yes, of course. Give me a break." Gabriela reaches for the bottle to fill my glass. "Here, have another glass and come back to your senses please." She then turns to Rosario. "You tell her. She doesn't listen to me."

Rosario is milder, but her message is along the same lines. "Roxy, look. You don't know how things are here, but we are here to help you. This is what we're saying. It was great you had some fun, but don't expect anything else. Don't expect him to call back."

"Why?"

"Because it's over," Gabriela announces in a decisive tone.

"But maybe—"

"Look." Even Rosario is losing her patience now. "Has he ever called you since?"

"No."

"Has he texted you?"

"No."

"Have you texted?"

"No."

"Thank God. That would have been the worst possible thing if you had."

I sense I've redeemed myself a little in Gabriela's eyes.

"And one more question—who paid for the lunches when you went out?"

"We split the bill."

"What?" Rosario's eyes widen in horror. Gabriela looks at her with that "I told you so" expression in her eyes.

"You paid?"

"Not just me. We split the bill."

"Roxy, this is not done here. I can't believe he asked you to split the bill."

"He didn't. The bill arrived. I took my wallet out. He didn't tell me not to. We split the bill."

"Fucking bastard." Gabriela decides she's heard enough.

"Why?"

"Roxy—" Rosario's voice has a motherly rhythm, as if she is talking to a toddler who can't be expected to understand much about life. "This is Argentina. Men pay for food here, they pay for drinks. They pay for everything. I can't believe you split the lunch."

"It's not a big deal. I've done it before."

"Not here. Not in this country." Rosario is now completely siding with Gabriela. "He doesn't deserve you."

"Do yourself a favor, darling, and erase his number, please." Gabriela comes up with the way forward. "And then let's have another drink and forget about this whole story."

We have another drink and I try hard to forget, as they say I should. But I don't delete his number. Because although he has neither called nor texted, I still hang on to a little thread of hope that he will.

Later that evening we leave Rosario's house topped up with Champagne and girly chat. We agree to go to the farm, have a shower, put some nice clothes on (as far as my cast allows), and then meet again for a New Year's party at another farm in the neighborhood. I don't know the people who are hosting the party, but Gabriela tells me it's no problem. We're in Argentina, people don't think twice about bringing friends to a party given by other friends. It's how things are done here, and particularly in the *campo.*

I smile. I love this *campo.* And I love all of its customs.

Later that evening a torrential thunderstorm pours down, transforming the dirt roads into a sea of mud. And even when

Gabriela announces there's no way we can get out of the farm in a car to go to the party, I still love it.

Because it's like this, the Argentine *campo*. Unpredictable, wild and real. Just like its inhabitants.

January

FRIDAY 1ST JANUARY

We spend New Year's Eve at the farm while a thunderstorm rages outside. It causes road blocks and a massive power cut just before nightfall, just as I'm in the middle of having a shower, with my right arm covered in a plastic bag. The lights suddenly go out and I freeze in the darkness under the water, which keeps on pouring over me. It's pitch black, and I don't dare make a move for fear I'll fall again, and break God knows what this time.

"Gabriela!" I scream instead. She usually has a solution for everything.

She doesn't fail, arriving after a short while with a candle in a porcelain cup. I'm still standing naked under the running water in the darkness.

"Don't scream darling, here I am. I had to find the fucking candle. The electricity has gone off. Not sure we can get it back while it's still raining."

It isn't just the electricity. The phone line and internet have gone, too. And even with no thunderstorm there's never any mobile signal at the farm. So we are properly cut off from the world.

"Not to worry, darling." Gabriela's optimism is hardly ever shaken by anything. "We have cake and we have Champagne and we will party."

And we do. The New Year arrives announced by thunder and lightning and we welcome it by candlelight, dancing to the rhythm of the music coming from a laptop that still has some battery left, glasses of Champagne half drunk in our hands and the smell of freshly baked cake filling the huge living room. And it feels just fine.

MONDAY 4TH JANUARY

In the end I decide to go back to Buenos Aires. I've had a great time at the farm and Gabriela has looked after me as if I were her invalid daughter. I suspect this is my new status at the moment. I've had plenty of rest. My body has recovered from the initial shock of the fall and the full anaesthetic I had in the hospital. There's not much I can do about the arm, though. It needs six weeks in the cast and only two have passed. But the rest of me is feeling strong again. The bruises have faded. The memory of that goal post, too. At least I think so, anyway.

I'm keen to get on with my life and I feel the best place to be is in the city. I want to go back to the language school for a few more weeks. I've given up on returning to England in early January as I'd planned. It's becoming clear that the best solution is to stay longer in Argentina, maybe another month until the cast comes off, and then a couple more weeks so I can do some recovery at the same physio place. It's much cheaper than having physio in England. Only when I'm fully recovered will I go back to London and look for a job.

So I change the date of my return flight to mid-February and tell my parents I'm going to stay a little bit longer. I don't tell them why. Very few people know the real reason. It's simply too embarrassing.

I still haven't heard from Rodrigo. It's been ten days, and I'm positive I'll never hear anything from him again. Thanks to the girls' support, I've come to terms with letting him go. He was my Argentine fling, and that was it.

Better to look forward, I tell myself, as the bus from Lobos starts the two-hour journey for Buenos Aires. Better to think about my plans for the new year. I should maybe make a new-year list.

Number 1: Recover my arm . . .

Ping. Message.

Hola, cómo estás? Happy New Year!

It's four days too late for that. Actually ten days too late overall. Rodrigo's message stares at me from my phone screen and all I can feel is anger.

I will not answer. I will not answer. I count to a hundred in my mind. I will not answer. My anger does wonders for my resolve and for the whole duration of my journey back I stick to my plan. I do not answer.

But then I enter my flat and the memory of him overwhelms me.

Hola, I write back after a long time.

Is everything all right? he asks immediately.

No, it's not. I'd rather die than admit how much I've wanted to hear from him.

But this time he does not wait for me to message back. He calls.

I keep my voice in check and tell him over the phone that I don't think it's a good idea that we meet again. Ever.

Silence. Then I hear him inhale sharply.

"If that's what you want, then we shouldn't meet."

Silence again. I can't bring myself to simply hang up. I'm waiting for him to do it.

He doesn't. A full minute goes by, second by second. And then I hear his breath again.

"*Linda*," he says.

I feel tears well up instantly. What is it with this damn word? How can I feel so weak in the knees just because a guy calls me beautiful? I don't even know this guy well enough. Maybe it's simply too long since anyone called me beautiful. Or maybe he's the one, and the warmth I feel in my heart right now is there to tell me I should trust him.

"I want to see you," he says. "Please. Tomorrow."

"OK," I say and I hang up before he can guess I'm in tears. Happy? Sad?

A bit of both.

TUESDAY 5TH JANUARY

I use the next twenty-four hours to rehearse my part well. I'm going to play the cool girl. Casual. *Whatever.* No feelings. So what if you didn't call for ten days. No offence taken. I was too busy to think about you, anyway.

We meet at a coffee place in the center of Palermo. He suggests we go straight there to meet up. He doesn't suggest coming to pick me up from home. Damn him. One more reason to damn him.

We greet each other with a kiss that's quick enough to count as friendly, although our lips touch briefly. He talks casually about his New Year's Eve party. With another girl, just a friend who came to stay with him. She's Brazilian. He likes Brazilian girls. I feel like fainting.

"*No pasa nada*." He shrugs, sips his Campari Orange and answers my unasked question. "She's just a friend."

I watch him leaning back in his chair, his shoulders relaxed, his face slightly tilted towards me as he talks. What is it that I like so much about him? His strong arms? Definitely those. His black hair and long face? Nothing out of the ordinary. He's wearing a black t-shirt again. Black suits him. I've only seen him in black or grey t-shirts and jeans. Maybe he doesn't own anything else.

He tells me that after New Year's Eve he went with his friends to spend a few days in another city. The Brazilian girl came along. Then he went to an Aqua Park for a day.

"With her?"

"Of course. She was here for a week. She's just left."

The same week he didn't bother to send me a message.

"*Linda*, why are you upset? I missed you."

"You didn't call me for a week."

"Of course I didn't. You said there was no reception at the *campo*. You told me you were going to be there for ten days, so there was no point calling, was there?"

Ah, such a convenient excuse. I'm getting angry again. "What about texting?"

"I didn't want to bother you."

I'm furious now. This guy takes me for an idiot. And the whole story with the Brazilian "friends only" girl is really not holding up well.

I decide I've heard enough and that I'm not going to let this story even come close to hurting me. It's going to end right now, right here.

"Tell me something. What is this for you? What is happening with us? What does this mean for you?" I ask him, looking straight into his eyes.

I can tell he didn't expect this. He gives me one long stare and his voice trembles a bit when he says, "Well, we are getting to know each other, right? I've only just met you. I like you. A lot. I want to see you again. It's early days still. We are getting to know each other," he repeats.

"So it's not like you think we are boyfriend-girlfriend?"

Silence. Not good. Silence is not the right answer for this question. He looks slightly away as if he's trying to avoid the answer.

"It's still early, no?"

He is not really sure where I'm going with this. Neither am I.

"Good. Good to hear we're not boyfriend-girlfriend. Because it would be a mistake to think so. Between us there can be nothing. Nothing serious," I add, "Nothing long term. I hope this is clear for you."

Silence. Is he shocked? Surely that's what he thought too. That's why he didn't call.

"So what is it then between us?" he asks me slowly.

"Nothing really. Fun. For a while. Possibly. But then I go."

"When do you go?"

"Twentieth of February. I've just changed my flight."

"That's in one and a half months."

"Seven weeks actually, until my bone heals and I've done some physio. Then I'll go home to London."

"And then?"

"Nothing. Then it ends. The day I board my flight it ends. Or sooner."

He gives me a long silent stare.

I keep my face cool. Chill. Relaxed. *Tranqui*. I'm proud of myself. It needed to be done.

"Why?"

"What do you mean, why? Why am I flying back?"

"Why does it need to be like this? Why have you already decided when it will end? And that it has to end?" His voice is cold. I bet he won't call me *linda* now.

"Because it doesn't make sense. Have you forgotten I'm fourteen years older than you?"

"No, I haven't."

"So? Do you think this problem will go away?"

"No, it won't go away. It will always be there. That's why I don't think about it."

"So it doesn't bother you? At all?"

"It doesn't matter if it bothers me or not. It's not going to change so it's pointless thinking about it."

I'm still not sure whether it actually bothers him, and if so, how much.

"And no, it doesn't bother me," he adds after a while. "Why? Does it bother you?"

The thought of it does bother me. Thinking about what others will say bothers me. But right now, while I'm having a drink with him on this terrace, it doesn't matter. It didn't bother me when we were making love, either.

"No, not right now. But it will, sooner or later," I decide to answer.

Silence. I can tell he's hurt.

"Look, try to reason," I tell him, more softly this time. No need to play the tough woman now that the point is made. "You have a life to live. All these fourteen years I've already lived. You want to go and see the world. I've already seen the world. You have your life and I have mine, and right now for some weird reason they've crossed, but it's nothing more than a short intersection. It can't be anything more."

He's still silent. I want to go home. This conversation is not really going the way I'd planned it, and in any case there's nothing to add. And I don't think there will be any passionate lovemaking between us after today.

"I'll come to see you tomorrow," he tells me, just before I jump in a taxi. "If seven weeks is all we have, we'd better make the most of them."

And I can't bring myself to tell him not to come. I just can't.

FRIDAY 8TH JANUARY

The best thing about Buenos Aires in January is the sales. Dozens of boutiques are piled with tons of summer clothes. Bright colors in dazzling combinations—reds, oranges, and pinks grouped together alongside bright blues and deep greens, in a whole myriad of silks and light cottons that fill the windows of the shops. The dresses are either long and flowing like the beach dresses we wear in Europe, or extremely short. Some styles are very original. Take the shoes, for instance. Almost evey pair of women's shoes has a thick platform. Or the miniskirts. They are way more mini than any miniskirt I've seen in Europe. Under Cristina, the former president, Argentina lived with very tough import constraints. As a result, the fashion industry was protected and developed. In Europe, you find the same styles hanging in the windows of the high-street shops whether you're in Germany, England, or Spain, whereas here the clothes are as unique as the Argentine soul.

With an arm in a cast to my shoulder, I go shopping for summer dresses. The shop assistants come into the changing room with me and help me try things on. They don't mind my cast. No one seems to mind my cast. It's taken me three weeks to understand that the only place my cast is a problem is in my own mind.

It's not a problem for shop assistants, even if they have to dress and undress me as if I'm a doll. It's not a problem for Santi at the language school, who carries on writing the new words in my notebook. And it's not a problem for Rodrigo, who comes to see me every other evening and makes love to me with a mixture of tenderness and passion I find irresistible.

After our conversation about my imminent departure, neither of us has brought up the topic again. We don't need to. All that needed to be said was said then. In a way, we've already broken up. We have a deadline, the twentieth of February. Until then, we can just have some fun. If we want to. If we don't, we can break up sooner, no offense taken. I would prefer that we don't do that—that is, break up earlier than the twentieth of February. There are a lot of things one can do with an arm in a cast, but I doubt going out in a bar and charming a new guy is one of them.

Rodrigo has already come to see me twice this week and stayed over. He woke up at 4:30 am to drive the one-hour journey back to his town to get to work by 6. It didn't seem to bother him. I didn't wake him up for snoring again. I discovered he turned on one side in his sleep if I pulled his arm around me, and then he would call me "*mi amor*" in a delicious half-asleep voice, and the snoring would stop. After all these years of sleeping alone I have learned to sleep next to a man again in a matter of days.

Life is good again. My arm doesn't hurt and I have only three weeks to go before the cast will be removed.

SUNDAY 10TH JANUARY

I wake up in Rodrigo's arms. He's been with me since Saturday lunch time. He's never stayed so long before. I wonder when he'll leave.

But he doesn't seem to be in a hurry. His phone rings and he chats to a friend in bed, next to me. It's a woman. Apparently she's having problems with her boyfriend. Rodrigo sounds understanding and patient with her. Maybe he's another girl's "Marco." For a second I wonder if Marco had ever taken my tearful calls lying naked in bed with a woman. If he had, it never seemed to influence his ability to give advice.

"Oh, I'm sorry about her," Rodrigo tells me as he hangs up. "It's not going well with her boyfriend and she doesn't want to see it. She will eventually. All I can do is be a good friend and listen when she needs to talk."

Just like Marco. Maybe he, too, saw the end of my relationships way before I did.

"I'm surprised you have girlfriends. I mean girls as friends. They say there's no friendship between women and men in Argentina."

"Whoever told you that is wrong," he says. "Of course there's friendship between men and women here. I have many women friends."

Maybe he isn't that much of a typical Argentine, I think.

We're still in the bed and he looks relaxed. We've never spent twenty-four hours together and this time we're getting close to it. He seems in no hurry to go anywhere.

He asks me if I've seen any Argentine movies. I haven't, but Santi has given me a long list of movies I have to see. To practice my Spanish, he says. Rodrigo takes a look at the list and tells me I absolutely have to see one of the them. *El Secreto de Sus Ojos. The Secret in Their Eyes.* A thriller.

He finds it online. I'm still expecting him to leave any minute, but he spends the next two hours holding my mini iPad in his hand so we can watch a movie that he's already seen. It's good for my Spanish, he says.

Definitely more than twenty-four hours now, I think, as we start kissing again at the end of the movie. And he's not going to go anywhere right now, either.

MONDAY 11TH JANUARY

I get a call from my parents. They still don't know about my broken arm. Very few people back in Europe know about my broken arm. I make an excuse. I tell them we can't do Facetime because it doesn't work in Argentina. All we can do is a voice call on WhatsApp. Everyone uses WhatsApp in Argentina. With no camera, my arm can continue to remain hidden.

My parents tell me their friends are on a cruise ship and will be stopping in Buenos Aires in two days' time. They want to see me. They'll give me a call when they arrive so we can arrange to meet.

"Sure, Dad. Tell them to call me." I keep my voice cheerful until I hang up.

Then I turn my phone off for the next two days and hope that the chances of me bumping into them on the street of this huge city are close to zero.

WEDNESDAY 13TH JANUARY

Today I'm meeting Jonny for a coffee. Jonny is my polo training buddy in England and the professional player in my team when I play a tournament. He's also a friend. He's in town only for this afternoon and I really want to see him. There are few people in this world who care about my polo as much as Jonny does. There's the Old Man, of course. He's my main trainer and he cares too. But the Old Man owned the club I trained at and he had a lot of other things to care about. A lot of other clients. I was just one of them and not really a good player. I needed time to develop my game and he knew that and gave me lots of time and two good horses. And he sent Jonny to help me out.

Jonny was young. He must have been about twenty-one when he came to the club in England. Originally from Mar de Plata, the same town the Old Man comes from, he was a young professional player, at that time handicap two. I was a minus two. That meant a hell of a lot of distance between us. When we first met, I was coming back to polo fresh from the broken-arms episode. I had spent the winter recovering and got back on a horse in April. I was determined I was going to make the best of that season. And Jonny was there to make sure I did.

I trained with Jonny two to three times a week. I played practice chukkas with him and I played tournaments with him. The only two occasions I ever won a cup in a polo tournament were while playing with him. Sometimes I played with the Old Man too, but playing with Jonny was special. I felt he cared. He cared about my game, he wanted to see me improve. He spent hours on the field with me as we did stick and ball together, shouting at me, correcting my hits, correcting my timing.

"Now," he would shout. "Not like that. Sooner!" and "Again. Now. I said now!"

Jonny liked to talk a lot. About the game, about the horses, about the weather, about life. We used to start our training session with a couple of wide circles in slow canter around the field to warm up the horses, and we would talk, rising and falling to the rhythm of the horses, in the same way other people might have chatted in a pub while sharing a few beers. In no time at all, Jonny became a friend.

He knew I had broken both arms the previous season and he knew I needed to regain my confidence. And he made sure I did. We trained together, we played together and we talked about a lot of things on that field. But as they say in polo, "What happens on the field stays on the field." That includes conversations.

Now Jonny was here in Buenos Aires for one afternoon only to get his visa for the UK. Next summer he would be back to train and play professionally at the Old Man's club in England. I had to meet him, firstly because I really wanted to see him, and secondly because I wanted him to reassure the Old Man that I really did have a broken arm.

I'd called the Old Man as soon as I returned to Buenos Aires after my recent fall. Once I managed to recharge my phone, I discovered he'd left me three voice messages. All on the same day of the fall. It was like he had a sixth sense.

"Finally, Rosanna. Where have you been?" he said, when I called him back at last.

"I have to tell you something—"

"Yes, when are you coming? I've got good horses waiting for you here."

"No. Wait. Where are you?"

"In Mar de Plata. What do you mean?"

"No, I mean where are you right now? Are you sitting down?"

"No."

"Sit down, please sit down. I need to tell you something."

Sitting down didn't help. He was furious. "Why do you keep on playing without me?" he shouted. "See what happens to you if you play without me?"

I wasn't sure this was the problem, but I had a nagging feeling he somehow he didn't believe I really had broken an arm and had it in a cast. Again.

So I needed to see Jonny so he could testify to the truth of my story.

"So tell me, Roxana." Jonny doesn't call me Rosanna. He's one of the few Argentines who can pronounce the awkward "x" in my name. "Have you fallen in love yet?"

I smile. Our conversations on the polo field used to include frequent updates on my single status as well as on my desire to have that changed.

"Yes, I have."

He grins. "Argentine?"

"Of course."

"Well done."

"I'm not so sure. There's a problem."

"What do you mean?"

"Well, he's younger than me."

"So what? You look younger, too."

"But he's much younger. Fourteen years younger, in fact."

Jonny's smile gets wider. "So what's the problem? We Argentines believe in love. When love strikes, age doesn't matter."

"But Jonny, fourteen years!"

"Are you happy?"

"Yes."

"Then that's all that matters."

Jonny leans back in his chair with that cheerful, honest look he always has on his face. He is like this, Jonny—he speaks the truth and makes it sound like no big deal. I take another sip of my drink and try to come to terms with getting love advice from a man twenty years younger than me, regarding another man fourteen years younger than me.

"Anyway, it's nothing. When I go it will be over. We've agreed."

"How can you agree this? How can you know when something is over before it is actually over?" Jonny looks at me as if I'm out of my mind.

"Because I know." I suddenly feel impatient. "I have a flight ticket with a date. Twentieth of February."

"Roxana. You cannot put dates on love."

He is twenty-two. What does he know about love? I decide to change the subject.

"Listen, please tell the Old Man you have seen me. Please tell him you've seen my arm and it really is in a cast. I'm not lying. Please tell him I'm sorry."

"Roxana, you'll play again. I'll make sure you do. Don't you worry about anything. Just see you recover properly. And in April we'll ride together again. I promise you that." His dark brown eyes look at me seriously from his young face. But he's not too young to make a real promise. I know he means it.

Just like the Old Man, just like Patricio, Jonny is another Argentine polo player who is promising to help me get back on a horse. And just like them, he cares.

"Thank you, Jonny," I say, my voice trembling a bit. I'm feeling grateful but there's not much else to say, and he dismisses my thanks anyway with a wave of his hand, just as he always does when I thank him after a game.

"*De nada.*"

But right now I don't want to think about how it will be when I get back on a horse again. The goal post still haunts me. If I let myself think about it, even for a second, I'm back on that field hitting that goal post again and again. And it doesn't feel good at all.

"And thank you for your love advice too." I smile. "We'll see what happens. But enough about me. Your turn now. News? Any girl who's taken your fancy?"

He gives me a wide smile and I can tell there's a story on the way, and it's my turn to listen and give advice. Just in case he needs any. But that isn't usually the case, because Jonny, unlike me, is very confident about what he does, be it on the field or off it.

THURSDAY 14TH JANUARY

They say there's no friendship between men and women in Argentina. Well, they are wrong. There is friendship with Jonny. And there's always Patricio, of course. My Argentine brothers.

But for the rest of the encounters, they are right. There isn't much friendship between men and women in Argentina, no matter what Rodrigo says. And that's mainly because men court women. Openly. Clearly. Straightforwardly. By no means aggressively. But they do it constantly. All the time. All the men do it. Even the married ones. And they do it to all the women. Even the married ones.

Gabriela told me how one day she was walking on the street with a friend of hers. The friend was obviously pregnant—six months or so. A guy walked past, then turned around and told the pregnant lady, "*Ay, mi amor. Perdón. Llegué tarde.*" I'm sorry, love. I got here too late.

The girls continued their walk, unimpressed by this typical display of Argentine courtship.

Before I broke my arm, I'd been slowly becoming accustomed to the constant interest I received from men here. Even if I didn't get many requests for my phone number, like Andrea did, I'd begun to understand the effect my presence had on men. And it wasn't just me. I understood the effect the presence of any woman had on any Argentine man. Their eyes would instantly light up, as if to say, "I see you." In Argentina, men see you just because you are a woman.

In London I often used to feel like a piece of wood. I often felt that for a guy drinking his beer in a pub my presence would have the same effect as the chair on which I was sitting. But this isn't the case here. Here, all a woman needs to do is be a woman. Wherever she goes she will get noticed. She will be approached.

The other Argentine thing is that they do it really well. Never aggressively. Never pushing. Always in a laid-back, half-joking and friendly manner. Always taking a "No" graciously. Never insisting if you don't feel like talking. Absolutely never harassing. The message they send is, "I'm here and I see you. If you want to talk to me, great, if you don't want to talk to me that's OK, too, I just want to tell you I've registered your presence."

This approach has an incredible effect on a woman's self-esteem. Especially one who is forty-one years old, has been through a divorce and a number of failed relationships, and has been single for a long while. I felt I was blossoming. I didn't understand why Argentine women were so matter-of-fact about this style of courtship, dismissing it with a wave of the hand. Nothing serious, just flirting. Even if it was just flirting, it was still too good to be true!

I thought it would stop as soon as I had my arm in a sling. After all, who would try to chat up an invalid? But no. Rodrigo was right. I was still *linda*. And Emi was right, too. The arm didn't matter. In fact, it provided a good topic of introduction.

I wait to cross the street at the traffic lights. On the other side of the street, he waits too. A guy like many others, dressed in a t-shirt and jeans. Handsome, with that unshaved, half-wild look I like so much. They're all handsome here. He may be in his mid-thirties, but I wouldn't bet on it. My ability to estimate ages hasn't proved very accurate recently.

He starts chatting me up even when he's too far away to actually chat. He points to my cast, looks straight at me and makes a gesture as if to ask, "What happened?"

I smile and shrug. What can I say? In between us, three lanes of busy traffic.

He makes the motion to fall, his hands outstretched. "Did you fall?" I read his silent question again.

Of course he can read minds. He's Argentine. Or maybe in this case, given my huge cast, it's pretty obvious.

I nod. Yes, I did fall.

"Ay. Did it hurt?" The pantomime goes on. I can see the horrified expression on his face, even from all that distance.

I nod again. Yes, it did.

The traffic lights turn green and we start crossing the street. He smiles at me. I smile back. As he passes, he turns and says, "Your pain is my pain. I can feel it in my heart. Because you are as beautiful as an angel."

And then he walks straight on by.

I've never seen this guy before. I'll never see him again. He hasn't asked for my phone number. He hasn't asked for anything. He simply paid me a compliment and left. He saw me.

For the rest of the day I walk around with a big silly smile stuck on my face, and it's just because a guy I'll never see again thinks I'm as beautiful as an angel.

FRIDAY 15TH JANUARY

I meet a girl from London. She is a friend of a friend. Our mutual friend has put us in contact, because he knows she's travelling by herself and he knows I'm alone here. Or so he thinks. There are very few people who know about Rodrigo. Not that he counts, anyway. I'm still technically alone. But not the same alone as before. A different alone.

I meet the girl for dinner in Plaza Serrano, the square at the heart of Palermo, where about ten restaurants and bars compete for outside space for their tables. There's always a crowd in Plaza Serrano, and every night here is like a party night.

I tell the girl about my experiences in Argentina. I tell her about the constant male attention you get here as a woman. She doesn't believe me.

"Seriously?" she says, looking unsure.

I tell her it's not like London. I tell her about the taxi driver, stuck in a traffic jam, who leaned out of the window and told me as I passed that morning, "*Mi amor.* Listen, I'm serious, you know? I'm really a serious guy. I want to get married."

My new friend is still not convinced. "It can't just be like that."

I tell her that of course it doesn't mean anything. I tell her about the heat of the Latino dances in the *bolliches*, which is what they call the discos here, where people dance and kiss casually, then dance with other people and kiss them too. Then they come back to dance with the same people again and kiss them again. I tell her about Rodrigo, and I tell her that he doesn't mean anything.

"Does he call you *mi amor* too?"

"Yes, he does."

And then something happens that makes her believe me. A guy approaches our table. He tells her something in Spanish. I explain to him that my friend doesn't speak Spanish.

He then turns towards me.

"Ah, *bueno*. Never mind. I can't speak English, so never mind."

He turns around to leave, but then he changes his mind and says, "Would you please just tell her one thing from me? Please tell her I think she is very beautiful. Thanks."

He leaves.

I translate his sentence faithfully to my new friend. She looks at me, stunned.

"This has never happened to me before," she whispers. "I'm now seriously considering moving here."

I laugh. "Welcome to Argentina, darling!"

SATURDAY 16TH JANUARY

And of course my story with Rodrigo doesn't mean anything. It can't. It's just supposed to be laid-back and fun. Only fun. No love. I promised Rosario I wouldn't fall in love. I promised myself too. And I promised Rodrigo, the day I told him we would break up on the twentieth of February.

I thought he got it then. I thought we had a deal.

So why is he asking me this now?

"Are you coming back to Argentina next summer?"

"I think so," I reply. "I love it here. I've already been here four times in two years. I'm sure I'll be back."

"And when you come, will we live together?"

I stop breathing. I feel dizzy and for a second I'm scared I might just faint. Right there in my seat as he drives through the mayhem of Palermo traffic.

"No, we won't."

"Why not?"

"Because we won't be together when I come back. Remember my flight date? Twentieth of February."

In a second the temperature in the car drops to freezing. He carries on driving without saying a word. We get home and this distance between us is still there. I try to kiss him tentatively, so as to ease the moment and ease away the stupid question. Why did he have to ask it?

"And what if we don't break up on the twentieth of February?" he asks me later, after we've made love in silence. "Will you move in with me when you come back?"

"*Mi amor.*" I laugh. "Come on. Why do we need to talk about this right now? I'll probably have another boyfriend by the time I come back to Argentina."

Another temperature drop. I can feel goosebumps on my my skin as he slowly lets go of me and gets out of bed with calm, precise movements.

Silence. Why did I say that? Why did he need to ask?

"I don't know if I can do this any longer," he says, his voice low. He's not looking at me. He's looking straight at the floor. "I really don't think I can do this any longer."

"Do what?"

"This." He makes a vague gesture to the room and me. "Come to see you. Make love to you. I'm sorry, but I don't think I can do this again."

"Why not?"

"Because that date we have means we've already broken up. Even if it's in the future. I can't be with someone I've already broken up with. I'm sorry. I thought I could. But I cannot."

He starts to get dressed.

I'm hardly breathing. This is it, then. This time I'll never see him again.

"I'm sorry," he repeats.

He leaves without looking at me. I still haven't said a word.

Marco calls later that evening. I really don't know how it happens, but there's a mysterious signal that Marco gets, wherever in the world he is, that tells him when I'm in a breakup situation. Maybe we had a deal before reincarnating, and his part of the deal was that he was going to be there for me every time I go through a breakup. I'm still not sure what my part of the deal was meant to be.

"*Ciao imbecille, come stai*?"

It only takes one sentence in Italian to wipe away all my Spanish, no matter how confident I am about speaking it. It just can't stand up against a full frontal attack of Italian.

It also only takes one "*imbecille*," Marco's favorite form of addressing me, to make me feel life is not that bad. With Marco on the phone I can make it through this, just as I've made it though many other breakups in the past.

"How the hell did you know I really needed to talk to you right now?"

He sighs. "Tell me. What have you got yourself into this time?"

I tell him, all of it. The fall, the arm, the guy. It was only supposed to be fun . . . It wasn't anything else but fun.

"He walked out two hours ago. I don't think I'll ever see him again."

"Why did he go?"

"I'm not sure." And then I tell him about my ticket and the date looming ahead. And about men being such strange creatures, and how I'll never understand them.

"Are you telling me you already broke up with him before you actually broke up?"

I'm not sure if he's surprised or amused. His voice has that slight hint of exasperation he sometimes uses when I tell him about something silly I've done.

"But Marco, it's in the future. We still have five weeks to go."

"It doesn't matter. If you agreed to break up, you've already broken up."

"That's what he says."

"Of course he does. Only an *imbecille* like you can't understand this."

I don't mind Marco's insults. This is how he expresses love.

"But Marco—"

But he doesn't want to listen. He's heard enough.

"And then you tell him you'll be with another man? And you tell him this while you're naked in bed, just after you've made love? Are you out of your mind? Are you completely insensitive about how a man feels?"

"Marco! This was supposed to be just fun."

"It doesn't matter. You can't tell that to a man. Even worse to a Latin man."

For a second I feel this is as absurd as the rule about not waking up a man when he snores. "Why not?"

"Because he will simply not want to touch you again."

"Well, he left."

"Of course he did."

"What can I do?"

"What do you want?"

"To have him back."

"Forever?"

"No, until twentieth of February."

"And then?"

"It's over then. Things between us can't last longer than that."

"Why not?"

"Marco, are you crazy? Have you forgotten about our age difference? Among other things. There's an ocean between us. Literally."

He pauses. "The only way you can get him back is if you're

willing to ease off on this control madness you're imposing on the whole thing."

"What control madness? I don't understand."

"Of course you don't. Go to his place. Now. Tell him you're sorry."

"I can't. I don't know where he lives."

"Then call him. No, wait. Better if you text him. Tell him you don't know where this story will go and when or whether it will finish. Tell him you're willing to wait and see."

"But Marco, I do know. Twentieth of February."

"No you don't, *imbecille.* No one knows what will happen on the twentieth of February. Not even a control freak like you. Believe me, it's the only way to get him back. And I'm not even sure it will work. But if you want to try, do it now. And by the way," he adds, "I'm coming back to Buenos Aires in a couple of weeks. I've got a business trip. I'll take you out for dinner. It sounds like you need it."

I hang up and I spend the next couple of hours staring at a blank text message screen. My mind is racing, thoughts come and go. I let them come and I let them go. And only once they're all finally gone and my mind is empty, and I'm too tired to think any more, do I type in the words, slowly.

I will live this story as it comes. I promise. No more deadlines. I will let it be and follow it . . . Hasta donde nos llega. Wherever it wants to take us.

I press send, still not sure I really mean it. But Marco said it's the only way to get him back. He must be right. He's always right.

And I do want him back.

TUESDAY 19TH JANUARY

For the past couple of days I haven't been sure whether I'll get Rodrigo back. His lukewarm answer to my text ended with "*Después vemos.*" I'm not quite sure how long a period of time that *después* refers to.

But I've got something else back. I've got Andrea.

Andrea has been traveling round southern Argentina and has done a long tour of all the tourist attractions of the country—Bariloche, the mountains, the glaciers, the south, Mendoza, and the west—and then, just to finish off in style, Uruguay and Punta del Este, the party hub of trendy Argentines.

She's returned suntanned, happy, bubbly, and full of stories. She also came back determined to find a place in Buenos Aires, settle down for a month and go to a language school to brush up her Spanish. Which means we're going to be spending lots of time together.

It couldn't have been better timing. My whole fling with Rodrigo is under a big question mark, so I have plenty of time on my hands. Too much time. January is a holiday month in Argentina, like August is in Europe. My friends in Lobos have gone away. Gabriela has gone to Europe again. Patricio and the rest of the family in Lobos have gone down to the south to visit the sister who lives far away. They'd invited me to come with them, but I had language school and a handsome guy waiting for me in Buenos Aires at the time, so I said no. The language school is still there, but I'm not sure about the handsome guy any longer. Rosario has gone away, too, with her boyfriend, touring the north of the country. Once more I found myself *Sola in Baires*. But now, with Andrea back, this is no longer the case.

We go out for dinner. Andrea always dresses up when she goes out, so I do too. I wear a long, black, backless summer dress, more suited for an evening on the beach than in the city. But it's glam enough for a night out, and Argentines love long, flowing summer dresses. I have lots of makeup on and my hair is done. My hair is now always professionally done, thanks to my inability to wash it myself and to the proximity of Sol's salon. My cast is covered with a glittery scarf wrapped all round my right arm. It looks a bit weird, but better than the crude white cast on its own.

A glass of wine and a girly chat, and all of a sudden life is good again. It's past midnight, but the restaurants are only just starting to fill. Customers are leisurely walking by in big groups, taking their time to check out menus and discussing where to go. Perhaps the *asado* place which is responsible for the odor of grilled meat spreading through the street? Or maybe that other lively pizzeria place? Or the Mexican place next door, where a couple are tucking into two big burritos topped with guacamole? Or maybe the terrace selling beer and burgers? Definitely not there, it's got a bight neon light. Better to go to the cozy pizzeria, where candles in small glass bowls burn on the tables.

People take their time here for everything, and selecting a restaurant is just one of those things. Waiters take their time to attend to customers too, but no one minds. Everyone is out to have a good time and rushing isn't part of it, even on an ordinary weekday. Even if they have to go to work tomorrow.

As Andrea puts it, "Every night is a New Year's night in Buenos Aires."

"Listen, Roxy. You can't carry on like this," she says, after hearing the latest developments between Rodrigo and me. "You are dangerously close to falling in love. It's not a good idea. You need to date others."

"What? But I'm already dating Rodrigo."

"Yes, precisely because of this. And it's not clear if you are still dating him, by the way. You need to go out with other men. At the same time. So you don't think about him all the time. And so you don't fall in love."

"I've never been out with two guys at the same time."

"Well, maybe now it's a good time to start."

WEDNESDAY 20TH JANUARY

There's still no sign of Rodrigo. I try hard not to think of him. I fail. I go to Sol to have my hair done and all I can talk about is him.

"What's wrong with you?" She seems really annoyed. "Look at you, beautiful, sexy, single."

"Not sure about single."

"Yes, single," she says firmly. "A guy needs to do a lot more than this guy is doing at present, for you not to consider yourself single any longer. Stop thinking about him. It was fun, but it's over. He's probably never going to call back."

"How do you know?"

"Because this is how it's done here. They disappear. They always disappear. For no reason. One day you wake up and they're not there any longer. You wonder what happened. But you'll never know. No explanations. No discussion. *Nada*. They just go."

I can't help but think of Mr. Perfect and the way he disappeared. I've never heard from him since that night he left the pizzeria in a hurry. As far as Rodrigo is concerned, there's a reason for his disappearance, but I'm not telling Sol the whole story.

Another client, getting her hair done next to me, nods in agreement.

"She's right. They are all like this."

"They who?"

"Men," Sol clarifies. "Argentine men. Never trust them, darling. Never. They promise the world and then they vanish from sight. Like they've never been."

The client takes over from there. She's a woman in her late thirties, wearing a long, pretty skirt with red and orange flowers printed across it.

"I was in love with a guy. I dated him for three years. We were talking of moving in together. Then one day, he vanished. Just like that. No calls, no explanations. Nothing. I tried calling him, but he wouldn't pick up. Then I noticed he had blocked me on Whatsapp. Gone. Like he'd never been. I still don't know the reason."

I felt for her. "And what happened then?"

"I cried for two days. Then I got over it."

"See?" Sol points her hair straighteners at the client approvingly. "I told you. You have to believe us. We know them."

Then she turns around and tells the client, "This girl comes from London. She doesn't understand a thing about how men are here. Imagine, she went out with this guy and they split the bill in the restaurant. He actually let her pay half the bill!"

The other woman gasps. "No. Seriously?" She looks at me with pity in her eyes.

Oh, God. Why did I have to share everything with Sol?

"I can't believe it." The woman with the pretty skirt is still digesting the last bit of information.

"See, I told you." The hair straighteners come back, pointing at me this time. "I told you no one would believe it here. You've got to stop being silly. You've been silly enough, no more. You deserve a man who treats you right. And . . . Sto-o-op," she screams suddenly. "*Stop* this. Now. Put it down."

The hair straighteners are now pointing menacingly at the waiting area seats, where one of her little boys is trying to squeeze a bottle of hair oil over his toddler sister's head. And then Sol screams some more, but I don't quite understand the rest. Oh, I really need to talk to Santi. I need a full lesson on Argentine slang. Reading Jorge Luis Borges has its limits when it comes to day-to-day speech comprehension in this city.

I go home and I check my phone for the hundredth time today. There's still no text from Rodrigo. But there's one from Andrea.

Come join me in the swimming pool. Super hot day today.

Andrea has rented a flat in a block with a communal swimming pool. I haven't got one in my block. I would love to go in the water, but I have two slight problems—I have a full arm in a cast and I have just done my hair.

Oh, come on. Don't worry. You won't get either the cast or the hair wet. Come try it out!

Andrea is like this. She doesn't see obstacles.

It's either that or waiting the rest of the afternoon for messages that are never going to come. Even taking into consideration my arm in a cast, the swimming pool seems a far better idea.

THURSDAY 21ST JANUARY

Finally there's a message from Rodrigo. He's too tired to come over. He's been really busy at work. Maybe another time, he writes. I text back saying I don't mind coming to his place.

Too far, he replies. *It's a nightmare to come here on public transport.*

I'll take a taxi.

Estás loca. You are crazy, he writes back. *It's more than one hour from Buenos Aires. They'll make you pay a fortune. Let's leave it for another time.*

I bite my lip and don't offer any more solutions. I text Andrea instead.

Shall we go out tonight?

Of course we are going out, she answers. As always, Andrea has options lined up involving various groups, and she's always on the guest list. The only question is, which one to choose? She lists the alternatives and we decide to go for a pizza with a group from London and their Argentine friends. Andrea only knows one person in the group and I know no one, but it's not a problem here.

Perfect, I think. Anything that stops me thinking of Rodrigo is just perfect right now.

We go out and I find some extra support to help me stop

thinking about Rodrigo. His name is Juan, I discover, as I give him the customary kiss on the cheek. He's a tall, dark-haired guy with a bright pink shirt. I like guys who aren't afraid to wear pink. I walked into the pizzeria feeling conscious of my cast and aware I didn't know anyone, but Juan immediately puts me at ease. He sits next to me at the long table, talks a lot, and he wants to know all about me.

Andrea had reassured me they would all be friendly, and she's right. After only half an hour I feel I already know everyone. About the same amount of time it takes for our drinks to arrive.

The waitress finally appears and asks us where we are from. Half of us from London, half from Argentina, we explain. She says she would love to go to London.

"Do you think I would be able to get a job there?" she asks one of the guys.

He pauses. "Well, actually . . . quite frankly no, I don't think so, if you ask me. You see, in London things move fast. If you take thirty minutes to deliver the drinks to one table, you won't have a job any longer the next day."

She seems surprised. "Is that so?"

"Yes, I'm afraid it is."

"Why are people so impatient in London?" she wonders.

I have long ago given up complaining about how long it takes to get service in Argentina. A very long time. Much longer than anywhere else I've been to. I'm used to this by now. But my new friends, freshly off a flight from London, are not.

The waitress doesn't take it personally. She probably secretly pities these stressed-out people who can't wait for a drink. I hope for her sake that she also secretly decides not to go for a waitress job in London. She won't last, for sure.

The pizza arrives and I can't cut it. My right arm is perfectly useless, hidden under the table in its sling. Juan cuts it into little pieces for me, taking a very long time and making sure the pieces are small enough for me to eat them without effort.

"*Gracias.*" I smile.

"*De nada, guapa,*" he answers.

Juan is from Spain. They don't say *linda* there. They say *guapa*. It really doesn't sound as nice as *linda*.

But there hasn't been a message from Rodrigo the whole day, so I decide that maybe *guapa* doesn't sound too bad after all.

We laugh, we drink, we talk. Andrea winks at me. Juan wants my phone number. Life is not so bad. In this country, men might have a habit of suddenly disappearing from your life. But there is always another one waiting just around the corner.

FRIDAY 22ND JANUARY

I've avoided this for three weeks now, but I can't put it off any longer. I need to take my laundry to the wash.

My mentor is there, at the launderette. He's not seen me in my cast yet. His eyes widen in shock as I enter, and there follows half an hour's conversation about what happened, and precisely how it happened. People are waiting in the queue. Occasionally he serves someone else but carries on talking to me. I can't leave in the middle of the conversation, it wouldn't be polite.

With the arm situation fully discussed, understood and pitied, he then asks me about love.

"Like this?" I indicate the arm in a cast.

"What's the problem?" He looks amused. "It's not going to stop love."

I admit that it hasn't. Then I tell him about my last three weeks and how my latest love seems to have disappeared. I don't tell him about the age difference or the tense exchange we had the last time I saw him.

"Don't worry, there will be others," he concludes.

He's said this before. Actually, it was just before I went out and kissed the football player. Maybe he'll prove right again.

LATER THAT EVENING

I'm going out with Andrea and the same group of friends again. Including Juan, who has texted me three times in two days. He's looking forward to seeing me. Where the heck is Rodrigo? Why is he not getting in touch?

I take a deep breath in and decide there's nothing to be done about Rodrigo. My launderette mentor would kill me if I try to contact him, so I won't. I just focus on Juan's messages to distract my thoughts.

But there are plenty of other opportunities to distract my thoughts.

"*Hola, linda*," the taxi driver says. He's friendly, as all taxi drivers are in Buenos Aires.

I tell him where we need to go. As usual, it only takes one sentence for him to grasp that I'm not a local.

"Where are you from?"

Bloody Santi, I think. He still hasn't sorted out my accent.

I tell him the whole story of where I'm from.

"And what happened to your arm?"

I tell him that too.

"And are you married?"

"No."

"Boyfriend?"

"Uh, no. I don't think so."

"Thank God."

Now that's original. I was expecting the standard "How come?"

"Why is that good?"

"Because imagine if you had one. Poor guy. Imagine what he would have to go through."

"Like what?"

"Like *si, mi amor, no, mi amor,* are you comfortable, *mi amor,* do you need to go to the hospital, *mi amor,* do you need anything from the pharmacy, *mi amor.* Don't touch this, *mi amor,* I'll do the dishes, *mi amor.* You can't, not with an arm in a cast. I'll look after you, *mi amor.* All these things he would have to do and he would only hear complaints and grumpiness back. Ah, I can't bear to think about it. If you had a boyfriend, he would have no life—poor him!"

I'm silent. Rodrigo hasn't done any of these things. There have been no lifts to the hospital. No questions if I need anything from the pharmacy. No offers to do any shopping for me. No washing of dishes. Actually he's never washed the dishes in all the times we have eaten at home. I wonder if he thinks I can do them with one hand, or if he knows I have a cleaner that comes in regularly.

"How do you know it would be like that?" I ask the taxi driver. "Maybe I'm not that difficult."

"Because that's what an Argentine man would do. Whether you are difficult or not, it doesn't matter. And when they treat you like this, you will become difficult anyway. All women are difficult."

Silence again. The questions build in my head. Why does Rodrigo not behave like an Argentine man? What's wrong with him? What's wrong with me?

And then, the big one. What if they're right? Sol, Rosario, Gabriela, all of them. What if this guy is treating me badly and I put up with it because I don't know any better?

OK, enough of this. I will flirt with Juan tonight, I decide, before I jump out of the cab.

"Ay, *mi amor,*" the taxi driver exclaims, turning round to give me the change. "Don't look at me like that. I won't be able to forget your eyes the whole night. They have a magnetic force in them."

No, my friend, I think. You're mistaken. It's just anger. And if the object of my anger were here right now, you would be right to feel sorry for him.

LATER THAT NIGHT

The great thing about going out with a group of glamorous people is that you have a reason to dress up. In my case a short, pretty, green evening dress, glittery heels, and lots of makeup. I don't even bother to cover up the cast. They all know about it, anyway. Including Juan.

The other great thing is you can take group photos. At the restaurant, at the bar, outside the bar, on the street as we go to another bar. And the advantage of group photos is that you can disguise your broken arm by hiding it behind other people. I get myself a decent set of party pictures that I can send to my parents, to illustrate the great life I'm having in Buenos Aires. They still don't know about my fall. I am determined that they will never know.

The last time I broke my arms, I told them about it immediately. I didn't know any better. I called home just as I arrived from the hospital and told my mum without much preparation.

"Listen, Mum, I'm OK, but something happened. I had a fall while playing polo."

"And ?" she screamed.

"I broke an arm. Not a big deal."

I could hear the sobs on the other end of the line.

"Well, actually, I broke two. Both of them." I hurried on to deliver the rest of the story. Better to do it in one go, I thought. Plus my mother was now crying, anyway.

She wanted to take a flight the same night and come over to London to look after me.

"No Mum, please, please don't, please."

"Why not? Who's going to look after you?"

"I have a nurse. Not really a nurse. I've hired a nanny. My friend sorted it out while I was in hospital. She's going to come every day."

"Why a nanny? I can come stay with you." My mum can be stubborn at times.

"No, Mum. You'll tell me to give up polo."

"Of course I'll tell you to give up polo. I hope you never touch a horse again after this."

"We'll see about that, but you see, Mum, I can't have you here for six weeks telling me I have to give up polo."

Especially as I have no intention of giving up polo, I added in my mind.

It was quite a struggle to convince my mum to stay away, but I managed it. The experience left me wiser. This time, I decided not to say anything. I couldn't risk having my mum here on the first intercontinental flight straight from Romania. If she came, what would I do about Rodrigo? He was another piece of news I hadn't shared. In fact the only thing I told my parents was that I played a little bit of polo, not too much, and that I was enjoying partying in Buenos Aires. And the set of party pictures were just what I needed to make my story stronger.

I'm really enjoying the night out. We drink, we chat, we flirt. Juan flirts, actually, and I flirt back, just enough to tell him I'm interested, but not too much to make me feel bad about flirting with someone other than Rodrigo. At 3 am they go on to a disco and I go home. There are still some limits to what one can do with an arm in a sling. And I'd had just enough flirting for one evening, anyway.

SATURDAY 23RD JANUARY

Message from Rodrigo. *Lunch today?* Neutral tone.

OK, I reply. No big deal, I think.

Message from Juan. *Dinner today?*

Can't, I write back. Just in case Rodrigo stays, I think.

Rodrigo comes, but things seem different between us. Awkward. Like he doesn't really want to be here. Why did he come? We eat in silence. He doesn't call me *linda*.

We go home and make love. It's not the same. The distance is still there.

"What's going on?" I ask him. "Look, I sent you that message, didn't I? No more deadlines. Isn't that what you wanted?"

He sighs. "Yes, but—"

"But what?"

"Maybe it's too late."

"What do you mean?" I feel a stab of pain.

"Look, I've been hurt. Pretty hurt by everything you said. Then you sent me that message and yes, it helped. But I'm still hurt. I can't change that. Not overnight."

"It's been a week," I say.

"It's not enough. I need more time. I'm really not sure if I can feel again . . . how I felt before."

How did he feel before? I wondered. He never told me how he felt.

"Is there anything I can do?"

"No," he says. "We need time."

Time. We don't have time. We have exactly four weeks until the twentieth of February. Whether I talk about it or not, the deadline is still there, strong in my mind.

"I can promise you one thing," I say. My voice is trembling a bit. "I won't talk about breaking up with you any longer. I will keep things open and see what happens after twentieth of February. But you need to promise me one thing in return."

"What is that, *mi amor*?" he whispers. His arms tighten around me.

He cares. Maybe he still cares.

"Promise me that you won't talk about it, either. We won't

make plans. We won't discuss anything. Whatever happens, happens. If I agree to keep things open, you do too. No more plans. No discussions about when we're going to meet again or how. Nothing. *Nada*. We don't talk about it either way. OK?"

"OK, *mi amor*." He pulls me closer, the weight of my cast resting on his chest again. "I promise. We won't talk about it."

And then he kisses me and we can't talk about anything anyway.

Later he gets dressed and tells me he has to leave.

"Are you not staying?" My voice is trembling again. I know this tremble. It means I'm hurt. Damn him. I'm not going to let myself get hurt by this story. I'm not.

"No, I can't stay. I've agreed to meet some friends later. We are going out."

Ah, OK. I don't say anything else, just in case the tremble comes back in my voice again. Going out dancing, he means. Discos. I know how discos are in this country. And obviously he's not going to go to a disco with a woman with one arm in a cast.

"How about tomorrow? Will I see you?" I ask.

"I can't. I'm having lunch with a friend."

This time I don't say anything. He'll hear the tremble for sure and I can't risk that.

"*Linda*," he tells me, just before he goes. "Just give me a little bit of time, OK? I haven't got a switch to turn on my feelings immediately. But they will come back, I think. Just give me some time."

If he still calls me *linda*, it can't be that bad.

SUNDAY 24TH JANUARY

I'm having brunch with Juan. This time he's wearing a bright green t-shirt. He says he likes bright colors. He is fun. He is my age. He has been coming to Argentina for the winter every single year for about ten years. He's looking to buy a flat here. This idea has crossed my mind a few times, too.

He would be perfect for me. Gabriela would approve. Rosario would approve. He pays for brunch. Sol would approve too.

And yet. In my heart I think of someone else. And I really hope I'm not going to bump into that someone else as I walk around with Juan in Palermo. That someone else said he would be having lunch with his friend in Palermo, too. In my heart, two different desires fight each other: I want to see him. I don't want to see him. I can hardly concentrate on what Juan is talking about.

LATER THAT EVENING

I go out again with Andrea and the same group. Juan is there too. He sits next to me, buys me drinks, and talks to me nonstop.

We go to La Catedral, a place where people gather to dance tango. It's not clear why they call it La Catedral, because before it became a bohemian tango place the building used to be a grain silo, and then a refrigeration warehouse. We get there by 11, which is too early for dancing. It doesn't get animated until around 1:30.

The tango scene in Argentina doesn't get cooler than this. The building is run down, the chairs battered with worn-out covers. Half-torn tapestries hang on the walls. The ceiling seems miles away, maybe more than ten meters high, and the bare lights hanging from it on metal chains do little to penetrate the darkness. It's better that way, otherwise I'm sure I would spot cobwebs. Tourists and locals alike sit on broken chairs and drink Sangria or Fernet with Cola, or Campari Orange in my case. Or wine. Argentine red. And they dance.

Ever since my tango lesson I have longed to go back to the dance school, but it's impossible with an arm in the cast.

In my black evening dress I cross over the dance floor, casually carrying my arm in a sling. Nobody minds. Live and let live seems to be the mood.

I'm not here to dance. None of us are. It takes years of practice to be able to move like they do, swinging your heels around in that rhythm without breaking your ankles. It's all in the heel when dancing tango, they say. Women dance with their eyes closed. They probably feel that same flow my tango teacher was trying to describe. Men dance with their eyes wide open, as they're supposed to lead. No one struggles. Their movements flow as the music leads them. And it looks like they feel every single note.

Because they are like that, the Argentines. It finally hits me. They are not afraid to feel. Whatever comes, the good, the bad, the joy, the pain. They let it in and dance with it.

TUESDAY 26TH JANUARY

Santi is becoming a friend. He's been my Spanish teacher for two months now. I'm his first-ever student, he says. He had just started working in the school when I came. After a week of Curly Hair I got Santi, and I've kept him ever since.

It only took two days for Curly Hair to start flirting with me. After two months, Santi is still not flirting. To me that's great. To Andrea, it's unbelievable. All Argentines flirt, she says. They always flirt with her. They sometimes flirt with me, too. But not everyone. Santi isn't one of them. He is just fresh out of university with a degree in literature. This makes him about twenty-five years old. Older than Jonny. But unlike Jonny, he doesn't offer advice. He just listens.

I tell him about Rodrigo. I tell him the whole story during the conversation part of our two-hour session. He smiles. He suspected I'd fall in love here.

"I'm not in love, actually. It's only a bit of fun," I assure him.

He is still smiling. "We'll see about that."

I'd closed the windows of the classroom before I started to tell him the story. Outside in the courtyard the other teachers are smoking. I didn't want to risk Curly Hair eavesdropping on my romantic adventures.

The classroom is stifling. We can open them again, I think. There is nothing else to add.

As if he reads my thoughts, Santi gets up and opens the windows. Of course he reads minds. He's Argentine.

"Shall we continue with the verbs now?" he says.

I nod. No advice. No dos, no don'ts. None of that, "Argentine men are like this or like that." Nothing about *trust them* or *don't trust them*. He just listens with a wide smile on his face. What does he know about love anyway? He's only twenty-five.

My homework from that day onwards is to watch Argentine soap operas on TV. I'm not sure if this is Santi's plan to improve my Spanish or whether he's trying to help me build some basic knowledge of how Argentine men behave when in love.

WEDNESDAY 27TH JANUARY

I've been given three days' notice to vacate my apartment. That's because Argentines do things at the last minute. I'd initially rented the flat on Airbnb, then carried on paying cash to the landlady—sometimes weekly, sometimes every two weeks. I just carried on extending indefinitely, and she seemed fine with it.

Until one day, "Sorry, Roxana. You need to leave. At the end of the week. We need the flat back."

In the meantime I'd found out my landlady was not really the landlady. She'd been renting the flat from the real owner, but instead of living in it, she'd decided to put it on Airbnb to make some extra income. It was the owner—the real owner—who wanted the flat back, because his son was getting married and he would be living there with his new wife.

I search for other flats on Airbnb and ask around. No one has anything. It's too short notice. I only have three days to sort this out. I also only have three more days until I'm out of my cast. On Friday I'm going back to the hospital—the same hospital where they put it on. I can't believe six weeks have passed already.

Andrea doesn't know of any available flats. Airbnb proves useless. Some don't respond, some tell me it's too short notice. I need to move somewhere on Friday and I need this new place for three weeks. To some it's a lot, to others too little.

Rodrigo is nowhere to be found. He has no idea of my struggles. His texts are short. No *linda*, and nothing about when we will meet next.

He's probably still looking for that damn switch to turn his feelings back on.

Gabriela is in Europe, Patricio back at the farm. I know I can go back to them any time I want, and they will welcome me. This fall-back option makes me feel better as I search and search and search for a place, silently wondering, *what am I doing here*?

Yes. The old question is back.

THURSDAY 28TH JANUARY

I'm getting another taxi. This time, a woman is driving. In almost three months in Buenos Aires, this is the first time I've seen a woman taxi driver.

"Where are you from?"

Three months here and they can still tell I'm foreigner after just a couple of words.

I tell her my story.

"Are you single?" This is no different to the question a male taxi driver would ask. Same questions, same order.

"Sort of," I say. "Actually I'm not really sure. Maybe not."

"Look, let me give you some friendly advice. Don't fall for an Argentine. It's not worth it. The men here are not serious. Yes, they're charming and handsome but they are not serious. Do you understand? Don't believe them. Whatever they say, don't believe them."

If one more person tells me not to trust an Argentine man I think I'm going to explode.

Later that day, I've found it. A new apartment, ten minutes from where I was renting, still in Palermo and closer to Plaza Serrano, which is the center of everything in Palermo. I feel great. It has a swimming pool. And a washing machine. And I will use both. My cast comes off tomorrow and I'll dive straight into the swimming pool. I can't imagine how I'll feel without it. After six weeks it has become part of my body.

With nothing else to do for the rest of the day, I lie down on the sofa to watch a soap opera on TV. I'm taking Santi's homework seriously.

Ping. Message. Rodrigo.

It's your last night in the flat, right? How about I come over? We can have a last dinner there.

My heart beats fast. *OK.*

He comes. We hardly speak. We head straight into the bedroom and make love, and it feels like before. Maybe he found the switch.

Later, Rodrigo holds me in his arms and tells me about his troubles with his car. Something about a garage not being able to sort out the clutch, or maybe another piece of the engine, I'm not sure. I'm never quite sure where the clutch is and what it does anyway.

His voice is serious. I think he actually feels in pain.

I try to laugh. "Come on, it's just a car. They'll sort it out."

"No, *mi amor.* It's my car. I love my car."

"Like you love a person, you mean?"

"Like it's important. Very important. A car is very important to an Argentine man."

"Ah, yes? And what else is important to an Argentine man?"

"Football. And women."

"In this particular order?" I'm no longer sure if I'm amused.

"The order depends. On the car. Or on the woman. Or what happened at the last football game. The priority varies, but this is what an Argentine man will talk about when he meets with another Argentine man."

"Cars, football, and women?" I repeat.

"Precisely. And right now my car is in trouble and I can't take my mind off it."

I'm not sure what type of car he drives. All I remember is that it's red. I've no idea what model. And I don't know anything about football anyway. But I know one thing. When we make love there are no cars, nor football on his mind.

He stays the night and for the first time we talk long into the night. Well past midnight. I find out that in football he's a fan of River Plate. It's so strange to hear the name in English, rather than Rio de la Plata, but even though it's an Argentine club, everybody calls it River Plate. Rodrigo tells me this is an important piece of information, something critical to his identity, and that alliances to football clubs in this city are often passed down the family line. Being a River fan or a Boca fan is one of the most important decisions a man can make. One usually inherits this allegiance, but there are men who break from the family tradition and become a fan of the other club if they feel in their heart that they belong there.

I commit this to my memory. River Plate. I may not know what car he drives, but I should at least remember this. Thank God the football player I kissed that night in the disco was from Boca. At least I think he was, since we met in La Boca. It doesn't matter, anyway. The football player vanished long ago and I'm in Rodrigo's arms and we talk in the darkness, in the last night I'll ever spend in the apartment that was my first real home here. Then we make love again, and at 4:30 precisely the alarm goes off on his phone. Time to go to work. How does he do it? I wonder sleepily, as he whispers *linda* in my ear and gives me a good-bye kiss. His lips are soft.

Maybe it's possible things can work out for us, after all, I think, before falling back to sleep the moment he's gone.

FRIDAY 29TH JANUARY

Rodrigo leaves without offering any help, though. The night before he asked me where I was moving. I told him. Then he said I could have come to stay in his flat if I wanted, for the remainder of my time in Buenos Aires. I didn't tell him I'd been waiting for him to offer and I'd got really angry when he didn't. Instead I told him it was too far away. Not that I knew exactly where his place was, but a one-hour drive from Buenos Aires wasn't what I had in mind. He told me he could see my point and didn't insist. And then he didn't offer to help with the move. No offer to take me to the hospital to take my cast off, either. Just nothing.

So I do it all alone. Actually with the help of Jorge, a driver who occasionally works for Gabriela. Even though she's far away in Switzerland, she's still looking after me from a distance, making sure there are people around to help me out.

My cast comes off. Under it, my arm is shrunken. My muscles are gone. A huge blue bruise is still visible. My skin has come off in layers like the shredded skin of a snake. It looks horrible. I can't move it. My wrist is frozen.

"But it's fine," the doctor says, looking at the new set of x-rays. "The bone has healed well. Go and do some physio and the wrist will move again."

I'm back to square one but I'm grateful, so grateful. He hadn't cut my arm, so I have no scar.

"We have no screws here," he'd told me at the time. "We don't need to cut if we have no screws." He'd used only his knowledge and experience to put the bone back so that it healed properly.

And as hard as it is to believe, my ugly, bruised, and stiff hand is actually perfectly healed. Without screws.

"Thank you."

"*De nada,*" he answers. "I'm glad it worked out well. We have a lot of polo injuries here, you know. We've even seen Cambiaso a few times in this hospital."

"Oh. I feel honored to share the hospital with Cambiaso."

"He's just one of many."

Many other polo players, he means. For a second I wonder how many more he's seen. Talking about broken bones is common in polo.

I ask him if there's anything to pay. He says no. Then I remember what Gabriela told me after my fall. That all the treatment at the hospital had been free. The ambulance, the anaesthetic, the nurses who dressed and undressed me, the x-rays, the doctor who put my bones together in a miracle surgery without any surgery. All of it.

I didn't believe her then. I suspected she and Patricio had paid for it and wouldn't tell me. I insisted, until she told me she was "fucking telling me the truth."

"This is Argentina healthcare. It's free here."

"Free for Argentines," I said. "I'm a foreigner."

"Free for everyone."

And this is what this doctor is telling me now, again.

"It was a pleasure," he says. "And it is free. Welcome to Argentina. We may not have screws," he added, pointing to the marks from the previous surgery on my other wrist. "But we still know how to put a bone back together."

A lot better than with screws, I thought, looking at my right arm with no scars. A lot better.

And a lot faster too. In England, when I broke my two arms it took about five hours in the emergency unit of a hospital to be seen by a doctor and put in a cast. Here, it took ten minutes from when I entered the hospital door until I found myself on the surgery table.

"Thank you," I repeat. A kiss on the cheek does the rest. Because we are in Argentina. People kiss, even in hospitals. And people don't spend too much time with formal thanks.

"You're welcome. *No pasa nada*."

SATURDAY 30TH JANUARY

Rodrigo doesn't even call to find out how my appointment at the hospital has gone. It's the last straw for me. To make matters worse, he suggests meeting at midnight.

"What are you doing before that?" I ask, irritated.

"Working," he says. He tells me he's taken a second job at the Spanglish language exchange event where I met him.

"So what do you have to do for that?"

He tells me he's in charge of the organization. Sitting people at tables, announcing when they need to change languages, making sure they move around after ten minutes and so on.

"By midnight I should be free," he says.

I'm still irritated, so I arrange to go out with other people first. Flirty Juan is still messaging me but has left town already. He's gone to the coast to spend a few days on the beach but will be back soon. He says he would love to take me out for dinner when he's back. Even if he's not available now, others are. There are always others available for a good night out in Buenos Aires.

I go to a *milonga*, a tango party, organized by the tango school where I took my lesson before I broke my arm. With my arm out of a cast I'm looking forward to some more lessons, and their tango students' *milonga* seems the right place to start.

I meet new people and chat freely. I don't dance, because I'm not able to. But at 11:45 I find myself with an Australian guy and a German girl having a drink on a terrace in Palermo, a couple of streets away from the bar where I'm supposed to be meeting Rodrigo at midnight. The Australian is a top executive in a big tech company who has taken a three-month sabbatical to think about his career options. He came to Buenos Aires, rented himself a flat and decided to use the time to learn tango. A bit like me with polo, only that tango doesn't usually result in broken bones. The German girl is between two jobs and backpacking throughout South America for a couple of months. She's only here for three days and had decided to try out a tango *milonga* because everyone passing through Buenos Aires should try out a *milonga*. So says the guide book.

To go or not to go. That's the question swinging in my mind with the precise rhythm of a pendulum. To go or not to go . . .

11:30 pm. They order more drinks. They're talking about going on to a disco. Disco. This is where they dance cumbia or maybe reggaeton and kiss as they dance. Rodrigo or disco? This is my choice. And what if I go to the disco with them?

11:52 pm. It will teach him a lesson if I don't meet him as promised. He didn't call to ask how my hospital appointment went. He doesn't care. He didn't offer to help me move my stuff. I had to ask Jorge to do it. If he cared he would have offered to help me.

11:55 pm. No, I won't go. I can't possibly. I—

My body moves without my permission. It simply jumps off the chair with an urgency that shocks me.

"Where are you going?" They both look at me, not understanding what's going on.

I don't understand either. My body wants to go and it has taken control.

"I have to go. Now. Sorry." I glance at my watch. "I need to meet someone."

"Now?" The Australian guy stares at me in disbelief. "Who on earth are you meeting now?"

"Sorry. I have to go," I repeat. "Enjoy the disco. They dance cumbia in discos here. Or maybe reggaeton," I add. And they kiss while they dance, I think, but don't say it. Let them find out for themselves.

"Just like Cinderella, she disappears at midnight!" They laugh.

"I'm sure there's a man behind this," the girl says.

I leave. Actually I try to catch up with my body, which is already running like a lunatic down the streets of Buenos Aires at midnight to make sure I get there, in that bar down the street, just in time. Because a guy with deep brown eyes asked me to be there and I simply couldn't say no.

SUNDAY 31ST JANUARY

I arrive out of breath. Three minutes past twelve. He isn't here. For a second I think maybe he's come and gone, but that seems unlikely. Argentines don't take time that seriously.

I walk around and then sit down at a table, but I can't stay there long. I feel restless and I walk around some more. He's still not there. I'm starting to get more and more annoyed. I'm checking my phone every other second. No message from him.

What if he doesn't come at all and I'm here like an imbecile still waiting for him? Where's Marco? I need Marco. This is serious enough that I need to talk to him. But I can't remember what country he's in, and so I can't calculate if it's too late to call.

Rodrigo shows up at exactly ten minutes past twelve. I'm already furious after seven full minutes of waiting. Polo has taught me what seven minutes mean. An eternity. A chukka in polo lasts for seven and a half minutes. It's a lifetime when you are on the horse in the middle of the action. A lot can happen in this time. You can win or lose the game, break arms or not. You can break up with someone or not. Actually, another half a minute and I would probably have gone.

I don't care that it's only seven minutes. I'm already trembling with rage when I see him. And I don't care that it may seem irrational. I don't even care exactly why I'm feeling that furious, and why all this rage has decided to come out of me right now because of these seven minutes of waiting.

"Where the hell have you been?"

"*Tranquila,* I'm here. It's twelve, isn't it?"

"It's ten past twelve."

"Same thing. It's still twelve, not a big deal. Sorry I couldn't leave earlier. I had to sort out some things at the last minute and it took ages. But I'm here now. *No pasa nada.*"

"The hell with *no pasa nada.*"

I have never been so furious with him.

He offers to buy me a drink. It still doesn't calm me down. I wait for him to get back from the bar and then with the Campari Orange in my hand I say it all.

How he hasn't called me once. Not one single call to ask how I've been doing these last few days. My arm came out of the cast yesterday, and he didn't even call to find out how that went. He didn't offer to drive me to the hospital, to be there with me. He doesn't care. He doesn't give a fuck.

And the flat. I carry on with all the rage that's built up inside me.

"You didn't give a shit about the fact I had to move. You didn't think I might need some help. Do you have any idea how hard it is to move three huge suitcases with one hand in a cast? Thank God Gabriela's driver came to help me out. And I don't care, you hear me, I don't care about your bloody light switch. The one you've lost. You'd better find it or go to hell. With or without that switch."

He listens to me in silence and suggests that maybe we should go home. The noisy bar makes it difficult to have a proper conversation. Is he shocked? I don't know. I don't care either. There are too many things bottled up inside waiting to come out.

We go, but I'm still trembling with rage. By the time we reach my flat I've calmed down and I just feel immensely tired. I look at him. He looks tired too, and sad. Very sad. In the short time I've known him I've learned that he's not very good at hiding his emotions. There's no *linda*, no kissing, and there will be no making love either tonight. Just two tired people who have lost the light switch and have no idea how to find their way back in darkness.

Still he tries a timid *linda*. I'm not impressed. I tell him he can go to hell and take his *lindas* too.

And then he explodes. He tells me that I don't understand anything. That I'm here on holiday without a care in the world. All I'm worrying about is where I'm going to go out, how much fun I'm going to have, and when I can play polo next, so I can break more bones. That people have a life here. That he has a job to do. That he has been working double shifts this week because a colleague at work had been injured and he had to cover for the guy as well. That the country has gone mad. That the electricity prices have gone up forty percent in the last week. That inflation is skyrocketing.

"Have you got any idea how hard it is to live in this country? Have you?" he shouts at me.

I haven't, actually. So I say nothing.

"Can you understand that what's happening right now in this country is crazy? That we voted this new president with big hopes and now it's all going to hell? No one understands what the fuck this guy is doing!"

He is now pacing up and down in my living room. I've never seen him so angry.

"Do you understand that there's more to life than going out and playing polo?" he shouts.

I had never heard him shout until now, either. His voice trembles with emotion, but he hasn't finished.

"Do you understand that the prices for the highway tolls have doubled overnight and no one can do anything about it? Do you understand? No one!"

"Why no one?"

"Because this is how things are in this country. Screwed up!"

A deep breath and then the last frustration comes out in an accusatory tone.

"And all you care about is if I'm ten minutes late going out."

I had no idea about any of these things he is talking about. I've not been reading the newspapers. I'm indeed here to party and to play polo. To recover my wrist, to see the Abierto, to fall in love. Ah, no. Not to fall in love. I forgot I erased that.

We both stare at each other in silence. There's nothing else to say. His look tells me he is a million miles away and has no intention of coming back. Ever.

"Maybe I should go home now." He sounds tired.

"Yes. Maybe you should go home now," I agree.

He leaves. This time, I'm sure I will never see him again.

February

MONDAY 1ST FEBRUARY

Marco is in town this week. I'm not sure how it happens, but it does. He simply shows up in my life whenever I need him. Actually, he'd told me two weeks ago when we spoke on the phone that he would be coming over for a short business trip, but I'd forgotten. Things are never definite with Marco. He may show up or not. Plans change, flights get delayed, business calls him elsewhere. It's like this, his life: planes, hotels, airports. Always on the go.

We meet for dinner. I'm looking at him in desparation over the table. I can't speak Italian any longer. I try. I say a few words and then they end up being Spanish. I try again. Impossible. In my mind, Spanish has taken over and completely and utterly defeated the rival Italian. I can't believe it's gone, but it is. My mind is blank.

He laughs. "Speak Spanish, then. It's OK."

I can't speak Spanish to Marco. I have always spoken Italian to him. I try, but I can't.

"English then, anything you like. Just talk to me."

English saves me in the end. I tell him the latest developments in my love story. Not really a love story, only-supposed-to-be-fun story.

This time there's no more encouragement. No more warm voice on the phone. No more "Go to his place tonight," no more advice as to the type of messages I should send him to get him back. Marco has reverted back to his cynical self.

"Roxy, listen. It is time you wake up from this . . . let's call it infatuation. A few weeks of it is OK. But it's been longer than that now. I have no time to listen to this nonsense any more."

"But Marco, how about if it's possible?"

"*Amore*." Even when we speak English, Marco is still Italian. He calls me *amore* with the same friendly ease with which taxi drivers here call me *mi amor*. To be honest, I prefer *amore* to *imbecille*.

"If it's possible to do what, exactly? Can you elaborate?" His voice has that hint of amusement I know so well. He knows what I mean and I know he's losing patience.

"To, well . . . to be with him."

"You're telling me he just left again yesterday. It doesn't sound like the two of you left each other on the best of terms. Maybe that's it, this time. Maybe you'll never hear from him again."

"No. He'll be back." I'm utterly shocked at my fresh conviction. I've got no idea where it came from. "Well, I think so anyway. I think that's just the way he is. Emotional."

"They all are," Marco says with a sigh. "Argentine men. Drama kings. Worse than their TV dramas. And it's not that they get their inspiration from soap operas. Here, in this country, it's the other way round. Their real lives inspire their soap operas."

Yes, emotions seem to run high here. I think of the soap operas I've been watching on Santi's instructions. They're just one long series of breakups, make-ups, more breakups, more make-ups. "Happily ever after" has the shape of a rollercoaster here.

"But anyway, let's go back to your infatuation. What exactly do you have in mind when you say to 'be with him'?"

"Well . . . you know."

"No, I don't. Can you explain?"

"Marco, don't be silly."

"You are the silly one, my dear. And this story with your . . . uh . . . toyboy. It's about time it ended."

"Don't call him that."

"How much younger did you say he was?"

"It doesn't matter."

"Since when does it not matter?"

"I'm not quite sure."

Thankfully I have to stop here, because the waitress is ready to take our order. The process takes ten minutes and I use the whole time to prepare my line of defense on why the age thing doesn't matter any longer.

"So what are you planning to do with him?" Marco comes back to his question once the stiff waitress with the bored air is done taking our order.

We are back at the same pizzeria where we met last time. Marco is right, they do really good pizzas here.

"I don't know. I think we should go somewhere on a short break. You know, like a mini-holiday. Somewhere hot and relaxing. I'm thinking the seaside."

Marco looks at me as if I'm out of my mind. "That is, if he ever texts you again."

"Yes, if he does. He will."

"And even if he does, do you really think going on holiday is the answer?"

The answer to what? I think silently. To fixing this relationship? To trying to bridge a gap between two incompatible lives? Rodrigo thinks my life is shallow—he made that pretty clear to me—but am I ready to give it up for him?

I keep quiet but this doesn't stop Marco from rubbing it in a bit more.

"Roxy, haven't you had enough of these ups and downs? Don't you think it's about time you woke up and got back to your life? Look, your arm is out of its cast. Two more weeks and you can get on that plane."

"Three weeks."

"Same thing. You get on that plane. You go back to London, you get a new project. You need to work. You need to earn some money. You get that hand moving again. You even go back to your polo if you really want to. But you go back to your place in the world."

"And what is my place in the world?" I ask. I'm not quite sure any longer.

"Your place, *amore*, is like my place. It's no place. We don't have a place. We get a new project, we deliver it. We go where it takes us. Then we get another project and we do that one. We make money. We spend money. We live well. We travel. We work. We move. That is exactly the point. We don't have a place."

He is right. This is his life. Living in hotels, traveling to three countries in a week. I'd done it too, for a long time. Too long. Management consultants. Our dream when we were studying together for that MBA degree, fifteen years ago. We had achieved it, and we were living this dream. Only it didn't seem like much of a dream any longer.

Marco was divorced, with two kids who were living with their mother on the other side of South America. He was traveling the world, living in hotels, juggling eight-hour flights to get to see his kids at the weekend. No time for any romance. I, on the other hand, was getting good projects in London for big-name companies and making lots of money. Spending all the money I was making on luxury holidays, travel, and polo. Breaking arms and recovering arms. No time for romance, either.

We've both achieved our dream of fifteen years ago. We have the lifestyle of jet setters. We are the envy of many. And nobody but us knows the true loneliness of our worlds. Problem is, this world has a strong grip on him, as it does on me. It isn't easy to leave it.

"You go back to floating, darling. In your world. And your world is not his world. He doesn't float. He's stuck in his maintenance department in a factory that produces cables. He in his world, and you in your world. And in three weeks' time you board that plane and it will take you back to your world. The world you belong to."

"And what if I don't want it any longer?" I whisper.

"Well, you'll have to find something else to replace it with. And it doesn't look to me that staying here with this guy is the answer."

The pizza arrives. Napolitana for me, with big round slices of fresh tomatoes. I love how they do pizza in Buenos Aires, with lots of cheese and a thicker crust than in Italy, but not so thick that Marco might refuse to eat it. But I don't feel like eating any longer. I have tears in my eyes. Marco is right. He's always right.

"It's OK, Roxy. The holiday is almost over. Talk to him if you want. Text him. Call him. Go to the seaside with him, if you want. It doesn't matter. Whatever you do, you know you'll board that plane and you'll go back to your life."

"But Marco, two weeks ago you told me I didn't know what would happen after the twentieth of February."

"Yes, I did." He sighs. "Because it's nice to live a story like this when it comes. It's refreshing. It's different. But then you need to wake up. And deep down in your heart you know it. And I know it too. You'll go back to your world. And all there will be left of this story will be the memory of a holiday fling. A summer romance. Nothing more."

I hate him. I really hate him right now as he sits there in front of me, slowly sipping his glass of red wine. There's nothing else left to say.

Yes, I will go back. I'll be sad for a while. He'll be there for me, just a phone call away. Like he has always been, in case I need a shoulder to cry on. There's nothing else to do but go back to my world while Rodrigo stays here, in his world.

I hate Marco because he's right.

TUESDAY 2ND FEBRUARY

Rodrigo sends me a text message to say he's sorry. He wants to see me. He's stressed out, he says. He's been working double shifts and the occasional job at Spanglish on top of it. He needs a holiday. Next weekend is a long weekend and he's off on Monday and Tuesday. Why don't we go away?

But the discussion with Marco is still going around my head. Rodrigo has no idea another volcano is about to erupt.

We need to talk. I text him back. *When are you back from work?*

He calls me straightaway. In the background I can hear the noise of heavy machinery.

"Are you still at work? We can talk later. I don't want to disturb you at work."

"No, let's talk now." His voice is cold. "I can't carry on working knowing there's something we need to talk about."

I spill it out again. It's the same story as last time. About how he didn't help with my move. How he's not the same. He is distant. I can feel there's something in the air. We are arguing all the time. I'm not happy. Not happy, really not happy any longer. Maybe there's someone else? Another woman?

"Don't be silly. There is no other woman."

Yes, there is, I can feel it. I can feel it in his energy field. I know when a man pulls back. I tell him I can feel he's not really there any more.

"Yes, I've pulled back, that's true," he says. "When you told me there's no way we can be together after you leave, I pulled back. I don't want to be hurt."

"And I don't want to be hurt, either," I shout back. "That's why I did it. Because . . . I just can't, can't carry on like this. Because I don't want to be hurt, and look, I'm hurt and I don't want this any more. Not any more."

"You don't want what any more?"

I ignore his question and carry on with my incoherent complaints. "And you don't treat me right. You never pay for meals, we always split the bill, and it's not supposed to be like this in Argentina."

"No, it's not. We split the bills because you are European."

"What?" I can't believe what I'm hearing. "So what if I'm European? Does that mean I'm I supposed to pay? Am I less worthy to be bought dinner than an Argentine woman?"

"Don't be silly. It's because I don't want to offend you."

"What?"

"European women like to pay the bill fifty-fifty. They are offended if a man offers to pay for them."

"Who told you this?"

"My cousin. He knows. He's married to a German and lives with her in Europe."

I take a deep breath. "Not everyone in Europe is like that. I come from a Latin country, for God's sake. Men pay for women when they take them out in my country."

"And how am I supposed to know? All I know about Europeans is from my cousin. I've never dated one."

"What else did he say?"

"Only this. That I should split the bill. Ah, and that I shouldn't send too many messages or call too often. European women are independent. He said they get annoyed if you call them too often."

I would pull his cousin's eyes out one by one if he were in front of me right now. Bloody idiot.

I'm not quite sure where this discussion is going. Rodrigo isn't sure, either.

"Look, I want to see you," he says. "I want to go away with you next weekend. We have less than three weeks left before you go. Let's not spend them arguing."

"Rodrigo, do you love me?"

I can't believe I asked this question. Someone else must have entered my body and opened my mouth and let those words out. Completely against my will.

The words hang there in the silence. I would give anything in the world to be able to take them back.

"Yes I do," he says after a while. "I didn't mean to. I really didn't mean to fall in love."

Silence again. I'm not breathing.

"But it happened," he finishes.

WEDNESDAY 3RD FEBRUARY

The owner of my new flat gives me one day's notice to vacate the property. The notice comes via text message. The deal was supposed to cover the three weeks I had left in Argentina. But the owner has received a better offer, someone who wants to stay for two months. So I get told I have to vacate the property by noon that day. I have only been here a week, which isn't even enough time to feel properly at home.

I stare in shock at the screen of my phone. I'm in Sol's salon, having my hair done. My hand has been out of its cast for five days, but it's still stiff, so I'm still coming to Sol every other day to have my hair done. I'm starting to think that this is one of the best things that has happened to me in Argentina.

I tell Sol my landlord is breaking up with me via a text message.

"Typical," she says. "Argentine men. They will let you down because they have found someone better. Just like that. They will drop you in a blink of an eye. They all do it. I told you not to trust them."

"Sol, this is my landlord. Not my lover."

"Same, all the same." She dismisses them with a wave of her hair straighteners. "I've seen it all. Don't trust them. Don't rely on them."

"Even when they tell you they love you?"

"Especially when they tell you they love you." She narrows her eyes suspiciously. "Why, what's happened now?"

"Oh, nothing," I say casually. "Just wondering."

I'm not going to tell her about the conversation I had with Rodrigo yesterday. About how embarrassing the silence felt after he told me he'd fallen in love against his will. About how I couldn't open my mouth to say anything. Not a word. And how he then said "Anyway, it's very noisy here. Shall we talk later?"

We hung up. We didn't talk later.

I wonder if he's still waiting for me to say something back.

I'm not going to explain all this to Sol. It would take too long, plus I have an emergency to deal with. I need to find a place to move to by the end of today.

I call Patricio as soon as I get out of Sol's shop. Why him? Because he's Patricio. Because I know that whatever happens to me in Argentina, I can call him and he'll have an answer for me. And because he's told me a hundred times already to pick up the phone if I need something. Anything.

I do it now. I haven't seen him for a month. He was in the south of the country visiting his sister with his family, then he went back to the farm in Lobos. Right now he's on his way to the airport to pick up Gabriela, who is returning from Europe once again. Ah God, how I've missed that girl and her constant "fucks" every other word.

"*Cómo estás*, Roxy?"

I tell him I'm on the street. Literally. I have to vacate my flat in a few hours and I'm not quite sure where to go. Any ideas?

Of course he has ideas. "Come to ours."

"Not Lobos. It's too far. I need to be in Buenos Aires."

"Come to our place in Buenos Aires, then."

It turns out they have a flat in the city. They, as in the whole family. Currently one of his sisters is using it. The same sister who found me sleeping in her bed.

"Let me talk to her to find out what her plans are. I'll call you back."

"But Patricio, I can't kick your sister out of her own flat. Not again, after I've already kicked her out of her bedroom."

"Nonsense. *No pasa nada.* I'll call you back. Let me find out whether she's there or not. If not, I'll send you a pair of keys via the bus that comes from Lobos this afternoon. Don't worry, one way or another you'll have a place to go to."

He calls me back half an hour later. His sister is in the flat waiting for me. He says she'll give me the keys and leave the flat to me.

"Was she going to use it? I can't have her leaving Buenos Aires and giving the flat to me just because I need a place to stay!"

"*No pasa nada.* Don't worry." He hangs up and texts me her number. *Call her now*, he instructs.

They are like this, the Argentines. They talk a lot until a friend is in trouble. When that happens, there's no need for words. They just act.

I call his sister and agree to move in that very afternoon with my two suitcases and my two-meter-long polo gear bag, which holds five mallets and the rest of my polo equipment. I've also got various plastic bags filled with all the stuff I've bought here—food, drinks, toiletries, detergents, one yoga mat, and a huge blue Pilates roll. A full household.

LATER THAT DAY

I go to physio before changing flats. With my arm out of its cast, I have resumed my once-a-day physio sessions. I do them with the same therapists, in the same rooms, and we're doing the same exercises. It's ridiculous.

"At least you know what to do now," my therapist says encouragingly. "Exactly the same exercises, but with the other wrist. You're an expert now."

Yes, I am. The good thing about having gone through this before is that I'm absolutely sure my wrist will move again. I'll make sure it does.

I'm still doing my wrist exercises when the second text message of the day arrives. It's even shorter than the one about the flat. It's one sentence only. *Te amo.* I love you. No signature. No need for it. I know where it comes from.

I stare in shock at the screen and then I close it and put the phone away. I don't answer. Not then and not for the rest of the day.

I pack my bags. I call Jorge to help me carry them. I meet Patricio's sister and get the keys from her. I tell her I'm very embarrassed to intrude and hope she wasn't planning to stay a few days in Buenos Aires. I get the "*no pasa nada*" reply, and that she had been intending to go back to Lobos today, anyway. I kind of doubt it.

I then call Patricio to thank him. He dismisses me and puts me through to Gabriela, who has just landed.

"*Hola*, darling, how the fuck have you been? We need to catch up. I need to know all about your love affairs—and your hand? How is your hand?"

I sigh. Yes we are definitely due a catch up.

We have a long chat, then I unpack my bags and find a place for everything in my new home. Even the huge blue Pilates roll somehow fits in. In a few hours, it feels like I've got a new home. I do some more wrist exercises, answer some emails and review my verb charts. I do all these things and everything else I can possibly think of, but there is one thing I make sure I don't do. I don't answer that message.

THURSDAY 4TH FEBRUARY

He calls in the morning. He doesn't mention the message. I don't mention it, either. I tell him about the flat, the emergency move and Patricio saving the day.

"You could have come to stay here at my place," he says. "You know that, right?"

Yes, I know, he said that before, but it's too far from the city.

I tell him I'm fine now and that I'll stay a few days here and then find another place.

"Why look for another place? You have only two weeks left. Why not stay where you are for the rest of your time here?"

"I don't want to intrude. They have been so nice to me."

"Nonsense," he says. "They are your friends. They won't let you leave. You'll see."

I have a feeling he's right, and I'm really not confortable with occupying their flat any longer. But then he changes the topic abruptly, and now there's something new for me to worry about.

"So, what are we doing? Are we going somewhere this weekend?"

At least he hasn't mentioned the text message. This is good. I'm not prepared to talk about that text message. The problem is, I'm not prepared to talk about going away for the weekend, either.

"I don't know. I'm not sure it's a good idea. Four days is a long time. We've never spent four days together."

"Precisely."

"And what if we don't get on? What if we argue?"

"We'll find out."

"Maybe it would be better not to push it."

"*Mi amor*, listen."

He hasn't called me *mi amor* for a while. Perhaps now he'll mention the text message. My body tenses.

"We've got only two weeks left. We can use this time now and go somewhere together, or we can spend the rest of our lives wondering whether we'd have got on."

"But even so, where would we go?"

He tells me we could go to the seaside. I tell him I've heard Uruguay, the neighboring country, has a better seaside than Argentina. The sea is much warmer. That isn't surprising, since Argentina's sea is freezing. Uruguay has fewer windy beaches too, which again is not surprising. I still remember the sandstorm-on-the-beach experience I had in Mar de Las Pampas two years ago. Plus, there are lots of parties on the beach, but then Argentina has that, too. If there's one thing Argentina is not lagging behind in, it's parties.

"Let's go to Uruguay then," he says matter of factly, as if we were talking about going to the supermarket next door.

"Just like that?"

"Yes, why not?"

I'm still not convinced. This was the very thing I suggested to Marco, the very thing I've been dreaming of, but now that it's actually happening I have cold feet. So many reasons why this isn't such a good idea pop up in my head. We haven't got anything planned. It's too last minute. And I don't really know him. I tell him all this and he can probably hear the doubt in my voice.

"Let's do one thing," he says calmly. "Let's hang up now. You think about it. Take all day to think about it. Tonight I'll call you again. Let's say at 8 pm. And you can give me your answer then. If you say yes, we leave tomorrow."

"Can you wait until tonight? Is it not too late for you to know?"

"*No pasa nada, mi amor.* It's just a weekend away. Of course I can wait until tonight."

Argentine. Likes to keep the future open. Must be a by-product of the *después vemos* phrase, I guess.

LATER THAT DAY

I'm sipping a coffee on a terrace in the sunshine. It's hot, very hot. I like it, though. After thirteen years of British weather, I'd take hot over cold every time.

I'm thinking about Uruguay. Punta del Este, the posh party resort on the seaside everyone says I should see. Andrea loved it. She said it was the playground for the rich and famous. I'm not that convinced I'll like it. I've seen the world of the rich and famous. It's not my world. I still have no idea which one is my world. Maybe Marco's right and we have no world. Maybe our world is just an empty concept, a sort of floating device in between other worlds . . .

My thoughts are interrupted by a cute dog, a boxer, who decides to stop and sit by my leg. There's something about dogs and my legs. They like leaning against my legs. Whenever I stop to pat a dog, he'll want to rub against my legs.

This one doesn't rub. He just sits there patiently as if stuck. I look around for his owner, then I spot him. He's an Octopus. I mean a professional dog walker. I call them Octopuses.

Dog walkers are a common sight in Buenos Aires. They are licensed by the City Hall and their license is valid for up to twenty dogs of one size only. There are licences for small dogs, medium dogs, and big dogs. Hence all dog-walkers walk around with a pack of similar-sized dogs. They go around collecting dogs from houses like a school bus collects kids to go to school. They walk them to one of the parks, where the dogs can find a little bit of grass, run, play, and socialize with other dogs. Then they go back through the busy roads and return the dogs home one by one. There are many of these dog walkers in the city. Argentines love to have a dog, even when they live in a block of flats and have no time to walk them.

One can spot dog walkers all over the city, with their pack of dogs all around them. It is a weird sight, like an octopus with many arms—the human in the middle, and all the dogs on leashes, distributed in a perfect circle all around them. That's why I call them Octopuses. A stange creature, floating down the streets of Buenos Aires.

The cute dog beside me is not on a leash. Therefore he can ignore the orders of the Octopus. He has decided my legs are a better option, and he clearly doesn't want to go anywhere.

"He likes it here," I tell the guy.

The dog walker gives me a frank look, up and down.

"I don't blame him. I wouldn't move from there either, if I were him."

Argentine. Of course he will think of something funny to say. I simply can't feel offended.

Then he asks me where I'm from. The same old irritation bubbles up inside me that Santi has still not sorted out my accent. And the same pleasure washes over me, the pleasure that comes from talking to a handsome man who seems very interested in everything I have to say.

He asks for my phone number. Just like that, casually. I hesitate.

"Why don't you give me yours instead?" I say.

He writes his name and phone number on my coffee napkin.

"Please call me," he says before he goes. "I'd really like to see you again."

As he leaves I stare at the napkin with his name and number. I'm not sure what I'll do with it. But it doesn't matter right now. I only need a backup. If it goes badly with Rodrigo on this trip I'm about to agree to, I need the reassurance there'll be another man who'll want to see me. "There will be another one," as the launderette man says. Curly Hair hasn't texted since he saw my arm in a cast, and Juan, the sexy Spaniard who cut my pizza into small pieces and repeatedly invited me to dinner, is still out of town.

So I think a handsome dog walker will do as a fallback option.

And at 8 pm that evening, with the name and number of the Octopus safely tucked into my pocket, I find the courage to tell Rodrigo that I want to go with him to Uruguay tomorrow.

FRIDAY 5TH FEBRUARY

I wake up in a panic. What was I thinking? Why did I tell him I wanted to go? It's going to go wrong. It's a terrible idea. We haven't even got anything planned, not even hotel accommodation. It's a long weekend here, and everyone will be on the coast. There's no way we'll find a room. And then, Rodrigo, well, we don't really know each other. The longest we've ever spent together is twenty-four hours. Maybe Gabriela and Patricio are right to worry about this guy. And why does he want to go away with me, anyway? Doesn't he have anything better to do with this life?

I call him and tell him maybe it's not such a good idea to go. He's at work. I can hear the same sound of heavy machinery in the background.

"*Tranquila*," he says. "It'll be OK. Trust me. *Linda*."

It's the *linda* that does it. As usual I can't resist this word. I relax. I can't worry about anything when he calls me *linda*.

"But still, the hotels?"

"We'll find something. Have a look if you can find something online. I'm at work until late today."

"And how do we get there?"

"We drive. Don't worry."

"How long does it take?"

"Eleven hours."

"What?"

"About eleven hours," he repeats. "We'll leave tonight and drive through the night. Tomorrow morning we'll be there."

"But you are at work today."

"I'll finish work about 4 pm. Then I'll go home and have a few hours' sleep. Then I'll come to pick you up, around 8, and we'll start driving. By morning we'll be there."

Fresh alarm bells start to ring. A night-long drive. And he probably doesn't understand I can't drive here.

"But Rodrigo, I . . . I can't help you with the driving. I'm not used to driving on this side of the road. In London we drive on the left."

"I know. Don't worry, I'll drive. *No pasa nada*."

We hang up. I call Patricio next with the surge of adrenaline still in my body. I'm really not sure this is a good idea.

"What's up, Roxy? All fine in the flat?"

"Yes, perfect. Thanks. Listen, I have another problem. I need to ask for some advice."

"*Qué pasa* this time?" He sounds amused.

I take a deep breath. "I'm considering going with Rodrigo to Uruguay. Tonight. He wants to drive there. He says it's eleven hours. He wants to drive all the way. Throughout the night."

"Yes. So?"

"Is this normal?"

"Of course it is."

"Eleven hours? Throughout the night?"

"This is what we do here. Everyone drives at night. There's no heat, it's more comfortable, no trucks on the roads."

"So . . . you mean it's ok?'

"I mean what he wants to do sounds normal to me. I'm not sure if it's OK, though. Are you sure you want to go with him?"

"Uhh . . . yes . . . I think so."

"Roxy, how well do you really know this guy? You know nothing about him. You can't just go away for four days with a guy you know nothing about."

"I know enough. Look, we've been dating for almost two months now. He's not suddenly going to stab me in Uruguay."

"Have you got his home address?"

"No."

"A copy of his identity card?"

"No, why would I?"

"Because I need it. In case something happens. I need to know where to find this guy."

"Nothing will happen." I laugh. "*No pasa nada*. See? I'm Argentine now."

He laughs. "OK, Roxy, but listen. Listen to me very carefully. Go have fun. Enjoy, but promise me one thing."

"Yes?"

"The first little thing that this guy does or says that you are not confortable with, you get out of the car. Do you hear me? You get out of the car immediately. And then you call me. I'll pick you up wherever you are. Four days' drive away if need be, it doesn't matter. You call me, OK? You don't wait for the second thing that makes you feel uncomfortable. You get out of the car immediately. You got that?"

I nod. I'm silent. I have tears in my eyes.

"I can't hear you," he says.

"OK, I promise. And thank you. *Gracias*."

~

Gabriela calls five minutes later.

"What the fuck is going on, darling? Are you running away with this guy now?"

"Gabriela, it's just a weekend away. We're going to Uruguay. *No pasa nada*."

"Don't give me this Argentine shit. This is serious. It's four full days. Are you sure? How well do you know this guy?"

"Gabriela!"

"I mean it, darling. How the fuck am I to sleep when I know you are away with a potential serial killer?"

"Gabriela, I have known the guy for two months now."

"You still don't know where he lives," she points out. "Have you ever been to his home?"

"No."

"See? Listen, I'm worried. If you go, you have to text me all the time. I want updates. Life signals. Just tell me you're OK. This is all I need to know. I'll worry like crazy if I don't hear from you."

"Yes, I know. I will." The memory of the Christmas Eve manic messages is still with me. "I'll text you, I promise, and I'll be OK."

"And one more thing—one thing this guy does or says, one thing you are not happy with—"

"Gabriela, I know. Patricio told me I should call him and he'll come and pick me up."

"No darling, you call me first. I'll come and pick you up too. I mean, we'll come together."

"Gabriela, *tranqui . . . No pasa nada.* Seriously." My voice is steady. "Everything will be all right."

But there is no way I can know this for sure.

LATER THAT EVENING

He arrives at 8, just like he promised. He kisses me tenderly. His mouth is warm. He carries my bags to the car, telling me I've packed for four weeks, not four days.

Of course I have. I need my beach dresses, my evening dresses, my just-in-case dresses—but men don't understand these things, and in this respect Rodrigo is a very typical man. His bag looks barely enough for an overnight stay. For him, it's jeans and t-shirts, whatever he does.

The traffic is mad, cars are at a standstill, and since we're in Argentina, there's a lot of honking. It's not surprising, since everyone has had the same idea—to get out of the city for the long weekend and drive through the night. When we finally reach the highway, it's pitch black outside. Rodrigo puts the radio on, then takes his hand off the gearstick and reaches out to grab mine.

We drive into the night listening to music, his hand holding mine tightly, and a big, wide, irrational smile spreads across my face.

SATURDAY 6TH FEBRUARY

By 2 am my eyelids are heavy.

"*Mi amor*, why don't you get some sleep?" Like all Argentines, Rodrigo is a mind reader. "Just close your eyes. I'll lower the music."

"And you? Are you going to be all right?"

"*No te preocupes, mi amor.* Don't worry. Of course I'll be all right. I'll carry on driving."

He woke up at 4:30 today to get to work. He did an eight-hour shift at his factory under the huge noise of the big cable-cutting machines he repairs. After that, he went home and got a couple of hours' sleep, woke up at 7 pm, drove one hour into the city center to pick me up, then drove another hour out of the city exactly the same way he had come in. And right now he's been driving for the last six hours with no break, except for the quick stop for the border formalities when we entered Uruguay.

I close my eyes and get some sleep. I warned him I wasn't going to drive anyway, so I shouldn't feel guilty.

At 4 am I wake up again and the music goes back on. We hold hands. Every now and then he turns to me, smiles, and calls me *linda*. About four times an hour, to be exact. I know, because I time him. I wonder if he has a secret alarm on his watch, alerting him when the next one is due. But my heart is singing. I really like it when he calls me *linda*.

At 6 am we stop at a petrol station near Montevideo, the capital of Uruguay. Rodrigo tells me he needs to close his eyes for a bit, because he can't keep them open any longer. He tells me to wake him up in half an hour, no more.

He falls asleep instantly on the driving seat. I watch him as he sleeps under the growing morning light. I watch his thick black hair, his long eyelashes, his muscular arms folded against his broad chest, which rises rhythmically with every breath. His beard, unshaved for at least a couple of days. A typical rugged Argentine look. I love it. I love him. It hits me there as I watch him sleep. I love this guy.

I'm relieved he's asleep and I don't have to say anything about this. Not to him, and not to anyone else either. I just sit there in silence, watching him sleep.

By midday, and after we have driven all across Uruguay, we arrive in Punta del Diablo. I picked this place. I heard it was a hippie surfer place, the complete antidote to the stylish, posh Punta del Este just three hours away along the coast. We had driven past Punta del Este and carried on. He was happy to go wherever I wanted to go, and I wanted to come here.

Punta del Diablo is just how I imagined it: rough, unspoiled, and wild. The long stretches of beach with golden sand are bordered by wooden huts selling food. Dirt roads lead to beach cottages with no resemblance one to the other—some are painted in bright colors, others are plain white, some are made from stone, others are wood. A lot of them are still under construction. Big waves break across the bay, where fishing boats are moored. There are a lot of surfers around—Argentine or Uruguayan, I still can't tell the difference. They all drink mate in the same way. And Brazilians. We are very close to the Brazilian border here, Rodrigo says.

We hit the water with the thirst and the sweat of the last sixteen hours in the car upon us. And then we find a room in a beach hut just for one night. Tomorrow we will have to sort out something else.

But tomorrow is another day. For now, the world outside doesn't exist any longer, it has melted in the darkness of our room.

I kiss his salted lips and we melt together too. And the words I did not dare to text finally find their way out and sing and dance on my lips before they are kissed away and echoed by his. *Te amo . . . te amo . . . te amo . . .*

SUNDAY 7TH FEBRUARY

"*Mi amor.* Listen. You can't carry on talking like that. You speak Spanish well enough now to finally understand the difference between *ser* and *estar.*"

This is a hard one. Santi has struggled with this for close to three months now. Unsuccessfully. I just can't understand why the Spanish language has two words for the verb "to be"—*ser* and *estar.*

I'm also not sure I'm ready for a Spanish lesson right now, on this boiling hot beach, as I'm trying to warm up after a swim in the cold waters. The water here might not be as cold as in Argentina, but it's still freezing by Mediterranean standards.

"It's easy." Rodrigo tries to explain it, just as Santi has tried before him. "*Ser* is for things that are always the same and will never change. You are a woman. You are from Romania. The world is round. You are beautiful."

"Just like this?" I laugh. "You cannot say *estás linda*?"

"You can," he admits. "If it refers to someone who is beautiful one day and the other day not. But this is not your case. You are beautiful all the time. It does not change. *Sos linda*. The verb *ser.*"

I laugh. I love it when he calls me *linda*. I give him a kiss. There's sand on his face. He's lying in the sand next to me and the towel isn't wide enough for both of us. He doesn't seem bothered by the sand, though. He kisses me back, then goes back to the Spanish class. His lips are salty.

"*Estar*, on the other hand, is about things that change. One day they are, the next day they are not. Like *estoy en la playa*. I am on the beach. Later I won't be on the beach any longer. *El agua está caliente.* The water is hot. Tomorrow it may not be. The weather is nice. I am happy. I am sad."

"I am in love," I whisper. "Is this an *estar* sentence as well?"

"It is," he admits.

"Because it can change?"

"Because it's a feeling. All feelings go with *estar.*"

I'm not so sure I like this verb.

"But you, *mi amor.* You always use *ser.* Always. This is a big mistake in Spanish. Remember most things are *estar.* There are very few things for which you use *ser.*"

"That's because most things are changeable—they eventually pass?"

"Precisely."

And then he kisses me again. "So that you remember," he says.

We had this deal early on. Whenever he taught me something in Spanish, he would seal it with a kiss. So that I would remember, he said. We did the same when I taught him something in English, but I have taught him very little English. We never speak English. I don't like speaking English with him.

"But why, *mi amor*? It is not fair," he used to say at the beginning. "Look at how much your Spanish is improving . . . And look at me—no progress with my English."

"I don't like speaking English," I said. "Please let's just speak Spanish."

He never really understood why, and I never told him it was my secret way of staying away from the world I lived and worked in, the world that eventually would take me away from him. In Spanish I could still be with him. In English, we had no chance.

LATER THAT DAY

We're looking for another room because the owner of our one-night-of-passion beach hut has asked us to leave. They have another booking.

Finding a room in the middle of a long weekend in a beach resort is not an easy task. We've asked everywhere. There are simply no rooms. Rodrigo is relaxed about it. He says if the worse comes to worst we can just sleep in the car. I'm not too keen on this idea. I have passed the age when one sleeps in the car and enjoys it. So we continue the search.

After a couple of hours we find a surfers' hostel further down the beach which has one room free. I can't believe our luck.

"Do you want to see it?" the receptionist asks.

"No, it doesn't matter how it is, we'll take it."

"It's small. Shared bathroom."

"*No pasa nada*. We'll take it."

It's either this or sleeping in the car, and I'm determined not to sleep in the car.

"Can I have your passports, please."

I watch as the receptionist enters the data from my passport into the computer. He's a young surfer guy with tousled blonde hair to his shoulders. He's only wearing swimming shorts and his toned chest is on display, smooth and tanned. A few bracelets dangle on his right wrist and his skin has the color of dark honey, making his blond locks even brighter. I swallow and try hard to take my eyes away from his chest, with its rounded pectorals. He's really handsome. It's not surprising. All Argentines are handsome. Hang on, this one is Uruguayan! Same thing. He's young, very young. Younger than Rodrigo? Maybe. Sexy though. More sexy than Rodrigo. Unfortunately. Rodrigo looks like a normal guy on the street, well built, but nothing like this athletic god with broad shoulders, strong arms and . . . perfectly designed muscles on his abdomen . . . Stop it! He's just a surfer . . . a sun-kissed surfer. Sun kissed . . . kissed in the sun . . .

Stop it, silly. Rodrigo is next to you!

"Oh, wow," sexy surfer says. "I can't believe this."

He looks at my passport.

"I can't believe this." He looks again. "No way!"

"What's wrong?" He has my British passport in his hands. Maybe I should have given him my Romanian one. Maybe he doesn't like British passports. Argentina and the UK had a war in the eighties, which is probably before this cutie was even born, but still, a lot of Argentines are not that fond of British passports.

"Your date of birth. What a coincidence!"

"Why?"

"You have the same date of birth as my mother."

My mouth feels suddenly dry. "You mean seventh of November?"

"No, the whole thing." He points to my passport. "Seventh of November, 1974. I've never registered anyone with the same date of birth as my mother before."

I feel as though I've suddenly been punched in the stomach. I blink. For a second I hope the earth will part straight at my feet and swallow me up, so I can get away from this embarrassing moment, from this sexy surfer guy and from my passport, open on the page that contains my birth date.

"How incredible." He goes back to entering my data in the computer.

I have the same birth date as his mother. The enormity of these words slowly sinks into my brain. His mother. Impossible!

I take another look at him. Yes, it's possible. I'm forty-one. If I'd had a baby when I was eighteen, he would be twenty-three by now. This sexy, sun-kissed surfer in front of me could easily be twenty-three. Older than Jonny. About the same age as Santi. A few years younger than Rodrigo.

Oh, my God, Rodrigo. He's next to me and he's heard the whole thing.

For the second time in the last five minutes I pray the earth will part and swallow me. And for the second time my wish isn't granted.

"All done." Sexy surfer smiles. Then he turns to Rodrigo. "Your passport too please."

Oh, no. I close my eyes. He will now see his date of birth too.

I give up on my wishes to have the earth part and swallow me, since it's clear it isn't going to cooperate. Nothing can save me from the agony of the next five minutes, as sexy surfer enters the data from Rodrigo's passport into his computer. There are no further comments, though.

He shows us to our room. I climb the stairs with the broken moves of a mechanical doll.

"*Mi amor. Qué pasa*?" Rodrigo is back to reading my mind. I guess it's not that hard. All the blood must have drained from my face.

"Did you hear him?" I say in a hoarse whisper. "The birthday of his mother?"

I don't say anything else, because I'm afraid I will just start crying.

"*Mi amor. No pasa nada.*" His hand finds mine and squeezes it reassuringly.

"And then he picked up your passport, and he will have seen your date of birth too."

"It really doesn't matter. It's not his business anyway." He leans over and kisses me. "*Tranquila*. I'm here, with you. Nothing else matters."

And it's true. Soon, everything else is forgotten as we make love on the squeaky bed in that small room which happens to be located directly above the reception desk of the sexy surfer. *No pasa nada*.

LATER THAT EVENING

We're having Campari Orange in a beach hut bar. The internet is slow. I really need the internet. I need to reply to several messages from Gabriela. There's one from Patricio, too.

I'm OK, I text them both.

It's been twenty-four hours with no sign from you. Are you fucking crazy? Gabriela replies.

I can tell she's annoyed and I'm sorry about my lack of messages, but at the same time I'm irritated by the constant surveillance.

No internet sorry, I text back. My last message to Gabriela was when we crossed the border. I didn't want to use my phone on roaming in Uruguay.

I tell Rodrigo I need some time to deal with some emails. He goes inside the bar to be closer to the router, where his phone picks up the signal better, so he can also reply to a few messages.

I search for a room for tomorrow in Punta del Este. We had planned to spend the last night in the posh resort before heading back to Buenos Aires on Tuesday.

No rooms. Nothing. All booked. I search again and again. I have to find something.

Rodrigo comes back. He's done with emails. I'm not. Not yet.

"I need a little bit of time," I tell him, concentrated on my search. "I need to finish this. Give me ten more minutes. Maybe just go back inside."

"*Tranquila*," he says. He sits on the bench next to me. "*Tranquila*. I'm not going to disturb you. I don't want to do anything. I just want to be with you here, next to you."

He picks up my legs, which are resting on the bench, and hugs them to his chest as he sits next to me.

'I just want to be here, close to you," he repeats. "Do what you need to do, I'll be quiet," he adds, my feet now in his lap.

We are out on the terrace of the beach hut bar. In front of us the large, empty beach stretches uninterrupted, and I can feel the cool breeze of the evening. There's no sound other than that of the waves breaking against the shore. It's getting dark.

He stays there, quiet just as promised, holding my feet in his lap and watching the sea. And I stay there too, the phone with the precious internet dangling useless in my hand. He wants to be with me, my mind repeats. Just be.

I watch him and feel his hands on my feet and I don't think of anything any more. I just learn to be.

And yet . . . he used *estar*, not *ser*. Does he mean he only wants to be with me now, and tomorrow this may change?

MONDAY 8TH FEBRUARY

Rodrigo has decided that this beach holiday is to be dedicated to improving my Spanish.

"What are you studying there?" he asks, as he gets out of the freezing water and throws himself in the sand, next to the towel I'm lying on.

I can't believe how long he can stay in that freezing water. For me it's just a quick in and out, and back to studying the subjunctive. The past subjunctive, to be precise. The one I have serious trouble with. I'm reading Santi's handwriting in my notebook and trying to do the exercise from the text book.

Rodrigo takes a quick look and then declares confidently, "Nobody speaks like this."

"What?"

"These complicated tenses. Bullshit. No one really speaks like this."

He can't be right, surely. Jorge Luis Borges writes like this. I know, because Santi gave me his novellas to read. But I'm not sure Rodrigo and Jorge Luis Borges would agree on verb tenses.

"Seriously, you need to learn some proper Spanish. How people really speak."

"But I know proper Spanish. Look, I can speak with you."

"That's because I make an effort."

"To what?" I look at him doubtfully.

"To speak neutrally. I use easy words. Boring words. So you can understand. If I spoke like I really speak you wouldn't understand a thing."

"How do you really speak?"

He tells me something. I have no idea what.

"You see? This is how we speak. This is true Argentine street talk. You don't get it in these books." He points to my open textbook. "You can tell your teacher he can stick them up his ass. Useless."

"And how do you say that again?"

For the next hour Rodrigo teaches me the basics of Argentine slang, carefully punctuated with kisses. So that I remember.

I repeat diligently each and every phrase.

"And when someone asks you where you have been this weekend you say *Me fui a la mierda*," he says.

Mierda means shit.

"To a shitty place? Why? I love it here!"

"No, it means I have been very far away."

"But *mierda*—doesn't it mean shit?" I ask, proud of my slang vocabulary.

"Yes, but in this case it means far. And the more you roll the *rrr* the further the distance. So *mierrrrda* is further away than simply *mierda*. Got it?"

I nod and write this and everything else in a new section in my notebook. I will impress Santi, I think. And I might finally understand what Sol shouts to her kids too.

LATER THAT DAY

After a long drive, which takes up most of the day, we arrive at Punta del Este. We head straight for the famous beach of Los Dedos, the fingers, named after the huge sculpture of a hand which emerges from the sand. We go for a swim and discover the water is even colder than in Punta del Diablo. I suppose it's because we are closer to Argentina.

After the swim we have a quick drive around, but Punta del Este seems to me a collection of impersonal skyscrapers, and roads so busy with traffic that everyone's at standstill. Unimpressed and chilled to the bones after our swim, we decide to head back to our room to watch a movie in bed.

At least we have a room, booked the previous night in the beach hut as I woke up eventually from staring at Rodrigo as he was staring at the sea, holding my feet in his lap. It's great to just be, but sometimes one also needs to do.

"I've brought a movie for you," Rodrigo tells me. "It's one from the list your teacher gave you. It's called *Wild Tales. Relatos Salvajes.* It's very Argentine. You have to see it."

I can't believe he remembers my list of movies. Rodrigo is like that. Sometimes he surprises me with the way he remembers various small details or things I've told him.

So we watch the movie in bed. It consists of six short, stand-alone stories. In the first one, a vengeful pilot brings down a plane full of passengers. In the second, a waitress poisons an innocent teenage boy in an attempt to bring about justice. The third is about a man who makes the mistake of having an argument with a truck driver. Things escalate so badly they end up killing each other.

The fourth movie is about a normal middle-class engineer who ends up putting a bomb under the office of the police department in his city. Just because he was refused a refund.

The fifth is about a rich boy who kills a pedestrian in a road accident. He has his parents bribe the gardener to pretend he did it and go to prison instead.

I'm not sure I want to watch any more of these stories. I'm already horrified. Rodrigo has seen the movie already, but he's still laughing as people kill each other, detonate explosives and bring down planes, each story a cocktail of strong emotions.

"I told you. This movie is great. It's about us. Argentines. This is what we're really like."

I guess he's referring to the intense emotions that bubble just under the surface in these nice, friendly people. They feel everything to an intensity which keeps on surprising me. And this movie, horror-comedy or not, gets across this trait very clearly.

The sixth and last movie is about a bride who ends up having sex with a waiter at her own wedding party as revenge on her new husband, who has invited an ex-fling to the wedding. They have a huge row, declare eternal hatred, break mirrors, scare the guests away and end up having sex on the same table as the wedding cake as guests leave the room, horrified. This one is called "Till Death Do Us Part."

By now I'm seriously alarmed by the insight into life in Argentina which Rodrigo has decided to share with me.

"*Mi amor*, it's just a movie. The reality is not that bad," he whispers, kissing me again just as the crazy bride and her groom kiss on the remains of the destroyed wedding cake on screen.

Actually, reality doesn't exist any longer. It's gone away for a wander, as it always does when I feel Rodrigo's lips on mine.

"They might be wild, but they are passionate," is my last thought of the day.

TUESDAY 9TH FEBRUARY

We start driving back towards Buenos Aires around lunch time. Rodrigo says it will take about twelve hours to reach the capital. It would normally be quicker, but the traffic will be horrendous so twelve hours is a conservative estimate. But he'll get me home by midnight. After that, he'll have to drive another hour to his place, then get a few hours' sleep before his alarm goes off at 4:30 am. Tomorrow is a working day for him.

The music is playing and he has his hand in mine again. Yet something has changed. Things just feel different. The surreal space of these days is coming to an end. We are heading back to Buenos Aires, back to work for him, back to less than two weeks until my flight for me. Back to the unanswered question as to what will happen after February twentieth, when I board that plane.

As promised, neither of us has mentioned the future beyond that looming date. We haven't questioned it, we haven't made plans. We've just acted like it didn't exist.

So when Rodrigo casually asks the question, just after we begin our journey back, I almost drop the bottle of water I'm drinking from.

"So. Your flight. Is it still on the twentieth of February? Saturday?"

"Yes."

"What time?"

"Midday, I think."

"How about we do one thing?"

He's staring at the road ahead. I can't read his expression. I wonder what he's about to say.

"How about I pick you up from your place the night before, luggage and all, you come to my place? I cook you dinner, you stay overnight, and then the next morning I take you to the airport."

"Will you take me to the airport?" I mumble.

"Of course I will. What did you think I'd do? Let you take a taxi? Plus I want to be the last person you see before you board that flight."

I'm hardly breathing. I'm expecting a full discussion about what happens after I board that flight. But no, that appears to be it. He doesn't ask anything else.

"OK," I say.

And at least I'll finally find out where he lives.

Later we stop to fill up at a petrol station. I tell him I'm hungry. He tells me to buy sandwiches and we'll eat them in the car. I want to stay and eat them there, at a table, properly. He says there's no time. I buy the sandwiches, dump them on the back seat and don't speak to him for the next twenty minutes.

By the time we speak again, we argue, with emotions unchecked. We scream. I call him selfish. He calls me stupid. He says I don't understand how much traffic there'll be on the way back after a long weekend, and how long it takes to get home. I have no idea where this is all coming from, but we both scream like we're out of our minds. Maybe it's that little conversation about the twentieth of February that's to blame for the outburst.

Eventually he stops the car on the emergency lane of the highway and gets out slamming the door with an intensity that shocks me.

For a second I remember Patricio's voice. "You call me, OK? If anything happens, anything at all, you get out of the car and you call me."

I look around. We are surrounded by nothing but fields. There's nothing else as far as the eye can see. No petrol station, no town, no house, nothing. Uruguay seems a deserted country, except for the occasional few cows. Where the hell do I wait for Patricio here? In the middle of the fields? It's going to take him twelve hours to get to this place. And that's only if I have a signal on my phone to call him, and if I can manage to explain where I am. I have no idea where I am, actually.

No, it's not feasible, I decide, and I move on to plan B. Make up with Rodrigo, before he either explodes or cuts my throat. And by now I know the only way to do this is the Argentine way.

Rodrigo is outside, still breathing heavily. He looks like a bull mortally wounded, about to strike the last blow. I can't see, but I'm sure his eyes are bloodshot, too.

I approach slowly. He watches me with a wary expression, as if to warn me off coming closer.

"*Mi amor,*" I whisper. "*Tranqui. No pasa nada.*"

The next second, he melts in my arms, apologizing and embracing me until my ribs crack, and I feel I can't breathe any longer. And then we kiss and it feels like we never really argued at all.

As we start driving again, hand in hand, the music back on, I remember Marco's warning. "It's not that they get their inspiration from soap operas. It's the other way round. Their real lives inspire their soap operas."

Well, in that case, I have become a soap opera character too.

WEDNESDAY 10TH FEBRUARY

Gabriela comes to town. She wants to go out for dinner with me and she wants a full update on the situation. I haven't seen Gabriela for a month. We have lots to catch up on.

She tells me she has been worried. They all have. Everyone at the farm. She tells me word for word the dialogue that passed between them all at the dinner table.

"Patricio asked me if I had news from you. I said I didn't. This is when you didn't bother to send a fucking text message for twenty-four hours." Her voice adopts that accusatory tone again. "We were worried like crazy. So I told Patiricio I was worried. He said he was worried too. And then his father asked why we were worried. We said you had gone to Uruguay with a guy and we hadn't heard back from you. 'With a guy? Which guy?' his father asked. 'A guy she met in Buenos Aires,' we explained. 'They've been dating for some time.'"

"Have you met this guy?" the father asked Patricio.

"Uhh, no, actually. No, I haven't."

Has Gabriela met him?

No. Gabriela hasn't met him either.

"Has anyone at this table met this guy?" the father continued.

Nobody had.

"Do we know anything about this guy? Where he lives? Where he works? Who his family is?"

No information.

"But son, how can this be?" the old man exploded. "Roxy goes to Uruguay for four days with a guy and you haven't met this guy? No one from this family has met this guy? How can you possibly have let that happen?"

"We tried to explain to him that we had no time to meet him beforehand, but that we'd surely meet him once you were back, but the old man was furious with us," Gabriela concludes.

I laugh until I'm crying. If I'm honest, the tears aren't just from laughter. I can feel the care of these people all around me, every single moment I spend in their country. My Argentine family.

"Tell them to chill," I say. "I'm fine. He was fine. We had a nice time."

Gabriela looks at me. One long stare and then she finally asks, "Tell me, Roxy. What the fuck is it with this guy? Why do you like him?"

"I don't know, I just like him. I like to be with him. He kisses so well. And when we make love the world melts. I have never felt like this before."

"So, it's just sex?"

"No, not sex. We make love, not sex."

"Give me a fucking break. You only met him two months ago. Don't talk about love. There's no love here. There can't be."

It's hard to argue with Gabriela, so I don't say anything. Maybe it isn't love, after all.

"And what happens after you go, in ten days' time?" She carries on with her questions.

"I don't know, Gabriela. I really don't know."

I tell her about Marco and about his predictions. About my world back home, actually the lack of a world, about my sadness at letting him go, about my impossible dreams of being with him. I tell her everything. I spill my heart out there on the table amongst the many Campari Oranges we share that night. She listens, and even her ever-present "fucks" seem to go into hiding for a while.

Because it's like this in Argentina. When your life turns into a drama and you need to talk about it, there's always a friend nearby willing to listen.

THURSDAY 11TH FEBRUARY

Juan is back in town. He wants to see me. He wants to have dinner with me. He still calls me *guapa* and sends me countless text messages.

Not only that, but Curly Hair is messaging me again too. While I had my arm in a cast there were no messages from Curly Hair. But now my arm is free and he knows it. So the text messages reappear. He, too, is calling me *linda*. He wants to meet up.

But there is very little communication with Rodrigo. He warned me on the long drive back that it was going to be a crazy week for him at work and that he would not be able to see me much. We had agreed to meet on Sunday for lunch. Sunday is the fourteenth of February. Saint Valentine.

I miss Rodrigo, but it's better I don't see him now. I have a small problem. I'm still in Patricio's family flat in Buenos Aires. Just as Rodrigo predicted, they've told me I should stay there until

I leave the country, and they won't hear of me looking for another place to stay. And just as I feared, they will absolutely not accept any payment for it.

So I'm still using their flat for free. As they haven't met Rodrigo, I feel it would be disrespectful to have him spend the night with me in their flat. I tell Rodrigo we won't be able to spend the night together until our last night, which will be at his place, as he offered.

He seems fine with this. Maybe too fine, if you ask me. After the closeness of our time away, he now seems distant and busy. He's barely sent any texts and there have been no calls. One or two *lindas* maybe. Not enough, definitely not enough *lindas*.

He's suggested meeting for Sunday lunch. Not Friday, or Saturday, or any other time during the week. It definitely isn't enough.

I suppose he's protecting himself, creating some distance to avoid getting hurt. By now I know him well enough to read this. He doesn't want to feel too sad in ten days' time when I board that flight. He's learned my trick—breaking up a little before breaking up—and he's using that trick to protect himself.

So I decide to protect myself, too.

I text Juan back, saying I'd love to go out for dinner.

I text Curly Hair back, saying maybe it's time he invited me for a drink.

Then I put the phone away and I carry on with my day. Language school, physio appointment, a massage in the afternoon. And I try hard not to feel the sadness inside.

FRIDAY 12TH FEBRUARY

Santi laughs out loud when I give him a full rundown of my newly acquired slang expressions. He says I'm getting dangerous now. I know too much. He asks about Rodrigo. I tell him I'm in love. I don't tell him I've agreed to have dinner with Juan on Valentine's Day, the same day I've agreed to have lunch with Rodrigo. I don't tell him about my secret protection mechanism. I don't tell him about Curly Hair, either.

Not that there is too much to say about Curly Hair. He answered my text straight away, saying he wanted to see me tomorrow after school. Fine, I said.

But today in school I didn't see him, so I left and went to have lunch on a terrace.

I've barely sat down when I receive his text.

Where are you?

Having lunch on a terrace.

Which terrace?

Ten minutes later he is there on my terrace, seated in front of me.

The waiter comes and asks him what he wants to drink. A Coca Cola.

I can't believe how daring his text messages are and how reserved he is in person. Right now, for the first time ever in twelve weeks, we are seated face to face at a table, having a drink. To be exact, I'm drinking the water I'd previously ordered with my lunch, which doesn't even qualify as a proper drink.

I push down the sense of guilt that's bubbling up my throat. Rodrigo. No Rodrigo, I think. No Rodrigo. Nothing. I'm not doing anything wrong. I'm just having a glass of water with a guy who has been sending me sexy messages for the past three months. I want to see what's in this story. I'm ready to see.

And because I'm ready, I see. Finally, I see it. The nothingness of it. A vast abyss of nothingness. He talks a bit about the city, the weather, the traffic. Then abruptly he says he wanted to see me.

He doesn't look at me but rather awkwardly around me. Like he isn't really sure what he's doing there. I'm not quite sure either.

"Well you are seeing me now," I say. "You could have seen me before, too. Why did you never invite me anywhere?"

"It's not that easy. I wasn't sure what you would say."

"There's one way to find out, right?"

"Well, maybe one day . . ."

"I'm leaving in ten days, for good. The one day has passed."

"Well, not yet. Maybe we still have time."

I watch him, this man who seemed so passionate in his text messages and so empty in flesh and blood. I watch him until I see clearly the emptiness of this whole situation, until I see it clearly enough never to forget the sight.

And when I reach that moment, I ask for the bill, pay for his Coca Cola as well, and get up to leave.

He gets up too and tries to take my hand. But it doesn't work. It'll never work. Because I've finally seen the void and I won't forget it.

I leave him there as I jump in a taxi. I feel his eyes on my back and I continue to feel them following the car as we drive away. I have no idea what he's thinking about or what that weird encounter was supposed to mean.

But I'm sure of one thing. He'll never send me text messages again. Maybe this is all it was supposed to be. Closure.

The taxi driver is chatty, as they all are. I tell him where we're going. I've got a physio appointment. I'm late. I've spent too long chatting to a loser.

"Where are you from?"

Here we go again. Santi, my accent!

He chats away as he navigates the crazy midday traffic. In ten minutes I know all about his life. He is forty-five, he likes tango. He likes meat, a good *asado*. No surprises so far, typical Argentine. But he is divorced. This is not so typical here. It didn't work out, so they separated seven years ago. No kids. Bloody traffic . . . Loves what he does. He likes talking to people and you talk to people a lot as a taxi driver. Would love to have a family. One day soon. He's certain it will be really soon now.

"Why soon? How do you know?"

"Well, I'm waiting for my partner to appear. My lady. She is close."

"How do you know she is close?"

"I can feel it. I can feel her."

"So what are you doing about meeting her?"

"Nothing. I'm waiting. You can't do much about these things. They happen."

"What do you mean?"

"You don't go out there deciding who is to be your partner. You don't go out on a hunt. You wait. They will come."

This is very unlike Argentine behaviour.

I smile. "And how does that happen?"

"It just happens when you're ready. You don't need to do anything about it. And I'm ready. So she will come." And then he smiles. "We've arrived. Just in time for your appointment. You see? I told you not to worry. It all happens as it should."

SATURDAY 13TH FEBRUARY

Thirteen is my lucky number. It has been for years. A lot of things have happened to me governed by this number, so whenever I see a number thirteen I expect something big to happen.

And, as always, something does. Today Rosario comes over to Buenos Aires to spend the evening with me.

This is a big deal. It's the first time she's come to see me in the city in the three months I've been here. I've seen her in Lobos, but she's never come to Buenos Aires. I've invited her countless times, but she kept telling me, "Look *amiga*, my life is crazy right now." And it was. She was juggling two jobs, a rebel teenage son who was in constant danger of not passing his exams at school, and a new man in her life. All kinds of complicated.

But Rosario is an artist at heart and artists love complications. I also suspect all these complications arise from the countless pictures of Frida Kahlo all over her house. Frida's life was full of complications as well. I told Rosario she should bin the pictures and pick another artist with a less complicated life, but she replied that one couldn't dictate one's passions. Frida remained triumphant all over the place.

We go out for dinner at midnight, then back to the same tango place I'd been to when I had my arm in the cast—La Catedral. This time I don't have my arm in a cast, so I get invited to dance. My partner is an older gentleman, but then the tango scene in Buenos Aires is most popular with people well past midlife.

At first I almost fall off my tatty chair when I get asked to dance, and I quickly decline. I tell the guy that he'll be sorry to have asked me, that I can't move, that I have taken a couple of tango lessons only, that—

But my vague attempts aren't strong enough ammunition against an Argentine man who is determined to have a dance with me. He waits patiently for me to finish my speech on why not, and then he smiles.

"*Tranqui. No pasa nada*. It's just a dance."

So I go. By now I have learned what *tranqui* means. Chill, woman!

I step on his toes a few times. Then I burst out laughing in the middle of the dance floor as he attempts to lead me into a *planeo*, a complicated type of pirouette, and I tell him my basic tango lessons didn't cover pivoting on one leg with the other one stretched out. Again I suggest that maybe he would be better off dancing with someone who really knows what she's doing.

But no, he wants to dance with me. He grabs my right hand, determined to push me into a pirouette and I gasp as the pain shoots up my stiff wrist. There's no time to explain what happened to my wrist or that it only came out of a cast two weeks ago.

I carry on mortified, missing steps, falling out of rhythm, then back into rhythm again. I try to guess his moves, and then

I remember my instructor telling me that under no circumstance should I try to anticipate. And that I shouldn't think, at all. I should let myself go wherever my partner takes me. And then I remember about closing my eyes.

I close my eyes and stop thinking. And then my body finally takes over, freed from the obsessive thoughts, from trying to compare my timid moves to the expert steps of the dancers around me. Just like in polo, as soon as you let the body take over, it just knows what to do.

With my eyes closed, I finally dance.

SUNDAY 14TH FEBRUARY

I wake up with Rosario on Valentine's Day and we spend the first cup of coffee analyzing my love life. I'm feeling uneasy. I'm supposed to meet Rodrigo for lunch and Juan for dinner today.

"Of course you have to go out with both of them. Look, it's not a big deal, everyone does it here. You have to protect yourself, Roxy. You're leaving in one week and you can't get on that plane with a broken heart."

This is what friends are for. To encourage you in whatever you do, however crazy it seems. And she does it well, my Argentine sister.

So I meet Rodrigo for lunch. And because I feel really uneasy about it, I make sure Rosario is with us, and her boyfriend too, which makes it a friendly get-together rather than a romantic lunch. Rodrigo is surprised to meet me with my friends, but he accepts it graciously. Afterwards we have a walk through Palermo, hand in hand. We stop for a drink, we talk a little, but it feels like there isn't much to say. We're both clearly uncomfortable. At least I know why I am.

A brief kiss and he's driving me home.

"You can't stay," I remind him as he drops me in front of Patricio's family flat.

I'd already told him about not feeling confortable staying with him in my friends' flat. Besides, it would be quite difficult to go out with Juan in the evening if Rodrigo decided to stay for the rest of the day.

"I know, I know . . ." He kisses me as I'm still struggling to explain. "*No pasa nada*. I'll pick you up on Thursday and take you to my place. We'll spend your last night there together."

He goes. I go home and prepare for my next date, trying hard not to feel anything.

By evening I'm ready. Or I think I am, because I managed to get myself to look decent. I'm wearing a short, sexy dress with high heels, complete with careful makeup and perfume. I'm not really sure what I'm doing and I don't want to think about it. So I just go through the motions. I've put more effort into how I look for dinner than I had for lunch, I think, as I finish applying my mascara. I had no makeup for lunch.

Juan has picked a cozy Italian restaurant with tables outside on the pavement. Every place has tables outside on the pavement in Las Cañitas. I love this neighborhood, and when he asked me where I wanted to go I didn't hesitate in suggesting it. It reminds me a little bit of the pizza with Mr. Perfect, but that was a long time ago now. The main thing is that it's not Palermo. Not the place where I've just been walking hand in hand with Rodrigo.

The food is great. Juan tells me he researched the place before he booked it. The wine is exquisite. Juan is attentive, kind, funny, and witty. We talk about our love for Argentina and about how we have each come back here a few times already. Juan is a freelancer just like me. Computer programmer. This is why he can take time off, just like me, and he choses to spend it in Argentina. Just like me.

I smile. He seems perfect for me. I enjoy his company, his manners, his conversation. But I hate the situation.

After dinner he wants to take a walk, hand in hand. I feel like fainting. He will try to kiss me soon, I can feel it coming, and I can't, I really can't imagine kissing him. Even though I think he's a nice guy, I just can't possibly kiss him after I kissed Rodrigo only a few hours before. I mumble an excuse and get a taxi back home without too many explanations, leaving him wondering what he'd done wrong.

"I tried, at least I tried," I tell myself as I finally get home. I tried to do what everyone told me I should do—to keep my options open. I tried to date a more suitable guy for me, for my age at least. I tried hard to avoid a broken heart in the few days before my flight to London. I haven't done anything wrong, I tell myself. I only tried to protect myself.

But the sadness inside tells me it hasn't worked.

THURSDAY 18TH FEBRUARY

My last days in Buenos Aires pass in a blur. I even manage to squeeze in a last minute trip to Iguazu Falls for two days and a night, just to give myself something to do. Anything to keep my mind from thinking too much.

I return from the top tourist attraction of Argentina unmoved by the experience, as though I haven't really been there. And maybe I hadn't. My heart had stayed in Buenos Aires. But I can't afford to think about the heart. Numb inside, I go though the motions of one big Argentine tradition—saying goodbye.

In Argentina, saying goodbye is a long and complicated affair. If you're leaving a party or an *asado* you're supposed to say goodbye and give a kiss on the cheek to every person present, children included. Often the kiss on the cheek is accompanied by an exchange of goodbyes, a personal "*despedida.*" Some of these exchanges are brief, some more lengthy. There are countless assurances and reassurances that we are going to meet again soon, much "*cuídate,*" take care, and even more "*nos vemos,*" we will see each other again. Sometimes there's a hug thrown in with the kiss on the cheek. This leaving ritual takes anywhere between thirty minutes and one hour, depending how large the party is and how well you know the people. But however long it takes, it's essential to go through the motions. Not doing so would be considered extremely rude.

Tourists, and especially Northern European tourists who come from cultures of colder social interaction, find it hard to deal with this lengthy kissing-and-hugging parting culture. Some tourists simply ignore the customs, utter a general "Bye" and disappear. Others try to sneak out through the back door without saying goodbye to anyone. Others try to reduce the interaction to a minimum.

I decide to be Argentine about it. I'm going to properly say goodbye.

So I spend my last hour of physiotherapy talking to every single therapist, receptionist, or personal trainer who has attended me over the past three months. We joke about my wrists. We admire the progress—the left one bending back, close to normal, the right one much improved since the cast was taken off almost three weeks ago. I recall how three and a half months ago I had arrived in Argentina with this one big wish—make my left wrist bend as much as my right wrist. Be careful what you wish for, I think. The Universe is listening. After three months, my left wrist is bending far more than my right wrist, and my biggest wish now is to have the right one catch up with the left one.

Next, I go to the language school and chat to all the teachers, receptionists, and directors. We laugh about my arm in the cast story. We look back at the progress I've made. I came into that school pretending I could speak Spanish, when in fact I was using Italian words to which I would simply add an "s" at the end, just to make them sound more Spanish. Now I'm leaving completely fluent, as if I've been reborn here with a different language.

And Santi . . . well, Santi is someone I'm going to miss. He tells me I was his first-ever student and that I set the bar really high. It will be difficult to replace me. He doesn't tell me why, though, so I take it as a general compliment meaning he really enjoyed his time with me. I tell him I'll forever think of him when speaking Spanish. I speak several languages and I find it helps a lot to keep a person in mind when I switch languages. Someone I always speak that language with, someone I can associate with that language. Someone who will live in my head, forever entwined with the language they represent. I have my grandmother for German, my teacher from when I was a kid for English, Marco for Italian, and another friend for French. And now Santi for Spanish.

I say goodbye to each and every one of them until there is no one left. Well, actually there's Curly Hair, but he isn't there. He left early that day. It's better that way.

Afterwards I head over to Sol's to have my hair done one last time. She told me to come at midday. She said she'll make me *linda* for my last date tonight. Rodrigo is coming to pick me up at 6. What she didn't tell me is that she cooked a tortilla, bought *empanadas*, and would be waiting for me with a big bottle of Campari on the counter of her salon. She locks the door behind me, pours the drinks, puts the music on, and toasts to me. Her aunt is there as well, and she has a glass too. Her toddler daughter only gets the orange juice, but gets to toast with us.

I find myself in tears.

"Sol, are you crazy? It's the middle of the day. You're turning customers away with that locked door."

"Ah, they will come back." She dismisses my remarks with a quick gesture. "*No pasa nada.* But you're going tomorrow. I'm not going to see you for a long time. Of course we need to say goodbye properly."

By the time I've finished my third glass of Campari Orange, I can barely walk. But the party is only just beginning. Sol puts the music on loud and suggests maybe we should dance.

But I can't dance. I'm too tired. Too drunk. Too emotional. I don't want to leave this country. I really don't. I content myself with taking many pictures of her, of us, of the daughter, of the glasses, of the food, of everything I could possibly think of, pretending I'm a crazy tourist and this was just a holiday.

My list of goodbyes would have naturally brought me to Lobos next, to my Argentine family. But fate decides otherwise. Gabriela called in the morning to say the roads to the farm are bad, as it has rained again.

"It doesn't make sense for you to come, you'll end up stuck in mud halfway across the field," Gabriela said. "Enjoy your last night with Rodrigo instead."

So I don't get to say goodbye to them, not at all. Like a tourist disappearing from an *asado* via the back door, I vanish without the customary kiss on the cheek and hug. A phone call doesn't count. Phone calls don't count for such things in Argentina.

But speaking with Gabriela and Patricio on the phone, leaving feels less like leaving.

I'm emotional, but I know they won't let me be emotional. I try nevertheless.

"Guys, thank you so much. For everything. You . . . well . . . the flat here . . . thank you. And the fall . . . And you looked after me—"

There are no more words. When words are not enough, they simply stop flowing.

No pasa nada. Cuídate. Nos vemos.

My Argentine family. They've been there for me this time, like they were there for me before. And they'll be there for me next time

I come. And I will come back. They know this. I know this too. So there's no need to say anything else.

Then Gabriela adds just one more thing.

"And I want to know everything, you hear me? Everything that happens with Rodrigo tonight. And what the fuck, you are going to his place? Finally? What if something happens to you? How do we know you're safe? How will we find out where you are?"

Gabriela's practical mind has turned to more down-to-earth things.

"Yes, Roxy, Gabriela's right, send me the address of this guy as soon as you get there," Patricio echoes her.

I guess some things never change.

MY LAST EVENING

I'm still thinking that some things never change as Rodrigo parks in front of my flat and comes up to get my luggage. I feel just like I did when we went away for the weekend to Uruguay. It's different now, but neither of us can admit it, so we both greet each other matter of factly, as if all that's happening is that we're spending another evening together. We can't talk about the fact that I'll board the flight tomorrow with no plans as to when or whether we're ever going to see each other again. We can't bring ourselves to talk about anything that happens after that flight takes off tomorrow. We can't say goodbye.

So we don't. We pretend it's just an ordinary Friday evening. We stop on the way to his place and do some grocery shopping. We get to his flat, a studio in a small town one hour away from Buenos Aires, and I feel shocked as I step in. The place is seriously unkempt. Dirty floors, dusty shelves, unwashed dishes piling everywhere. Dust. Lots of dust.

"A man living alone doesn't clean up that often, you know." Rodrigo reads my mind as always. "It's a bit messy, sorry."

It's a poor excuse. It's far worse than messy, but for me it's good news. I did spend some time worrying whether there was another woman in his life, and if that was the reason he never invited me to his home. But now, looking around, I know there is no other woman. No woman would be able to put up with this mess.

I go to the bathroom and take a shower. The towel is so dirty that I end up drying myself with toilet paper. I start to feel seriously uncomfortable in the place and I wonder if he'd take it badly if I suggest we go to a hotel.

Then, just to take my mind off things, we attempt to make love, but there are no condoms in the flat so we have to stop what we're doing, get dressed, and go back into the street to find a little kiosk that sells everything. Including condoms. He goes in and tells me to wait outside, too embarrassed to buy condoms holding my hand. I wait outside, feeling like a teenager. By the time we go back to the flat, neither of us feels like sex any longer. Great, I think, this story is ending just how it started—with a missing condom.

Then he cooks pasta with tomato sauce.

"Vegetarian dish especially for you," he says. No *asado* for him this time. The dirty dishes scattered everywhere don't make for an appetising background, so I decide I'm not that hungry. My mind is racing, trying to find something to do. I'm feeling awkward and I know he is too. I don't need to be Argentine to read his mind right now. What are we doing here? Together? What are we going to do until tomorrow? Sex is out of the question now.

Salvation comes in the form of a sci-fi movie. We watch *Lucy*, who at the end leaves planet Earth disintegrated, sending a text message to her would-be lover saying, "I am everywhere." Just not there with him. I feel it's a ironic prediction of the future that will begin tomorrow.

Then we go to sleep, barely touching each other. I ask him if he has clean bed sheets and he manages to produce some from the wardrobe.

In the darkness of the night, I listen to his snoring and this time I don't wake him up nor expect his embrace as he turns over in his sleep. There will be no hot whispers tonight, no passionate kissing, no world melting away. All that is suddenly gone. And all that is left now is a big sense of emptiness engulfing me slowly as I finally fall asleep.

SATURDAY 20TH FEBRUARY

And then it happens. The last goodbye, the one we'd most tried to avoid, the one we'd both decided to suppress, comes out to find us. It takes us by surprise, while we're unprepared and ill-equipped to deal with it. It sneaks up on us as we sleep and have our defenses down. And we surrender.

The night is turning into day when I wake up with his kisses. And then it doesn't matter anymore where we are and what's going to happen later that day, because the world melts once again, and all that's left are our souls dancing together in the light of the breaking dawn.

We don't talk afterwards, and we don't talk much on the way to the airport, either. Just the usual practical things. What time are you boarding? I hope the flight isn't delayed. The small stuff. The stuff designed to keep us safe.

We manage that well. We park the car, check the bags in, have a coffee, and talk a little bit more. We utter the customary *cuídate* and *nos vemos* and how nice it has been to spend that time together.

We even manage a brief kiss and a hug and still with no tears. I would have made it to the end without crying if it wasn't for the last word he said.

"*Linda.*"

I look into his deep brown eyes and serious face, his warm gaze absorbing me as if he wanted to burn all my features deep into his memory.

"*Linda.*"

I turn around and walk briskly ahead, towards my flight, through security, through passport control, through the long grey corridors of the airport. I walk on and on, holding on with all my strength to that one last word, still warm inside me. I walk on with a veil of tears blurring my vision.

Then I reach the safety of the British Airways flight and here the tears dry up, because they've put the aircon on and one can't cry too much and freeze at the same time. Plus, my tears feel really out of place here.

So I stop crying just as the plane starts to move towards the take-off stand. I find my notebook and pen and start preparing myself for my own take off—my plan for London:

1. I will recover my wrist. The right one. It's pretty good since I had three weeks of physio here. But I need to have some more. Probably another month or so. It's not as bad as the previous break. This one had no screws in. Thank God they don't do screws in Argentina. I really have to get this wrist going, because I need it for the next point.

2. I will play polo. It's almost the end of February now. The polo season starts in mid-April in England. I have about two months to recover, which is perfect. Just what I need. I'll do physio sessions, some gym, and then I'll be ready. Jonny will be back at the Old Man's for another season. He'll help me get my confidence back, I know he will. And the Old Man—well, I hope he's not upset with me any more. It's just an arm and these things happen in polo. He'll know that. He had his own broken bones.

3. I will find a job. A new consulting project, ideally for six months. Ideally a big brand company, like the ones I've done projects for before. Ideally paying me more than before. Or at least the same. Definitely not less. My rates only go up, I always used to say. I need to earn money, because I haven't been earning anything for the past six months and Marco is right. Mostly right, I mean. Well, about work he's definitely right. I need to make money and I need to get back in the job market, otherwise my skills will become obsolete and who will employ me then . . . and . . . OK, enough. I will get a project and I will make money. I know I will.

4. I will forget him. Rodrigo, I mean. I will let him go. Well, he is already going. As the plane took off, the last of the strings connecting me with him snapped. I will not dream of him. I will not think of him. I will not remember his kisses, his caresses . . . Especially those. This was a fling, a holiday fling. Nothing more. It can't go anywhere. It won't go anywhere. I will never see him again and I will not talk about him, think about him, or dream about him. I am determined.

I put the pen down, contemplating my list. I'm feeling pretty satisfied. I think the key things are there. Wrist, polo, job, let go. Yes, I feel good about this list.

And yet, there's one more point. There needs to be one more point. I like lists that have five points. I think it's the ideal length for a list. Three is too short and seven is too many, but five is just perfect. I need to have five points on my list.

I sit there with the pen in my hand and wait. I wait for the fifth point to come to me. I wait all through the time it takes the plane to reach the cruising altitude after takeoff. I wait until the fasten-seat-belt sign is turned off, and then it comes. My fifth and last point.

5. I will not write lists any longer. I will not force myself to live a predetermined script. I will not try to guess what comes next and attempt to control reality. I will live life as it comes, take things one step at a time, like they do in Argentina. I will take my seat belt off.

And I will let myself fly.

Epilogue

The funny thing about lists is that once you make them they tend to get ticked off, whether you believe in them any longer or not.

My wrist got fixed. It took about two more months of recovery, just as I'd imagined, but it looked perfect in the end. It bends in just the same way as the right one. I'm not sure if that's as much as it did before the break, but I have no point of comparison left. What matters is that both are fine and I feel balanced once again. My left wrist bears the scars of screws. People ask what happened. I tell them I recovered in Argentina at the Institute for Sports Medicine, Recovery, and Rehabilitation and that they have done a great job. My right arm bears no scars and only a few trusted friends know its story. But both are fine and I intend to keep them so. I am determined.

I did play polo again. I got back on a horse in April next to Jonny, who was freshly returned from Argentina. The Old Man watched me with a critical eye, mentally assessing how long it would take me to get back into the speed of the game. It did take a while—many hours cantering around with Jonny on the stick and ball field, many conversations, many fears repressed. But Jonny, being Argentine, didn't need too many explanations. He could read minds. And he did read all my fears. Fear of scoring. Fear of hitting a goal post. Fear of falling. Fear of breaking a bone again. So he devised an exercise that I was to rehearse hundreds of times: full gallop to the goal, hit the ball, ideally score a goal (not always done), then pass very close to the goal post in full gallop while trying to get the horse back under control. Again. Do it again. Faster this time. Faster! And then one day the fear was gone and I played a tournament again, in Jonny's team. We played together, just like he promised me in Argentina that we would.

I got a job. It was a project-management assignment with eBay. It was a good company to work for. Just like I wished, the project lasted for six months. They allowed me to work remotely and I spent a lot of time in Spain. Although it bore a different accent, hearing this language all around me brought me back instantly to the place my soul calls home—Argentina.

And I did forget about Rodrigo. We wrote a few short, neutral messages to each other along the lines of "all is good." Just friends, nothing more. No dramas, no soap operas, no broken hearts. No crying. I thought about him for a couple of weeks and then my life in London fully kicked in, and the work started too, and I had no time to think about him any longer. He was gone, like he was supposed to be.

Then, in June, he texted me to say he would be in London for a few hours in between two flights. He was traveling to Germany to visit his cousin, then he would backpack in Europe for a month. He wanted to see me.

I didn't want to go. It took Jonny a full hour of stick and ball to convince me I should.

"It's not nice if you don't go, Roxana. You had a story with this guy. He's done nothing wrong."

More balls got hit and more reasons found. In the end, he won. I agreed to see Rodrigo at the airport.

It was just supposed to be a coffee, but it ended up far more than a coffee. His lips were soft and I remembered their taste as if it had been yesterday. He asked me if I was still single. I was. He said he was too, and then he promised he would come back to London in two weeks' time to spend a weekend with me. I told him I wasn't sure I was going to be there.

I went back to stick and ball with Jonny.

"Roxana, you have to be here when he comes. Otherwise you'll break his heart. Seriously."

"How do you know? You've never even met him."

"I know love is like that. Everyone knows this. Don't you?"

No, I don't, I wanted to tell him, but decided to hit some balls in silence instead. I have no idea how love is any longer. In the absence of my lists, I'm not sure at all how to deal with what comes up.

In the end, Jonny managed to persuade me to see Rodrigo again. He is a good coach, Jonny. I always do what he tells me on the polo field. No questions asked—I just do it. In the heat of the game, if I hear his shout from behind to "Go for it!", I go for the ball. I know it's safe to do so. I trust him. If he shouts "No!" as I'm about to hit the ball, I obey. I leave it, even if I don't really know why and I feel I could have had a good shot. I trust that he is right to tell me to leave it, and that it would probably have been a foul. When he shouts "Back!" I do a backhand. When he tells me "Under the neck!" I lean out of the saddle and try hard to not fall off the horse as I send the ball under its neck. It's like this with Jonny. Whatever he says, I do. No questions asked. So when he tells me I should spend a weekend with Rodrigo, it's hard to do otherwise.

So I did. We spent five days in London and then five more days in Barcelona at the end of his backpacking tour in Europe. We lay on the beach and walked hand in hand on the cozy streets of the old neighborhood of Barcelonetta. We got drunk on Sangria and made love in the small attic rented out on Airbnb. And every time we made love, the world around us melted, just like it always had.

And four days later, when he flew back to Buenos Aires, I felt more in love than ever.

All in all, it's not bad for a list that I'd decided to stop following...

Ah, and one more thing. The deal I made with the Universe delivered in the end. You remember my trip to Paris? The Astrolines? My birthday trip last year, when I went to spend the night in Paris in a romantic hotel overlooking Notre Dame, because someone had told me my Venus lines were passing through Paris and that Venus governs love?

Well, Venus kept its deal in the end, just not in the way I had expected. You see, when you make a deal with the Universe, you need to be precise. I had done this. I made sure I was right in the center of Paris, kilometer 0, Notre Dame. But you need to read the fine print of the deal too. This, I didn't do. I was just happy with the first point, that Venus was supposed to deliver—one romantic, sexy love of my life. I didn't read the fine print that said there were additional ways Venus could fulfil the deal—developing self-love, enhancing self-expression, fostering creativity, providing a life lived in beauty, harmony, friendship, pleasure. And the arts. Venus apparently governs artistic expression, too.

So Venus was keeping its options open as to how it would deliver its side of the bargain.

But I think it must have been the deal I made in Paris that brought me to Mallorca this summer. I felt at home here immediately and stayed for nearly twelve weeks. I rented a flat from a guy called Paris which was located on a street called Nuestra Señora. This is Spanish for Notre Dame. I still didn't get the message. I thought I'd come here simply to enjoy life and my newly found freedom to work remotely for a consulting project. I told you eBay was a cool company to work for. So I enjoyed the island, the beauty, the peace, the pleasure of swimming in the sea each morning. I made new friends.

And then one day, I got it. I was here to write. And I did. In my last two months here, I wrote two books—a business book, and then this one, the story of my Argentine adventure. And Venus made sure I had enough fuel to see them through.

I'm leaving Mallorca now. I'm going because it's time to go. It's the end of October, the beach is empty. My books are finished. Both of them. And my flight is waiting for me to board. Next week, I'm going back to Argentina.

Rodrigo tells me he will be in the airport waiting for me. We did talk about the future a bit when we met in Barcelona. We talked about how it could be if we really got together forever. About how we could solve the huge differences that kept us apart. But in the end we decided to leave the future open. And we did, all these months when I've been in Mallorca writing and he's been back to his life in Buenos Aires. We kept in touch with short text messages, and then one day I told him I was coming back. He didn't ask how long I will be staying this time. I didn't tell him I didn't know. As I get ready to leave, I sometimes catch my mind racing ahead, wanting to know what will happen, trying to make plans, trying to guess where the story will go this time, trying to prepare . . .

But then I take a deep breath and remember to not think too much. Because in Argentina the future can't be planned and there's only one possible answer to all of these questions.

Después vemos.

—Mallorca, October 2016

About the Author

Roxana Valea was born in Romania and lived in Italy, Switzerland, England, and Argentina before settling in Spain. She has a BA in journalism and an MBA degree. She spent more than twenty years in the business world as an entrepreneur, manager and management consultant working for top companies like Apple, eBay, and Sony. She is also a Reiki Master and shamanic energy medicine practitioner.

As an author, Roxana writes books inspired by real events. Her memoir *Through Dust and Dreams* is a faithful account of a trip she took at the age of twenty-eight across Africa by car in the company of two strangers she met over the internet. Her following book, *Personal Power: Mindfulness Techniques for the Corporate Word* is a nonfiction book filled with personal anecdotes from her consulting years. The Polo Diaries series is inspired by her experiences as a female polo player—traveling to Argentina, falling in love, and surviving the highs and lows of this dangerous sport.

~

Roxana lives with her husband in Mallorca, Spain, where she writes, coaches, and does energy therapies, but her first passion remains writing.

www.roxanavalea.com

Other Books by Roxana Valea

Through Dust and Dreams, 2014

At a crossroads in her life, Roxana decides to take a ten-day safari trip to Africa. In Namibia, she meets a local guide who talks about "the courage to become who you are" and tells her that "the world belongs to those who dream".

Her holiday over, Roxana still carries the spell of his words within her soul. Six months later she quits her job and searches for a way to fulfil an old dream: crossing Africa from north to south. Teaming up with Richard and Peter, two total strangers she meets over the internet, Roxana starts a journey that will take her and her companions from Morocco to Namibia, crossing deserts and war-torn countries and surviving threats from corrupt officials and tensions within their own group.

Through Dust and Dreams is the story of their journey: a story of courage and friendship, of daring to ask questions and search for answers, and of self-discovery on a long, dusty road south.

www.throughdustanddreams.com

Personal Power: Mindfulness Techniques for the Corporate World

This book is about your power. The one you were born with, the power that is always in you waiting to be used. Blending concepts of psychology, mindfulness and practical spirituality with the author's over twenty years of experience in the corporate world, it presents a simple yet powerful seven step framework to connect with your power and use it to manifest the life that you want.

You will learn to ground, cleanse and protect your energy. You will tap into what you already know and learn how to make decisions using your power base. You will be reminded how to direct your energy to manifest abundance and to reflect on and constantly improve your process.

If you want to achieve a sense of self-determination and inner peace while still working in a hectic corporate environment, and wonder how some people do this effortlessly, this book is for you.

www. personalpowercorporate.com

Other Books in The Polo Diaries series

A Horse Called Bicycle
Seven and a Half Minutes

46200526R00181

Printed in Poland
by Amazon Fulfillment
Poland Sp. z o.o., Wrocław